P9-CDE-618

RICHMOND HILL PUBLIC LIBRARY
NOV 22 2013
OAK RIDGES MORAINE
905-773-5533

PRAISE FOR
MORE THINGS in HEAVEN and EARTH

"Told through the eyes of Dr. Luke Bradford, a newly minted MD, the story of the little town of Watervalley, Tennessee, and its inhabitants comes vividly to life. Jeff High's medical background gives him that cutting edge in the technical details of his tale and his love of his native Tennessee and the human face shines from every page. Dr. Fingal Flahertie O'Reilly is delighted to welcome Luke, a transatlantic colleague to be fiercely proud of."

—Patrick Taylor, MD, *New York Times* bestselling author of the Irish Country novels

"The best of small-town Americana and the eccentrics who live there are brought to life in *More Things in Heaven and Earth.* This story warmed me, made me laugh, and then kept a smile on my face. It's delightful, compassionate, humorous, tightly woven. If you're looking for a feel-good read, spend an afternoon with Jeff High's novel."

—Charles Martin, *New York Times* bestselling author of *Unwritten* and *When Crickets Cry*

"A well-spun story of the mystery and microcosm that is small-town America. Jeff High skillfully captures the healing places, the hurting places, and the places where we so often find out who we are truly meant to be."

—Lisa Wingate, national bestselling author of *Tending Roses* and *The Prayer Box*

BOOK SOLD
NO LONGER R.H.P.L.
PROPERTY

MORE THINGS in HEAVEN and EARTH

A NOVEL OF WATERVALLEY

JEFF HIGH

NEW AMERICAN LIBRARY

RICHMOND HILL
PUBLIC LIBRARY
NOV 22 2013
OAK RIDGES MORAINE
905-773-5533

New American Library
Published by the Penguin Group
Penguin Group (USA), 375 Hudson Street,
New York, New York 10014, USA

USA | Canada | UK | Ireland | Australia | New Zealand | India | South Africa | China

Penguin Books Ltd., Registered Offices: 80 Strand, London WC2R 0RL, England
For more information about the Penguin Group visit penguin.com.

First published by New American Library,
a division of Penguin Group (USA)

First Printing, October 2013

Copyright © Jeff High, 2013
All rights reserved. No part of this book may be reproduced, scanned, or distributed in any printed or electronic form without permission. Please do not participate in or encourage piracy of copyrighted materials in violation of the author's rights. Purchase only authorized editions.

 REGISTERED TRADEMARK—MARCA REGISTRADA

LIBRARY OF CONGRESS CATALOGING-IN-PUBLICATION DATA:

High, Jeff, 1957–
More things in heaven and earth: a novel of Watervalley/Jeff High.
p. cm.
ISBN 978-0-451-41926-2 (pbk.)
1. Physicians—Fiction. 2. Small cities—Fiction.
3. City and town life—Fiction. 4. Tennessee—Fiction.
5. Domestic fiction. I. Title.
PS3608.I368M67 2013
813'.6—dc23 2013018662

Printed in the United States of America
1 3 5 7 9 10 8 6 4 2

Set in Adobe Garamond Pro
Designed by Spring Hoteling

PUBLISHER'S NOTE

This is a work of fiction. Names, characters, places, and incidents either are the product of the author's imagination or are used fictitiously, and any resemblance to actual persons, living or dead, business establishments, events, or locales is entirely coincidental.

The publisher does not have any control over and does not assume any responsibility for author or third-party Web sites or their content.

ALWAYS LEARNING PEARSON

For Page Chamberlain and William Pollard,
the men who helped me learn.

And for Dawn,
the one who helped me understand.

All service ranks the same with God—
With God, whose puppets, best and worst,
Are we; there is no last or first.

—*Pippa Passes* by Robert Browning

MORE THINGS
in HEAVEN and EARTH

PRELUDE

A drop of water.

Carried up from the vast ocean a world away and pulled by chance wind across earth and sky. In time it is released from the swell of a thunderhead and plummets through the open air, landing on the high hills. It finds a leaf, then a rock, then a blade of grass. It passes through the forest floor, then down below into the infinite web of roots and loam. Falling through layers of limestone and minerals, it is cleansed from the impurities of the world behind. Now pristine, it finds bedrock and pools in long-undisturbed caverns.

But time and pressure pull it downward toward the valley. It permeates the rock and surfaces again from a small spring. At first, part of an unhurried rivulet, then a toppling brook, then a wide, shimmering stream. It leaps over smooth stones and shallow falls until reaching the clear lake at the heart of Watervalley. Now its journey will end for a season, having found the way here through time and space and earth by the chaos of forces that were unforeseen and random.

Or were they?

CHAPTER 1
The Clinic

Watervalley, Tennessee

In medical jargon it's called a Code Blue.

It's a nice way of making hospital staff aware—and without panicking everybody else—that someone's in cardiac arrest and preparing to catch the angel bus. During my residency at Vanderbilt I had run dozens of them.

Even still, trying to revive someone whose heart has just flatlined puts a real cog in your day. It's always borderline chaos. You practice for it, plan for it, but it never happens the way it should. I hate a Code Blue.

To make matters worse, a Code Blue always involves a strange, spontaneous assumption of roles. It's confusing. Who grabs the crash cart? Who starts an IV? Who pulls the drugs? Who does compressions? Who charges the paddles? You're in a crowded, disorganized room with frenzied voices, frantic activity, rapid commands flying everywhere. And all the while some poor soul's life is in the balance. So in the back of your head is this scared whisper nagging at you, reminding you that you will make the difference between some guy staying alive and an awkward conversation with the family about how "it was just his time." Yeah, I really hate a Code Blue.

Weeks earlier, when I had been at Vanderbilt, a trained team of professionals had always been on hand to respond quickly to someone coding. But now that I was the new and only doctor in Watervalley, things were different. Here a Code Blue has to be carried out by unrehearsed clinic staff and panicked bystanders. It's pretty much a guaranteed disaster.

And one final thing. Regardless of where and when it happens, regardless of the disorder and fluster, there are three cardinal rules to follow when you're "coding" a patient: Always keep your cool. Know when to call it. And never—and I mean never—ever let the family be present while you're trying to revive the guy.

But this is Watervalley, and things like a Code Blue happen differently. They don't follow the normal order. Here they happen randomly, almost comically. And sometimes, beyond all reason, they happen miraculously.

Because on that July afternoon during my first week at the Watervalley Clinic, when Sawyer Wilson went into cardiac arrest in the waiting room, I didn't break just one of the rules—I broke all three. In hindsight, thank God I did.

It was nothing that med school could have ever prepared me for.

Sawyer Wilson, or "Hoot" as he was known, had come to town in the middle of his workday because his ten-year-old daughter, Wendy, had an earache. A single parent and a third-generation dairy farmer, Hoot had an expansive, mischievous humor, a perpetual smile, and was a good three hundred pounds. Ducking as he came through the clinic entrance, he was wearing overalls tucked into knee-high rubber boots and smelled of silage. In Watervalley, for dairy farmers like Hoot, coming to town held no requirement to change from his work clothes, much less wash or shave.

Holding Wendy's hand, he checked in with the receptionist, and after broadcasting a buoyant "Afternoon, everybody!" he plopped down in a corner chair and fell fast asleep. It was July hot outside and the air-conditioning had made him drowsy.

At least, that's what everyone thought.

The first sign of a problem came when Wendy walked up to Nancy Orman, the receptionist, and announced in a small voice, "Mrs. Orman, something's not right with Daddy."

Nancy leaned over the counter and glanced at Hoot sleeping dreamily in the corner. She responded with an impish laugh. "Sweetie, I don't want to hurt your feelings, but we've all known that for years."

"No, you don't understand. I don't think he's breathing."

This got Nancy's attention. After a minute of shaking Hoot and fussing at him to "cut it out," she realized that something was drastically wrong. She burst into the exam room where I was taking a patient's history.

"Dr. Bradford, I need you to come to the waiting room immediately."

Her panicked tone told me more than the words themselves. I grabbed my stethoscope and followed.

A quick assessment told the ugly story. Hoot was in V-fib, ventricular fibrillation. His heart was quivering, not beating. In a matter of minutes he would be dead. The clock was ticking.

"Nancy, call the EMTs over at the fire station. We're going to need them." I turned to the staff nurse. "Mary Jo, get the defibrillator off the crash cart. It's in exam room one."

Mary Jo didn't move. Her words seemed to ooze out one by one, thick with her dawdling Southern drawl. "Don't you want the whole cart?"

I responded firmly, calmly. "Mary Jo, if we have to run a full code on him, I don't want to do it on the waiting room floor. Go!"

She frowned and shuffled away.

"Cindy, go find the gurney and get it out here. We may need to move him to an exam room quickly." The frail little lab tech gave me a panicked nod and headed off. Meanwhile, I sent Camilla, the phlebotomist, to get the oxygen tank and bagging mask.

I enlisted some men from the waiting room to help me ease all three hundred–plus pounds of Hoot onto the floor, where once again I listened to his breathing, or lack thereof. One whiff and I shuddered. His gaping jaw emanated a toxic smell that could take the bark off a tree. I did a finger sweep, pulling out a large plug of chewing tobacco. My day just couldn't get better.

Cupping my hands over his mouth, I gave him two hard rescue blows, filling his lungs, and began doing chest compressions, hard and fast. Unbelievably, three more rounds of rescue blows and compressions ticked by and no one had returned. It was a damnable eternity.

"Where's the defibrillator?" I half yelled. People crowded silently around me, staring with anxious faces.

Mary Jo finally returned with it. She pulled up Hoot's T-shirt only to discover a chest hairier than a sheepdog. The shock pads would never find skin to stick to.

"Mary Jo, get the pediatric pads and put them on him first."

Again she argued. "Why? He's way too big for those!"

I was practically bouncing up and down doing compressions on Hoot's massive chest. I didn't need a debate. "Mary Jo, get out the pediatric pads and put them on him now!"

She reluctantly tore open the foil package and placed the two small pads on Hoot's upper right and lower left chest.

"Now rip them off."

Mary Jo gaped at me, confused.

"Go ahead—rip them off quickly."

She complied. It worked as a spontaneous wax job, leaving a clear surface for the adult pads.

It was time for another round of mouth-to-mouth. Two blows into the poor man's noxious oral cavity almost asphyxiated me. I looked up to see the arrival of the oxygen tank and had the fleeting notion that I might need it first.

"We had a hard time finding one that wasn't empty," said Camilla sheepishly.

Precious seconds were flying by. Still bouncing up and down, I snapped out instructions. "Camilla, hold the mask tightly over his mouth and nose and start bagging him."

She complied with a vengeance, squeezing vigorously on the oxygen bag, pumping him full of air.

"Camilla, we're not trying to inflate him like a flat tire. Just give him one slow squeeze every eight seconds." She was wide eyed and scared to death, but nodded obediently with quick bobs of her head.

Finally, the defibrillator was ready to analyze Hoot's heart rhythm. But when I stopped compressions to allow for the test, I noticed the valve of the oxygen tank sitting on zero. Camilla had been pumping him full of room air.

"Camilla, you need to cut the O_2 tank on, wide open." I was still calm but the aggravation was beginning to show. With quick, birdlike movements she looked back and forth between the tank and me, her face in a blank panic. I looked over to Nancy, speaking quickly.

"Nancy, turn the valve counterclockwise as far as it will go." She nodded and turned it so hard I thought she might twist it off.

Mary Jo hit the analyze button. Above the din of the small crowd the mechanical voice of the defibrillator announced, "Shock advised."

"Set it at two hundred fifty joules. Everybody step back!" I nodded to Mary Jo.

The shock caused Hoot's body to jolt, almost lifting off the floor. Finally, his quivering heart was getting smacked back into rhythm. All eyes were on the defibrillator, waiting, watching. Magically, after a few sputtering waves, it began to show a sinus rhythm, a normal heart wave. Once again Ol' Sparky had done his job. I exhaled a deep breath. Crisis over.

That is, until five beats later, when the rhythm went flatline. No quivering, no V-fib, nothing.

This was bad news—really bad news. The small voice of panic began whispering in the back of my head. For a moment I stood there, frozen in disbelief. All eyes were on me. The only solution for jump-starting a flatliner is drugs, delivered quickly and methodically in a timed sequence, and then shocking him. The voice was now screaming: *Get moving, Luke—Code Blue! Code Blue!*

"Camilla, keep bagging him." I searched the room and pointed to a lanky fellow in his late thirties. "You—Did you see the way I was doing those compressions?"

He nodded.

"I want you to start doing them just like I was. Press hard—he's a big fellow. Try to do a hundred a minute."

I turned to Mary Jo. "We need to get him to the exam room and run a full code. Where's our lift stretcher?"

"We don't have one."

"We don't have one?" I responded incredulously. We had to

get him off the floor and onto the gurney, which, I now noticed, wasn't there.

"Where's the gurney?" I looked down the main hallway of the clinic. Nancy was waddling toward me, her short legs moving as quickly as they could. I met her halfway.

"Cindy's getting it. It was back in the storage room covered with the Christmas decorations. She's cleaning it up."

I pressed my lips sternly together, squelching back a fuming desire to scream, loudly and with gusto. "Nancy, I don't care if it's clean or not. Bring it now and bring an extra bedsheet."

I returned to the waiting room and recruited three men and two of the heftier farm women to help lift Hoot. We got the extra bedsheet under him just as Cindy arrived with the gurney. The air was thick with confusion and tension. Hoot's life was slipping away.

With three of us on each side, we yanked him up so hard he almost went airborne. Stepping quickly, we dished him onto the gurney in a smooth, sweeping motion that was perfectly executed—except for the small detail that no one had thought to lock the gurney's wheels. Upon landing, Hoot scooted across the floor like a roller skate, his massive limbs dangling from all sides. I dove and caught him. We moved swiftly.

Including the staff, about ten of us crowded into the small exam room. I stood at the head, calling out orders, timing the intervals, running the protocol. The passing minutes became a surreal blur as events moved with an unbelievable rapidity.

Everything imaginable went wrong.

Camilla, who normally had a rock-steady hand, was so shaken she took forever to get an IV started. This forced me to give the first two doses of epinephrine by direct injection into his jugular, creating no small mess of blood. No one could find a blood pressure cuff big enough to fit Hoot's arm. We pulled his boot off and put one at his ankle. I couldn't intubate him because the battery in the laryngoscope was dead. The only atropine available was a month out of date. I used it anyway. With no way to get quick lab results, I was left desperately short of critical metabolic information. It wasn't that the clinic's resources were primitive; they were nonexistent.

To top it all off, the EMTs had yet to arrive because they had been far out at a friend's farm helping to deliver a calf. Only in Watervalley.

Minutes passed. Numerous times the drug protocols sparked some sputtering waves. When that happened, we quickly shocked him, desperately trying to revive a normal rhythm. But nothing was working. Panic was seizing everyone, permeating the frantic voices of those around me. My frustration and anger mounted. Hoot Wilson was an otherwise robust, healthy man of forty-three. To my thinking, it just wasn't his time yet. But he was about to meet his maker because remote Watervalley lacked the fundamental equipment needed to keep him alive and all of my training couldn't make up the difference.

In my head I had been doing the math. It had been over thirty minutes since Nancy had first shaken him. By all the odds, he didn't have a chance. I needed to think about calling it, but I just couldn't. My irritation and fury surfaced. I took over doing the compressions and yelled audibly.

"Come on, dammit. Get a rhythm going." Sweat poured down my face. Everyone in the room was standing, staring with lost expressions. This ad hoc group had followed my instructions as best they could, but the drama had left them shell-shocked and exhausted. Everyone knew the inevitable was coming. We had given multiple doses of epinephrine and atropine, we'd done continuous compressions, multiple shocks, and yet nothing. No sustained rhythm. I had lost him.

Finally I stopped and stepped back, heaving deep gasps in and out, trying to catch my breath. I searched the long, somber faces of those in the room, particularly that of Mary Jo, the staff nurse. I was looking for confirmation. It was time to call it. That was when I noticed something that made me feel like an even grander failure.

It was Wendy, Hoot's daughter. All the while she had been sitting quietly in the corner of the exam room watching the terrible drama of her father's last minutes. But something was remarkably odd. Instead of being in a state of panic and tears, she looked placid, curious. She sat and waited patiently for me to break the silence. I needed to call it, but her presence stopped me.

Hoot was gone. At this point it made no sense to send her away, so I motioned for her to come closer. Her face expressionless, Wendy walked up to her father and with her pudgy hand she squeezed his large, bare foot and spoke in a soft and determined voice.

"Don't go yet, Daddy."

I exhaled deeply. It was the final straw, an epitaph to my failure.

And then I heard the beep, a singular heartbeat on the cardiac monitor. The room held its collective breath. The beep was followed by another, then another, then another. We all stood in stunned, shocked silence.

After ten more beats, Nancy Orman, a devout Baptist who for all of her fifty-three years had lived, walked, and breathed a mile away from the nearest known sin, blurted out in a low, weak voice, "Holy shit!"

Everyone else was speechless.

Miraculously, the heartbeat continued.

About this time the EMTs arrived. We loaded Hoot into the ambulance and I rode along for the forty-five-minute drive to the regional hospital in the next county. It was the closest facility available.

Hoot's heart rate remained constant. He even began to regain a drowsy consciousness on the ride over. A few days later he got a pacemaker and within a week he was back on the farm. It was a miraculous turnaround, one for the medical journals. But to the people of Watervalley, it seemed to be no big deal. To their thinking, it was just providential timing and grace.

For me, it was more complex, a combination of critical elements. Yet still, I couldn't completely account for it, just like so many other things about Watervalley that in time I would come to realize were simply not explainable.

Being dead on the exam room table for that long normally impacts mental function. But with Hoot's loud and happy personality, no one noticed a difference. He was just glad to be back among his cows and with the darling jewel of his life, his daughter, Wendy.

From then on, every day after school, Wendy would go and sit in the corner of the milk parlor and calmly do her homework while Hoot went about his work. Engrossed in her lessons, she would quietly study, seemingly oblivious to the incredible noise and clamor of the milk machines and baying cows. But every so often she would look up from her book, and sweetly, proudly gaze over at her immense father and, with a face of pure love, smile.

Hoot's Code Blue happened on the Thursday of my first week as the new doctor at the Watervalley Clinic, my first job out of med school. I'd like to be able to say that the days leading up to it since my Saturday arrival had not been quite so eventful.

Unfortunately, that just wouldn't be true.

CHAPTER 2
Arrival

When I had left Nashville the previous Saturday morning, I was reasonably confident that by most standards I was fairly smart. At least . . . well, something above average. But that day, my first day in Watervalley, proved otherwise.

It began when I stopped at the country store: a narrow shotgun building of flaking white paint, patchwork tin roof, and sagging concrete blocks fronted by a porch cluttered with rusted soft drink machines. A small cushion of dust stirred as I pulled my worn-out Corolla into the gravel lot. The small, wispy cloud hovered in the stagnant air, covering the faded sign that read COUNTY LINE MARKET AND GENERAL STORE. Given the absence of any other vehicles, it was clear I was the only customer.

The storekeeper was a tidy little man with neatly combed gray hair, heavy black-framed glasses over a small pinched face, and a white short-sleeved shirt buttoned to the neck. As I entered, he was standing at the cash register talking in a nasal monotone.

"Come in, stay a while, don't rush off, awful hot out there. Got a special going on cold drinks, candy bars on this shelf are half priced if you like candy."

His barrage was nonstop, leaving me no chance to speak.

The cluttered store was thick with an old but agreeable aroma of many years. Shelves on the twelve-foot-high walls overflowed with canned goods, fishing lures, brooms, rakes, seeds, hardware bins, hand tools, coveralls, and a pair of winter sleds.

I smiled and nodded, moving cautiously away toward a drink cooler. He followed, hovering next to me, meekly talking in the general direction of my shoes and only occasionally glancing up with a squinting face of childlike hope.

"Got some Western shirts in the back at a real good price. If you need any pet supplies, we got them too—you got a dog or anything?"

The little fellow was my first contact with Watervalley, so despite his troublesome persistence I felt the need to at least pretend interest in his unwanted inquiries. I couldn't bring myself to tell him that I had stopped only to ask directions.

Although I'd left Nashville five hours earlier, I had traveled only 120 miles and was as lost as last year's Easter egg. My portable GPS was proving to be of little help. To make matters worse, the air-conditioning in the old Corolla had died months before, making a misery of the hot hours down the ragged two-lane roads.

I had just graduated from my Vanderbilt residency, and my education had left me two hundred thousand dollars in debt. I'd received several offers at the university for research assistant positions, something I would have loved. But the pay was notoriously low and I had lived off peanut butter and jelly long enough. Small, doctor-deficient towns in Tennessee would pay off your college loans if you set up practice there. I had been part of a small town many years before. It hadn't ended well. But remote, small-town Watervalley was my only option. It was a three-year commitment.

So that morning I had left Nashville with its offers of research grants and fellowships and headed, for all practical purposes, to the dropping-off point of God and all creation. I had accepted my departure from civilization and was determined to make the best of it. But for hours I had traveled the narrow back roads into an endless maze of fields, farms, and woodlands. The drive into rural purgatory had left me exasperated. I was lost in more ways than one. It was a tricky balance. My head was looking for a place that my heart didn't want to find.

"Wanna hear about the daily special? It's called the Sandwich Meal Deal, comes with a bologna sandwich, chips, and a Coke. Bologna is fresh cut—got salami if you don't want bologna. Got lettuce too if you want that."

I couldn't get away. Despite my frustration at spending the entire day off course, I couldn't help but listen patiently to his lowly but persistent inquiries. Finally I succumbed to buying a six-pack of beer, which evoked a crestfallen look of grateful disappointment. I grabbed a couple of candy bars and tossed them on the counter for good measure. This lifted his mood, but only slightly. While handing me the change, he began a liturgy of thank-yous in the same droning voice.

I nodded and made a hasty departure back to the afternoon heat. Two steps out the door I halted and spoke audibly, "Crap, I forgot to ask directions." I stood for a moment, trying to decide if I was up for another round of Watervalley's answer to Zig Ziglar. Then the situation resolved itself as a battered pickup truck pulled into the gravel lot. Its driver, a tall, tautly built, middle-aged fellow in work khakis, emerged and began to walk up the steps, oblivious to my presence.

I blurted an emphatic "Sir."

He stopped abruptly, his strong-featured face regarding me with a look of suspicious irritation.

"Can you tell me how to find Watervalley?"

He stood for a long moment, appraising me coolly with a calculated sophistication that I hadn't expected to find this far back in the sticks. Finally he spoke in a relaxed voice of raw disdain.

"Yeah, sport. Just keep driving down that road there till you start feeling stupid." He walked away, shaking his head in an expression of permanent contempt.

I retreated to the Corolla and tossed my purchases into the passenger seat. As I pulled onto the blacktop, it occurred to me that I'd arrived at feeling stupid three exits ago. I was miles past that.

After a long run down a deeply wooded lane, the road made a sharp bend and opened up to a spectacular view of the valley below. The trees continued up the steep slope to the right, but to my left was a wide overlook offering a complete vista that stretched for miles. I stopped the Corolla to take it all in.

I had stepped into a different world. A broad floor of velvet green rolled toward tall hills in the distance. Along the wide plane were small dots of houses that grew closer and closer together as they progressed toward the town. In the far distance was a lake and in between stood Watervalley, outlined with the prominent points of church steeples.

A sweet, warm breeze swept up from the valley and rustled the high leaves of the nearby trees. The air was filled with an incredible clarity and an amazingly unfamiliar silence. The common cacophony of the city was distinctly far behind me.

So this is Watervalley, I thought, curious. Admittedly, the view was captivating, almost mesmerizing. The shoulders of the distant hills framed the stunning panorama before me, the wide sweep of the incredible Tennessee Valley. I stood at the precipice of my new life as a small-town doctor. And I felt in that instant, if only for a second, that something in the wind and sun, the endless roll of green fields and meadows, and the magnificent blue of the vast sky held an unspeakable enchantment for me. The scene was beautiful beyond words. For a brief moment, my regrets were forgotten.

But despite its splendor, I didn't want to be here. My dream was to do research, lead groundbreaking studies, find miracle cures, make a name for myself. Instead, I was about to drive into a Terry Redlin painting. I sighed, climbed back into the Corolla, and began the five miles of hairpin turns down into town.

The scorching July wind breathing past me provided little relief from the heat. With no air-conditioning, the old Corolla was like an oven with wheels attached. Glancing at my watch, I noticed it was still a couple of hours before my informal meeting with the mayor. The day was hot as hell, and I felt that I was barreling headlong into it.

I was parched. I had downed my last bottle of water some miles back and had forgotten to grab a few more when I stopped at the market. Tempted, I looked over at the cold beer and thought, well, why not? So I popped one of them open.

In hindsight, I believe that as I descended farther and farther into the valley, my IQ was the only thing dropping faster than the elevation.

CHAPTER 3

First Impressions

Winding down that last stretch of road, I was blissfully unaware that my coming to Watervalley was a matter of significant anticipation. The town had been without a local doctor for three years and everyone was eagerly awaiting my arrival. Having learned the make of my car, Warren Thurman, the sheriff, was parked on the outskirts of town along with two of his cruisers, ready to meet me with a police escort. He wanted it to be a big surprise. It was.

Right after I threw back the first swallow of beer the three patrol cars with their blues flashing popped out on the road in front of me and drew me to an instant halt. I was shocked, paralyzed with disbelief. Admittedly, I was stretching the law, but how could they be on to me that quickly, and after only one swallow?

I had to slam on the breaks to keep from hitting the sheriff's cruiser. In my panic, the bottle slipped from my hand and beer shot out, completely drenching my shirt and pants. The sheriff, a giant of a fellow with a spontaneous smile, emerged from his car and strolled up to the Corolla.

He spoke in an amiable, drawling voice. "Hi there. I'm Sheriff Thurman. You Dr. Luke Bradford?"

I looked slowly up from my soaked shirt and pants, the unmistakable aroma of spilled beer wafting through the open window. His smile faded.

"Are you drinking a beer?"

"Yes—well, actually, no, sir, Officer. I think I'm mostly wearing it."

"You are Dr. Bradford, aren't you?"

"Yes, yes, I am," I responded.

"How many of those you had to drink, Doc?"

"Well, I only opened one and after that sudden stop I pretty much just took a bath in it."

Sheriff Thurman looked at the six-pack with the single missing bottle, and at the thoroughness of my drenching.

"Oh." His broad smile returned. "You're okay to drive, then. I thought I might have to put one of the boys behind your wheel and have you ride with me. Looks like you'll be all right. Just follow me, Doc. Lots of folks wanting to meet you."

As he ambled away it occurred to me that maybe I should turn the car around and head back out of town. But obediently I pulled the Corolla in behind the sheriff, who led the way with blue lights flashing and an occasional blip of the siren. The two other cruisers fell in behind me, barring any chance of escape. My relief at not being handcuffed and hauled off to jail was followed by the panic of being in beer-soaked clothes and on my way to meet the mayor.

The sheriff had also said something about folks wanting to meet me. I wasn't sure what that meant, but decided to make a quick change at the next stoplight. I reached over and grabbed a clean shirt and pants from my duffel bag. After spending many seasons playing varsity sports, I considered myself pretty agile. But my six-foot, two-inch frame didn't allow for easy maneuvering inside the small Corolla. That's when the blurry bad dream began.

I had just struggled out of my soaked pants when I realized that even though Watervalley did have two stoplights, the sheriff had posted officers at each one to usher the welcoming convoy through to the courthouse steps. Furthermore, the pants-changing maneuver made for rather sporadic handling of the steering wheel, causing me to weave considerably on my approach down Main Street.

I was in the process of trying to get the clean khakis up from my ankles when the sheriff stopped abruptly in front of me and I darn near hit him again. But the real panic came when I noticed that to my left was a crowd of about twenty people standing on the steps of the courthouse, waving hand-painted signs reading WATERVALLEY WELCOMES DR. BRADFORD.

Someone had a boom box with a recording of "Rocky Top" playing loudly in the background. In the next instant the mayor, Walt Hickman, jerked open the car door and extended a big smile and an eager handshake toward me.

A low gasp rose from the crowd, which understandably had expected their first view of me to include pants. It didn't help that the now empty beer bottle rolled from the car floor and clanged loudly onto the street.

The mayor, a portly gray-haired fellow in his fifties, retrieved his hand, shut the door, and turned his back to the car in a spontaneous effort to shield me from general view. He had a shocked look on his face. As I would later learn, it was one of the few times since infancy that Walt Hickman was at a loss for words.

Some agonizing moments passed while I managed to get my pants on and tuck the beer-soaked part of my shirt into them. I tapped lightly on the window, now with the mayor's backside pressed to it, letting him know I was ready to get out.

Walt peered cautiously at me over his shoulder. Having regained his composure, he turned around, opened the car door, and with his large, pudgy-fingered hand extended said, "Welcome to Watervalley, Doc," as if the previous two minutes had been erased from history.

Sporting my wet shirt, khakis, and flip-flops, I got out of the car to what was now a rather halfhearted round of applause. After nodding awkwardly to the crowd, I sheepishly raised a hand in a gesture that was part wave and part self-defense. Immediately I was plunged into a battery of introductions.

I smiled and did my best to make conversation, all the while thinking about the picture they were getting of this beer-stained, underdressed new doctor in whom they would be entrusting their health and the health of their children. It was something short of an ideal first impression.

The reception dwindled quickly and afterward Sheriff Thurman led the way to my provided housing, a quaint white cottage several blocks away in a well-groomed older neighborhood. My new home at 205 Fleming Street had been completely renovated and furnished. Inside it was fresh and clean and comfortable, with shiny hardwood floors and soft couches and chairs. The living and dining rooms and eat-in kitchen were on the main floor, with two cozy bedrooms in the gabled upstairs. I had to admit, it was delightful. For the past seven years during med school and residency, I had lived in dumps and dives and in a hollow tree with the Keebler Elves. Watervalley had given me a place to call my own. Yet still, I met the whole business with a certain reluctance.

Sheriff Thurman helped me unload my few possessions from my car and casually followed as I made the tour of my new residence. With his ready smile and patient, easy manner, he had an accommodating way about him. He made me relax, let down my guard. But very quickly I came to realize that the first thing Warren Thurman wanted you to do was underestimate him. Hiding behind that huge smile was a very observant mind.

"What do you say, Doc? Think you'll fit in here okay?"

"Sure. Seems plenty big for a single guy. I've got some family furniture in a storage facility in Atlanta, but doesn't look like I'll need it here."

Warren nodded in a kind, thoughtful way. Yet something in his countenance spoke of a more calculated assessment. His question about fitting in here had a subtle duplicity; it was imbued with meaning. He was gauging my response on a larger level, weighing my words, trying to read my thoughts. The question didn't seem to be driven by meanness, but rather by caring. In time I would learn that in the vernacular of Watervalley, he was dumb like a fox.

"Well, we're glad to have you in Watervalley, Doc. Maybe in time you can get all of your things here. The valley has a way of growing on you, getting into your bones." I suspected Warren sensed my reluctance, but was too considerate, too respectful to ask me about it directly. He extended his massive hand and offered an even larger smile, if that was possible. We shook and I thanked him, after which he departed to the patrol car.

I spent about an hour settling in until, as planned, the mayor came by to give me a short driving tour of the town. Proudly chauffeuring his old Cadillac Sedan de Ville, Walt, with his broad face and double chin, chatted nonstop about the town's history, the schools, the few local industries, and the variety of shops Watervalley offered. But he spoke mostly about farming crops and raising cattle, the businesses that had been the financial mainstays of the valley. The vast rolling, fertile fields had afforded the farmers and townspeople a prosperous living for decades, despite droughts and blights and seesaw markets. He occasionally asked me questions, but seemed more preoccupied with supplying information than with gathering it.

"That's the Farmers Bank over there, Doc. Good people, good people. You probably want to set up an account with them."

"Yes, I'm sure that's something I should take care of in the next—"

"Hey, see that over there? That's the Depot restaurant. Best food around. Used to be the actual depot when the train ran through here years ago. Lida Wilkins owns it. You met her earlier at the reception. You remember her? Short gal, reddish hair?"

"Yes, I seem to recall—"

"Lida also owns Society Hill."

"Society Hill?"

"Bed and breakfast. It's an old, rambling mansion built by a fellow named Hiram Hatcher back in the twenties. Watervalley is not exactly a convention center, so we really don't have any hotels. Society Hill Bed and Breakfast pretty much handles all the visitor traffic. We thought we might have to put you up there for a spell, but Public Works managed to get your house ready in time."

"Yes, and it's very nice. I want to—"

"By the way, Doc. Not to pry, but have you got a girlfriend back in Nashville? There have been several inquiries." Walt glanced over at me with a gleeful, openmouthed wiggling of his head. It was a look of baited anticipation.

"Not really anything permanent. I guess I was a little more focused on—"

"Well, that's good, that's good. I'll put out the word that hunting season is open." Walt exhaled a low-pitched chuckle, shaking his head. He was quite amused with himself.

We drove around the balance of the town, with Walt

dispensing tidbits of history and some colorful gossip about a few of the local personalities. He pulled the Cadillac back into my driveway and handed me the keys to the clinic. Although he had interviewed me at length on the phone, I always expected that there would be some further evaluation, some additional review process after I arrived. Apparently, the only test I had to pass was listening to the long version of Walt's chronicle of the community. I took the keys from him and, with no more ceremony, I was Watervalley's new town doctor.

"I know Watervalley's not Nashville or Atlanta, Doc, but I think you'll like living here. We're sure proud to have you."

I shook his hand and nodded. As I stood in the shade of my front lawn and watched Walt drive away, the thought occurred to me: I knew more about living in a small town than Walt might have guessed.

Later that evening I stood on the back stoop admiring my newfound kingdom and reflecting on the day. As the sun began to set I pulled the Corolla onto the grass behind the house out of sight from the street. A soft breeze kicked up and long shadows began to play across the back lawn. Lightning bugs started to flicker in the mystical half-light of dusk. Turning on the radio, I sat in the driver's seat with the car door open and channel surfed. It was a long-held ritual. As I absorbed the smells and sounds of the summer evening, my mind wandered, bouncing seamlessly between the decades.

My affinity for summer evenings and radios was rooted much deeper than my years at Vanderbilt, even deeper than my teenage years living with my sophisticated aunt Grace in urban Buckhead. It called up warm memories of being a young boy, listening to Braves baseball games, and playing in the open fields beyond my parents' back porch in rural Georgia. Perhaps deep within, it reminded me of those incredible early years with them before the accident, before everything changed. I was only twelve years old when it all had come to its tragic end.

The mayor's assumption was mostly correct. I had spent the better part of the last two decades in Atlanta and Nashville. But I knew small towns. I knew them well. Yet when I had abruptly moved to Buckhead—as a tall, gangly, emotionally splintered boy—and found myself enrolled in an upscale private school, I had quietly learned to slough off my rural skin. During those years in Buckhead my future self had been forged.

The local radio station hummed and crackled in the background, permeating the summer evening with a mix of classic country music songs. I climbed out to stretch my legs, leaving the door open. The sagging Corolla sat tiredly in the dewy grass, looking as if it would be quite happy for me to leave it parked there permanently. I stared mindlessly into the evening, mesmerized at the play of light and shadows. I was transported away to forgotten places, forgotten voices. Over the years those memories, those early childhood experiences had been pushed to the periphery, only scantly and obscurely viewed, never looked upon directly, because doing so primed up a deep well of confusion and loss and broken understanding. Time had taught me to silently tuck those feelings away.

A bursting twang from the radio brought me back. As twilight spread above, I thought of the day's absurdities and could only laugh. It was a rather undecorated start. Even so, I knew my parents would have been proud. I had followed in my father's footsteps and become a doctor. In spite of myself, I was a doctor in Watervalley, Tennessee.

I leaned against the car and closed my eyes, listening for a long while under the wide canopy of evening stars. When the weariness of the day finally set in, I turned the radio off, locked the back door behind me, and went upstairs to bed.

I lay in the orderly confines of my bedroom, pondering, brooding, staring into the shadowy darkness. The first night in a new place always feels peculiar, dark with uncertainty and strangeness. It's not that I was consumed with any notion of fear or dread, just one of ambiguity. Although the townspeople's welcome had been enthusiastic and warm, I saw myself as a permanent visitor. With a mixed heart I listened to the random pops and groans, the nocturnal noises of the house.

Outside, the night was unseasonably cool. From a distance, the random streetlights blended together, giving a soft glow to the wide valley floor. At the far rim of the county, the moonlight cast a rich shadowy luminescence on the grasses of the high hills. Up above, a million stars twinkled brightly. A whole universe was moving about its order.

I drifted in and out of a fitful slumber, sometimes simply lying there. After midnight, the headlights of a few cars rolled along Fleming Street and then slowly faded into darkness. All now quiet, Watervalley had gone to sleep for another night. And in the small upstairs room at 205 Fleming Street, I finally slept, peacefully, blissfully unaware of the disaster awaiting me the next morning.

CHAPTER 4
Breakfast

It was ten a.m. and I lay there in disbelief. Having pulled weekend emergency room duty for the last couple of years, I hadn't slept for so many hours in a single spell for a long time. I stretched luxuriously.

Normally I went for a run, but the sound of nearby church bells reminded me that taking a jog on Sunday morning was likely not the way the people of Watervalley showed a little reverence. My thoughts turned instead to breakfast.

I ambled downstairs to the kitchen and rummaged through the fridge, finding eggs, bacon, and a can of biscuits. When I turned on the old gas oven it made an odd hissing sound. In my drowsy morning state this struck me as curious, but I thought little more of it.

I found an iron skillet and started the bacon. A short while later I opened the oven door and turned toward the kitchen table, where I had set the baking tray of biscuits.

That's when the explosion came.

As I was about to learn, the oven flame had never ignited and gas had been pouring into the closed compartment for the last several minutes. When I finally opened the oven door and made an about-face to retrieve the tray of biscuits, the gas streamed out and was ignited by the flame on the cooktop.

Like the mouth of a dragon, the oven spewed a huge ball of fire five feet out with an incredible boom that shook the entire house. It was just for an instant, but enough to sear my boxers and singe the hair off the back of my legs. The blast sent me sprawling across the kitchen table, knocking it over and propelling everything on it across the room.

As quickly as it had come the flame was gone, leaving me in shock on my backside on the kitchen floor. The flash had set off the fire alarm, and complicating my confusion even more was the deafening sound of the siren blasting from the attic gable.

What I didn't realize was that the system had automatically triggered an alarm at the fire hall. It was later explained to me that since the house belonged to the town, Ed Caswell, Watervalley's fire chief, had made sure it was equipped with a state-of-the-art alarm system. So at ten twenty-eight in the morning, while I was fumbling around in burned boxers, twenty-four different pagers were going off in the middle of sanctuaries and Sunday schools all over Watervalley. Every one of them read "205 Fleming Street," which of course created no small stir.

Ministers in three different services interrupted their sermons, requesting immediate prayers for the emergency. Knowing their congregations' natural curiosity, both the Episcopal and Baptist ministers communicated the location of the fire so that petitions to God could be as specific as possible.

Meanwhile, I managed to gather my wits enough to scramble up from the floor and shut off the gas to both the oven and burners. But the pan of bacon on the stove was now a small grease fire. In my panic, I used the tablecloth as a potholder and, without thinking, put the flaming pan in the sink, dousing it with water. This put the fire out, but created a choking fog of smoke. The control panel to the fire alarm and security system was beside the back door, and after a few painful minutes of pushing several button combinations, I fortunately managed to get the siren to stop.

By now the smoke in the kitchen was almost intolerable, forcing me out onto the back porch steps, leaving the door open to air out the place. I bent over with my hands on my knees, coughing violently to get the sharp pinch of smoke out of my throat. Standing straight again, I found myself face-to-face with Ed Caswell, whom I had met at the bungled courthouse reception the day before. A no-nonsense and orderly little man, he had cut through backyards, running directly from the Episcopal church after radioing the station to see if the pump truck was on the way. He had rounded the back corner of the house with a fire extinguisher in one hand and a first aid kit in the other.

"Doc, you okay?" was his immediate response to all the smoke coming out the back door. I waved my hands in a gesture of dismissal.

"Fine, fine. Everything is fine." It was a futile attempt. The last thing I wanted now was to attract a lot of attention to this small disaster. "It was the stove. The gas stove. It sort of blew up and caught some bacon grease on fire, but everything's okay now. No need to do anything. So I guess you can go back to, you know, whatever you were doing."

Ed walked right past me into the house as if my words didn't register. In the distance, I heard the slow, steady rise of a fire truck's siren, followed by a sudden foghorn blast. I stood listening in total disbelief. There were two blasts, each lasting a good fat second. I turned and looked into the kitchen, where Ed now stood, staring calmly at me.

"They do that when they go through an intersection. The horn blast."

"So I guess that means they're on their way here?"

"That would be correct."

"Well, can you call and tell them that everything is okay and just, um, not to worry about it?"

Ed was polite, but very matter-of-fact. "I could. But by my calculations they just passed the corner of Main and Church, and they'll be here by the time I get dispatch on the radio."

At that moment Chick McKissick, a local mechanic, and two other volunteer firemen rounded the back corner of the house. Sunday shoes, fire coats, rubber boots, and loosened ties had been flying everywhere as the men tried to change into their fire suits during their sprint from the First Baptist Church. Seeing Ed and me on the back porch brought them to a halt.

"Everything okay here, Ed?" asked Chick.

"Yeah, boys, everything's fine. Just a little stove mishap. Doc here's still in one piece too."

I stood silently, my arms folded with one hand held casually over my mouth. I was certain that even if I lived to be 110, this would be the most embarrassing moment of my life—quite a thought given my entrance to Watervalley the day before. With scorched boxers, singed hair, and soot-covered legs, I tried to look unfazed and in control. But given my sad state, there was little room to stand on my dignity.

I couldn't help but notice that Chick and the other men were grinning at me and muttering to each other, studying my burned underwear with undisguised delight.

Chick spoke up. "Hey, Dr. Bradford, you sure you're okay?

'Cause if your legs get much darker, I may have to call you a brother."

This produced further laughs from the three. I sensed that it was all in good fun and simply nodded and said, "Yeah, well, if I get much darker, you can call me well done."

They all smiled. Meanwhile the pump truck could be heard screeching to a halt in front of the house.

Ed Caswell said, "Chick, if you don't mind, go around front and tell them it's all clear. Oh, and tell Charlie to leave the blow fans."

The high-powered fans were unloaded from the pump truck and placed at the back door to suck the remaining smoke out of the kitchen. Chick stayed with Ed to help maneuver the fans. Within a few minutes, they had done their job.

As they turned to leave, Walt Hickman came around the house in a fast waddling trot. Fortunately, I had already gone inside to put on some jeans, avoiding yet another encounter between the mayor and my underwear. Upon my return downstairs I saw Walt and Ed standing outside the breakfast room window in an intense conversation. The mayor had a frustrated look on his face and was shaking his head from side to side. Ed was speaking firmly, pointing to him and then at the house.

I couldn't make out their words, so in the absence of information my imagination began filling in the blanks. I was certain Ed was using words like "dimwit" and "moron." My status as an idiot now seemed confirmed. These people were going to come get me in the middle of the night, drag me out to the street, and beat me. Or, even worse, they were going to bury me in some ditch with a backhoe and call the residency program at Vanderbilt saying, "Dr. Bradford never showed up. Would you please send us another one?"

Finally Mayor Hickman pursed his lips and nodded reluctantly in reply to some last point Ed was making. With that the mayor looked up at the house, right toward the window where I was standing. I immediately ducked down so as not to be seen eavesdropping. What I really wanted to do was get into the Corolla and drive away. But by now the mayor was climbing the steps to the back porch.

"Hey, Doc, you in there?"

"Sure, just a minute." I took a deep breath and tried to gather my thoughts. Within twenty-four hours of my arrival in Watervalley, I'd already been center stage to not one but two disasters. A wretched queasy feeling began churning in my stomach. I was about to get fired. I knew it. I hadn't spent five minutes on the job and already I was getting canned. Admittedly, part of me almost liked the idea, while another part was sick with failure. Stepping out the back door, I stiffened my neck in preparation for the worst.

"I'm real sorry about that stove, Doc," Walt said. "Ed told me all along we should have had that thing replaced."

This of course took me aback. "Well, no—I mean, I should have paid more attention. Look, Mayor, instead of the stove, maybe you should just have me replaced. I've really gotten off to a bad start here."

He gave me an incredulous look. "Nonsense, Doc. You're going to be just fine. I tell you, though, what you need is a housekeeper. You're gonna be awful busy and it might be good to have somebody keep an eye on this place. I know just the lady. Connie Thompson is her name. I'll tell her to come around to the clinic about seven thirty in the morning. You two can talk things through."

I stood in disbelief.

"That sound okay to you, Doc?"

My stunned response was a mix of relief and skepticism. "Sure, sure—seven thirty would be fine."

That said, he turned and left. For several moments, I stood on the back stoop, still in a state of disbelief. Returning to the kitchen, I stared at the charred mess before me. I exhaled a deep sigh, found a dish towel, and began the arduous task of cleaning up.

CHAPTER 5
The Housekeeper

Monday finally arrived. It was to be my first day at the Watervalley Clinic. Given the disastrous events of the weekend, I met the morning with no small amount of trepidation. But I was determined to take control of my world and begin this unwelcome new job on my terms.

I rose early to take a run. It wired me, served as a wake-up call. Running was a habit I had acquired some time back when the hungry years of med school had forced me to forsake the expense of barista coffee. Afterward I showered, ate a piece of toast, and walked over to the clinic, arriving before seven. I was the first one there.

The clinic had been a grand private home dating from the 1850s before it was bought by the town and converted to a clinic in the 1920s. True to its antebellum style, it had a considerable front porch supported by broad-shouldered columns. Original plate glass filled the fan transom and side panels surrounding the front door. Astonishingly, the glass had survived years of wear and storms and even war, and still it remained to weakly obscure the interior.

The hinges groaned as the massive door swung inward,

revealing a broad entry hall with imposing cased openings on all three sides. Straight ahead was a receptionist counter and beyond it was a grand central hallway that ran the length of the old home, with a massive stairwell down one side. The rooms were heavily trimmed with moldings painted crisp white, and all had twelve-foot-tall ceilings and shiny wood floors. Despite the near echoing spaciousness, I felt an unexplained ease, a warm welcome within the walls. On either side of the front entry hall were orderly waiting rooms filled with comfortable chairs and interspersed with low tables stacked with old magazines and picture books of children's Bible stories.

I moved quietly down the center hall and found a door with my nameplate already attached. The office was cavernous with dark mahogany paneling, handcrafted shelves, a polished wood desk, and a wheeled leather chair. The decor spoke of an older South, a steady, enduring gracefulness. Behind the desk, two large windows flooded the room with brilliant morning light.

Shutting the door behind me, I stood frozen, absorbing everything. The room was a stately, breathing presence, a quiet sentinel to the many years of service and duty. There was a captivating smell of accumulated time filling the room with a fragile wonder, an air of expectancy. The office resonated with the lives of Watervalley from decades past. Echoes of simple, rustic voices were whispering hopes, fears, worries. For Watervalley, this office, this room had a significance I had not foreseen.

I moved tentatively to the large leather chair and sat there brooding. It was difficult not to be impressed, not to feel some small measure of pride in the stateliness of my office and the implied respect Watervalley gave to my new role. And while I had done my best to school myself away from regret over my circumstances, I still had mixed emotions. My gifts were academic, better suited for independent research. Engaging the masses was an honorable calling, but I wanted it to be calling someone else. My ill-fated antics of the last two days weren't helping either, especially when compared with this imposing room. I kept telling myself that it was only for three years, only a thousand and ninety-five days, give or take a leap year. I felt little consolation.

I heard several staff members come in through the back entrance of the clinic. The lights were still off, so no one realized I was there. Through the office wall I heard the unmistakable sound of very animated and very Southern female voices emanating from the adjacent staff kitchen. I listened to see if I could hear what was being said, curious to know if my weekend humiliations were the hot topic of conversation. I could barely discern anything except for the word "NASCAR," which I was certain was repeated several times.

The plan for the day was to meet the clinic staff and discuss the caseload with Dr. Curtis, who had been filling in on Thursdays in rotation from the regional hospital in Gunther County, some forty miles away. I was also scheduled to take a tour of the town hall and talk with, among other people, Ed Caswell. After yesterday's pyrotechnics, I was well ahead of the game on that one.

I sat in the chair mindlessly thumping a pencil on the desk. Reality kicked in when the door burst open and a woman I had met the previous Saturday stepped in to turn on the lights. She was five feet, three inches, noticeably overweight, and a virtual cyclone of energy. She flipped the switch.

"Oh my!" she said with a gasp, her hand flying to her chest. "Doc, you gave me a start. I didn't know you were in here."

"Hi—sorry. I came in earlier and was just gathering my thoughts for the day. By the way, I know we met Saturday, but names were kind of a blur. Nancy Orman, right?"

Nancy bubbled. "That's right, Dr. Bradford! I'm the receptionist, clinic manager, shoulder to cry on—pretty much whatever is needed."

"Well, Nancy, it's good to see you again."

"Same here, Doc. We sure are glad to have you here. We heard that you finished first in your class."

"Yes, that's true. But I'm starting to think maybe it was a pretty dumb class." I smiled, trying to think of a nice way to say I was glad to be here without lying.

"Oh, by the way, Doctor, your seven-thirty appointment is here."

"I didn't think I had any patients scheduled for today."

"It's not a patient, Dr. Bradford. It's Connie Thompson. I think she's here to talk to you about keeping house."

"Oh, that's right. Mayor Hickman said something about her coming by. Please send her in."

"I'll do that, and then after you two are done I'll introduce you to the rest of the staff."

"Sure. I'll be right here," I replied. *Dying a slow death,* I thought to myself.

As she opened the door to exit, she turned to me with a large smile and lifted eyebrows. "So excited. We're all so excited."

The condition was not contagious.

She left and I stood there thinking to myself, *Connie . . . Connie . . . Connie?* I didn't remember meeting a Connie on Saturday, which was probably a good thing. For a moment, I delved into a slight daydream. Every Connie I'd ever known was blond and pretty. Maybe this Connie was someone the mayor was subtly trying to fix me up with. I had dated various girls along the way, but since I had no significant attachments back in Nashville, I liked the idea of having an attractive young woman to look after my house and home. Two sharp knocks on the door brought me back to earth.

"Come in."

The woman standing before me profoundly shattered the Connie vision. Connie Thompson was a large and robust black woman in her mid-fifties. She wore a neatly pressed cotton suit and carried a black patent leather purse in one hand and two soft white gloves in the other. With an exceptionally handsome face, she had near perfect brown skin, the whole made even more distinctive by an arresting glare. Her black-rimmed glasses trimmed with gold inlay rested above a firm mouth and elevated chin that communicated a look of pure disdain. Without doubt she was quietly putting me through a critical assessment and showed little sign of liking what she saw.

"You must be Connie Thompson," I said. "Should I call you Connie?" I stepped toward her with my hand extended. She looked down sharply at my hand through the lenses of her glasses and then up at me, clearly with no intention of accepting my handshake.

After a long, awkward moment she looked directly at me and said, "You may call me Mrs. Thompson."

Realizing that my hand was still dangling in space, I withdrew it and placed it on my chest, pretending to rub something off my shirt. With an uncomfortable nod I replied, "Please have a seat."

She sat in one of the two tall leather chairs across from my desk. I considered sitting in the other one beside her but instead chose to retreat to my desk chair.

I folded my hands and sat quietly for a moment. Connie's gaze bore in hard, with no change in her expression. The silence was excruciating.

"Okay, I understand Mayor Hickman recommended you. Did you bring a résumé?"

Connie stared impassively at me, then answered in a calm but firm voice, "No."

I thought about this for a moment. "Okay. Well, then, maybe you could give me your verbal résumé. I guess you could tell me about your experience as a housekeeper, for example."

Having rarely conducted an interview before, I was painfully unfamiliar with what to ask. Thus far Connie Thompson hadn't moved a muscle or changed the terse look on her face. With this question she turned and stared toward the wall for one moment to contemplate an answer. After what seemed like a month, she returned her gaze toward me.

"I kept house for Mr. Thompson for twenty-seven years. I raised four children, all of whom are grown, educated, and with careers. They have families of their own, except for my son Rayford in New York and my baby Angelica, who lives and works in Nashville."

Lucky her, I thought to myself. I pondered her response and something about her past-tense description of Mr. Thompson raised a question. "I gather you and Mr. Thompson are not together anymore?"

"I'm a widower. Mr. Thompson passed seven years ago. Heart attack."

Again I thought, *Lucky him*. The interview was not going well. This woman was in full contempt of me and had apparently been weaned on a dill pickle. Hiring a housekeeper had been Mayor Hickman's idea. I wasn't sure I even wanted one, much less could afford to pay for her. I was out of questions and not sure what to say next. As I tapped a pencil on the side of the chair and tried to avoid eye contact, another question finally came to me.

"What other experience do you have?"

"Other experience?"

"Yes, for example, have you been a housekeeper for anyone else?"

Once again Connie looked away for a brief second. Then she answered, "No."

I didn't know what else to ask, so I simply repeated her response. "No. Okay, I guess that's a fair answer." I smiled, but her expression was still one of firm disapproval. "Let me think for a moment. I'm sure there are several other things that I need to ask you but they don't exactly come to mind." I was trying to phrase another question when Connie Thompson spoke.

"Dr. Bradford, do you go to church?"

"I'm sorry. Do I do what?"

She slowly repeated her words as if my hearing was geriatric. "Dr. Bradford, do you go to church?"

The question threw me. "Well, yeah. I mean, in the past. Why do you ask?"

"I'm not interested in keeping house for any man who won't at least make the effort to go to church from time to time. I realize that sitting in church doesn't make you a moral man any more than sitting in a pumpkin patch will make you a pumpkin. But at least it's a step in the right direction." She said her words with clarity and crispness, more lecture than conversation.

I sat for a moment, both puzzled and amazed. Connie Thompson was not at all what I had expected. But what could I do? The mayor had recommended her. There was no way to avoid hiring her unless I wanted my things to be moved out of the house and left on the front lawn before the end of the day. Attending church along the way wouldn't bother me, but the audacious tone of the demand took me by surprise. I returned from my brief mental fog and realized I was sitting on the edge of the chair. I slumped back between its cavernous shoulders and exhaled deeply. So much for taking on the new job on my own terms. With something of confused resignation I replied, “I’m sure that won’t be a problem.”

I had said the magic words. Instantly, Connie’s face took on a sweet and pleasant demeanor. “Very well, Dr. Bradford. I’ll start this afternoon.” She began to rise from her chair.

Relieved to have the awkward meeting over, I rose also. “Okay,” I said. Then it struck me. “What about a key and pay and that sort of thing?”

Connie was already headed toward the door. She spoke without turning around. “Oh, don’t worry about that. Walt already gave me a key.” By now her hand was on the doorknob. She paused and faced me. “Let’s see how it goes for a week. Then we’ll talk about money.” I joined her at the door and merely nodded.

Then Connie did something completely out of keeping with her previous frostiness. She extended her hand and said, “You have a good first day, Doctor. I’ll see you when you get home.” Her voice was almost warm and motherly. I instinctively shook her hand and smiled.

“Thank you, Mrs. Thompson,” I said. And then, feigning enthusiasm as best I could, I added, “It’s been good to meet you.”

Connie’s head tilted down. She looked at me sharply above the top of her glasses and the powerful look of disdain returned. She didn’t speak, but the whole of her face said, *Cut the bull, Doctor.* I felt like a truant in the principal’s office. She turned to leave, then hesitated and looked back at me again, this time with an air of stern reprimand.

“One more thing, Doctor. Around me you will keep your pants on. None of this parading-around-in-boxers foolishness.” In a tone of detached finality she added, “I am a lady.” Then she nodded her head and was out the door.

I leaned back against the closed portal and exhaled deeply, still a little stunned. *Boy, now wasn't that just a bucket of fun?* I stood gathering my thoughts. It was time to introduce myself to the rest of the staff, but I needed a moment. My meeting with Connie Thompson had left me in a slight daze. Eventually, I shook my head and chuckled, endeavoring to laugh off the encounter. For a split second, lying in a dark corner in the fetal position also seemed like an attractive option.

The rest of my day went surprisingly well. That morning I met all the clinic staff. As it turned out, Camilla, the phlebotomist, and Cindy, the lab tech, were sisters, not a difficult guess given that both of them were small, quiet women with mousy faces and slightly bowed shoulders. They were sweet natured, with soft, amiable voices.

In contrast, the staff nurse, Mary Jo Marshall, reminded me of the middle-aged women in Nashville who would perch in bars, wearing stylish outfits, predatory looks, and condescending glances. She was broad shouldered and thin, with hair so blond it undoubtedly came out of a bottle and skin so brown it was clear the tanning bed industry had found its way to Watervalley. She wasn't particularly pretty, although her facial features were sharp and well painted. And while I had heard her mention that she was pushing fifty, I highly suspected that she was pulling it. She typically had a laconic expression that bespoke a deep-seated boredom. She said little, but when she did speak, it could be venomous. Her uncensored opinions were not tempered with any sense of restraint. I had known a few people whose tongues had been dipped in acid, but I sensed Mary Jo gargled with it. I would later find that, paradoxically, with the patients she smiled pleasantly, always seemed to find the right level of compassion, and ultimately knew her business through and through.

But it was Nancy Orman who was the heart and soul of the staff. Full of boundless energy, she seemed to have a spiritual and emotional need to exhaust herself in the service of others. In time I would also come to learn that along with her relentless smile she had an unsparing generosity, with the incredible knack for knowing just the right thing to say to whoever came through the clinic door. Having lived in Watervalley all her years, she knew everyone's name, nickname, and hat size.

I also spent a considerable amount of time reviewing the equipment and supplies, which were notably limited and outdated. This concerned me, but my first day didn't seem to be the best time for making critical observations.

Late in the afternoon Chick McKissick, the volunteer fireman I had met the previous day, came in with a nasty cut, having snagged his leg on some metal banding from a shipping box down at his auto repair shop. For Chick, it was probably the only five minutes of the day when he wasn't smiling about something. Short, wiry thin, and always grinning, he was a guy you couldn't help but like. He just radiated friendliness.

I injected lidocaine around the cut to numb it before closing it with stitches.

Chick let out a low wail.

"*Ooooooh weeeee*, Doc. That's got some sting on it."

I could see him wincing, bravely trying to choke back the stinging pain. After a moment, the medicine took effect and the relief was easily read on Chick's face, an easy, brilliant smile against his dark skin.

I stitched him up, for which he thanked me profusely.

"Sorry to be causing you trouble like this, Doc. Thanks so much. I owe you one—I surely do."

"Not at all, Chick. Although I might give you a warning call before I fire up my stove again." I wanted to make light of the previous day's mishap.

Chick grinned. "You're covered on that one, Doc. I hear you got Miss Connie keeping house for you now. She can fire up the stove by just looking at it. She's a mighty good woman, but mind you now, she'll fire up your backside too if you cross her." He laughed heartily. Given the propensity for gossip in a small town, it shouldn't have surprised me that Chick already knew about the housekeeper. And yet somehow it did.

I nodded and smiled. The thought of being home with Connie Thompson standing over me like a disapproving specter gave me a queasy feeling. Chick wasn't helping.

When I arrived home a car that I assumed was Connie's was parked in the driveway. I walked up the front porch steps and stopped at the door, momentarily gathering my wits. I pursed my lips, sighed, and with trepidation turned the door handle. I was met with an almost palpable wave of incredible aromas wafting from the kitchen. Connie had prepared a veritable feast, including meat loaf, corn casserole, collard greens, and macaroni and cheese. It was the pinnacle of comfort food, all from a woman who pointedly made me uncomfortable.

She gave me little more than a sideways glance and spoke with a breezy indifference. "Afternoon, Dr. Bradford." She had on a striped cotton dress and a long white baker's apron. Clearly, this was a woman who was content in the kitchen, although little about her expression revealed it.

"Hi, Mrs. Thompson. Dinner certainly smells fabulous."

"It's ready. Plates are in the cabinet. Serve yourself up." Her voice was as impassive as ever.

"Actually, if it's okay with you, I was thinking about going out for a short run to unwind from the day. You've gone to a lot of trouble here, so would it hurt your feelings if I were to just heat some up later?"

Connie looked at me flatly. "If I were an eight-year-old girl I guess I would be crushed about right now. But since I'm past that, no."

It was answer enough. In reality, I really just wanted to keep my distance from Connie's critical air. "Okay. I'll be back later and will fix a plate then. But thank you so much. I'm sure it's all great."

Her response was deadpan. "Mmm-hmm, it is."

I nodded.

She continued, "Well, I've got to go. There's Jell-O in the refrigerator. And, Dr. Bradford, make sure you bless your food before you eat."

Again, I nodded obediently.

"I'll be back in the morning around six thirty to get your breakfast. Put the leftovers away and leave the dishes in the sink. I'll catch them in the morning."

"Okay, sounds good." I paused. "Do I get breakfast in bed too?" I was ineptly trying to dispense a little charm, to do something to soften Connie's hard exterior.

She stared at me warily, offering only a noncommittal grunt. As she turned to leave, she said in the same breezy, lilting voice, "I'd say there's a better chance disco makes a comeback." With that she was out the door.

I went for a short run, showered, and returned to the kitchen. I filled an overflowing plate of food and ate heartily. It was heaven, absolute bliss. Despite her critical demeanor, Connie Thompson was quite the cook. I wondered if her delicious but calorie-laden meals had put her late husband into an early grave. It was probable, but I shrugged and filled my plate again, deciding it wasn't such a bad way to go.

After dinner I got to work setting up my wireless network, eager to connect with old friends and to make sure the world hadn't ended in the last twenty-four hours—the kind of news that probably wouldn't reach Watervalley for another day or so. After a few short minutes I was online and bouncing around to some familiar sites.

Then an odd thing happened. A blip went across my screen, something I didn't recognize. Maybe because I was in Watervalley, it hadn't occurred to me to set up my Wi-Fi with password protection. As a precaution I immediately went to the DHCP clients table, the setting on my computer that revealed who was using the wireless network. My jaw dropped. Just that quickly, somebody had slid in on my network, potentially peeking into all my personal accounts. Not knowing what else to do, I reached over and pulled the power to the router, shutting the whole business down. I set up the wireless network again, but this time established password protection. It was odd, and a little unnerving. I checked and rechecked but no other users were getting access. Notably, somebody nearby was reasonably tech savvy. Perhaps Watervalley wasn't as far off the grid as I had thought.

Eventually, I let the matter drop and made my way to bed. I had other concerns. Tomorrow would be my first day with patients, a reality that nagged at me with a small amount of trepidation. It was my debut as a real doctor.

CHAPTER 6

A Day with Patients

I awoke early and anxious, opting to take a morning run to start the day. As I passed them, the sleepy, majestic houses on Fleming Street spoke of old money from the town's more robust years, when the railroad was still in operation. Within only a few blocks the quiet street gave way to a two-lane blacktop that shortly after became a country lane. On either side were broad, rolling pastures with grazing Holsteins, well-kept fences, cornfields, large gardens, white-painted hay barns, and boxy red tobacco sheds. From a distance came the low drone of a tractor moving about the fields. The sunlight spreading across the sloping hills gave me the sense I'd stepped into a different century, a faraway land. No doubt, Watervalley had a pastoral charm. It was a delightful start to the day. But it was short-lived.

Returning home, I noticed Connie's car once again parked out front, filling me with a low apprehension. I stopped on the front porch, standing with both hands on my knees to catch my breath. From inside I heard a voice singing a vaguely familiar hymn in a rich, deep contralto. The voice was powerful, mesmerizing. Regrettably, my entry through the front door silenced it.

"Is that you, Dr. Bradford?"

"Good morning, Mrs. Thompson. Certainly smells good in here." I was soaked with sweat.

She, however, stared at me dryly. The delight that a moment earlier was driving the song in her heart had been derailed on the way to her face. Nevertheless, it privately revealed something about Connie Thompson. It occurred to me that her scornful nature might be only a veneer.

"Hmm-hmm. Aren't you just a daisy? Been swimming in the lake?"

"I went for a run. I do it every morning." I paused to catch my breath. "In med school we called it exercise." I couldn't resist nudging her a little. "As your doctor, I would suggest that you consider trying it. A little running or walking could be a very healthy habit for you."

"Humph," replied Connie. "First of all, you're not my doctor. Second, I've seen lots of people running. Never seen the first one smiling. They're all wearing a pained look on their face. Soon as I see someone running and smiling, I'll give your advice some thought."

I couldn't help but be amused. "Okay, fine—make a joke. But you know as well as I do that exercise is a good thing."

She stared at me passively and then grabbed a towel to retrieve a pan of biscuits from the oven. As she continued with her breakfast preparations, she spoke generally to the room.

"Every fool knows that exercise is good for you, Dr. Bradford. But for a woman my age, running would accelerate my heart too quickly into an anaerobic rate. It'd also push me past my lactate threshold. Now, it's possible I could convert lactate to pyruvate and use it to fuel the citric acid cycle or I could get rid of the lactate with the Cori cycle by converting it to glucose in my liver. But uhh-uhh—neither are good for a woman my age."

She let that soak in for a heavy moment. Then she added in an unaffected and airy tone, "Any ol' doctor ought to know that."

For several moments I stood with my mouth open, speechless. "Whoa whoa whoa. Where did that come from?"

"Where did what come from?"

"All that. That talk of pyruvate and the Cori cycle. That's not stuff you pick up while making casseroles."

"Oh, that. Well, my youngest, Angelica, is a nurse and I used to help her with her studies when she came home on the weekend. Anyway, enough of this foolishness. Get your soaked, smelly self upstairs and get showered and ready for work. Otherwise you're gonna be late on your first day with patients."

It was clear that beneath the stern exterior Connie was subtly amused with herself. Her half smile had something of a forced, accommodating quality, the kind people use when they're looking at ugly babies.

I was still dumbfounded, staring vacantly.

"Heavens, boy—shoo. Go defunkafy yourself!"

I looked back at Connie as I retreated up the back stairs. I could have sworn I saw a broad grin emerge across her face.

At ten minutes till eight I was out the front door walking the three blocks over to the clinic on Church Street. I passed through the Episcopal church parking lot, which, oddly, was filled with cars. I didn't think much of it since churches often had breakfast meetings during the week for various committees or groups. But as I walked to the back door of the clinic, I noticed that the entire clinic lot was also full of cars.

Nancy greeted me with her normal hurried exuberance.

"Morning, Dr. Bradford. Big day. Big day today. Lots of patients here to see you. Lots of patients."

From the rear entrance I stepped into the wide central hallway and stopped short. The front reception area was standing room only with a mass of solemn-faced people peering back at me. A few low-toned conversations could be heard, but mostly they all stood grimly like a group of strangers at a train stop. I stepped back into the small rear entrance room.

"Ms. Orman, how many appointments do I have today?"

"Forty or so. We schedule them ten to fifteen minutes apart."

"Oh," I responded, only modestly relieved. "Must be a lot of family that came along, because it sure seems like a bigger group than that out there."

"No, no, Dr. Bradford. They pretty much are all patients. The clinic has always had a policy of taking walk-ins since there's really not any other place for them to go. So people come early to get their name on the list. First come, first served, you know."

"And how many have signed up on the walk-in list?"

"Oh, about another thirty, so far." Nancy grabbed my hand and spoke in an excited yet confidential tone. "People just can't wait to meet the new doctor. They just can't wait."

I studied her for a moment, slowly taking a deep breath. I forced a smile and spoke with resignation. "Okay. Well, let's get started."

"Your first patient is here for his annual physical. He's in room one and his chart is hanging outside the door."

"Just a physical? Shouldn't we be putting well-patient care off till we see the sick ones?"

"This one is kind of a special case."

"I'm not sure I understand."

"Mr. McAnders is the oldest resident of Watervalley. He's sort of the—well, the grandfather of the community. Letting him go first just seems like the right thing to do."

I had to agree. But the idea of seventy-plus patients waiting had me on edge. In an effort to be lighthearted I responded, "Okay, then. But let me know immediately if anybody out there is bleeding, convulsing, or grabbing their chest."

"Yes, Dr. Bradford," Nancy responded, and half bowed in an act of obedience.

Outside exam room one I glanced at the chart. There was an obvious typo that showed the patient's year of birth as 1912. This would make him almost a hundred years old. The little man sitting on the end of the exam table was clearly an octogenarian or better. He wore a flannel shirt and khakis and probably weighed no more than 140 pounds. As he turned his head, a pair of shining blue eyes glinted at me.

"Good morning, Doc. I'm Knox McAnders." He held out a hand that wavered in space until I was able to set down the chart and grab it.

"Luke Bradford, Mr. McAnders. Good to meet you."

Knox had a warm smile and remarkably smooth rose-colored cheeks. He had a full head of short, neatly cut white hair and bushy white eyebrows. But what struck me most was the clarity of his eyes, which were light blue with a perceptible mischievous spark in them. He seemed a man in which humor was never far away.

"Mr. McAnders, your chart says that you are ninety-nine years old. Is that correct?"

"Sounds about right. Way I see it, Doc, I got two choices: old or dead. So I guess I'll just take old." His mouth had a slight quiver when he spoke, as if his small, slightly protruding jaw had to get started before the words actually arrived.

"Well, you look pretty good for a man of your years."

"Well, not really, Doc. If you want to see someone who looks good, you should see my dad. He's the one who drove me here."

He turned his head to catch my reaction. I was about to speak but stopped abruptly with an incredulous look. It was long enough for Knox to know he had successfully hoaxed the young doctor, even if just for a moment. I smiled and began to reach for my stethoscope.

"You had me for a second there, Mr. McAnders. Take a few deep breaths for me."

"Ah, hell, Doc. Call me Knox."

As I continued with the examination, Knox told me briefly of his family history. His father had immigrated to America from Scotland in 1898 at the age of thirty-eight. The high hills surrounding Watervalley reminded him of his native Highlands, so he bought land and began to farm as well as make Scotch whiskey on the side.

Knox also spoke about his older brother.

"His name was Cullen. I think he was born in 1900. When the Great War broke out, Dad couldn't stop him from joining up, what with our Scottish cousins fighting the Germans. He survived the war but caught the influenza on the train ride back to Watervalley. He lingered for about a week, but it got the better of him. Everybody in the family took the flu, but Cullen was the only one who died from it. Broke my dad's heart. Three boys from Watervalley were killed in the Great War, but two times that died of the flu epidemic of 1918."

I remembered studying about the Spanish flu, which had devastated millions. But its history was long in the past. Knox's other comment intrigued me. "So your dad made Scotch?"

"He did up till the war. When my brother died, my mother and her Presbyterian roots somehow convinced him that the making of spirits had brought calamity on the family. So my dad shut it all down. Silly, I guess. But that's just how tragedy affects people. They look for something to be the cause."

I nodded, understanding Knox's words better than he knew.

"My dad was also in the ice business. The farm has this big cave that goes into the rock face on Akin Ridge. In the winter he would cut blocks of ice out of the lake and store it deep in the cave. Then he'd sell ice all summer long. Something about the mineral content in that old cave kept it cold, sort of a natural deep freeze. He would have ice that never melted all summer and was still there when the first frost hit in October."

Once again Knox paused. "A lot of old shafts in that cave. I think my dad stuck all his distillery stuff and whatever whiskey he was aging back in one of them and walled it up after Cullen died. Least, that's what I heard. I was just a boy and had gone to Primm Springs to convalesce after the funeral. When I got back, the distillery was gone from the barn and my folks never talked about it."

His story was interesting, but something more important was grabbing my attention. While listening to his heart, I was convinced I heard a slight irregularity.

"What do you do for exercise, Mr. McAnders?"

"I walk down to the high-water mark and back. It's about a half mile from the house."

"The watermark?"

"The river borders the northwest edge of the farm. There is a high rock bluff on the far side. Kids like to jump off of it. Dangerous, I think."

Knox paused for a moment, collecting his thoughts. I was fidgeting, but listened patiently.

"Anyway, when the big flood came in 'twenty-nine, the river rose thirty feet above where it is now. You can still see the watermark on that rock bluff after all these years. It colored the rock differently, like a paint line."

Knox spoke on reflectively, but with clarity. "I remember it like it was yesterday. Rained for seven days. I was nineteen. Two weeks later the stock market crashed and the local bank failed. Had my savings on deposit there. Wasn't much, but I never saw a dime of it. I was just starting to take over the farm from my dad. He died a week after Christmas, cancer in his lungs. Everything was ruined. Flood got two of our barns. We lost half our cattle. It was a bad time. But we got past it. So I like to walk down there and look at that watermark. It reminds me that you can get through anything. You just got to use your head and not give up."

I smiled and nodded. It was time to move on. "Knox, sounds like you've had quite a life. Look, overall you seem fine but I want to run a couple of tests just to be sure. I'm going to get the nurse to do a twelve-lead ECG to see if it tells me anything more specific."

"Is that where they strap those wires to me?"

"Yeah, it's painless. It measures the electrical activity of your heart."

Knox shrugged his shoulders. "Whatever you think, Doc. I'm hoping I can hang on for a few more months till I reach a hundred years. The mayor's told me we'll have a big parade to celebrate when the Fall Festival comes around."

"Sounds like a pretty nice gesture."

"Not really. It's an election year. Mayor Hickman's no dummy." Knox's eyes twinkled. He spoke confidentially. "Still, could be a good way to meet some women."

I had to laugh. "Okay. But first let's get that ECG done to make sure your heart's up to all those celebrity moments."

"While you're at it, check my ears. I keep hearing rumbling sounds in the night. It wakes me up."

This was odd, but not particularly alarming. "Anybody else hear these sounds?"

"I don't really know. My grandson Toy lives with me and sort of looks after things. He drove me here this morning. I pay him a little. But he doesn't get off his work shift till almost midnight. So sometimes it's just me there. It's only happened a couple of times."

"Well, let me think about that a little bit. Meanwhile, I'll get the nurse for that ECG." I needed to move along. "If everything looks okay, I'll see you again in about three months."

"Good to meet you, Doc. If you're ever out Ice Cave Road, drop in and see me. Name's on the mailbox."

We shook hands, but as I began to leave he spoke again.

"Doc, I'm glad you've come to Watervalley. I'm not an educated man, but I do read the paper. I figured there must be some reason why a summa cum laude graduate would come here. Can't be for the money."

He stared at me. His chin was firm but his eyes were soft, wise, discerning. I smiled and departed, quietly amazed at the uncanny, almost magical insight of this little man. His gaze had penetrated further than he knew. It had gone right through me and deep into the voices of my past.

CHAPTER 7
The Apple Tree

The balance of my first day with patients was long but uneventful. Determined to take my time with each one, I didn't get home till after eight. Connie wasn't there, but as on the evening before she had left an incredible dinner of meat loaf, potatoes, green beans, and chess pie. It was the best of all possible worlds—at least, all possible worlds if you had to live in Watervalley.

Wednesday morning proved to be a lighter day for patients, and, much to my delight, my arrangement with the town gave me Wednesday afternoons off. At noon I stopped by the Depot to grab lunch. The place was buzzing with the clatter of dishes and animated conversation. On the way in I said hi to a couple of familiar faces, but names were still a challenge. I received some friendly nods in response. Ironically, it seemed that despite their general openness and courteous nature, many of the people of Watervalley acted with an awkward reluctance toward me, as if uncertain about what to say. Privately, it was amusing, because I found myself in the same situation regarding them. I found a stool at the counter and read the paper over a plate of chicken fries.

I came home to an empty house and was restless, not so much for company as for space and time. I went upstairs to my bedroom, where I noticed Connie had done the laundry and neatly stacked it on my bed. I changed clothes and headed back downstairs to ponder my options for an afternoon escape. I had heard there were some old trails by the lake, so I dug out my hiking boots, hopped in the hot Corolla, and headed in that direction.

Watervalley Lake was a large kidney-shaped body of water that stretched a half mile in length. I eased the car onto the gravel parking lot and was quietly thankful that at present I was the only visitor.

The area was well kept save for a dilapidated structure built out over the water. It was an enormous old bandstand with weathered railings and a sagging roof, clearly much past its glory days. A locked gate had been installed at the mouth of the short pier with a rusty NO TRESPASSING sign hanging on it. The scale and majesty of the building were fascinating. The old structure evoked a tremendous sense of story: a doorway into long-elapsed decades. It was puzzling. From what I had seen, most of the public structures of Watervalley were kept in pristine form, yet this one was a notable exception.

On the far bank, a narrow stretch of grass bordered the lake at the edge of the woods. From there the hillside rose abruptly. I selected a trail that ran beside a creek and began to plod my way up. I eventually emerged upon a small pasture, a beautiful field of orchard grass. On the far side were several openings with no sure marking as to which trail to take. I choose one haphazardly, knowing that if I got lost, the way back would be always downhill.

After a while I came upon an old farm road that was little more than two dirt tire tracks with tall, broken grass in the middle. I followed it a short distance and came upon a fence with an old metal farm gate. Beyond it was a perfectly groomed apple orchard, a picturesque meadow of meticulously trimmed trees standing in crisp rows above lawn-tight grass. I was intrigued, but the orchard did seem out of place. It had a stately, eerie presence, as if it had somehow risen magically out of the tangled undergrowth and confusion of the woods.

I climbed over the gate and walked around the lower perimeter of the grove. The trees were heavy with green apples, some showing the slight blush of ripening. About halfway down the length, I saw a lone apple that had fallen from its branch, lying enticingly in the short grass. When I bent over to pick it up, I heard a gun cock and a deep, firm voice say, "Just what in hell are you doing?"

I was startled. I stood up and turned around in a single motion, dropping the apple in the process. Standing a few feet away was a tall, large-boned man in his late fifties shouldering a rifle aimed straight at me. He had thick, loosely parted gray blond hair, and despite his wild appearance, his scowling face had a certain handsomeness, albeit a hardness as well. He wore weathered khakis and a sweat-stained white button-down shirt over tautly muscled arms. I recognized him. He was the man who had given me directions at the County Line Market.

"Whoa whoa whoa," I blurted excitedly. "Don't shoot." I held up my hands in a defensive gesture.

"And why shouldn't I? You're trespassing." The voice was threatening yet without tension. It was the confident voice of a man who knew he was in full control of the situation, or perhaps any situation for that matter.

I spoke rapidly. "Okay, fine. I'll leave. But point that gun somewhere else." I stood frozen.

The man kept the gun leveled straight at me. "Where did you

come from anyway?" His relaxed inquiry had the same controlled focus.

"From town—from Watervalley." I hesitated a few heavy seconds. Now that the initial shock of the moment had passed, a subtle defiance was welling up in me. "Look, I said you need to point that gun somewhere else. I'll leave, but you're inviting something stupid to happen. I'm not moving till you put that thing away."

A faint grin pressed through the scowl. The man stood for a moment, sizing me up. Casually he took the gun by the stock and rested it over his shoulder with the barrel pointing to the distant woods behind him.

"Ballsy. I like that. What are you doing up here? Hold it—I hope you're not another jackass for Jesus sent up by the little steeple people. Because if you are, I really am going to shoot you in the ass."

"Hey—" I said firmly. I stood square shouldered to the man. "Nobody sent me. I'm new to town. I'm a doctor. I just wanted to get out of the house, take a hike. So chill out and I'll be gone in a minute."

Now his entire countenance changed. He manner wasn't exactly pleasant, but more one of reserved amusement.

"Oh, good grief. You're Bradford, aren't you? Why didn't you tell me that earlier? It would have saved this little tête-à-tête out here in the hot sun."

"I think it had something to do with you pointing a gun at me."

The man moved toward me. "Relax, Doc, it's just a BB gun. I use it to shoot the grackles and crows that get in the orchard." As he came closer, it was clear he was holding an air gun replica of a Winchester rifle. The realization provided little comfort. Whoever this man was, it seemed a good time to part company.

"Yeah, well, you can get back to your bird safari and I'll be making my way out of here." I nodded and stepped past him toward the iron farm gate where I'd entered the orchard. After I walked several steps, he spoke again.

"Hey, Doc."

Disgusted, I turned around and faced him. "What?"

He was standing casually, grinning, the gun still propped over his shoulder. He looked into the distance. His words were calculating. "I'm guessing that you're not completely sure how you got here, because if you were, you sure as hell wouldn't be trespassing on my property. That tells me you're not completely sure how to get back."

I considered the comment for a moment. It was, of course, entirely accurate. This guy might be slightly nuts, but he wasn't stupid. It still didn't matter. I was ready to skedaddle.

"I'll figure it out."

"Yeah." He scratched his chin and nodded, again looking toward the distant valley. "You probably will. Then again, there are a lot of old cow paths and blackberry thickets between here and the lake. It could make for a hot, miserable afternoon."

We stared at each other in cool assessment. It was clear we each knew the language of competition and assertion. But it seemed that, for both of us, the opposite ground—the realm of conciliatory and accommodating behavior—was much more foreign and much less attractive. For both of us, it was easier to start a fight than to end it, to declare war than try to negotiate peace. A long, silent moment of appraisal passed. I held the edge of my lower lip lightly between my teeth, deliberating. "So what do you propose?" I finally asked.

"Well, come on up to the house. It's a short walk up the hill. I can either draw you a map or give you a ride. Your choice."

I pondered the offer and nodded. "All right. Fair enough." As he spoke, I stepped toward him. Now within arm's length of each other, we stood in silence. Oddly, the encounter had invoked a subtle air of camaraderie. Yet there remained a lingering contention between us.

"Harris. John Harris." He held out a large, weathered hand. I took it.

"Hello, Harris. John Harris. Luke Bradford." I had always been an athlete and had a strong arm, but the man's grip was so hard that it almost made me tear up. He nodded over his right shoulder.

"C'mon. The house is this way."

I stood solid.

He stopped and looked back. "What?"

I returned a wry smile. "Before we go, I want that damn apple."

This evoked a large grin and an appeasing nod from John. He bent over, picked the apple up, and tossed it to me. "Suit yourself. But if you eat it, I hope you know a good doctor. Pretty green."

"The apple or the doctor?" I responded flatly.

"One for sure. Too soon to tell about the other." He headed up the hill.

The thought occurred to me to bean him in the head with the apple and make a run for it. Instead, I followed him.

CHAPTER 8
A Most Interesting Man

We walked through the grove, ascending a modest hill. On the north side of the fenced orchard was a rusted ornamental iron gate that opened onto a well-laid rock path. It cut through a stand of thick woods and undergrowth. The path climbed sharply to yet another elaborate wrought-iron gate mounted into a waist-high rock wall. Past the wall was a large, level yard covered with thick grass and shaded by generous oaks and maples.

Rock-lined wildflower beds framed the contours of the estate, and across the wide lawn stood a stunning, steep-roofed house that sat perfectly on the small rise of the yard. Not massive, but large enough to be imposing, it was a complication of multiple rooflines, wood siding, stone foundation, and large exposures of glass. The design reminded me of a farmhouse I had once seen in the French countryside during a summer jaunt in my undergraduate years. The rock wall extended around the whole of the open area, likely a full two acres.

We had negotiated the climb in silence and now continued across the soft grass toward the house. Despite the grand size of the yard, I noticed that careful design and forethought had been given to the selected plantings. In a far corner of the yard stood a modest English-garden-style greenhouse, the glass lightly streaked with chalky stains and the ornate copper long since turned to verdigris. The entire grounds and house wore a rustic elegance that spoke of educated taste, understated grace, and clear evidence of substantial money.

As we neared the house, I felt the first wave of a soft breeze. Off the back was a large redwood deck that pushed out over the sharp drop of the yard and overlooked a generous opening in the trees. From the deck one would be able to see a perfect vista of Watervalley. It was from this opening that the breeze poured onto the yard.

In the nearby grass sat a pair of white but slightly weathered Adirondack chairs with an antique wrought-iron table between them. The location offered an ideal vantage point from which to view the expanse of the valley below. As we passed I noticed on the table a short round drinking glass holding about an inch of what appeared to be diluted tea. A dead insect floated on the surface. It was the only thing out of place.

Despite the mature appearance of the landscaping, the house looked new. The wood siding was a rich chestnut and the white trim was fresh and spotless. I broke the silence.

"Nice place."

John continued walking and looked up momentarily as if to survey his property. "Yeah, it ain't bad."

I stopped to take in the view. He took another step or two and then instinctively stopped to look also. I stared into the distance.

"Quite a sight. You have a complete overlook of the town."

"Yeah, it's like watching an anthill. Except ants have

demonstrated some forms of intelligence. The verdict is still out on that bunch down there."

"So let me guess. You don't have a real high opinion of the people of Watervalley."

"Med school certainly honed your assessment skills. You've been here now—what, less than a week, and you haven't figured that out for yourself?" His voice was matter-of-fact, absent sarcasm.

"I didn't exactly start off on the best foot. So I guess I'm not particularly judgmental quite yet."

He continued to gaze out over the landscape and nodded.

"So I heard. Not to worry, Doc. Idiots are a protected group in Watervalley."

"That's very comforting. Thank you."

"Think nothing of it. You want something to drink?" He looked toward the door as a signal for me to follow him.

Through the side mudroom we entered a massive kitchen with rough-hewn columns and a soaring vaulted ceiling with exposed beams. The kitchen ran along the entire back of the house with French doors leading outside. It was spectacular. Something about the place was inviting and pleasing, the obvious work of a decorator, which once again spoke of understated wealth. Someone with an eye for color, light, and space had clearly brought the elements of furniture, pictures, and finishings together. Even though I'd grown up in the affluent neighborhood of Buckhead, I thought this was probably one of the most beautiful rooms I had ever seen.

"You want a beer?" John asked.

"Think I'll pass on that. If you don't mind, water actually works for me."

"Suit yourself." He reached into the refrigerator and brought out a bottled water for me and a beer for himself.

"This is well put together. Have you lived here long?"

"A little over three years. That's when we built the house. But I've owned the land a lot longer. Probably about twenty years."

On the kitchen counter was a framed black-and-white photo of John and a very attractive brunette, taken at the beach. The couple appeared to be fortysomething. Given the changes in John's appearance, I gauged the photo to be about ten years old.

"This your wife?"

John stared at the frame for a moment. "Yeah, that was her."

"Was?" I responded lightly.

"She passed away. Couple of years ago."

"Sorry." I gazed at the photo. "She was very pretty."

"Yeah, she was. She was quite a gal." He took a long swallow of the beer. "Well, Doc, if you're not in a big hurry, I'll give you the ten-cent tour. I can draw you a map of the trail back, but you'll be heading off right into the heat of the afternoon." He paused, waiting for my response. Then he grinned and spoke again. "Besides, it's rare to find someone in this county with an IQ above room temperature. Might be interesting for you to stay around a while."

I easily accepted the offer, the idea of returning to the empty house on Fleming Street presenting no immediate appeal. John's manner had become more affable, and besides, the place was stunning. The house and grounds I had just seen were by far the most elaborate I had experienced thus far in Watervalley.

We spent the next half hour ambling from the deck to the greenhouse to the small raised-bed garden, and then around the perimeter of the long rock wall. Surprisingly, John talked quite readily, going into modest detail about various plants, the origin of certain antiques, and the engineering difficulties they'd encountered in building the house.

On a couple of occasions he mentioned his departed wife, Molly. Apparently, she had designed almost everything I had seen, including decorating the home and selecting the various flowers in the gardens throughout the property.

The tour left John more relaxed. His tone became animated and he asked me about my education and background. It was not a probing interrogation, but a polite, methodical inquiry. He had a sharp intellect and, when he chose, was well accomplished in the art of conversation. At first I kept my responses somewhat clipped, not sure what to make of this curious, brooding man. But the exchange began to flow easily between us. Eventually, we wound up beside the two Adirondack chairs. Once again, I absorbed the tremendous view.

"So there's Watervalley."

"Yeah," responded John, his tone of disgust returning.

"Why all the angst about the folks in town?"

"What? Those idiots? Humph. You live here long enough, you realize that you're dealing with pretty narrow-minded people. And that's all fine and good until you have to swallow a healthy dose of their Bible-thumping morality as a substitute for common sense."

"So I take it one or two of the folks from the congregations below have tried to pay you a visit. You know they do that here in the South. It's not uncommon. You don't usually have to point a gun at them to make them leave."

He smiled. "Yeah, but it gets much quicker results."

I laughed under my breath. "Maybe so. I don't particularly care for that kind of thing either. But they're hardly dangerous."

John took a last long swallow from his beer. He looked at me solemnly and then turned, gazing distantly toward Watervalley, pondering my words. Oddly, the long silence that followed felt in rhythm with our conversation. I instinctively knew that, with John, this was not a failing of social tact but rather an acceptance of my company, an understanding that there was no need to fill the gaps. A gloomy intensity began to tighten in his eyes as he stared at the rim of the far hills. Something in my comment had poked the cinders of a smoldering memory, a subdued but angry release of uncertain sparks. A seething voice seemed to be welling up from within him. When he finally spoke, his words were delivered coolly, penetrating the air with muted invective: " 'The devil can cite Scripture for his purpose.' "

I glanced sideways at him. "So, do you make a habit of quoting Shakespeare?"

John looked at me, surprised. Something in my question had pleased him, releasing him from the spell of his thoughts. "Not bad, sawbones. *Merchant of Venice*, to be exact. Apparently you studied more than germs."

"Lucky guess, maybe. I have something of an uncanny ability to remember things. Still, I don't get the connection."

John inhaled deeply and nodded toward the town. "There is no idiot more dangerous than the one who is convinced that he must undertake his purpose because God has whispered in his ear to do so."

"Wow. Don't sugarcoat your insights on my account."

John cut his eyes toward me, his face a haughty smirk, his words delivered with an almost amused detachment. "You can rest your ass assured on that, sport. Besides, it's not just the steeple people down there. I don't like the people of Watervalley in general. For the most part, their minds either jump to conclusions or don't move at all."

"Are you saying they're a bunch of racists or rednecks? Because I haven't seen any of that."

"No, for the most part they've pretty much gotten the news that Lee has surrendered. They're simpletons, that's all."

"And you know this because . . . ?"

"Because I grew up here. Graduated high school here. It's where I met Molly. We came back for a few years in my late thirties, when I ran one of the local manufacturing plants. In those years I was in the thick of it—Chamber of Commerce, school board, Athletic Boosters, Boy Scouts. Hell, I even sang in the choir. It was just the two of us, so we pretty much devoted all of our time to the community. We were immersed in all things Watervalley."

"So I take it you have no children?"

John hesitated before answering. "We wanted to, but that never worked out." He let that comment hang briefly in the air before continuing. "Anyway, eventually I took an assignment overseas. But Molly always wanted to return. It was home to her. So we bought this property. I took early retirement four years ago and we moved back. So, yeah, I've spent a lot of years in the company of the good citizens of Watervalley."

"I get the impression something specific happened?"

John stood quietly. "Ah, it's a long story. And I don't like long stories."

I let it remain at that. We stood in the breezy shade of the yard and, for the moment, I was mesmerized by the sweeping splendor of the valley. Even through the heat and haze of the July afternoon, the details of the lake, the town, the distant rolling fields, and the far hills held the mind captive, no matter how often or intently one looked upon them.

I found myself trying to fill in the blanks about John Harris. But I was uncomfortable in asking any more personal questions. Without doubt, there was a smoldering intensity about him. I had my own misgivings about where my life was at that point, but they were nothing like what I sensed in him. His was a soul burning with conflict.

He clicked his tongue in an unspoken signal to move on.

"Come with me, Doc. I've got a little something I need to do around the greenhouse."

I followed. "You need some help?"

"Nah. Bring your water and you can park it. You can sit and we can talk of many things."

I responded casually, " 'Of shoes and ships and sealing wax, of cabbages and kings.' "

John walked on ahead of me. Without looking back, he immediately added, " 'And why the sea is boiling hot, and whether pigs have wings.' "

We exchanged wry grins but did not break stride or speak another word along the path to the greenhouse. As with much of the encounter, the exchange had served as a weighing out, a testing of each other's complexity. The ability to quote lines from Lewis Carroll's *Through the Looking-Glass* registered an understood mutual approval.

When we arrived at the greenhouse, he pointed toward a small shaded bench a few feet away.

"Take a load off, Doc. I'll be right back."

He stepped inside and emerged a moment later with a shovel and a wheelbarrow. He went on to explain the need to dig a small trench along the side of the structure to cure a drainage problem.

"I meant to get to this sooner, before the ground got hard. But so much for that." He placed the shovel in the grass and stepped on it with the full weight of his right foot. The ground gave way with a firm crunch, his satisfaction reflected in his demeanor. He popped the slice of earth up and tossed it into the wheelbarrow. Placing the shovel for a second time, he repeated the process.

"So what was it like growing up here?" I asked.

He reflected on the question for a moment, still focused on the shovel. "It was a small town, just like it is now. There weren't a lot of things to do. You could drink some beer, or you could drive a car fast down Beulah Road, or you could take a girl out to Moon Lake and try to get somewhere with her, which you generally never did. And of course that made you feel pretty stupid. It was not, I imagine, quite like growing up in Buckhead."

I smiled. "So you heard."

"So tell me, Luke Bradford—why did you become a doctor?"

I pondered the question. "No one reason, I guess. I played a little college basketball, but that was never a viable career option. Studying medicine came easily to me. I could help people in practical ways. The money's potentially good. And besides, my dad was a doctor. I guess I never seriously considered being anything else."

"Rumor is you finished top of your class."

"Yeah, well, that's the rumor."

John stopped and leaned on his shovel, assessing me directly. "Oh. So you're pretty smart, huh?"

"Smart enough, I guess. At some point I'd like to do research. But seems that getting some practical experience is what's in the cards right now."

He placed the shovel on the next bit of unbroken ground and resumed digging. "Not smart enough to keep your ass from landing in a place like Watervalley."

"There are financial reasons as well as some other commitments. It's complicated. Besides, looks like you're here too, and I'm not the one digging the ditch."

A smile forced its way across his face.

I spoke again. "What did you used to do anyway? You know, what was your career?"

"I have a PhD in chemical engineering. I worked for DuPont. I did some university teaching on the side. I helped write a couple of textbooks. I own a few patents."

"Okay, I'm impressed." This explained some unanswered questions. From the beginning, John Harris's rustic appearance had an underlying sophistication to it. So it came as no great revelation that he was a learned man. Clearly I was talking with someone who could claim significant accomplishments in a very complex field.

John spoke again. "Yep, along with my deft shovel skills I can tell you the recipe for the covalent bonds of a dozen different polymers."

"Is that why you think so little of Watervalley's collective IQ?"

John methodically continued to work the shovel. "Glad to see you picked up on my frequent use of the term 'idiot.' That pretty well sums it up for that bunch down there. That is, of course, with one notable exception."

"You saying there's someone smarter than you in Watervalley?"

Again, John stopped and leaned on his shovel, giving me a curious look. "You don't know, do you?" He seemed surprised. "You'll find out soon enough, sport."

The afternoon moved forward. We talked leisurely on a number of subjects that hovered mainly around the categories of news, weather, and sports, the typical safe topics of new male acquaintances who want to avoid confrontation that might surface from the world of ideas. I suspect we both held a private wish to find common ground.

The sun's gradual decline toward the west had spread long fingers of shade across the lawn. Cooler breezes occasionally fluttered, bringing some welcome relief from the afternoon heat. A little before six, I asked John to give me a lift back to my car.

We walked to the large garage where John housed the old farm truck I had seen him in at the County Line Market. Next to it were two Mercedes Benzes, the only two that I had seen so far in Watervalley. The first was a long black sedan, clearly less than a year old. The other was a vintage two-seater with the top down. It was a 280SL Roadster, luxurious red with a creamy white interior. I gawked for a brief moment until John spoke flatly.

"Forget it, sport—we're taking the truck." He went inside to get his keys and returned along with a small, partially filled paper bag that he placed on the seat beside him.

The first mile or so of the drive back was along a chert top. I sat mesmerized by the uncanny familiarity of all the dust and honeysuckle along the roads that traced elusively into the far contours of Watervalley. The sounds and smells were stained upon me from the earlier years of dust and ditches and the endless drone of gravel battering the bottom of my father's truck in north Georgia.

Deep within I knew I had become a doctor because of my father. But, unlike me, my father had loved the rural life. And, unlike John Harris, my father had been a soft-spoken, straightforward man of simple components. John was not made of the normal elements. He was of heavier stuff on the periodic chart: isotopes susceptible to imbalance, inclined to volatility, and in danger of combustion. I liked him, but I remained guarded.

Eventually, he turned onto a paved road and angled the truck left toward the downhill run into the valley. The surface was roughly patched and was bordered by unkempt fencerows, woods with rocky outcroppings, and an occasional trailer complete with old cars and pastel flamingos serving as yard art. After another ten minutes of silent travel, we reached the outskirts of town.

When we arrived at the lake parking lot, John pulled the truck to a stop, leaving the engine running. Then, with an uncharacteristic politeness and an engaging look, he turned to me and extended his hand.

"Luke, really good to meet you. Come back up anytime."

I returned the handshake warmly. It had been a good afternoon. "All right. Same here. And I will." I paused for a moment. "I'll also stay clear of the orchard. Don't want you shooting me."

John returned a thin smile and a nod. I climbed out of the truck and shut the door. Across the heat of the gravel lot, the lake spread motionless, placid. A sudden curiosity hit me and I leaned one arm into the open passenger window.

"Hey—got a question for you. What is the story with that old bandstand? Everything else in Watervalley seems pretty well kept up, but that old place is being left to rot. Seems odd."

John's demeanor began to change. Something was welling up from deep within and he focused intently through the truck windshield toward the old structure. A smoldering and fiercely restrained anger was leaching through. When he finally did speak, his eyes never moved from their hard glare at the distant bandstand.

"To understand the answer to that question, Dr. Bradford, you'll have to take in a little more of the oxygen of Watervalley. You'll have to breath in the stupidity of the air that seems to have permeated the minds of the fair citizenry."

I glanced momentarily back at the bandstand and spoke again through the open window. "Okay, sorry I asked that one. Thanks again for the ride. I'll drop in sometime."

"Hey, Doc, don't forget this." John tossed me the brown paper bag he'd left on the seat beside him. I caught it in midair. With a sly, mischievous grin, he put the truck in reverse and within seconds was gone from sight.

Inside I found the apple I'd picked up in the orchard. I laughed at John's cleverness, climbed into the old Corolla, and headed home. Connie would be waiting.

CHAPTER 9
A Strange Boy

As I entered the front door I could hear Connie in the kitchen. There was the predictable sound of dishes clanging and cabinet doors closing, but I also heard her half of a robust telephone conversation.

"Yes, Estelle, I hear what you're saying."

There was a pause while Connie listened to the voice on the other end of the line.

"Yes, yes. I know all about not sitting in the judgment chair. But all I'm saying about that woman is this: nobody can be showing that much leg in church and expect to be getting guidance from the Holy Spirit."

There was another pause, but by this time I had entered the room. Upon seeing me, Connie spoke up immediately.

"Estelle, honey, I've got to go. Dr. Bradford finally got home and I need to get dinner. From the looks of him, he could use it. We'll talk more about this later." She hung up the phone on the wall cradle and stared at me, her chin slightly raised with her normal look of placid disdain.

"Take your boots off outside, Doctor."

"Oh, sorry." I halted in midstep and walked backward on tiptoe to the front porch. Somehow Connie Thompson could invoke a debilitating fear in me. Upon reentering, I was determined to strike a friendly chord with her, to see if I could bring her under the spell of some Luke Bradford charisma.

"By the way, Mrs. Thompson, I want to thank you. I noticed you did the laundry today. That was very kind of you."

Her response was deadpan. "You're welcome, Doctor. Now quit your schmoozing and get washed up before your dinner gets cold."

I shrugged, defeated. "You know, Mrs. Thompson, over the years I thought I had developed a workable capacity for dispensing a little charm and wit to, you know, kind of win people over. That doesn't seem to be working here."

This actually elicited something close to a smile from her. She spoke in a relaxed voice. "Charm and wit's got nothing to do with being housebroke, Doctor, unless you know how to charm mud stains out of the entry rugs."

I nodded and went to the refrigerator to retrieve one of the beers left from my infamous purchase at the County Line Market. Not finding them, I said, "I had some beers in here. Do you know where they are?"

Connie stared at me impassively for a moment, then began to gather her belongings to leave. "They're in the cabinet beside the sink."

"Why are they up there? They'll get hot in the cabinet. You can't drink beer that's hot."

Connie's voice remained flat. "That's why they're in the cabinet. There's a pitcher of tea in the fridge if you're thirsty."

I stared at Connie for a moment, then shrugged my shoulders, deciding to let it go. "Okay. Well, thanks for dinner. I'll see you in the morning."

Connie gave a perfunctory nod and turned to leave. But she paused at the kitchen door, obviously pondering something. She turned back to me.

"Dr. Bradford, I don't like to pry, but I'm curious. Those two pictures beside your bed—the one of the couple and the other of a woman in the convertible. Are they your people?"

"Yeah. The couple is my mom and dad. It was taken a month before they were killed in a car accident. I was twelve."

"And who is the other one?"

"That would be my aunt Grace. She raised me after they died."

At first Connie said nothing, but she looked at me reflectively. The firm lines of her face had slightly melted away and she nodded at me with eyes that now seemed patient and undemanding. Then she spoke softly.

"You have a restful evening, Doctor. I'll see you in the morning."

After eating, I grabbed my glass of tea and headed to the backyard to enjoy what was left of the day. In the quiet of the evening I thought of Aunt Grace and how much I missed her now that school was over. Although she had never married, she did not fit the spinster librarian stereotype of an old maid. Tall, elegant, and athletic, she dressed fashionably, traveled widely, and entertained with ease in the opulent social circles of Buckhead, our family having been part of that community for generations. I sat quietly in the warm air and thought of the day of my parents' funeral.

Luke, you're going to live with me now. I can never be your mother and father. We both know that. They're gone. So we will have to be family. I love you, sweetheart, and we're going to be just fine.

Even now I remember her words vividly—she'd said "we" instead of "you." I think secretly she was talking to herself as well—that she was just as scared as I was. Not that she didn't love me; she never made me feel that. But she was scared about becoming a parent to a heartbroken twelve-year-old, scared about making the right decisions. My aunt's voice—soft, sweet, compassionate—had not matched her appearance. She, on the other hand, was a perfect blend of long, slim, sophisticated lines and an austere nature. She had been in the dining room going over papers with men in suits, discussing the affairs of my newly dead parents. She had come into the living room, where I was sitting, and had crouched down beside the large chair so she could talk to me at eye level. In years before, I had always been afraid of her, but now she seemed gentle, vulnerable.

She died of breast cancer two months before I started med school. She was only fifty-eight.

An odd noise brought me out of my thoughts. I looked around but saw nothing out of order. I did my best to discount it, but there was no denying the feeling of another presence.

Instinctively I turned my head to gaze up at the maple tree in the adjacent yard. Two eyes behind thick glasses were staring intently at me. It was a boy of about twelve sitting motionless on a limb, wearing a white bicycle helmet and a solemn, inquisitive expression. I stared at him for a minute in much the same way I would have examined an unusual rock formation. It was the boy who broke the silence.

"You like to think a lot, don't you?"

"Hello to you too," I responded. "How long have you been up there?"

"Does it matter?"

"Well, no. I guess not." I stood for a moment, replaying the last few minutes in my mind, quickly assessing whether I'd done any brainless acts. Somehow the last few days had reinforced the idea of doubting myself first.

"You didn't answer my question," the boy said.

"What question?"

"The question about thinking."

"Oh, that one. Well, I don't know. Sometimes I sit and think, and sometimes I just sit."

The little fellow continued his emotionless stare.

"You know," I said, "it's a little creepy to have someone sit and watch you like that. What are you doing up in that tree anyway?"

"Sitting and watching." A slight grin was now forming in the corners of his small mouth.

"Who would have guessed?" I responded dryly. "Why aren't you riding your bike or something?"

"Haven't got one."

"Then why are you wearing a bike helmet?"

"I like it."

"So you wear it when you climb trees?"

"No, I pretty much wear it all the time. It protects my brain."

I thought about that for a moment and smiled. "You're kind of a dorky kid, aren't you?"

"I'd say that pretty well sums it up."

"Good for you. Dorky is okay with me. Matter of fact, it's pretty much been my experience that the dorky people end up with all the money."

The boy smiled approvingly. "Dorky people and doctors."

"That remains to be seen." I paused for a moment. "What's your name?"

"Will."

"Good name for a guy. Is it a family name?"

"It was my grandfather's, except his was Wilhelm."

"You have a last name, Will?"

"Yup."

"You want to tell me what it is?"

"Fox."

"All right, then, Will Fox. I'm Luke Bradford. Good to meet you. You have any brothers or sisters?"

"Nope, just me."

"How old are you?"

"Twelve."

"Do your folks know you are up in that tree?"

"It's just my mom, and she doesn't care."

"Is your dad not home?"

"He died last November."

This caught me by surprise. He was so young, his father's death must have been tragically premature.

"I'm sorry to hear that. Being twelve without a dad is tough." I paused, considering for a brief second about elaborating. But it was not the time. "How old was he?"

"Forty-three, I think."

I nodded. Although annoyed to have my privacy invaded, I felt a genuine empathy for this odd little fellow.

"So how is your mom taking all this?"

"She seems sad a lot, and she worries about things."

"I guess that's understandable. By the way, speaking of worrying about things, I think she would be worried to know that you are up in the tree like that. How did you get up there anyway?"

"It's easy," the boy said with detached determination. "There's a limb over there by the fire escape." He made a head gesture toward the house behind him.

I walked into the neighboring yard to get a better look. Next to the upstairs window was a black metal fire escape complete with stairs and landing. The maple tree had a sizable branch that reached beside it. It would have been little trouble for the boy to climb over the rail and walk along this branch while steadying himself on the upper limbs. I studied the situation and then looked up at him, still perched in the same position in the tree.

I smiled again, speaking casually. "Okay, Will Fox, here's the deal. What say you climb back over to the fire escape while I'm watching, just so I'll know that you got there okay?"

Will thought about this for a moment. "What if I don't? It's my tree."

"That's true—it is your tree. But if you fall and break your arm, you'll be my patient." I put emphasis on "my." "So let's just say I'm practicing preventative medicine."

"Are you trying to get rid of me?"

"Not at all. Come on down. We can still talk, just face-to-face."

With that the boy reached for a limb above him and began the process of clambering back to the fire escape. Despite his small, gangly appearance, he moved nimbly and was quickly over the rail and onto the metal landing. He came down the stairs and walked over to me, staring up with curiosity. I stood a good two feet taller than him.

"This isn't exactly face-to-face." There was an injured quality to his voice.

"Point taken." I walked over and took a seat on the remains of a stone wall that stood between the two properties. "So, what grade are you in?"

"Sixth."

"You like school?"

"It's okay."

"You play sports?"

"You ask a lot of questions."

"I'm a doctor. It's my job."

"You're not at work right now."

"Sorry, force of habit."

"I have a question," he injected.

"Okay, shoot."

"You have a girlfriend?"

"That's none of your business," I said flatly.

"It was a fair question."

"It was a fair answer."

"You don't have to be embarrassed. I don't have a girlfriend either."

"Who said I didn't have a girlfriend? I simply said it was none of your business," I returned, amused by the little fellow's lively intellect.

"I think I know the answer," responded Will confidently. "Besides, it's no surprise with that piece-of-crap car you drive. What kind of doc are you anyway?"

"I'm sure there are many people in this town asking themselves the same question."

"Which question?"

"Well, not the one about the girlfriend or the car. You know, you have some pretty sharp opinions for a guy with a bicycle helmet and no bike."

"It's still a crappy car. So what about the doctor question. Are you any good?"

"I think my best advice to you is to stay out of trees so you don't have to find out."

A grin forced its way across his face. It was clear he was enjoying the banter. "You know, I bet you like being a doctor."

Something in his comment struck home. I did like being a doctor. It was being a doctor in Watervalley that I wasn't so sure about. This peculiar little boy was clever, maybe even too clever. I couldn't help but enjoy his company. I wondered if his quick mind had earned him some pounding by the larger, more dim-witted boys at school. That would certainly explain the bicycle helmet.

The moment was broken by a loud call from the back porch of his house. "Will?"

Clearly, from the tone and pitch, it was his mother. To my surprise, his face suddenly turned ashen, as if he were thinking about things a world away. "I need to go."

"Sure. But—hey, since we're neighbors, why don't I say hello to your mom?"

"Now is probably not a good time. Maybe later," Will said hastily. He sped off and disappeared around the back corner of the house.

I stood and scratched the back of my head, thinking about Will's sudden departure. His mother's call had panicked him in some small way and it was clear that he was truly nervous, wanting to hide something. It was intriguing, but then again, so was he. Just like Connie Thompson, he was a small bundle of complexities.

As I walked back to my yard the thought occurred to me that John Harris had it wrong about the people of Watervalley. They weren't simple at all.

CHAPTER 10

Getting to Know You

I sat on the steps of my back porch for a few minutes, pondering the day and watching the last dappling patches of sunlight play across the rear lawn. I knew I needed to start making calls. From the dozens of patients I had seen the day before, I had made a list of about fifteen or so who had issues that I wanted to follow up on. It was not something anyone had required me to do. It was simply a practice I remembered from years before. I had learned it from my father.

Every evening after dinner he would spend an hour on the phone calling patients, asking if they had gotten their medications, inquiring about their symptoms, or just listening quietly to a liturgy of minor complaints. When I was a child, it baffled me. In time I had come to realize that this was how he chose to run his practice. Now, despite my ambivalence about being in Watervalley, it seemed the right thing to do. I knew the staff could make many of these routine calls, but I was the doctor and they were my patients. I went inside, placed a chair beside the kitchen wall phone, and dialed the first number.

"Hello."

"Hi, is Doyle Dodson there?"

"Speakin'."

"Doyle, this is Dr. Bradford."

"Who?"

"Dr. Bradford, from the clinic."

"My God, Doctor. What's wrong? Have I got cancer?"

"No, no. Not at all. I was just calling to tell you your strep culture came back negative."

"Negative? Is that bad?"

"Well, no. Negative is good."

"Negative is good? That doesn't really make sense, does it, Doc?"

"I see your point. Look, Mr. Dodson. The test showed that you don't have strep. You just have a sore throat. Take your medications and you should be fine in a few days."

"Okay. I guess that's good. Man, you scared me, Doc. I never had a doctor call me at home before. You sure the test didn't show I have cancer?"

"We didn't test you for cancer. But if you're concerned, come by the clinic and we can do some blood work."

"Nah, that's okay. So, is that it? Is that why you called?"

"Yeah, I thought you might want to know the test results." There was a long pause with no response. "Mr. Dodson?"

"Yeah, I'm here. Okay, then, Doc. Thanks for the call. Hey—while I've got you. Do you have any way of testing whether or not a cow has strep?"

"Mr. Dodson, I'm pretty sure cows don't get strep throat. Any infection from cows is usually passed through their milk if they have something like mastitis."

"Well, he just sounds hoarse to me."

"I see."

"I mean, not like a horse, but like a sore throat kind of hoarse."

"I understand. I think."

Mr. Dodson proceeded on for several more minutes describing in great detail the symptoms of his vocally challenged cow. At one point I even held the phone out and studied it like a rare artifact, amazed at the endless words pouring out from the small speaker. I couldn't help but wonder what kind of conversations he and the cow had. Given Mr. Dodson's penchant for talking, I was surprised the cow got a word in edgewise. Eventually Mr. Dodson took a breath and I was able to end the call. Before I dialed the second number, I was beginning to get the vague notion that one of the hot beers in the cabinet might not be so bad after all.

Next on my list was Nadine Tomlin, a pleasant but rather forthright and seriously overweight woman in her late forties. Her chronic arthritis had been giving her a considerable amount of pain. I had prescribed some new medications. The phone rang seven or eight times before she answered.

"Hello."

"Is this Nadine Tomlin?"

"Yeah, and I don't know what you're selling but I probably already have three of them. Bye!" I heard a stout click, followed by the steady hum of the dial tone. I redialed the number. It rang even longer this time and the response was tinged with annoyance.

"Hello-oh."

"Nadine, this is Dr. Bradford. Please don't hang up."

"Oh, crud. Was that you who just called?"

"Yeah, but that's no big—"

"Gosh, Doc. I am so sorry. It's usually someone trying to sell me something."

"Not a problem. Listen, I was calling to follow up—"

But once again, Nadine broke into the conversation. "Doc, can I call you back in a few minutes?"

"Did I catch you at a bad time?"

"No, it's just that *X Factor* is on and I really don't want to miss who wins."

"Um, yeah, sure."

"Will it take long? Because I can call during the next commercial."

I exhaled and shook my head. "Just call when you get a free moment." We said good-bye and as I placed the phone back in the cradle I started contemplating what beer on ice might taste like.

It took another hour and a half, but I was finally able to make the rest of my phone calls. Like Doyle Dodson, a few of the others immediately responded with a voice of alarm, but generally I was able to put them at ease in short order. Some expressed polite trepidation and hesitation, not sure what to make of the doctor calling them at home. A few genuinely appreciated the call and the underlying attitude of care that had prompted it. And while even those conversations were often awkward, I felt assured that this was a good practice. I would do my best to make it a mainstay of my role as community doctor.

After I finished the last call, I flipped the paper over and noticed that I had written down one additional name followed by a question mark. It was Leo Sikes. He and his wife, Mavis, had come to the clinic because Leo had been experiencing a slate of changes in his demeanor. They were both in their early seventies and, other than some significant hearing loss, had been in relatively good health. But lately Leo was having trouble remembering things, he had lost his sense of taste, and he was experiencing increasing mood swings and depression. I had prescribed a few medications for these symptoms, but wasn't really satisfied. What troubled me about Leo was that these issues could be caused by a number of etiologies that were perhaps unrelated, especially given his advanced age. After they had left the clinic, it had occurred to me that his symptoms could also be signs of the onset of Parkinson's. I wanted him to come back so I could test him further.

Over the next half hour I dialed his number a couple of times but never got an answer. It was not a great concern, but it did seem odd that they were not there to answer the phone even past nine o'clock at night. I would have Nancy get in touch with them in the morning. Eventually I turned off the lights and went upstairs to shower and go to bed. Tomorrow would be another day of patients.

CHAPTER II
Haircut

Thursday morning brought only a modest number of appointments and we worked through them quickly. Despite her fondness for socializing, Nancy was a drill sergeant when it came to processing patients. She marshaled the staff into an invisible lockstep. They would have the paperwork filled out, the blood work done, and the patients ready for me, all to the beat of an unseen metronome.

Most of the patients were middle aged to elderly and much of what I saw could have been treated at home. More than a few were obese and seemed to have an affinity for tobacco in one form or another. It also became clear that a number of patients weren't so much sick as they were curious—that is, curious to meet the new doctor. And while most of them were plainly dressed and plain-spoken, I began to see the warp and woof of small-town Southern life. Vague in its presentation and elusive in its markings, the various strata of social ranking in the fabric of the town's tapestry were becoming evident to me. It was a complexity I had not expected to find in such a remote little place.

One lady who presented an air of high decorum was Mrs. Polly Fletcher, who had come to the clinic to have her blood pressure checked and for a review of her medications. She was a short woman of robust proportions, with a powdery, well-rounded face, graying hair that was clearly molded in a beauty parlor, and red lipstick so thick it bordered on that of a circus clown. With doleful eyes she spoke in a modulated voice that required her lips to barely move. Although somewhat stiff, she had an appropriately polite and receptive manner and took great delight in telling me all about the Society Book Club, of which she was a member. More than once during the conversation she reminded me that it was Watervalley's oldest and most prestigious book club, as if it were some great importance to me. She noted that the club was for women only, but that they would be delighted to have me come speak sometime. On what, I had no clue.

Another mainstay in town was the Chicks with Sticks Knitting Club, to which several of my patients belonged. Apparently this group was a vestige of what had once been known as the Home Demonstration Club, a group of farm women that had met once a month to learn about canning, cooking, sewing, child rearing, and anything else that provided an excuse to gather and gossip. The old Home Demonstration Club had played out its usefulness a couple of decades earlier, but the interest in socializing had not. This group also offered me an invitation to come and speak to them at some point in the near future. I appreciated the enthusiastic interest but was at a complete loss as to why or what to talk about. What did these people think I had to offer? It was a knitting club. Did they want a demonstration on suturing wounds?

And yet, while social tiers clearly existed, there was still a certain unity of spirit, a genuine openness and kindness I experienced from the patients who came to see me. With each new appointment, however, I came to realize that many of them cast lingering glances at my manner of dress and appearance. Which raised the issue of my hair.

During my residency I had allowed my hair to reach an almost shaggy state, but Watervalley was the land of buzz cuts and flattops. It seemed that a more conservative cut was in order. So at noon on that Thursday I walked downtown to find Maylen's Barbershop, which according to Nancy was pretty much my only option. Some men had been known to go to the Three Sisters Salon, but Nancy's raised eyebrows and wary face had offered an unspoken opinion of that idea. Maylen's would be fine.

With storefronts filled with colorful displays, signs, and merchandise, Watervalley's modest downtown had surprising character and vibrancy. The buildings varied in material and design and spoke of a more opulent bygone era. With the courthouse nestled among the trees and green of the central square, the town presented itself as a picture-perfect village of merchants and markets.

Maylen's Barbershop was on the modest side, a simple one-room structure made of concrete blocks smothered in clean, fresh white paint. The traditional spiraling barber pole was mounted outside the door and the glass front was covered with printed community announcements.

I entered and took a seat after offering a polite nod to the half dozen men situated around the small room. Maylen looked up from where he was standing at his barber's chair and, without expression, spoke with simple courtesy.

"Afternoon, Dr. Bradford." From the very first, just because he knew my name without an introduction, I liked the man.

I responded with a polite nod. "Maylen."

Snipping away with his scissors, Maylen Cook had the epitome of a hangdog appearance. Although a trim fellow, he had doleful eyes and heavy jowls that bounced lightly on the few occasions he chose to speak. Having been a barber for thirty years, he projected a lackluster disposition that suggested cutting hair had long ago become tedious for him. Nevertheless, he was methodical at cutting, gifted at listening, and an insightfully clever fellow as well. He treated me with a genuine politeness and an obliging humor. But that wasn't true for everyone in Maylen's world.

After only a few minutes it became apparent that not all the men hanging around the shop wanted or needed a haircut. Several were there to pass their time in idle conversation that endeavored not to offend God or man. That is, everyone except for Vernon Boshers.

Vernon was a squat, chunky little man who owned the coin laundry adjacent to the barbershop. Apparently he was a daily fixture in Maylen's place and had been so for a long time. With his round face and perpetual clownish grin, he was a loud, ill-mannered, opinionated talker. His gregarious nature and vacant intellect had remained undimmed despite many years of Maylen's disdain. He noisily rambled on without mastery of facts on any topic, preferring a broad amount of ignorance to a small amount of trouble.

Vernon sat in a chair across the small room and regarded me with focused interest; no doubt my presence was a novelty. It didn't take long for him to let his thoughts be known.

"Doc, you got a lot of hair. You might want Maylen to give you an estimate first." The comment raised only a few grins, but Vernon laughed robustly, delighted with his own small wit. I simply smiled. Meanwhile, I noticed that Maylen had discreetly and briefly looked up from his scissors and glanced at me. It was a discerning, protective expression.

Vernon continued, speaking again generally to the room but clearly directing his remarks to me. "Is that the way people wear their hair in the big city now? Kinda makes it hard to tell a guy from a girl." He chortled a short laugh and glanced at those around him, still quite pleased with himself. His inquiry was driven more by mindless probing than by malice. Several of the men gave me anticipatory looks, suggesting that a response was expected.

I had no desire to engage Vernon at any level, so I grabbed a magazine from the adjacent side table and began to feign interest in it. It was on bow hunting. Childhood arrows with rubber tips were the extent of my experience and knowledge.

For a short moment Vernon lost interest in me, but that didn't stop his stream of rolling commentary.

"Hey, I was up in Nashville not long ago and ate at one of those Mexican restaurants, and I swear to God they had moles on the menu. They put it in a sauce. I know people in other countries eat strange food 'cause they're hungry, but I never heard of such a thing. I could supply them up for a month just from my backyard."

He surveyed the occupants looking for confirmation, and finally attained several approving nods. I was doing my best to sit poker-faced and not outright laugh at Vernon's ignorance. Unfortunately, he felt that my input on the issue was required. So he redirected the entirety of his efforts of persuasion on me.

"Moles must be some kind of delicacy in Mexico, don't you think, Doc?"

I glanced up at Maylen, snipping away and unaffected by Vernon's remarks. Without looking in my direction, Maylen closed his eyes and shook his head for a brief moment. In his deadpan voice, never losing focus on his scissors, he said, "He's a doctor, Vernon, not a food editor. Meanwhile, we'll let you know if you suddenly become interesting."

This brought some muffled laughs and sideways glances from the men around the room. But Vernon Boshers was unfazed. He continued to comment on a variety of subjects, none of which interested me until I heard the name Knox McAnders.

"I tell ya, I've heard it all my life. There's a truckload of Scotch whiskey bottles hidden back in that old ice cave. Before we have the parade for his birthday, I think those caves need to be checked out. Then we'd have a real celebration. Ol' Knox's had that place boarded up for fifty years, claims he looked and never found it. But I bet they're still in there somewhere."

The man beside Vernon responded, "What makes you think so?"

"Why, all the talk I've heard over the years. There's lots of people think the way I do."

The other man continued, "Well, my grandmother knew Knox's mother and she claims every bit of it got poured out into the creek after Knox's older brother died."

As Vernon droned on, it was clear that his comments were based on little more than rumor and conjecture. Still, it did make for an interesting story.

"I bet a hundred-year-old Scotch would be worth a lot of money," Vernon continued, exercising great authority with his pronouncement. "What do you think, Doc? All you doctors drink Scotch, don'tcha?"

I smiled and shook my head. "Can't really help you on that one."

Vernon stared briefly at me, openmouthed and clearly surprised at my answer.

The conversation about Knox continued, and it was easy to discern from the others' comments that Watervalley looked on Knox McAnders with a regard bordering on reverence. For them, he was more than liked, loved, and respected. He was considered the standard-bearer of all things good about Watervalley—a love of the soil, a devotion to community, and an independent, self-reliant spirit.

Eventually, Vernon's rambling caught my attention once again. "I bet John Harris would know a thing or two about Scotch." He glanced at the others with a malicious leer. "Shoot, I bet he's got hundred-year-old Scotch up in his big house right now."

I kept browsing the hunting magazine as I discreetly tuned in to the conversation. The topic of John Harris prompted a lengthy discussion from the men in the room. Apparently he stirred emotions much the way Knox did, but with darker feelings mixed in with the light. It became clear that in years gone by John had walked among the people of Watervalley like a giant. A man of unspeakable gravity, he possessed the triad of wealth, education, and respect. The passing comments, the subtle innuendo, the animated faces all spoke of an odd combination of reverence and disdain for the man. Despite the general contempt for his arrogance, there was an undertone of self-importance to those who claimed to have known him well, and even those who didn't like John Harris wanted to know him. Once a major figure in the town's leadership, he was now a bitter recluse, all references to him based on experiences from years past.

My turn in Maylen's chair was coming up, but still in line before me was Vernon himself, who, unlike most days, was actually in the shop to get a haircut. Once in the chair, Vernon jabbered nonstop while Maylen clipped away with the same weary focus, offering only the occasional grunt in reply.

At the end of each haircut, Maylen had a standard practice of dousing a long horsehair brush with a green barber's tonic and lightly swishing each customer's head with this rather oddly scented concoction. Despite his expressionless demeanor, Maylen did this with a ritualistic flair and everyone seemed to accept it.

But just as Maylen had doused the brush and was ready to administer this final touch to Vernon, he blurted out, "No no no—don't put that smelly stuff on my head. My wife will think I've been to a whorehouse."

Maylen was caught off guard and noticeably irked to have his routine interrupted. He stood poker-faced and for a long moment looked at Vernon, then at the brush, then at Vernon again.

Then he simply shrugged and said, "Suit yourself. My wife doesn't know what a whorehouse smells like."

Yes, without a doubt, from the beginning I really liked Maylen Cook.

CHAPTER 12
Celebrity

On the way back from Maylen's I stopped in at the Waterval-ley library. It took up half of what was known as the Memorial Building, a beautiful Greek revival structure that sat a block off the town square. The Memorial Building had been built in the twenties, after the Great War. The other half of the building was a large hall, a gathering place for dances, meetings, and, during election years, political fund-raisers.

To my surprise, the library was quite extensive, with a large selection of magazines, audio books, Internet terminals, and a wide-ranging collection of books and reference materials. Perhaps what was most amazing was the number of people there—it was downright crowded. The head librarian, an energetic little fellow named Herbert Denson, was for all practical purposes the male counterpart of Nancy Orman, except with a bow tie. He was lively and personable, shaking my hand vigorously as he greeted me warmly, delighted that I had come in to get a library card. We talked briefly while I filled out the paperwork. I got my card and said good-bye. But as I was turning to leave, Herbert came up beside me, put his hand on my shoulder, and with great earnestness asked me if sometime I would come and speak at a library board meeting. I was vague but noncommittal, and as with other invitations was at a total loss as to what they wanted me to talk about. On the way back to the clinic, I intentionally walked on the opposite side of the street from the firehouse, fearing that Ed Caswell might come running out to ask me to speak to the volunteer fire department.

After I'd returned from my haircut, Nancy informed me that the lunch break had brought in a new round of walk-ins. It was going to be a busy afternoon. She still had not been able to reach Leo Sikes on the phone but seemed not to think much of it. I asked her to try again before she went home. I had just started my first exam when Hoot Wilson went into cardiac arrest out in the waiting room.

That event was a turning point for me as the Watervalley doctor. With all the absurdities surrounding my arrival and being so fresh to the job, I was certain everyone in town viewed me with some measure of skepticism. But Friday's headline in the Watervalley paper, *The Village Voice*, read "New Doctor Saves Local Resident." The story was only loosely correct and effectively credited my actions with saving Hoot's life. Privately, I knew better.

That morning the staff was almost walking on air. Irrepressible smiles burst from everyone's face—everyone, that is, except Mary Jo, who in her smirking, laconic way asked me if I had considered going down to the lake to see if I could walk on water. Mary Jo's sharp comments aside, I received a slew of kind praise from my morning patients. When I walked over to the Depot to grab lunch, a noticeable buoyancy entered my step as many animated townsfolk greeted me along the way. No doubt, I was enjoying a brief moment of celebrity. And while I was far from letting the perception go to my head, I found nothing wrong with taking some modest delight in the accolades. I was closing out my first week as the new doctor and my confidence was at its pinnacle.

I should have known that a large dose of humility would be served up before the day was out.

At five forty-five I walked out of what I thought was the last exam and crossed the hall to my office to make some final notes. I had just landed in my chair when Nancy knocked on the half-opened door. She spoke hesitantly.

"Doctor, there is one more but it's technically a physical." She paused, wanting to get my initial reaction before proceeding. I sensed there was something more and responded with a nod.

"Well, it's a Miss Akins and she is here with her two-month-old for his well-baby checkup. She just got off work and rushed over hoping you might see him before you go home."

I had just paced myself through a full week of mostly geriatric cases, so it hit me as a refreshing change to put on my pediatric hat. Moreover, what Nancy said called to something within me that I had known well in recent years.

During the long, fatiguing hours of internal medicine residency at Vanderbilt Hospital, it was my pediatric rotation that had taken me to the absolute limits of fortitude. I could never bring myself to refuse a child. A nurse's page alerting me to an elevated temperature or labored breathing or an accelerated heart rate would pull me from an exhausted doze in some random chair and I would find the strength and patience to go, listen, watch, and assess. Walking the long halls late at night, I would look with compassion into the anxious faces of drained parents. Through those tiring and surreal hours, each new child had kept me focused and compelled me to the next room, the next chart. They were the innocents.

I looked at Nancy. “Did you say ‘Miss’ as in M-i-s-s?”

“Yes,” she responded. There was a heavy pause. “Yes. That would be correct. Would you like me to have her reschedule?”

“No,” I responded, somewhat surprised. “No, not at all. Put them in room three. I’ll be there shortly.”

Nancy nodded and turned to walk out. As she reached for the door handle, I spoke again. “How old is she, Nancy?”

She paused as she pondered the question. “I’m thinking she just turned eighteen. She looks older. But I can check the chart.”

“Not important. I’ll look at it before I go in.”

Nancy shut the door behind her. For a moment I sat and stared out the window at the long shadows the afternoon sun was sketching across the lawn of the church next door. Actually, the mother’s age *was* important. A single mom in a small town such as this was always vulnerable to poor health. She was a child with a child.

I had already taken off my lab coat and tie and decided to conduct the exam with an open collar. Glancing at the chart for a moment while walking down the hall, I was relieved to find Mary Jo already getting the infant’s vitals while the mother held him loosely on the exam table.

Sarah Akins had gaunt but soft, pretty features and large, expressive eyes. Her posture was bowed with rounded shoulders, and something in her manner spoke of a gentleness, a simple desire to please. On the floor beside her was a cheap quilted cloth bag that no doubt carried diapers and formula. Her face and manner revealed a blend of adult concern and schoolgirl innocence. She wore little to no makeup and her hair was straight and stringy. She was smiling and cooing playfully with her chubby newborn, speaking cheerfully and tenderly to him. Below the surface, however, she was likely haunted by uncertainty and fear.

The young mother's weak smile and inquisitive gaze suggested she was awaiting judgment or disapproval. I gave her neither and greeted her warmly. Pulling up a low stool, I spoke admiringly of the baby, who sat looking at his mother through brilliant blue eyes.

"Okay if I call you Sarah?"

"Oh, sure."

"He is one beautiful little boy."

She smiled bashfully. "Thanks. I sure feel that way. But then again, I'm his mom. I guess all moms think that of their baby."

"His name is Samuel?"

"Yeah, Samuel Eugene. It's a family name. But I call him Sam."

I proceeded to ask her questions about his eating and sleeping habits and who cared for him. All the information Sarah Akins offered was encouraging. I learned that she worked as a clerk at a convenience store. During the day an aunt kept the baby and from all reports she took excellent care of him.

Mary Jo handed me the updated progress chart, which included information from the infant's newborn visit two months earlier. All the measurements for height and weight and head circumference were on track. I examined the child, listening to his breathing and heart, checking his flexibility, and performed a small battery of other assessments. Everything was normal. The infant's mother stood quiet and attentive, making no effort to interrupt.

Whatever problems this teenage girl had brought upon herself by the choices she'd made were not evident in the love and care she showed for her son. She seemed to possess a resilience of character, and the yoke of motherhood was one she wore with clarity and focus.

"Sam appears to be a perfectly healthy little fellow," I concluded. "All we need to do now is give him his two-month shots." This comment brought an immediate look of reservation from the young mother.

"Yeah," she spoke hesitantly. "I wanted to ask about that. I know there are several, but do you know exactly how many?"

I thought for a moment, wondering what was motivating the question.

"Let's see. I'm not completely sure—there is the second hep C, DTaP, rotavirus, and some others. I need to look at the schedule to be certain."

"Do you know how much they all cost?"

Mary Jo promptly spoke up. "All of the two-month shots together cost about two hundred dollars."

Sarah hesitated. "I don't have any insurance. So maybe I could pay for one or two of them and then come back in the next week or so for the rest. Which ones do you think are the most important, Dr. Bradford?"

Ignoring Mary Jo's frown, I stood and held up my hand in a gesture of embarrassment.

"You know what? I completely forgot. When I negotiated with the mayor about coming here, he assured me that the city was going to set aside a budget for community health vaccinations for the flu and whatnot. I'm sure that well-baby shots are covered in that. So there's really no charge."

Mary Jo appeared skeptical, but she said nothing.

I turned to her, away from Sarah, and spoke with a quiet nod. "I'll cover it."

I turned back toward Sarah, who was smiling with a flush of

relief. Her whole posture seemed to relax. "Well, okay. That's great. I guess we'll just go ahead and get all of them, if that's all right?"

"Absolutely," I responded. "Mary Jo, if you'll draw those up, I'll give them to Sam."

Mary Jo stood staring at me for a moment longer, her face unchanged. Then she said, "Sure. I guess I didn't get that memo."

I smiled and looked at her flatly. "Well, looks like you got it now. So, if you would, please get them drawn up."

Mary Jo exited the room without ever losing eye contact with me.

I continued to ask Sarah questions. She said she smoked and I encouraged her to stop. She stated that she rarely drank now, noting that drinking was what had helped get her into this predicament. And she said her appetite was fine despite her remarkable thinness. Ultimately, I calmly asked her the key question.

"What can you tell me about the father?"

Sarah looked down, refusing to meet my gaze.

"Why do you have to know anything about him?"

"I don't have to, to be quite honest. But it would be helpful to know his medical history."

She raised her head and glanced back into my eyes for a moment, but remained silent.

"Any chance he might be able to help out with the expenses and with taking care of the baby?"

"He gives me a little money when he can. He hasn't been able to afford a place for us yet. Besides, he has his hands full taking care of family."

I tried to sort through this information, but it didn't exactly present a clear picture. I deduced that the father must already be married with children.

"Does he have a name?" I asked in a low voice, still looking compassionately at her.

"Well, yeah, Doc. He's got a name," Sarah responded. "Half the people in this town would like to know it. It's none of their business."

"That means it's none of my business either."

"I didn't mean to snap at you, Dr. Bradford. It's just that me and him, we got our reasons and nobody else needs to know them."

I smiled and nodded my head. The fact that she had been a minor when she became pregnant was reason enough to be secretive. Tennessee, and especially small towns like Watervalley, had conservative opinions on this matter. Despite the feelings between Sarah and Sam's father, there was the looming possibility that he could be accused of statutory rape. Further questions on the matter would have been pointless.

Mary Jo came through the door carrying a sterile pan with two labeled syringes, but the needles were wrong.

"Get me a couple of twenty-three-millimeter needles if you would, Mary Jo."

While she was normally obedient with such requests, this time she responded flatly. "These are sixteen millimeter. They're thinner and shorter. It's what we always use on infants."

It was late and I was tired. I repeated the request. "Mary Jo, get me the twenty-three-millimeter needles, please."

"Dr. Bradford, that's an awfully long needle for such a little fellow."

I stopped her. My voice was low and firm. "Mary Jo, when we get a chance I will show you the literature that cites the benefits of the longer needle. But right now it's late and I think it best to get this done so we can all go home."

She shrugged her shoulders and complied.

I switched the needles and asked Sarah to hold Sam with his bottom exposed. After dabbing the target with alcohol, I gave the injection as I'd done a thousand times before. It was routine.

What was not routine was the volume of the wail that came from the infant. It started as a sudden gasp for breath quickly followed by a deafening scream. This, of course, brought a deeply condescending look from Mary Jo. But I was undaunted. I got the second syringe and proceeded to dab a spot of alcohol on the other pudgy pink buttock.

In three seconds the job was done, but Sam was clearly just getting warmed up. His screams brought the rest of the staff—Nancy, Cindy, and Camilla—to the open exam room doorway, where they stood with sympathetic looks for both the screaming child and the girlish mother who was desperately bouncing him and whispering soothing sounds into his ear.

My confidence running high, I remained unrattled. Even still, the commotion made for an awkward moment. I reached instinctively toward Sarah, who by reflex gave the bawling infant to me. In hindsight, I can't imagine what I was thinking or, for that matter, what Sarah was thinking. When comforting a screaming child, there is nothing that trumps the soft voice, warmth, and smell of his own mother. But for some reason, Sarah yielded Sam to me. It was an act of obedience to the myth that wisdom is automatically bestowed to the medical professional.

I cradled him and gently bounced him with his head on my shoulder. Within seconds, all was silent. For a brief moment, it seemed that the comforting touch of the doctor had worked its magic. A grand smile of satisfaction spread across my face as I glanced around at the women, all of whom were mothers themselves. I went from being treated with subdued respect to earning their deep, ogling adoration. I was a genius. I had started the week with an exam of Watervalley's oldest resident and was now finishing with Watervalley's youngest. For a few cosmic seconds, they gazed upon my prowess with enchantment.

Until Sam wrenched forth a tremendous burp, followed by an explosion of regurgitated formula that streamed all across my back and down my white shirt.

CHAPTER 13
Dinner

After rinsing out my shirt in the sink, I walked the few blocks home from the clinic. Strolling the sidewalks under the large trees, I collected the sounds and smells of people gathered for backyard barbecues. The sun was now falling behind the western hills and the heat of the day was beginning to melt away. Long shadows traced across the front yards of Fleming Street. Kids rode by on their bicycles, men were mowing their lawns, and women were standing along picket fences, laughing and talking with great animation, gesturing with their hands. Life was happening all around me.

These people of Watervalley, these patients I was getting to know—I knew my job was to listen and evaluate and recommend a cure for them. Nothing more. But their lives intrigued me, stirred something more in me. The names, the faces, the medical histories—I knew their numbers but not their stories, and what few stories I did know were unexpectedly captivating me. Their lives were rich with qualities I was just beginning to understand.

As I meandered down the sidewalk, I wondered if Connie would still be waiting. Soon enough, I had my answer.

"Mmm-hmm," she hummed softly. "Just look at you. What fool thing did you do? Walk through someone's sprinkler on the way home?"

"That would have been more pleasant. I'm going upstairs to change. I'll explain when I get back down. Something smells good."

"It sure isn't you. You smell like a dairy barn."

I retreated upstairs, washed up, put on some jeans and a clean shirt, and returned to the kitchen.

Connie was at the stove and without looking up she spoke to me in a deadpan voice. "How was your day, Doctor?"

"Long."

"Sorry your dinner is running late. I was delayed getting out of my yoga class."

"Did you say your yoga class?"

Connie looked up from the stove. "Yes, that's right."

I had to ponder that for a moment. "Wow. That's really interesting. I didn't know you took yoga."

Connie had retrieved a plate and was serving up portions of pork chops and an array of vegetables.

"I don't take yoga. I teach yoga."

I was gulping a large swallow of tea and nearly spit it back into the glass.

"You teach yoga? How did you learn to do that?"

"I spent three years in a Hindu monastery."

"I don't think I believe that one."

"Mmm-mmm, Doctor. Nothing gets past you," Connie replied in her breezy monotone.

I studied her for a moment. "You enjoy this, don't you, Mrs. Thompson? These little conversations of ours."

For the longest minute, she regarded me with purse-lipped

boredom. Again her response was deadpan. "Sure. I'm ecstatic about them, almost to the point of yodeling."

She turned away with a subtle grin, then put together a second plate and placed it on the table.

"If you don't mind, I'm going to join you. I haven't had dinner either."

"Sure." I was actually glad for the company.

Connie put away her apron and sat across from me. "I've already blessed it, Doctor. You can dig in."

I nodded and reached for my fork. Connie spoke again. "After Mr. Thompson died I just couldn't seem to relax. I was watching one of those infomercials on TV late one night and there was this ad on about learning yoga. It was a five-disk set for only twenty-nine dollars and ninety-five cents plus shipping and handling. Couldn't pass that up."

I stifled a laugh. "Wow. Yoga. Mrs. Thompson, you're a mess."

An almost perceptible smile began to inch across her face, but it vanished quickly. Meanwhile, I was trying hard to slow the pace with which I was devouring the food before me. Again, it was Connie who broke the silence. "So, what do you think about your first week, Doctor?"

I stretched back in my chair, cupping my hands behind my head. "I think I'm glad no one died. That episode with Hoot Wilson yesterday scared me to death. Didn't do him a lot of good either. I talked to his cardiologist today and he's doing fine. He'll probably get a pacemaker."

"I heard you handled that situation really well. Everyone said you knew exactly what to do."

There was a detectable tone almost of pride in Connie's voice. Since the first minute we had met, it seemed that Connie had looked upon me as little more than a tall adolescent, so this came as something of a surprise. I was gratified, but I knew better. I looked at her impassively and shook my head. "Actually, it was a disaster. The only thing I can figure is that Hoot is a direct descendant of Lazarus. I think Wendy did more to save him than I did."

"God works in mysterious ways, Dr. Bradford." Connie's voice had a certain oratorical, sermonlike quality; she seemed always ready to seize upon the opportunity for a teachable moment. She continued in a declarative tone. "Seems like your being here was providential."

I shrugged. "I can't say I can speak to that. All I know is that Hoot was dead as a rock and then came back to life when Wendy grabbed his foot. It might just be that the heart monitor was malfunctioning all along and then finally decided to work. That would certainly explain everything."

Connie continued to eat dinner in silence, choosing to ignore my last comment the same way you ignore someone who has just made an embarrassing sound. In time we finished and as she began to gather the dishes from the table she spoke again. "So, how was the rest of your week?"

"Well, it seems like I met half the town. Some interesting people, and, thankfully, none of them were extremely sick. Most of them could and should take better care of themselves."

"I'd say that sounds like Watervalley."

"I did meet one elderly gentleman who was ninety-nine years old. Really interesting fellow."

"Oh, that's Knox. That little Scotsman was born when Taft was president. A lot of stories about his dad and that old ice cave still float around. If we were in the big city, I guess folks would call it an urban legend."

"Since we're in Watervalley, what do folks here call it? A rural legend?"

Connie paused to give me a short look of reprimand. "No, they just call it an old story."

"Just what is this so-called old story?"

"There's supposed to be a tunnel full of his father's whiskey somewhere in the catacombs of that old cave. But the whole place has been boarded up for decades."

"You know, they were talking about that at the barbershop. I didn't think much of it. I just figured it was some kind of old folklore or myth. Or something of that nature."

"Mmm-hmm," responded Connie. "Jesus help us. If those bottles really do exist, there are plenty enough feeble minds around here that would love to get their hands on them. It's the syrup of Satan."

"I don't know. One-hundred-year-old Scotch might be a pretty prized possession. Some people would pay a lot of money for it."

"People fork out half their paychecks for lottery tickets. Doesn't mean they have good sense."

I smiled and nodded but I couldn't resist digging into Connie's indignation. "Okay, point taken." I rose to get the pitcher of iced tea from the refrigerator. "You know, the word 'whiskey' comes from old Scottish words meaning 'water of life.' "

"Mmm-hmm," Connie responded without looking up from her plate. "And the word 'intoxicated' comes from the Latin word *toxicum*, which means 'poison.' "

How does she do that? I thought to myself. Retrieving the tea pitcher, I headed back to the table. It was time to change the subject.

"This tea is incredible. What's in it?"

"Amphetamines," Connie responded. "Gives you a slight euphoric feeling."

"Fair enough. I'll make mine a double."

"Any other interesting patients this week?"

"Are you familiar with what's known as the HIPAA laws?"

"That would be the Health Insurance Portability and Accountability Act of 1996. It protects confidential patient information."

I stopped and stared at Connie for a moment. "Yeah. That would be the one."

"Get off your high horse, Doctor. I'm just trying to make conversation. You can change or even delete the names to protect the innocent if you want to."

I took another large swallow of tea and nodded. "Well, he wasn't a patient, but I did meet an interesting fellow on Wednesday when I decided to go for a hike in the hills around the lake."

"And you found your way back. I'm impressed. Those trails have never been mapped out. Even Saint Peter has been known to stop and ask for directions." Connie was definitely in a lighter mood now.

"Yeah, the trails were pretty bad, but I had a little help with that."

"Someone show you the way home?"

"I hiked up a pretty good ways and came upon this beautiful apple orchard. I met the owner. He wasn't very friendly at first."

Connie's puzzled frown was quickly transformed to a reserved smile and a slight nod of understanding. "So did John try to shoot you with his BB gun?"

"Sounds like you two have met."

"Oh, yes. I've known John Horatio Harris for over fifty years." She paused and looked at me for a moment. "Mmm-mmm-mmm, Dr. Bradford. You're just gettin' a real education about Watervalley—good, bad, and ugly."

I shrugged. "Not so sure about that. All I know about John

Harris is that he's pretty darn smart, pretty darn rich, and pretty darn intense. Doesn't seem to have a lot of lost love for the people in town either."

"I can assure you the feeling is mutual."

"What's that all about anyway? I understand he lost his wife, which might make anybody bitter. But all that animosity toward the town—that's driven by something else, something he didn't want to talk about."

Connie looked inquisitively at me. "So I take it you two actually spoke to each other. He didn't just shoot his gun off and send you running."

"Like I said, he wasn't exactly friendly at first. But eventually he invited me up to the house, gave me a short tour, and we sat and talked for a few hours. Actually, I kind of liked the guy. He definitely has a volatile way about him, but he ended up being friendly. Gave me a ride back and invited me to come up and see him again."

Connie's expression was one of pure astonishment.

"What?" I inquired.

At first she didn't speak. Then she began to shake her head. "Dr. Bradford, are you telling me that you actually befriended John Harris? This may be a sign of the apocalypse. He is not a man given to generous impulse."

"I guess I did." I paused. "Like I said, he's a little intense. But . . . I don't know. He's an interesting guy. And I guess you have to be a little impressed with the whole setup. He has one really beautiful place."

"Oh, yeah. That would be Molly's hand you saw. That gal had more style in her little finger than most people could ever attain, body and soul, in a lifetime."

"So what's the story?"

Connie sipped her tea and thought for a moment before speaking. "John Harris used to be one of the most beloved men in this town. He grew up here, was an All-State basketball player, smart, good-looking, cocky. Went to Carnegie Mellon on a full academic scholarship. He and Molly Cavanaugh dated in high school. She went off to Agnes Scott in Georgia. She was a short, cute brunette, always had a big smile for everyone and always had John wrapped around her little finger. They carried on their romance long-distance all through college and got married here in a big wedding the summer after they both graduated. The Cavanaughs were old-money people, big farmers. Good people, though. Threw one of the biggest weddings this town ever saw."

"What about John? I guess he came from money too?"

"Not really. They were respectable folk, but not rich. His dad was a mail carrier and his mom was a schoolteacher. Just solid workaday people. Both passed away a few years ago. John and Molly never had any children—not sure why. Anyway, John was an only child. Molly had a twin sister."

"So if John was so beloved as you say, what happened?"

"John came back here and ran the DuPont plant. What people don't know is that six months after he arrived, he got orders to shut the place down. But he refused. He managed to keep it open for another seven years. He worked like a dog getting the place retooled and retraining the workers, trying to make it profitable. Ultimately corporate made him close the doors anyway, and a lot of folks wanted to blame John. They had no idea how hard he had worked for them."

"Is that why he's so angry at the town?"

Connie regained her focus and shook her head. She spoke reflectively. "No. There's more to it than that. John Harris's anger is all wrapped up in that whole ugly business with the bandstand."

"The bandstand? You mean down at the lake?"

"Yeah, the one at the lake. You see, when we were kids in high school—no, even for many years before that—they used to have big dances down at the bandstand. That's where John and Molly had their first date. Anyway, about fifteen years ago a bunch of teenagers threw a big shindig down there and some young bucks with small brains and too much testosterone got in a knife fight. One almost died. A lot of beer and booze was floating around. Well, that was enough for the city to close the bandstand down. Too much liability."

"How does that play out with John?"

"When John and Molly moved back, she got the idea to have the old bandstand renovated. She was quite the romantic. At first she didn't get very far with the idea. But nothing ever stopped Molly. She was determined to have the old bandstand returned to its former glory. Then she was diagnosed with cancer. But that didn't keep her from pushing for the city council to hold a vote on the restoration. She really wanted to see that done in her remaining time. John even offered to fund it as a gift to the city. The proposal came before the council a month before she died. Despite being deathly sick, she was there with John, much against his will."

"I take it the vote did not pass."

"No, it didn't. What made it worse was that the main folks who spoke against it were some of my misguided brethren from several of the local pulpits. As if doing away with that bandstand would do away with sin and stupidity. John took it personally. Coupled with the bitterness of losing Molly, all he was left with was a lot of anger at the town, the people, and no doubt the Church."

"Why doesn't he just move away? He could live anywhere in the world. You'd think there would be some place more interesting, away from all the things that remind him of his dead wife."

"This is home to him. And it was where Molly wanted to live. He's holding on to his anger, but he's holding on to his home too." Connie's voice had been subdued, thoughtful. Then her gaze turned critical. She lifted her chin and focused pointedly at me through the lower half of her glasses. "Besides, Dr. Bradford, not everybody thinks that Watervalley is such an uninteresting place."

"You're kidding, right?"

Connie responded with a sullen face, clearly offended. "Where are your manners, boy? That's not exactly cotillion behavior. I would have thought a Buckhead upbringing would have taught you to be a little more polite."

I shrugged. "Well, it's not that. It's just that aside from the lake, the softball park, and Maylen's Barbershop, there's not a lot to this town. I guess I'm just more of a big-city guy. But it is what it is. So here I am."

Connie shook her head. "Mmm-mmm. Give it some time, Dr. Bradford. There's not a lot to see in Watervalley, but what you hear makes up for it."

Her comment provoked a question. "Okay, how does that work anyway?"

"How does what work?"

"How is it that everybody in this little town knows everything about anything the moment it happens? It's like you have to constantly watch your step."

"Oh, I wouldn't worry about that too much, Doctor. You're not going to control what people think. Besides, around here you'll find out pretty quick that the people who care don't matter and the people who matter don't care."

I nodded, then grabbed my tea glass and began to move toward the back door, thinking I might enjoy the evening shade from the back porch.

Connie's voice stopped me. "So how did your shirt get all wet?"

"The last patient of the day was a little two-month-old who needed a checkup and his shots." Connie immediately began to speak, but I didn't let her. "I know, I know. I'm sure you can guess who it was, so we don't need to call out any names. I gave him his shots with a deep needle and that kid let out a wail you could hear from space. So, like a knucklehead, I took him from his mother and tried to comfort him. That's when he ralphed all over my back. I had no other shirt to wear home, so I tried to rinse it out in the sink."

I had been gazing out the back door while telling the story. As I finished, I glanced back toward Connie, who was now staring at me, smiling with a beaming pride. The look threw me.

"What?"

"Sounds like you were trying to do the right thing, Dr. Bradford."

I responded with a low resignation. "Oh, I don't know. I was just trying to be a doctor."

"A baby's cry is a good thing. It means life. It means God hasn't given up hope in us yet."

I simply nodded my head and stepped out onto the back porch. It was well past sunset. I sat on the back steps and reflected on the day. For some reason, Knox McAnders was foremost in my thoughts—maybe because he'd been my first patient, maybe because I had a sense of his story, maybe because of his age and the subtle arrhythmias I had noticed. Time would tell.

After a few moments Connie stepped through the back door and stood behind me where I was seated on the steps.

"I'm leaving now, Dr. Bradford. I'll see you Monday."

"Thanks, Mrs. Thompson. Dinner was good."

"Get yourself to bed soon. You look tired."

"Sure. Thanks. I've got a few phone calls to make first." My voice was solemn and crisp against the night air.

I stayed seated on the back steps. For a moment, Connie remained behind me, gazing into the deep black of the yard. She reached down and softly patted the hair on the back of my head, smoothing it into place. "It was your first week with patients, Dr. Bradford. Sounds like it went just fine." With that she stepped back inside. A minute later I heard the front door close and then Connie's car start up. The sound of the engine faded into the distance as she drove away.

I sat in silence. But Connie's small act of kindness, the caring lilt in her voice were still drifting in the air, stirring memories from the distant years, stirring within me the voice of my aunt Grace.

My arrival in Watervalley had been so botched. But arrivals had never been a grand affair for me. Years earlier, when I had ventured fresh-faced into the new world of private school in Atlanta, neither I nor my classmates had looked upon my arrival with anticipation. It was a place of academic competition, clever banter, and high regard for social standing. I was a stranger, uncertain and turned inward, who had learned to sit in the back of the class and observe and assess those around me. In time I learned to adapt, to become part of the pack, to create an acceptable version of myself.

But during that difficult first year I remember Aunt Grace would sit on my bed each night, smooth my hair, and talk to me about my day, patiently listening to the ups and downs, the small victories, the abysmal defeats, the curious discoveries, and the occasional outpourings of my guarded heart. I was changing, casting away the boy of those early small-town years that had been so wrapped in wonder. Even though in time I had found a place in

Buckhead—a role to play—I think she knew that secretly I still counted myself an outsider, always looking for some point of entry into the light and fellowship. As the years passed I completely reinvented myself with my prep school demeanor, my seasoned urban self. Even so, part of me believed that my aunt always regarded me as an awestruck little boy from a small town. But now too many years had passed for that identity to still define me.

I sat and listened to the sounds of the night. It had been a good first week. Despite my dubious start, it seemed I had a charmed touch as the new doctor. I thought about the short list of patients I needed to call. For some reason, I considered calling Knox, just to check in with him, but there was really no need. More important, I remembered Leo Sikes, who Nancy still had not been able to connect with on the phone. Tomorrow was Saturday, and if I still couldn't get in touch with him, I would drive out to his farm.

I looked up and saw a million stars visible from galaxies far distant. It struck me as incredible that some of the stars I was watching no longer existed. They were there for me to see for this brief moment, but their fate had already been cast. It didn't occur to me at the time that the laws that bound the heavens also bound the life in Watervalley. Before another week would pass, I would understand.

CHAPTER 14

Lessons to Be Learned

By midmorning Saturday I still had not been able to reach Leo Sikes, so I drove out to his farm on Fatty Bread Road. I was far from any real sense of panic about him, but it was unsettling that we had been unable to contact him for three days. The long gravel drive led to a small farmhouse shadowed by a large barn in the rear. I knocked on the front door and waited for several minutes, but received no response. Something was wrong here, something afoul about the whole business, and I could start to hear my heart pounding in my ears. I walked around back, where an old Chevy Impala and truck were parked on a small concrete parking pad filled with years' worth of cracks and opportunistic weeds. I yelled out for Leo but heard no response.

With faster steps I walked toward the huge Dutch-style barn, noticing that the large sliding door to the central hallway had been left open about three feet. I stepped inside, my eyes adjusting to the dark corridor. A light was coming from an open door on the right a few feet down the long hall. I heard the faint sound of voices. Again I yelled out Leo's name and hurried in that direction.

"Leo? Leo Sikes?"

"Hey, back here." I had just heard his response when Mavis stepped to the open doorway holding, of all things, a glass of iced tea.

"Well, hello, Dr. Bradford. What brings you out here?"

"Hi, Mavis. Are you two okay?" I had reached the open doorway only to find that this room of the barn was finished out into a small office complete with desk, filing cabinets, and a small window AC unit.

"We're fine, I think," she replied, clearly confused by my presence. Leo was across the room sitting in one of two recliners, watching a baseball game on a large, boxy old TV set. He rose from his chair, looking as spry as ever, and greeted me.

"Hey, Doc. Didn't know you make house calls."

I exhaled, relieved to find them okay, and laughed sheepishly.

"Nancy and I have been trying to get in touch with you for several days. I want to run a few more tests. But we could never reach you on the phone."

"Oh my," Mavis responded. "I am so sorry, Dr. Bradford. For some reason we can't get the satellite dish to work on the TV in the house, so we've been out here a lot lately. I'm afraid we've missed your calls."

We talked for a few more minutes, during which Mavis offered several times to make a sandwich for me. I politely refused. They agreed to call the office Monday and set up another appointment. I departed amid a chorus of thanks and apologies and began the drive back to town feeling a mixture of relief and embarrassment. Watervalley simply lived at a pace and a remoteness that I did not understand. But the drive home revealed an even deeper revelation about the rural life I was coming to know.

Along Fatty Bread Road, I noticed a number of fresh-vegetable stands beside the long gravel driveways. Makeshift tables had been set up to accommodate the overflow of family gardens. Baskets of cucumbers, tomatoes, squash, and beans were proudly displayed. These were typically manned by a solitary child or an elderly man or woman. But some stands sat unoccupied, with only a price list and a jar where customers could put their money. I marveled at this, amazed that such a culture of trust still existed.

As the wheels of the old Corolla crunched their way down the gravel road, my mind was absorbed, deliberating. The owners either were naively trusting in those around them or simply saw it as a benevolence to those needing food and unable to pay. In either instance, it spoke of a deep well of common goodness. I drove the dusty roads in a state of wonder.

On Monday morning the alarm went off at six. I pressed the snooze button once. The second time, I managed to sit up and place my feet on the floor. I groaned my way out of bed and by a quarter past six I was out the front door and jogging west on Fleming Street.

Slowly, the aches and sore muscles loosened somewhat and I felt the strength to maintain my pace. But the morning was hot. The air was heavy, humid, motionless. Within a mile I was soaked with sweat and heaving deeply to find my breath. Usually I felt a certain awakening in running first thing, an unexplained illumination, a sharpening of focus. But this morning it was just work, a drudgery. After another half mile, I decided to turn back. I was hot and hurting. Pushing farther and harder seemed pointless. I walked the last couple hundred yards with my hands on my hips. Fleming Street seemed devoid of oxygen and catching my breath felt almost impossible. As I approached the house, I saw Connie's car parked out front.

The house was already rich with the smells of breakfast as I came through the front door. Connie was in the kitchen with her striped cotton dress, white apron, full makeup, styled hair, and inevitable sour face. She was holding a spatula, standing over a pan of frying eggs on the stove. Without looking up, she spoke in her usual breezy voice. "Good morning, Dr. Bradford."

I noticed a plate of cooked bacon cooling on a paper towel on the counter next to the stove. I walked over to grab a strip, but as I reached out Connie swatted my hand with the spatula.

"You best keep your sweaty hands back. I didn't hear anybody say breakfast was ready."

I recoiled a couple of steps. "Somebody's a little testy this morning."

"Humph," Connie replied. "Mind your manners, Dr. Bradford. Just look at you with your big sweaty self." Connie reached to the upper cabinet and retrieved a large glass. "Here. Pour yourself some orange juice and go get cleaned up. I'll have breakfast ready when you get back down."

Taking the glass from her, I returned her firm grimace with a wry grin.

"Good morning to you too, Mrs. Thompson."

"Humph." She turned back to the stove.

I downed the glass of juice and headed up the back stairs. Within minutes I was shaved and showered and returned to the kitchen. Connie had a plate of eggs, bacon, grits, and toast ready for me on the table. I grabbed a couple of paper towels and tucked them into my open collar.

Up to her elbows in dishwater, Connie made her usual announcement. "Dig in, Dr. Bradford. I've already blessed it."

I looked at her hesitantly, then nodded and grabbed my fork. The breakfast looked delicious, but was far larger than what I was accustomed to eating in the morning. I couldn't resist making a teasing inquiry.

"Mrs. Thompson, I'm sure this is tasty and I know you're a fabulous cook, but have you heard of this thing called a bagel?"

Connie turned toward me, holding the cast-iron skillet like a handy weapon. "Not sure. Have you heard of this thing called a mild concussion?"

I grinned and began to devour the plate of food in front of me. After a few swallows, I said, "Yes, Mrs. Thompson. Come to think of it, I have. But if I keep eating like this, I'm going to weigh over three hundred pounds."

Connie turned back to the sink and continued drying the dishes. "You're still a young man, Dr. Bradford. And skinny. Maybe even a little on the puny side by my standards. There are still plenty of years for yogurt and granola. But don't worry. I'll fix you some fruit and frittatas if that's what you want."

I took another huge bite and shook my head. "I'm not saying this meal isn't absolutely scrumptious. But if you keep this up I'll have to ask for a double XL lab coat for Christmas."

I finished and hastily began to gather my things for work. "By the way, what are we having for dinner?"

Connie looked at me deadpan, as if the answer was yet undecided. Finally, a subtle amusement spread across her face. "Bagels."

I smiled, shaking my head, and returned up the stairs to grab my tie. At ten till eight I was out the door. The thick August air hit me instantly, so instead of walking I drove the car over to the office. Having been parked in the shade, even with no air-conditioning, it at least held the promise of a cooler arrival.

I was slightly relieved to find the clinic parking lot relatively empty. Approaching the back door, I found Mary Jo Marshall discreetly smoking a cigarette on the stoop. It was likely not her first of the day. She stood like a bored statue, clasping the elbow of her cigarette-holding arm.

"Good morning, Doctor." Her voice was flat, unaffected.

"Good morning, Mary Jo," I responded. "I could be wrong, but seems like I read somewhere that those things are an impairment to your health."

Mary Jo was unmoved. "I know. I keep thinking I should switch to reefer."

Rebuttal seemed pointless. "I'll see you inside, sunshine."

As I entered, Nancy was trotting down the hall at a whirlwind pace, wearing an ear-to-ear smile on her excited face, bursting with her usual warmth. "Good morning. Good morning, Dr. Bradford," she called, as if one "good morning" was inadequate. "Sure is hot out there. Hope you had a nice weekend. Just a few patients lined up this morning. Do you want some coffee?"

"Good morning, Nancy. And no, thanks. No need for more coffee."

"Well, that's probably good. They say it's not really that healthy for you."

"Yes, they say a lot of things. I hope your weekend was okay," I responded pleasantly.

"Oh, yes, yes. It was just great. Mr. Orman and I went to that new steak house over in Hohenwald. They have the best salad bar. It had three different kinds of lettuce."

"Maybe later you can tell me all about it. So, not too many patients this morning?"

"Oh, not too bad. But your first appointment is over at the elementary school."

"The elementary school?"

"Yes, I'm sorry. I should have told you, but I have on my calendar that you need to be over at the elementary school at eight thirty this morning for the professional day in Mrs. Chambers's sixth-grade science class."

This news caught me off guard. "The elementary school, really? It's just early August. Is school already in session?"

"Watervalley went to a year-round schedule two years ago. They're just coming back from a three-week break."

By now Mary Joe had appeared through the back door, having attained her nicotine fix for the morning. Hearing Nancy's last comment, she immediately chimed in. "Hot dig, Doc, you're in for a real treat. Take the first aid kit. Mrs. Chambers is one sharp-tongued old battle-ax."

"Now, Mary Jo, be nice," responded Nancy.

Mary Jo smiled with a sneer. "Humph. I *was* being nice."

"I agree, she can be opinionated," replied Nancy, "but she's really good at what she does. Everybody says so."

I held up my hand. "Time out, ladies. Just who is Mrs. Chambers?"

Nancy responded, "She teaches science and math to the sixth graders at the elementary school. She has been there for over thirty years and has taught nearly everybody in this town. Very smart. Very, very smart. But she does have a bit of a sharp personality."

"Sharp and snooty, if you ask me," retorted Mary Jo. "They don't get much more uppity."

I looked at Mary Jo with amused curiosity. "Mary Jo, you're not being helpful."

She replied flatly, "I wasn't trying to be."

Nancy looked at Mary Jo and let out a disgusted sigh. "Well, anyway, every year she wants someone from the clinic to go and talk to her class about the medical profession and how science is used in what we do. Mary Jo went a couple of times when we didn't have a doctor. But I think Mrs. Chambers will be delighted to have you go, Dr. Bradford."

I stared at both of them. Whoever this woman was, apparently it was my fate to go and do whatever I was asked. "Okay, then. Sounds like a slice of heaven." I turned toward my office.

Shutting the door behind me, I retreated to my chair and sank into it, breathing out a deep sigh. Once again I was being tagged to talk to a group, not something I really cared to do. Apparently the title of new doctor in town carried with it the role of chairman of the Speakers Bureau.

The day had an odd feel to it, an unspeakable, unfathomable feeling of disarray. I leaned my head back and stared up at the ceiling, feeling slightly anxious about the school assignment. Surely eight years of higher education, three years of residency, and two hundred thousand dollars of debt qualified me to talk to a bunch of sixth graders. I rose from my chair and grabbed my keys. It was time to face another day as the Watervalley doctor.

"Dr. Bradford, do you know how to find the elementary school?" Nancy asked.

"I'm going to take a wild guess and say it's that big building over on School Street, about seven or so blocks down Main, right?"

"Yes, that's right, except it's to the left," replied Nancy in a sober tone of careful instruction. "It used to be the old high school. But they built a new one out on Shiloh Road, in the south part of town."

"So it's down on the left, right?"

"Yes. It will be on the left side of the street."

I smiled. My frail attempt at humor was utterly lost to her. "I'm sure I'll find it." Nancy walked with me to the back door. The early morning heat was already escalating toward the smothering oven of midday. "Think I'll drive. It's too hot to walk."

"I'm sorry, I don't know anything more about what to expect. Mrs. Chambers set this up over a month ago and since they were out for several weeks I wasn't able to call her to get more information."

"Oh, no problem. I'll just go and wing it. You know, pretty much like I do here."

This remark brought a pursed *Shame on you* grin from Nancy. She said good-bye and closed the door behind her.

I walked down the back steps and climbed into the hot Corolla. The soft of the morning dew had long since burned off. The leaves on the trees now had the wilted look of late summer and the lawns were beginning to show patches of brown. I rolled down the windows, but found little relief.

After parking at the school in a visitor spot, I made my way up the front steps to the double doors. There, a posted sign requested that all visitors check in with the office. The school secretary, a plump and pleasant woman in her early forties, greeted me. After introducing myself, I said I was there for a meeting with Mrs. Chambers. The woman looked puzzled and there was an awkward silence. I instinctively filled the void.

"Nancy Orman over at the clinic said that Mrs. Chambers set this up a little while back. Nancy seemed pretty certain today is the correct day."

The secretary smiled, shrugged her shoulders, and told me where to find the room down the west hall, apologizing for not being able to announce me to the teacher. "Our intercom system went down over the break. I'm sure if she is expecting you, it will be just fine."

"Okay, thanks," I responded, and proceeded to make my way to Mrs. Chambers's room.

Though freshly painted, the building was old with classic Greek revival details. Built decades earlier, it had a majestic grace that spoke of a more celebrated era. The central hallway had a tall domed ceiling and a well-worn but glossy wood floor. The heavily molded doors had opaque transoms above them. There was a pleasant antiquate smell of many years, a collective fermentation of cleaner, floor polish, and must. It seemed a fit setting for the elderly Mrs. Chambers I was about to meet.

I walked the long hall searching the nameplates until eventually I found the correct room and vaguely heard a woman's voice coming from the other side. A neatly engraved placard bearing her name was mounted next to the door. On the hallway wall were colorful displays of plant cell drawings, each bearing a child's name. I exhaled a deep breath and rapped on the door several times. Nothing happened. I knocked again, this time with a little added velocity. I mumbled to myself, "The old woman is probably deaf."

Finally the door opened, and with that simple motion, nothing would be the same for me for a very, very long time.

The person standing before me was not some well-pickled, stern-faced school madam, but a fresh and fully bloomed woman in her late twenties. She was a warm brunette with rich, deep brown eyes who carried herself with a poised, athletic bearing. She was stunningly beautiful and looked at me with an expression of pleasant inquiry.

"May I help you?" The lilt of her voice conveyed a quiet control, a subtle complexity of something from beyond the rural drawl of Watervalley.

I was dumbstruck. My chemical instincts betrayed me as I glanced down to the floor and then back up at her face. She wore a tight navy skirt and a fitted white blouse that only faintly masked the brimming curves beneath it. It wasn't the usual denim skirt, tennis shoes, and generic polo shirt that was the fashion norm in Watervalley.

I spoke abruptly. "Yes, hi. I'm Luke Bradford, the new doctor at the clinic. I was told by Nancy Orman, the office manager, to be here at eight thirty to meet with an elderly science teacher." I paused. "Do I have the right room?" I stepped back and looked at the nameplate beside the door.

The young woman looked at me with restrained curiosity. "An elderly science teacher?"

"Yes, a Mrs. Chambers. She was described as a stern old battle-ax. You know, evidently something of a sourpuss. But clearly that's not you." I smiled broadly, hoping to engage her with a measure of charm.

But the woman before me responded sharply, with the edge of polite irritation. "Yes, that's right, Dr. Bradford. That's not me. That would be my mother."

I felt the oxygen being sucked from my lungs. Once again I had managed to find a way to commit an incredible act of calculated stupidity.

"Wow, I am so sorry. I really didn't mean to be insulting." I struggled to regain my poise and searched for a way to turn the conversation into something more amiable.

The young woman folded her arms and took one step backward. She turned toward the class.

"Everyone, continue working through your questions. You have fifteen more minutes." She turned back and looked at me with subdued annoyance, then nodded for me to step into the hallway. She followed, partially closing the door.

"Look, again, I'm sorry about the whole 'battle-ax' thing. I guess I foolishly repeated a rather biased opinion. You just weren't who I expected, and—well, I don't think you told me your name."

"I'm Christine Chambers."

"Okay, good. It's nice to meet you, Christine." I held out my hand, hoping to extend some gesture of graciousness that would put the conversation on a different bearing. She briefly shook my hand and offered a perfunctory smile.

"So, your mother—has she retired?"

"No. My mother, Madeline, hasn't been well for the last several months, and lately has gotten particularly worse. I came back over the summer to be with her and help out. I teach at a private school in Atlanta. It doesn't start till September and the principal here asked me to sub for a couple of weeks until he can hire someone else to take my mother's place."

"I see. Looks like I did a complete job of adding insult to injury."

"It's all right. You can't always take everything you hear in Watervalley at face value." Her voice was less firm but still short of accommodating.

At that moment, one of the children from the classroom appeared at the door. "Ms. Chambers, I'm through with my paper. Can I go to the restroom?"

I recognized the boy as my next-door neighbor. "Hi, Will Fox."

"Hi, Luke Bradford," Will responded with an intentionally deeper and subtly mocking voice. He grinned mischievously at me.

"Where's your bike helmet?"

The boy nodded toward Christine with an accusatory grimace.

"Oh," I responded, looking over at her for confirmation. "Well, I'd say your teacher has a point. Don't really need a bike helmet to learn math and science." He rolled his eyes and stood loosely at attention.

Placing her hand on Will's shoulder, Christine spoke in a firm, gentle voice. "Will, run along to the restroom and come right back."

Will never looked at Christine but marked his compliance with an emphatic nod of his head, a perfunctory gesture. It seemed that he understood the drill of polite exchange, but it bored him. There was a childish aloofness to his actions, as if reality required only a small percentage of his attention and the majority of his thoughts were off in some imaginary land. He spun around whimsically and began to half skip down the hall. But after a few steps he turned back and spoke to Christine. "He drives a really crappy car."

Christine cut her eyes at me, unamused, and then addressed the little boy. "Will, you need to watch your language. Choose a better word next time."

Will obediently nodded his head with his eyes rolled up toward the ceiling in a gesture of subtle defiance. He proceeded on his way.

We both watched him disappear into the short corridor where the restrooms were located. Christine looked at me with an expression of inquiry.

"Oh, we're neighbors, over on Fleming," I explained. "Nice kid. A little odd, but a nice kid."

"Yes, my mother told me about him. Smartest child in the class by far. Brilliant at math and a whiz on the computer, but unsettled. His father passed away last year."

"Yes, he mentioned that to me. Apparently an accident."

"Yes." Christine nodded. The conversation paused. Then she spoke in a modulated, diplomatic voice. "Well, Dr. Bradford. It seems that there has been some miscommunication. I'm afraid you have made the trip here for no reason. I need to get back to my class. So sorry for your trouble."

My mind was racing. I couldn't let this conversation end. She was beautiful. Simply beautiful. "Oh, no trouble—no trouble at all. Perhaps at a later time?"

"Perhaps. Good to make your acquaintance." She nodded and turned toward her classroom.

I thought feverishly. "Listen, Miss Chambers—your mother. If it's not prying, what kind of illness does she have? I don't think I have seen her at the clinic."

Christine stopped and stared, evaluating me. She spoke with polite reserve. "Actually, Dr. Bradford, it is prying. Her doctor is in Nashville. And her situation is not the business of anybody in Watervalley, including yours."

I was taken aback. As a doctor the mantle of inquiry fell naturally upon me. But clearly I had overstepped some boundary. "Sorry—I just—Well, sorry."

After a short pause, Christine nodded. "Sure."

I knew at that very second that my chances with her were slim. I had never been one to push a relationship, to charm my way past a rejection. But the probability of seeing her for a second time, even in this small town, seemed little to none. I couldn't let go of the opportunity. I exhaled deeply. "Miss Chambers?"

"Yes?"

"I realize we got off on the wrong foot here. But the truth is, I haven't met many people our age in Watervalley because I'm pretty tied up at the clinic and so . . . I was wondering if maybe you would like to, well, go do something sometime?"

There was a short, awkward silence. Then her face melted into an expression of amused disbelief. "Are you asking me out on a date?"

I desperately tried to speak with a tone of ease, fighting the timidity bouncing around in my throat. "Yes—yes, I guess I am. Nothing too dramatic. Just, you know, go out to dinner at the Depot, go check some books out from the library, or we could think about getting matching tattoos. Whatever excitement Watervalley has to offer."

She responded dryly with a mixture of amusement and annoyance. "Wow, this may be a record. You manage to disrupt my class, insult my mother, and ask me out all in the scope of five minutes."

"Yeah, guilty as charged. Normally I don't tend to move this fast."

"Oh, I'm sure you have plenty of fast moves. But I think I'll pass, since, as you say, the town has so little to offer. You know, Dr. Bradford, you seem to make a habit of disparaging everything. First my mother and now the town." There was an undertone of judgment in her reply.

I was flustered. "Well, no. That's not the case at all. I mean . . . Watervalley is what it is. I wasn't trying to be critical about it. Look, you said you've been living in Atlanta, so I'm assuming you understand the difference between the two. And, well—"

Christine held up her hand. She cut me off and spoke with a bemused, controlled delivery. "Look, Dr. Bradford, I'm afraid you're trying awfully hard to spark a flame where—I can assure you—there is absolutely nothing combustible."

The offer was going nowhere. Now I could add one more humiliation to my new life in Watervalley. Frustrated, I spoke with resignation. "Right. Sorry to interrupt your class and for the whole date thing." I nodded and turned to depart, muttering under my breath, "I guess I need to learn how these things are done out here in the hills."

But as I said it, Christine's voice rang out crisply. "Excuse me? Did you say 'the hills'?"

I turned around. She was peering at me with an incredulous scowl. I walked back to her and responded in exasperation. "Yeah, sure, the hills. Oh, I get it. It's a valley." I looked to the side and gushed out a low chuckle. "You know, you've already put me in my place once today. Do you really think a second geography lesson is necessary?" I stared at her intently, wishing desperately she wasn't quite so gorgeous.

She smiled at me coolly. Her voice was crisp, controlled, full of feminine pluck. "Tell me, Dr. Bradford, did you take a class in arrogance at med school or do you just come by it naturally?"

I grinned, again briefly glancing to the side. "Wow. Arrogant. I see. Look, Miss Chambers, I said a dumb thing about your mom and I apologized for it. I innocently interrupted your class and I apologized for that too. I asked you out because I'm lonely and you turned me down. Fine. I'm new to town. In fact, for the most part, I'm new to small towns. And I'm certainly new to life in Watervalley. So, yeah, I tried to make a connection and I fumbled badly. Yet all I get from you is a healthy dose of your small-town contempt. So tell me, who's the arrogant one here?"

For a moment she was speechless, but she quickly gathered herself and spoke with resolve. "Dr Bradford, it's not like that. You don't understand. I'm just not interested in a relationship right now."

"It was the matching tattoo thing, wasn't it? Should I have waited till the second date for that?" It was a desperate last reach, a final grab at changing her mind.

She paused and exhaled, offering an unamused smile. "Dr. Bradford, I have a class to teach."

Shot down yet again. "Certainly, of course. You have a class to teach and here I am trying to teach you class." As soon as the words left my mouth, I realized what a gigantically asinine thing I had done. Somehow, for one split second it seemed like a clever thing to say, something that sounded a lot better in my head. But the incredible look of hurt on her face told the bitter story. Unwittingly, I had struck at the heart of the grandest of small-town insults. I was something beyond an idiot.

Whatever wound I had ignorantly inflicted now surfaced in a smoldering resentment. She spoke with fiery, disdainful composure. "Dr. Bradford, you can be assured that the devil will be singing Christmas carols before you and I hit the town together." With that she turned and slipped into her classroom, nearly slamming the door behind her.

I stood for a moment shaking my head, stunned, wild with regret. The exchange now seemed like a blur. I thought about knocking on the door and offering yet another apology. But enough damage had been done. I traced my steps back down the long hall out to the heat of the Corolla. I was in a daze. Once I was in the car, a singular thought occurred to me. Christine was mistaken. I had found plenty in her that was combustible.

By the time I'd made my way back to the clinic, I was aggravated, frustrated, soaked with sweat, and all the while thinking that this day couldn't get any worse.

I parked in the back and headed toward the stoop. Nancy was standing outside the rear clinic door with an intense and panicked look on her face.

"Dr. Bradford, we've been trying to get you on your cell phone."

I felt for my front pocket where I kept my phone and realized I'd forgotten to turn it on that morning. "Why? What's up, Nancy?"

"The EMTs from over at the firehouse are swinging by here to pick you up. Toy McAnders called about fifteen minutes ago—" Nancy paused and placed her hand over her mouth. Her eyes were wide and fearful, her face a fixture of stunned distress. "It's Knox McAnders. He died in his sleep last night."

CHAPTER 15
Ice Cave Road

I rode with the EMTs out to the north edge of the county. My mind was floating, occupied, assimilating. I had experienced the death of patients under my care before, but that was in the hospital, where acute disease and fading health had well telegraphed the inevitable end. In the previous week, I had seen Knox, assessed him, and sent him on his way, citing no acute issues. I rode along in a fog, oblivious to the twists and turns we were making. The only thing I noticed was the sign before the last turn, which read ICE CAVE ROAD, and the mailbox with the name MCANDERS stenciled on the side. It was mounted on an old plow handle that was cemented in place next to the long gravel driveway. It was strange, the details you absorbed in such moments.

As the EMT van pulled next to the house, a young man was standing on the side stoop smoking a cigarette. I gauged him to be in his mid-twenties. From a distance he looked of average height, with a wiry build. But walking toward him, I saw that he had arms and shoulders of a sinewy, cabled hardness and a strong, handsome face. He was tan, deeply tan—not the kind one gets at the beach or in a tanning bed, but the kind acquired from long hours of work in the sun. He had a full head of thick brown hair that fell partially across his face. We were introduced.

He was Toy McAnders, Knox's grandson. He nodded at me without expression. With his piercing blue eyes he was a younger replica of Knox. I suspected Toy had an easy grin, but at the moment he was reserved, quiet, dark. His was a face of genuine but suppressed grief. He stared at me for a few awkward moments and then flicked his cigarette into the nearby shrubs. He spoke with a nod of his head toward the side entry door.

"He's in there."

We passed through a mudroom into a wide central hallway that ran the length of the house from front to back. It was a typical farmhouse with ten-foot ceilings, heavy moldings, and the occasional sag caused by decades of settling. The rooms were large and square, each with a small fireplace. Oval rugs covered the wood floors. Curiously enough, the house was spotlessly clean, which told something of the character of the quiet and intense Toy McAnders. Even yet, the house had an old smell to it—not an organic or distasteful odor, but one of time, of aged furniture and old draperies. And while the house was orderly and neat, it lacked the softness that a woman's touch conveys to a place. There were no doilies, no flowers, no decorative items artfully displayed on tabletops.

Once in the main hallway, Toy looked at me with a somber face and pointed to a door on the back left. I entered first.

It was dark in Knox's bedroom. I immediately opened the curtains and turned on all the lamps, flooding the room with light. For some reason, people think the dead like shadowed rooms. From my hospital days I instinctively knew that these situations were morbid enough without the added darkness. Toy had covered Knox neatly with the bedsheet. I examined him, determining that the time of death fell somewhere between two and four in the morning. From all indications his heart had simply stopped beating and he had died quietly in his sleep. Since my role as community doctor included being the county coroner, I signed the death certificate. The EMTs carefully placed Knox in the van to take him to the local funeral home.

By the time we were ready to go, several other cars had arrived. A small crowd had gathered in the large kitchen at the back of the house. I was introduced to Trent McAnders, a man in his late fifties. He was Knox's son and Toy's father. Several other men and women of various ages stood clustered in the distant reaches of the room. They were talking quietly. Their solemn faces and lack of eye contact conveyed that they were not comfortable with engaging or introducing themselves. It made the moment all the more awkward.

Trent was reserved but amiable. "Thank you for coming out, Dr. Bradford. Dad said he had a nice visit with you last week."

"Certainly. I'm . . . um, I'm sorry for your loss. Knox seemed like a kind and wise elderly gentleman."

"Yes, yes. He was," responded Trent.

There was a moment's pause with all three of us exchanging uncomfortable looks.

Then Toy spoke with quiet authority. "Was there anything you saw in his checkup last week, Doc?"

The entire room picked up on this question and conversation ebbed as everyone stared intently at me.

After looking to the side and thinking for a moment, I responded with simple conviction. "No." I let the answer sink in for a few seconds. Trent nodded. I continued, "There was nothing that could have predicted this. He had an occasional irregularity in his heartbeat that he'd probably had for decades called a PAC—premature atrial contraction. We ran an ECG, but nothing else showed up. He was simply a man of many years. I'm afraid I have no better explanation."

I probably should have explained more about the ECG and what it was. But buried deep within me was the instinct to remain vague. I knew they were looking for an answer, a reason for the death, but there was little I could offer. And secretly, even though every bit of my training confirmed that my actions and assessment had been correct, I still doubted myself and wondered if I had missed something.

My answer brought another nod of acceptance from Trent, but Toy offered no such assurance. He looked at me deadpan, as if trying to read me more than my words. Trent broke the awkwardness once again by thanking me and offering his hand. I shook it, nodded to Toy, and left.

During the ride back, the mood was subdued among the two EMTs and me. There was little conversation. I stared vacantly out the window along the seventeen-mile return to town. The landscape was dotted with small houses and rolling hills. Some were well kept; others were not. There was the occasional large farmhouse with the accompanying shacks and sheds and farm implements sitting idly in tall weeds. Soon the countryside was a blur of gardens, overgrown fencerows, small tobacco patches, and fields of corn.

It seemed strange to me that behind the door of any one of the dozens of modest houses and tattered trailers were the lives of people I knew nothing about but to whom I held a bond of responsibility. I had been there for a week and had seen over two hundred patients, a significant cross section of the valley's inhabitants. Perhaps with each exam, with every new face, at work in the back of my head was a simple nagging question: why do you live here? For the most part, they were uncomplicated people whose lives were filled with work, fears, weariness, hope, romance, conversation, boredom, dreams, and simple entertainments. I thought about the endless labor that encompassed their everyday life. And yet, I had also witnessed during my brief time in Watervalley their unmistakable capacity for contentment in their small world. I wondered about their lives, but felt a world apart from them.

Knox's death was just part of the natural course of events, but it had shaken me. The town had been preparing to honor him on his one hundredth birthday in a matter of weeks, and, more than I realized, I had been caught in the collective spirit of that imminent celebration. He had been my first patient and now he was gone. It was impossible not to feel some sense of failure in my role, not to second-guess myself. I rode along in a daze trying to grasp what had just happened. The rural countryside flew by in blurry confusion, a haze of hills, woods, light, shadows, within which I felt a need to find some order, some meaning. Death was rarely a con artist, but invariably he showed his hand long before playing his cards. Hypertension, renal failure, respiratory disease—something usually foreshadowed the inevitable end. But that hadn't been the case with Knox. Despite his advanced age, his passing was unexpected. It seemed as if my life in Watervalley had lost some degree of innocence. One of those under my care was gone. It was impossible to regard his passing with indifference.

Lost in my thoughts, I felt as if only scant moments had passed when the EMT van pulled into the clinic's parking lot. I thanked the guys and got out, took a deep breath, and climbed the steps to the front door. I had patients to see.

The day passed without further incident. Nancy had no shortage of energy, but it was subdued. Somewhat to my surprise, the most compassionate face I encountered all day was that of Mary Jo. From her I half expected a look of curt indifference. Instead, she looked at me with an almost tear-filled empathy. At one point in the afternoon, she found me standing in the small kitchen, my hands on the counter, staring at nothing. She walked over and patted my hand, then lay hers on top of my own. When I looked at her, she pursed her lips and nodded. Nothing was said. She walked away, leaving me to my thoughts.

I arrived home a little before six. Connie had left a hamburger casserole and a note telling me that she was helping some friends take food to the McAnders family. I understood, but my heart was pain-struck. Connie was the one person in whom I thought I could confide. So I was left with my thoughts, the casserole, an empty house, and the blinding hot late-day sun.

The evening passed slowly. I moved about aimlessly, watched some TV, and drifted around on the Internet for a meaningless hour. The clock pushed past nine. The last of the twilight had melted away and the dark had quietly, eerily stolen across the trees and yards of Fleming Street. Sleep was still hours away.

I decided to take a walk. I went out the front door, pulling it shut and not bothering to lock it. I ambled down the long, empty sidewalks, past the silent houses and tightly drawn curtains. My mindless steps took me downtown. The night air was thick, warm, unsettled. A few cars would roll slowly past, then move steadily on, their taillights disappearing from view at a distant turn. I heard the faint, far-off hums and groans of the night. The streets seemed filled with sad and indiscernible whisperings. I walked for well over an hour.

Stopping in the shadows between the far-flung reach of the streetlights, I looked deep into the night sky at the distant, tender stars. I understood nothing. All of my pondering of Knox's death had yielded no revelation. Knox's life was simply a star whose light had passed. There was nothing more I could do, nothing more to understand.

Unconsoled and weary, I began my return to Fleming Street. As I passed back through downtown, something caught my eye. About fifty feet in front of me someone had emerged from the alley next to Morrow's Drugs. I heard a short gasp. Whoever it was turned and ran back down the alley. It was a small figure in pants wearing a ball cap. I felt no compulsion to run and certainly not to give chase. When I approached the alley, I stopped and stared into the narrow darkness, but couldn't detect anything.

Odd, I thought, and resumed my pace back toward Fleming Street, only occasionally looking behind me to see if I might catch a glimpse of the skittish man. But I saw nothing more.

Curiosity began to give way to uneasiness and I accelerated my steps. In a few short minutes I arrived back home. What an hour earlier had been a collection of lonely rooms was now a familiar and welcome haven from the unsettling encounter in the shadows of the downtown side street. I locked the front door behind me. Only one lamp was lit in the living room, but it was ample enough light to guide my way to the kitchen. The small measure of adrenaline from the walk home had passed, leaving me with a genuine exhaustion. I retrieved a bottle of water from the fridge and decided to step out onto the dark of the back porch to once again gaze at the night sky before climbing the stairs to bed. I walked a few feet into the grass to get the best view of the massive bowl of stars above me.

Suddenly, there in the cloaked silence of my backyard, I heard the strange, rhythmic, muted sound of footfalls. I walked to the side yard in the direction of the noise. The sound stopped. All was quiet and still. I had only imagined it. Returning into the house, I climbed the back stairs to my bedroom, washed my face, and crawled into bed, hoping sleep would come soon.

CHAPTER 16
The Funeral

The blaring phone woke me from a deep sleep. It rang enough times to kick on the answering machine downstairs in the kitchen. It was almost six. In ten more minutes the alarm was going to go off anyway, so I decided to force myself out of bed and check the message.

It was from Connie. She was not going to be there for breakfast but reminded me that there was cereal in the cabinet and a can of biscuits in the fridge. She added in a lecturing tone to be careful when using the oven to bake them. There was a pause. Then, speaking in a somewhat hesitant voice, she noted that the visitation for Knox McAnders was being held at three that afternoon and she would see me there. The fog of events had precluded my thinking about the funeral. I wanted to stay away from the whole business, but I caught Connie's suggestion. It would be best for me to go and politely offer the appropriate condolences to the family. After all, since I was the county physician, they were all my patients. Perhaps because Knox had been so full of life, so sharp and clever, his death felt out of place. I had been unable to erase my small sense of guilt regarding his passing. Despite my reluctance, I knew that attending the visitation was the right thing to do.

Restless, I showered, dressed, and headed to the clinic. Nancy pulled in behind me as I drove into the parking lot. We walked in together, Nancy as bubbly as ever. The appointment load wasn't heavy and I told her I'd be leaving around three that afternoon so I could attend the visitation at the funeral home. Nancy diplomatically said that visiting would be a nice gesture. The tone of her response made me ill at ease, but I said nothing and nodded in return.

The day passed quickly. At lunch I walked over to the Depot to see what the meat-and-three was for the day. I took a seat at the counter and ordered. Some familiar faces nodded, but no one spoke or called me by name. That is, until Warren Thurman, the sheriff, slapped me on the back and mounted the wide chrome-and-plastic seat next to me.

"How we doin' today, Doc? Anything good to eat?"

I was delighted to be greeted with such lack of reserve.

"Hey, Sheriff. I'm doing fine. As far as the menu goes, they say it's all good."

Warren grinned. "Well, they would be right. And I've got an extra twenty pounds of middle to prove it."

I nodded and smiled. "So how's the police business?"

"Never a dull moment. Got a call this morning from Mayfield Morrow, the pharmacist. He owns Morrow's Drugs—you know, over on West Main."

"Sure, I know where it is."

"Well, he thinks someone tried to break into his store again last night. When he opened up this morning, the alarm system had been turned off and the dead bolt on the back door was unlocked. Mayfield swore he had set the system and locked the dead bolt when he left last night."

"Was something missing?"

"Nope. That's why I'm making small talk of it. Nothing was out of place or stolen. Same thing happened several times in the last few months. Sometimes I think Mayfield is just getting forgetful about locking up. So, no crime no foul—just fodder for conversation. We've got a suspect or two, probably somebody who's pretty good with keys. But since nothing was stolen, it's not a police matter."

I sat quietly. It was next to Morrow's store that I'd seen the man in the ball cap the night before. Perhaps he'd been the lookout for a thief breaking in and my presence had spooked both of them.

Warren continued, "Mayfield's just turned seventy-two. I think maybe he's getting confused. Or hell, maybe I am. Never know—could be both." Warren breathed out a short but deep-throated laugh.

I thought about telling Warren about what I'd seen, but hesitated. What had I seen? Really nothing. Just someone in the alley, someone I could in no way identify. I let it pass. He and I exchanged small talk for the rest of lunch. Nothing was said about Knox, which again left me with a troubled feeling. Perhaps Warren saw no reason to talk about what was well known to everyone, or maybe he thought it best to let me bring up the topic if I felt the need to talk about it. With him, there was an odd mix of insight and politeness, a cleverness that left room for the other person to direct the topics of conversation. I finished up, paid my bill, and walked back to the clinic.

At three, I went to my house to change into my suit and go to the funeral home a short walk away. I took my time, not wanting to get there too early and be the first in line. When I arrived at a quarter past four, the building was already packed—front steps, front porch, all with more people than I knew existed in Watervalley. Clearly half the people in the county had known Knox, and the other half was related to him.

I worked my way into the front funeral parlor. It was an elaborate older building with floors covered in rich, deep red carpet. The entire place had an air of practiced decorum and muted dignity. I signed the guest register and moved toward the throng of people in the receiving line.

A tall, gangly young man in a poorly fitted dark suit approached me. He had a boyish face and was clearly in his early twenties. His general mien seemed stiff and rehearsed, as if he were stoically trying to look older than he really was. He introduced himself as Campbell Harrington, the son of the mortician. It became clear that I'd been spotted as a stranger and this fellow wanted to satisfy his curiosity. I told him who I was, which invoked an animated look of recognition. The effusive cordiality in his manner seemed to cover an underlying frostiness. I suspected he was privately passing judgment on me. It was unsettling.

The room buzzed with a muddled cacophony of low conversation. The people of Watervalley, in all their plain and modest finery, were here en masse. Some of the women were small with a hardened timidity in their thin, sour faces, but most were bulky, with putty-colored skin, big hair, wool suits or neatly pressed cotton dresses, and large clunky shoes. Some held small shiny purses in front on them, while others carried handbags large enough to contain a week's worth of laundry.

Beside them stood neatly shaven, rotund men in ill-fitting brown and gray suits, poorly polished shoes, nicotine-stained fingers, and blemished, leathered skin. There were numerous children: somber-faced little girls in Sunday dresses who whispered behind their hands to each other with great intensity, and boys of all ages, some with well-oiled and neatly combed hair, wearing short-sleeved dress shirts buttoned to the neck. They were all standing obediently with darting, inquisitive gazes that absorbed everyone and everything and seemed particularly interested in me as I entered the room.

The people in the receiving line were huddled in small confidences, wearing expressions of staid decorum. Old Knox McAnders was stretched out in his coffin, devoid of the youthful spirit for which he was so well known. He seemed to be only a frail shell of the alert, mischievous gentleman who, with a kind face and warm, twinkling blue eyes, had greeted me in the clinic the previous week. I heard the overflow of several conversations expressing regret about how Knox had come so close to reaching one hundred. It seemed absurd at first. The man had lived ninety-nine incredibly healthy years. Still, it occurred to me that the planned celebration wasn't so much the marking of time, but rather a heartfelt opportunity to truly recognize one of Watervalley's grandest old gentlemen. The laments I overheard were driven by a deep remorse that Knox had been cheated out of a tremendous outpouring of love and appreciation. It only deepened my own personal doubts about my handling of his last days.

I moved through the line expressing my condolences and was received with reserve and graciousness. Most of the family politely recited the labored and clumsy words that people say when speaking of the departed. As I made my way past them I noticed the curious absence of Toy McAnders. Having reached the end of the receiving line, I glanced around the room looking for a familiar face, but saw none. It seemed inappropriate to make an immediate exit out the front door, so I moved to one of the adjacent rooms where people were talking in more animated tones.

Easing into the crowded room and wishing privately to be

invisible, I tried my best to mask my awkwardness. But I felt painfully obvious and out of place. It seemed my presence had only brought further unease to an already heartrending situation. I felt foolish for having come.

As I maneuvered through the crowd, I saw from across the room a face of amused but sympathetic assessment. Christine Chambers, wearing a neatly cut black dress, was looking directly at me. She stood in a small gathering with her back to one of the large windows. The soft, filtered light fell fairylike on her bare arms and cast a glow around her face. She looked fresh, wholesome, firmly molded. She was intoxicatingly beautiful. I stood hypnotized, trapped in the gentle net of her gaze. I was pressed with an incredible desire to talk to her, to apologize for the awful, insensitive things I had said, to somehow start afresh and find some common ground. Something in her fleeting glance seemed to read a confirmation of my attraction. For a brief second, the agony of my embarrassing isolation was forgotten. I was drawn in, enchanted.

I looked away and moved to the far side of the room. Then I felt a friendly hand patting me on the back and turned to find Mayor Hickman.

"Good to see you, Doc. You doing okay?"

"Sure, fine. How are you?"

"Oh, fine, fine, fine. Hmm, tough business, huh? Knox was a good man. The best."

"I'm sure that's true. Can't say I got much of a chance to know him."

"Yeah, that's a shame. You would have liked him. Sad thing too—he didn't quite make it to his one hundredth birthday. We had a big celebration planned."

I nodded. "So I heard." The mayor talked nonstop for another few minutes. He had a remarkable ability to look you in the eye and, in a confiding manner, talk to you about absolutely nothing of importance. I never thought he was disingenuous; it had simply become his default mode of communicating, as if you were the one person he most needed to talk to. Even still, during the subtle nod, he would make quick surveys of those around him, working the room, assessing whom to talk to next based upon a highly refined calculation of influence and benefit. It was clear that Walt had a keen sense of political theater, but he was so darn friendly, so unreserved, you had to like the guy. At his core, he was a politician. Even still, the mention of Knox and the celebration only thickened the cloud of my own self-doubt.

We talked cordially for a few more moments, and while I heard his words, my mind was only half engaged. I desperately wanted to maneuver for a view back across the room at Christine. After what seemed an eternity I closed my conversation with the mayor and stepped politely away, giving a short, furtive glance in Christine's direction, but she was gone. I stepped into the crowded central hallway leading out the front and almost bumped headfirst into someone walking in the opposite direction. The man did not move, but instead looked at me with impassive reserve. It was Toy McAnders. Despite my clear six-inch advantage in height, his body language didn't give the slightest pretense of yielding. We stared sharply at each other. Finally, I pursed my lips and gave him a subtle nod.

"Toy," I said softly while holding out my hand.

Unlike most of his kinsmen, he had a well-groomed, polished appearance. His charcoal gray suit was well tailored and crisply complemented by a starched button-down shirt and silk tie. He was clean shaven, revealing the modest but handsomely strong facial features of his bloodline. He looked at me with a contemplative, calculating, and darkly confident face. Without the slightest change of expression, he lowered his gaze to study my outstretched hand. Then, in an awkward, deliberate motion, he extended his right hand in a firm grasp.

"Doc." He gave a slight nod.

We stood silently. Neither of us offered anything more. I nodded again and proceeded to walk past, pausing only long enough to say thanks to the funeral staff member standing sentry at the front door. The short, gray-haired man insisted on shaking my hand as I passed. After we shook, I once again glanced down the hallway at Toy.

At that moment I noticed something curious. He was rubbing his chin with the thumb of his left hand. This, coupled with the ungainly nature of his handshake, told me that Toy was likely left-handed. But what was truly interesting was the position of his left thumb. It curved backward at such an angle it seemed to be made of rubber. I couldn't help but wonder what was going on under his intense and brooding surface. Without access to that deeper knowledge, I found myself gathering only the physical minutiae my medical training would allow me.

I stepped onto the porch, exhaling a deep sigh. Moving slowly down the wide steps, I took off my suit jacket, threw it over my shoulder, and began to make my way back to the clinic. About a half block down the street I noticed a car parked with the motor running. In it was a young woman who was apparently waiting for someone. After looking in her direction for a few moments, I realized she was staring at me. I recognized her as Sarah Akins, the young mother with the infant I'd examined the week before. When she realized I was looking back at her, she pulled the car down a side street and was quickly gone from view. I didn't recall seeing her inside the funeral home. Yet it seemed clear she was either waiting for someone there or deliberating whether to attend. It was an odd, curious moment, but was soon lost to the larger shadows hanging over me: the looming sense of doubt about Knox's death that had taken over all my thoughts.

It was five in the afternoon. As I walked the few blocks to the clinic, I could see on the horizon the ominous black of a late summer storm front. Replacing the vibrant blue sky, the dark thunderclouds piling up in the west had thrown the streets into an eerie twilight.

I felt a desperate frustration. Clearly, from all the comments I'd heard earlier that day at the clinic and now at the funeral home, Watervalley was mourning the loss of one of its prized citizens, a beloved man who had been a mainstay of stability and strength. It seemed that there was now a minor tear in the fabric of life in this small town, one that would take a measure of time to heal. Idiot chance had placed me in Knox's path just as he was making his last step toward departure from the flesh. His death had been inevitable. But the sullen glances, the whispering huddles, the dropped conversations as I had moved about the funeral home plagued me with the feeling that, for some reason, I was being held to blame. I knew I had begun to doubt, in some small degree, my assessment of Knox, wondering if perhaps I had truly missed some indication of illness. It should be no surprise that others might be thinking the same.

I arrived at the clinic's back door at the very onset of a raging downpour that pelted me with a blowing fury. The clinic was closed and I let myself in, moving through the shadowed hallway to my office. The deluge poured against the large windows. Slowly I pulled my desk chair toward me. My charmed existence in Watervalley had been short-lived. With Hoot Wilson's miraculous escape from death, I had made a glorious entrance to center stage.

Knox's death had placed me there again, except now I stood under the glaring light of doubt and suspicion. I sat down and leaned forward, holding my face in my hands.

Eventually, I collapsed back against the chair and stared at the ceiling. In the silence of my office, a thought occurred to me. There was one person I could talk to. I grabbed my things and went home to change into jeans and a T-shirt. I decided to take a drive up to the hills.

CHAPTER 17
Questions

By the time I pulled the Corolla onto the brick driveway of John Harris's home, the rain had moved out, leaving the evening air cooler, thick with dewy moisture. It was the cusp of early twilight, with darkness still a shaded hour away. A small, professionally engraved wooden sign at the entry read SUMMERPLACE. This struck me as curious, because John didn't appear to be the estate-naming type. It would be a question for another time.

I parked the car and rang the bell but noticed through the side transoms that no one appeared to be inside. Instinctively, I walked around the house toward the rear deck, calling out a strong "Hello." I soon found John taking in the view from one of the two Adirondack chairs on the low plane of the lawn behind the house. He looked over his shoulder and immediately rose to meet me.

"Well, now, damn, Doctor. What brings you up here?" Unlike our first encounter, this time John offered me a large, engaging smile. Given the events of the day, I was elated. Clearly he, like me, was glad to have company.

"Ah, looking for fresh air, I guess. You said to come anytime."

"That I did," responded John heartily, still bearing a relaxed, pleased grin. "Come join me. I'm having a Scotch. A damn good one—twenty-year Ardbeg. Best Islay there is."

"Thanks for the offer, but how about I just have a beer?"

He gave me an incredulous look, not so much disappointed as surprised. He nodded in resignation. "All right, so be it. There's beer in the fridge. Go help yourself."

I smiled, knowing that for him such an offer was the apex of hospitality. I made my way to the kitchen, grabbed a cold beer, and rejoined him in one of the Adirondack chairs.

We sat quietly for a moment, staring into the far reaches of the valley below. To my surprise, it was John who broke the silence.

"Well, Doc, I'm starting to worry about your sanity. First you move to the armpit of Tennessee and now you're turning down twenty-year-old Scotch. Your condition is starting to appear serious." There was a slight slurring in his voice.

"How many of those have you had? You seem blithe and vocal tonight."

John smirked. "Blithe and vocal—rather linguistic of you, Doc. Humph. Well, I have explored the subtleties of the Scotch bottle with resolute thoroughness, if that is what you're asking, smartass."

I smiled, shaking my head lightly. I downed a long draw of beer and took in the well-crafted details of the strong rock wall surrounding the property.

"I gotta hand it to you, John. You've got a nice place here. Solid looking. With that rock wall, you could probably hold off a pretty good siege for several days."

"Why, is there a murmur in the village? Are they coming after me with torches and pitchforks?" No doubt John was in a state of full mirth.

"Not hardly. Right now they're all at Knox McAnders's funeral. I take it you knew him?"

"Hell, Doc, Knox was on a first-name basis with everybody in the valley and most of their pets. He was quite the man—friendly, smart as a whip, and completely dedicated to the community. Served on the school board for fiftysomething years. You look around this county, you'll see his handiwork everywhere. The soccer complex, the new high school, the new library, the renovation of the Memorial Building—all those things were accomplished because Knox was quietly working in the background, building consensus, finding the money, making things happen. Yet you won't find his name on a single one of them. That's just how he was. He had a way of reading people, knowing what made them tick. He knew how to get things done."

"I only saw him briefly, at the clinic last week, but I have to admit there was something about him. He had this charmed way of looking at you and you knew he was reading your mind. Anyway, if there is a murmur in the village, I think it is more pointed in my direction. Comes with the territory."

"Oh, really? So that's what has you all mopey looking. You believe they think you're to blame for Knox's death?" Even on the fringe of being sloshed, John's insight was painfully accurate.

"Oh, hard to say. I haven't quite figured these people out. They've all been nice. Still, I can't help but think that sometimes it's just a veneer. Seems to be an underlying mind-set of suspicion."

"Humph." John chortled. "Hell's bells, Luke. Did you think your Buckhead urbanity would stumble on many common denominators among these denominational commoners?"

"Clever. Anyway, looks likes news travels fast."

"Knox McAnders's death is a big event, Doc. You didn't see? The paper ran a special edition."

"Really? What did it say was the cause of death?"

Curious, John carefully read the tone and nature of my question. "Natural causes. Isn't that what your report said?"

I was considerably relieved. "Yeah—well, sure. Heart failure, to be exact. My God, you know the man was ninety-nine."

"Ninety-nine, ten months, and two days to be exact, according to the paper. And spry till the last. Pretty darn good if you ask me." John sat staring intently down toward the town, as if he could focus in on the steps of the funeral home. In a low and casually sarcastic voice he added, "And I'm sure the god of all the little people in the valley thought that was pretty darn good too."

"Well, now, that's interesting. Given your inference that he's not your god, you seem to have a pretty strong insight into what's on his mind."

"That's right, sawbones. We parted amiably several years ago. Since then we get along just fine. Besides, I'm looking for a new god."

"A new one?"

"Yep, a new one. I'll tell you what I want. I want a god who will stand up for jackasses. We don't get the support we need."

"Ha. Well, good luck with that." I shook my head and laughed. John loved it. He held up his glass.

"To Knox McAnders, a fine old Scotsman. He left behind some pretty good family and a lot of dumbass neighbors."

"Powerful speech, John. Thanks for sharing. Dumbass neighbors, huh? So where does that leave us?"

John looked over at me ponderously, drunkenly, still with his glass held skyward.

"Sport, that leaves us high on a hill, drinking damn good Scotch, overlooking all of them. You and me, a smartass and a jackass, respectively."

We laughed spontaneously, sympathetically, our voices echoing into the reaches of the growing darkness. Perhaps we both had been looking for something to laugh about, and John's wit and sarcasm were the only tonics available.

"Yeah, here's to Knox McAnders, my first patient in Watervalley."

"Oh, cheer up, Doc. Another ten or fifteen years, nobody will be remembering that."

"Thanks, John. That's very comforting."

"Glad I could help."

Bolder shadows were now covering the west wall of the valley, the last rays of sun hovering over the cathedral of trees rimming the tops of the far hills. My mind stirred.

"So John. I'm curious. How does this all work for you? You've got this great place, incredible view, a couple of great cars, but, uh . . ." I struggled with how to properly frame my words. "But you don't seem to be connected."

"Sawbones, if you have a question, spit it out."

"Why do you live up here all alone?"

"Well, I don't know. I've found a certain gratifying ease in living a self-centered life. There are a whole lot less birthdays to remember."

"I'll take that one under advisement."

John poured more Scotch into his short glass. "My life's no different from anybody else's. Things happen. You deal with them. I deal with them in my own way just like anybody. But I'm more of an up-and-outer than a down-and-outer."

I smiled at the remark. Then my thoughts took a different direction. "Hey, tell me something, Mr. Up-and-Outer. Toy McAnders—what do you know about him?"

John smiled. He spoke slowly, stoically. "Tough one to figure out, isn't he? Toy is one of the best athletes the valley ever produced. Made All-State in baseball and basketball several years ago. He's a lefty. Almost won the state baseball pennant single-handedly. Could have gone off to school, but never did."

"Not enough horsepower between his ears?"

"No, that isn't his problem. He's plenty smart. He just loves farming and loved his grandfather Knox."

"I guess there's no crime in that."

"Small towns have opinions on everything. They judge you pretty sharply if you do well and leave or if you do well and stay. Toy's a tough, quiet kid. His senior year a couple of thugs tried to steal Knox's wallet while he was waiting for Toy after a basketball game. It happened in the school parking lot. Toy waded into the middle of it and beat the crap out of both of them. As the story goes, each one had forty pounds on him. There was a beautiful swiftness to his sense of justice. For him, the time for inquiries was after the fight was over."

"Interesting story. So Toy is one tough fellow?"

John nodded. "Ever since, an entire mythology has grown up around him. I don't think he's mean or anything, but no doubt he's got a murky side to him. In towns like Watervalley, you have your mayors and councilmen, but you also have chieftains, people with weight and influence. I'd say for his generation: Toy is that guy. Everybody in the town knows Toy, just like they knew Knox. But I bet you not thirty of them have had a conversation with him."

I stared into the evening, taking in all that John had said.

"Anyway, not long after that, Toy moved in with Knox. He finished high school and worked the farm. Not much money there, though. I think he has an evening job at the cabinet factory."

"I met him yesterday morning out at Knox's place and again today at the funeral home. He's not a very talkative type."

"I suspect not. That degree in front of your name gives you a special status. But you're still an outsider, slick. You'll see. They'll lead you to water, but it doesn't mean they'll let you drink. Simple people, simple minds. You better get used to it."

"Well, don't sugarcoat it for me, John."

"What did you think Watervalley was going to be?"

I brooded on the question for a moment. "You said something a minute ago, about people having a sharp opinion—judging, I think you said, if you do well and stay or if you do well and leave. Is that what happened to you?"

"Getting a little personal there, aren't you, Doc?"

"You brought it up."

John stared into the distance and rubbed his chin. "Yeah, I did." He took a strong swallow of the Scotch. His gaze into the distant twilight grew sharp, focused.

"Growing up in a little town like this one is all fine and good. It gives you a sense of roots, of consistency. But it can also make you insignificant. Molly saw life here as something sweet and vibrant. For me, it was stagnant water, a swamp." He took another swallow.

"When I was ten, my dad took me to Nashville for the first time. We walked around downtown, saw all the tall buildings, visited the capital, the Parthenon, drove by all the big hotels. I was just a hick kid. I felt small, frightened. But I remember as we were leaving the city that night, I turned around in the backseat and looked at the distant lights through the rear window. I was hooked. It was like my first taste of an opiate. That is where I saw life happening. I wanted to be part of it, consume it, live right in the middle of it. Molly went along. But wherever we lived, from time to time I would catch her standing out under the stars, looking into the evening sky and wondering which direction was Watervalley. She loved this place beyond words. And, to be honest, it was beyond me why she did."

"But you loved her, so you came back."

"You don't miss much, do you?"

Darkness was now melting over the expanse of the valley and the last lingering fingers of twilight reached far into the rifts of the distant hills. Down below, the streetlights of the small town were flickering on one by one. Stars began to appear vividly in the wide sky above. I took the last swallow of my beer.

"Go get yourself another one," John said. "You look like you could use some cheering up."

"Well, I don't know, John. Somehow talking to you hasn't been the load of giggles I thought it would be." I could tell that he was reaching a saturation point. The alcohol had taken the edge off his anger, making him modestly jovial, randomly philosophic.

"Ah. You just need some stouter medicine. Knox was a good man. But it was time. Doesn't mean you're a bad doc." John took another large swallow of Scotch. He exhaled deeply. Then, again holding his glass toward the stars, he quoted: "'Stir up the Athenian youth to merriments; Awake the pert and nimble spirit of mirth; Turn melancholy forth to funerals; The pale companion is not for our pomp.'"

"I'm impressed. Half a bottle of Scotch and you're quoting *A Midsummer Night's Dream*. Seems to me the moment calls for one of Shakespeare's tragedies rather than a romantic comedy."

John chuckled. "Okay, explain this to me, Doc. How is it you know your classics so well? I figured you'd be all about zygotes and mitochondria."

"I guess I can credit my aunt Grace with that. After my parents were killed I seemed to have a lot of nightmares. I was just a twelve-year-old kid and was more or less thrust upon her. She had a pretty short on-ramp to the business of parenting. Anyway, she was a librarian and loved the classics. So for the first year or so she would read to me before going to bed. I was a little old for Dr. Seuss, so she read what she loved: Shakespeare, Homer, Jane Austen, even a little Washington Irving thrown into the mix. I guess the habit stuck, and I kept reading them after the nightmares went away."

John looked up at the stars now vividly cast in the evening's deepening blue. "Doc, you're a man of many facets. I'm glad your unlucky ass landed here."

"That's very reassuring, John. Meanwhile, I better head out. I've got patients to see in the morning. Thanks for the beer."

"Don't rush off. I might be able to cheer you up yet."

"I'll take a rain check on that."

As I began to leave, John rose with me, his gait somewhat unsteady. He staggered with the unmistakable markings of alcoholic gravity. As we proceeded to my car, I paused one last time to admire the incredible beauty of the moonlight on John's well-manicured world. A final question came to me. I leaned against the front fender, addressing John directly.

"Hey—one more thing. Since you know everybody in Watervalley, there's this girl in town, a schoolteacher. Absolutely gorgeous and feisty, all in the same incredible package. I met her earlier this week. Her name is Christine Chambers. You know anything about her?"

Suddenly John became stone-faced, staring at me intently. He inhaled deeply, lifted his glass and drained the last of his Scotch. Then, oddly, once again he quoted *A Midsummer Night's Dream*: "Oh my. 'So quick bright things come to confusion.'"

With that he turned away and walked drunkenly around the house, retreating into the darkness.

Standing alone in the night, I wondered what in the world that was all about. Knox's death, the stranger in the downtown alley, Christine Chambers and now John's odd behavior—the last twenty-four hours had just been filled with unanswered questions. I started the Corolla and began the long, winding drive down the hills back to Fleming Street. Being with John had been a good way to occupy myself, to distract me away from my sense of isolation. But now as I drove the dark curves of the wooded lane, all the uncertainty, all the doubt, all the awkwardness closed in upon me again.

It was then that I first seriously entertained the thought that perhaps I had made a mistake. That perhaps it might be best if I faced up to some tough realities and did what was needed to leave Watervalley and return to the world of medical research and grants, to the urban world that made sense to me. After a few lost minutes, I dismissed the thought. But in time, it was an idea that would begin to consume me.

CHAPTER 18
Autumn

I awoke the next morning to the smell of bacon. The enticing aroma wafted up from the kitchen and reached into my senses in my half dream state, prompting memories of my adolescent room, careless summer mornings, and my mother's soft, prodding feminine voice. I finally reached over and checked the clock. Quarter till six. Connie was early.

I placed my feet on the floor and paused, opening my eyes wide like a child, and stretched my arms high above me. After putting on jeans and a shirt, I made my way downstairs, drawn to the delightful smells of breakfast. My footfalls were inaudible against the clamor of activity created by Connie's orchestration in the kitchen. She had her back to me and was in a lively conversation on the telephone. The long spiral phone cord bounced across the length of the room as she moved between the stove and table. I stopped and sat at the bottom of the steps, unnoticed, taking in the intensity of her heated conversation.

"I'm telling you, Estelle, I had every right to do what I did. There we all were, seated at the restaurant, and Luther decided he wanted to be the one to say grace. That's all fine and good till he starts getting this sanctimonious air about himself, puffing all up and talking in such a low voice you'd think he was trying to force out a burp. You know the man hasn't hit a lick at a snake for thirty years, claiming all that stuff about weak legs and a bad back, and all the while his infirmity of limb hasn't done anything to stifle his appetite. Anyway, he was several minutes into it, praying over everything from dead relatives to the blight on the neighbor's tomato plants, and I finally just spoke up and hollered out 'Amen.' Heavens, girl, the food was getting cold. Well, that stopped him just long enough for everybody to scramble for their fork in case he wasn't completely derailed. Then he got huffy and started giving me the evil eye. That's when I told him that if he was behind on his prayer life, he could get caught up on his own time."

At that moment Connie turned and noticed me sitting on the back steps with my chin propped in my right hand. Her eyes narrowed to thin slits, regarding me with a puckered scowl. "Estelle, honey, I gotta go. The doctor is up and moving around in stealth mode."

She marched indignantly across the room and hung up the phone. Then, towering over me with hands on her hips, she spoke in a lecturing tone. "There are actions that separate a gentleman—particularly a Southern gentleman—from the lower creatures. Apparently you are not generally familiar with them. Just when did it become polite for you to sneak in on somebody's conversation without letting yourself be known?"

Staring sheepishly up at her, again I stretched luxuriously, lifting my right hand straight above my head and using my left hand to cover a deep and robust yawn. "The bacon is starting to burn."

Connie's glare remained locked. But I noticed a minutely perceptible line form on the right side of her tightly pressed lips. It was a grin screaming to surface. She recovered with a quick "humph" and turned toward the stove.

"We need to amend our contract. There needs to be a fine for bad manners."

"Don't stand on ceremony on my account," I responded mischievously. "Feel free to speak your mind."

Connie's sour look of disapproval continued. She reached into the nearby cabinet to retrieve a plate. "Get off those steps and get the milk out. Your breakfast is gonna get cold, burned bacon and all."

Moving with some measure of early morning sluggishness, I took my place at the table as Connie set the loaded plate before me. I reached for my fork but then stopped abruptly.

"If I begin to recite some lengthy homily, are you going to cut me off?"

A muted grin began to emerge, but Connie caught it quickly. Still, it told volumes. A telltale crack had shown itself on her often critical exterior. She countered quickly. "Watch yourself, Doctor. You keep acting too smart for your britches and I'll cut you with something other than words. I'll fix it to where you can say grace to the Lord face-to-face."

I took a large bite of egg and toast. "Good morning to you too, Connie."

This brought another "humph" from her, but it served no purpose in discouraging me. In the absolute, Connie Thompson was a loving, vulnerable softie. It had simply taken me a while to figure it out. She walked over to the counter, took off her apron, poured herself a cup of coffee, and joined me at the table. Now when she spoke her tone was milder, more conversational, though still unmistakably Connie.

"I looked for you at the funeral home yesterday. I heard you were there. Several of us went to dinner afterward. I was hoping you would join us."

"I appreciate that, but I don't know. Some of the McAnders family seemed to regard me rather warily."

"Oh, you're talking about Toy," Connie responded abruptly. "I wouldn't let him bother you. The verdict is still out on him. I'm not so sure that his part of the McAnders gene pool doesn't need a little chlorine."

"Toy McAnders is sort of a tough one to figure out. But it wasn't just him. I'm not sure where I fit into that situation." I was also thinking about Christine Chambers, but chose not to subject my interest in her to Connie's critical opinion, especially given that I had been, in fact, attending visiting hours for a dead man.

"I don't understand what you mean. You're the town doctor. That's where you fit in."

"Right, I get that part. I'm just talking about in the larger sense. I'm not sure how I fit socially with these people. Everybody's nice enough, but that's about where it ends."

Connie pondered my words. "Sorry, Doctor. Your welcome package to Watervalley doesn't come with a decoder ring. Where you fit in is something you're gonna have to figure out for yourself."

We sat in silence for a few lingering seconds. The conversation had hit a dead end. Connie drank her coffee. Her face was now reflective, with an underlying concern.

"So, what did you do after you left the funeral home?" she asked.

"I wanted some company, so I drove up to John Harris's place and chatted with him for a while."

"Good heavens, Doctor! You no sooner leave the angels floating around poor old Knox's casket than you skip on up to bend your elbow with the devil himself."

I was taken aback, surprised at Connie's intuition that alcohol had been part of the visit.

"Devil or not, he was a lot more friendly than the so-called angels floating around the funeral home," I said. She'd put me on the defensive. "Anyway, it's not like the devil, as you call him, and I were up there discussing *Beyond Good and Evil.*"

"Humph," responded Connie. "You're not going to find much room for Nietzsche in this part of the Bible Belt. Not even with John."

I did my best to muffle my stunned reaction. How did she do that? I was trying to think of a sharp reply, but, unfortunately, Connie wasn't finished.

"Oh, not that he couldn't handle it. He's always good for taking up an intellectual challenge, whether it's Schrödinger's cat, the Chinese room, or Occam's razor. It's not John's intellect that's in question. It's his anger you need to watch out for. Don't be bringing around here any of that salty language he uses."

As I had done on several occasions before, I stared at Connie with an expression of disbelief.

"Okay, first of all, what makes you think I am so impressionable?" I asked. "And you know another thing—" I stopped in midsentence. "Hold it—Schrödinger's cat? How do you know about this stuff? How do you pull it out of the air?"

Connie pulled her shoulders back and lifted her chin as I'd offended her. She looked to the side for a moment, clearly preparing her answer. "My youngest son, Theodus, is an associate professor of philosophy at Rhodes College in Memphis. We talk on occasion."

I nodded with resignation. "I think I better go get ready for work."

"Leave your dishes."

I rose from the table and headed upstairs. Halfway up I thought how nice it would be to reply to Connie with some clever retort, but nothing came to mind. I wished she wasn't such a good cook.

I went to work and moved through my day, listening and thinking and acting in the moment. The appointments came and went, and patient by patient I did my job. Work and life in Watervalley was becoming routine and the days began to roll forward.

As the hot weeks of August started to pass into September, I began to quietly bury my thoughts, my longings, and my deep, unspoken loneliness. I wished for distant places. I began to pour myself into the oblivion of work, the long hours, the repetitive cycle of daily assessments, and the drowning ritual of daily life. I would absorb the muddled histories of patients, listen to their stories, and piece together a medical chronicle of their lives. I would assess and prescribe and coach and teach. I began to know them by name and nickname and could speak to them with a voice of care, compassion, and quiet sagacity.

My greatest fear was that somehow the people of Watervalley would discover the level of my detachment. I had no disdain or contempt for the people here. They were my patients and by definition deserved my skill and attention as well as my concern and acceptance. But I longed to be elsewhere, pursuing a different life. I longed for the glorious promise of new places, new friends, lively music, the call of laughter and nightlife. For so many years my life had been confined to schoolrooms, marching to an invisible metronome of classes, exams, and deadlines as I bided my time for a grander day. And while there were small delights and satisfactions in my daily care of patients, I still found myself as before: marking time, in a hurry to get to the future.

My conversations with Connie became comfortable if not somewhat perfunctory. As the weeks passed, we slipped into an easier relationship. Although she continued to have a relentless scrutinizing nature, it came with a soft undercurrent of care. I had begun to be on call every other week, swapping the alternate week for referrals to the hospital in the neighboring county. I was pulled out of bed at all hours, and yet I still needed to see my regular patients every day, regardless of my lack of sleep and exhaustion. She worried about me.

Sometimes I would eat lunch down at the Depot, but I felt embarrassed sitting at the counter by myself, pretending to read the paper or look otherwise occupied. On one or two occasions Sheriff Thurman joined me. Curiously, he continued to mention some repeated occurrences of break-ins to downtown stores from which nothing was taken. Warren never lost his easygoing nature, but it was easy to see that these events troubled him.

Most days I fell into the habit of eating lunch quickly in my office, knowing that there were patients waiting. I had infrequent conversations in the side yard with Will Fox, and thought it odd that I caught only glimpses of his mother from a distance. On occasion I would drive up the hill and spend a few hours talking with John. But I went randomly and my visits were never reciprocated despite my many offers.

September flew by, and as the days passed, I came to know a profound loneliness, although, admittedly, it was foolishly self-imposed. Within me was a deep-seated determination not to embrace this provincial existence, not to define myself by Watervalley. Late at night, when my mind would drift beyond the pages of some medical journal, I dreamed of some chance circumstance, some lottery ticket, some magic door through which I could pass and find myself in a different, abundant, more exciting place. I was determined not to accept the smallness of my life. I had turned inward.

However, an event in late September started to change all of that.

CHAPTER 19
Rhett Butler

On the last Saturday in September I had decided to take a midmorning run out Summerfield Road, although I wasn't running with much conviction. Watervalley's Fall Festival was a week away and part of that event was the annual Tackiest Yard Art Contest. Locals would doll up their yards with everything imaginable, going well beyond the traditional pink flamingos and painted tires and invoking some very creative uses for discarded toilets and old washing machines. It was Watervalley's way of poking fun at itself, and on my run I passed several inspired entries. It was amusing, but I tended to follow these events from a distance, quite comfortable to keep the world at arm's length.

Eventually I made my way out to the more open farmland of Summerfield Road. Here the countryside was an orderly patchwork quilt of harvested crops, dreamy landscapes, and rambling vegetable gardens divided by crisp white fences and weathered rock walls. A soft gray overcast was painted across the wide canopy of sky. A cooler air had tumbled its way into the valley, offering an almost refreshing chill that was short of the sharp cold snap that presages the harsh days of winter. As I passed some of the farmhouses, an intoxicating smell of woodsmoke drifted in the air. After several miles Summerfield Road wound through a wooded section whose tall trees provided an awning over the narrow lane. I stopped in the middle under this cool, shadowy canopy to walk for a short way and catch my breath. I had taken a few steps with hands on my hips when I heard an odd sound, an eerie moaning in the thick greenery off to my left. I paused, staring and listening intently in the direction of the noise.

"Hello? Is someone there?"

Once again there was a low, nonhuman crying from within the dark shroud of undergrowth only fifteen or so feet away. An unease crept over me; I was uncertain of what was there but equally certain that I couldn't just ignore it.

"Who's there? Are you okay?"

Cautiously, I moved in that direction, carefully pushing back the undergrowth with each step of my advance. I heard a rustling a few scant feet away and froze. After a long wait, I took one more measured step and with some effort pushed aside a large tangle of thick hedge. That's when I heard the growl.

What I had been hearing came into full focus. It was a large dog with big teeth and apparent anger management issues. He exploded into a chorus of vicious barks that sent me scrambling for safety back on the road. But not before I noticed he had no collar and a smear of blood and mud across one side of his face.

Before I could decide what to do, I heard the sound of a truck approaching. The driver slowed to a stop and rolled down the window. It was Hoot Wilson.

"What's going on, Doc? You look like a bunch of hornets was chasing you."

"Hello, Hoot. I was out jogging and heard a noise in the woods. There's a big dog in there. I think he's hurt."

Hoot nodded his head with a wide-eyed look of understanding. "Well, let's have a look-see." He cut the engine and emerged from the truck, dressed in a warm farm coat, overalls, and his standard black-and-red knee-high rubber boots. With his generally unkempt appearance, bushy eyebrows, and thick mop of hair under his red co-op hat, Hoot exuded something of a homeless vibe. But he had an impregnable cheerfulness. His booming voice was mixed with a constant low chuckle that was amiable and accommodating. He rounded the back of the truck, rubbing his hands together, almost as if preparing for hand-to-dog combat. Without hesitation, he proceeded to push his way into the woods where I had just exited. I followed cautiously.

"Be careful there, Hoot. He doesn't seem too sociable."

Hoot moved forward undaunted. "Ah, he won't hurt me much." He paused for a moment as he worked back a stand of heavy thicket. He stayed keenly focused, speaking to me in a loud whisper. "I tell you, though, Doc. I know modern medicine has come a long way, but snakes have still got the edge in my book. Dogs are one thing, but you don't want to get a snakebite."

"Hoot, I wouldn't advocate getting any kind of bite. Be careful now. You're almost there." I spoke the last words in a low voice, as if somehow the dog wouldn't be able to hear a three-hundred-pound man stomping aside the bushes as he approached. Hoot pulled back the last of the undergrowth, revealing a full view of the animal lying before us. Again, the dog bristled and let out a low growl.

"Ah, heck, Doc—that's just a big ol' golden retriever. He ain't going to bite nobody."

"I wouldn't be so sure, Hoot. It's not like they've signed a treaty."

He bent down on one knee and began to make a low humming sound, talking to the animal and calling it to come to him. "He'll like us better if it's his choice to get close," he said.

I followed Hoot's example and bent down. The poor creature was thin and muddy with matted hair. Eventually he lowered his ears and attempted to crouch-step his way toward us, but something was holding him back.

"Look at that, Doc. I think he's got a piece of Bob-wire caught around him."

"You mean barbed wire, Hoot?"

Hoot turned to me, offering a sympathetic, humoring grin. "That's funny, Doc. I guess you don't learn about farm things in med school. It's called Bob-wire. Pretty sure some guy named Bob invented it. Anyway, looks like it's got him tore up a little."

I let this pass. Instinctively, we both started inching closer toward the pathetic creature. I reached him first and with some trepidation stretched to pat his head. The dog whimpered lightly, then yielded to the simple show of affection. Eventually, with some soft-toned encouragement, we were able to get him turned enough to see that a strand of barbed wire had gotten caught around him, cutting a small gash above his left ear and entangling his legs to the point where he couldn't move. Hoot retrieved some wire cutters from the truck, which enabled us to free him. With Hoot leading the way, I carried him through the woods and laid him in the back of the truck. He was bony and muddy, with a thick, earthy odor of wet hair.

"This ol' boy's gonna need some TLC, Doc. Whatcha want to do with him?"

I looked at Hoot and then into the huge brown eyes of the wretched, smelly creature before me. There was really no choice.

"You mind driving us back to my house? I want to get him cleaned up, and I've got a suture kit at home to close up that cut. I'll figure out the rest from there."

Hoot was glad to accommodate.

We felt convinced that the retriever would lie quiet in the back of the truck for the short ride. So I climbed into the cab with Hoot and he turned around and headed back to town. Hoot explained that he had brought Wendy in to the library—her favorite place to visit on Saturday mornings—and was returning to the farm for a couple of hours before picking her up with this week's stack of books.

"Doc, I got part of a chili dog here. Think he'd like to have that? Or is that just wrong, a dog eating a dog?"

I couldn't help but laugh at Hoot's earnest inquiry. "Probably best if we don't put anything spicy in his stomach just yet."

"Yeah, I imagine you're right."

"So how have you been feeling, Hoot?" It had been several weeks since I had seen him.

"Doc, ever since I got that ticker tune-up, I'm a new man. I've been walking around the track over at the high school. Don't much care for it, but Wendy puts her foot down about it."

I smiled. "Good for Wendy."

"So I guess you like running out in the country rather than on the track, huh, Doc? You're more of a free-range doctor?"

"Never quite thought of it that way, but, yeah, I guess so."

"Hey, you like huntin', Doc? Deer season opens next Saturday. I love huntin'. It's like God's grocery store 'cept it never closes. You ought to come huntin' with me."

I appreciated the kindness of Hoot's offer, but simply had no experience to draw upon. "Hoot, I love being out in the woods, but I'm afraid I'm not much of a hunter. I don't even have a gun—at least, not with me. I think there's a couple my dad owned back in storage in Atlanta."

Hoot could do little to mask his surprise, having obviously assumed that everyone hunted. He grew silent for a moment. It was clear he wanted to be accommodating but was having a hard time finding a topic of common interest. I probably wasn't helping much, being somewhat preoccupied with the dog in the truck bed and glancing back occasionally to check on him. Soon, however, a ready grin spread across Hoot's face.

"Doc, I guess you're probably spending more of your time huntin' for two-legged animals." He chuckled to himself, turned, and winked at me.

I exhaled a slow laugh. "Yeah, well, Watervalley is not exactly a target-rich environment. I guess maybe I'm a little too picky."

"That's too bad. Still, I don't blame you for keeping your standards high. I used to be the same way. I wouldn't date a woman who thought she was smarter than me."

I nodded and turned to look out the window, stifling an outright choking laugh. As likable as Hoot was, it seemed to me the bar he had set eliminated dating all known women and half the animal kingdom.

"Yeah, back in the day I had lots of girlfriends. There were plenty of women chasing ol' Hoot." Again I kept my thoughts to myself, but the only scenario in which I could imagine a woman chasing Hoot involved security at a mall. Knowing the "after" picture, I found it hard to envision the "before." We talked on during the ride back to my house and Hoot spoke openly about his ex-wife, his life, and the great delight of his life, Wendy.

All in all, I liked Hoot. Once you got past his large and loud nature and his rather sloppy use of the tobacco spit bottle, underneath his barbarous exterior were some pretty noble capacities. He was a single parent, his wife having abandoned him and Wendy when the girl was less than one year old. He worked hard and lived frugally and possessed an irrepressible hearty friendliness. Toward Wendy he was a devoted father—tender, patient, and encouraging, especially regarding her education, as witnessed by his clear pride at her love of books and her straight-A record. It also seemed likely that his bravado about his early dating life was a compensation for the residual pain of his wife having walked out on him years before. Yet like many of the folks in Watervalley, he had an unsparing generosity. Like so many I had come to know, he possessed an inexplicable optimism that kept a short memory of past setbacks and was able to look beyond an uncertain future.

After pulling into my driveway Hoot offered to help me get the dog inside and cleaned up. I thanked him but refused. The dog was going to be issue enough, but the prospect of Hoot's muddy boots raising Connie's wrath was worse. I ran in to grab a towel to wrap around the poor fellow. I picked him up, thanked Hoot, and returned inside, making my way upstairs to the bathtub.

The dog now had a completely submissive manner, staring at me through those large brown eyes and a most pitiful face. He stood obediently as I filled the tub with warm water. It took three rounds of scrubbing, rinsing, emptying, and refilling the tub, but I was finally satisfied that he was thoroughly clean. After the last rinse he must have thought the same, because he proceeded to initiate a systematic full body shake that splattered all four walls of the small room. Something in the action also cast off his lowly demeanor and he wagged his tail and perched both front paws on the side of the tub, looking at me with an air of exuberant anticipation. I exhausted every towel I had but finally got him dry. Meanwhile, he attempted to return the grooming favor by constantly licking and playfully pawing at me.

I examined the small cut above his ear and decided it would be best to put a stitch or two in it. I thought this would be problematic, but once again he stood obediently as I injected some lidocaine and managed to sew the wound.

The only thing in the fridge was some leftover casserole, hardly appropriate for a half-starved dog. I gave him a few pieces of bread, which he swallowed whole, and poured some milk in a bowl, which was consumed with equal vigor. Once finished, he looked up at me with the most innocent face, full of wonder and rapt attention. I never knew an animal could say so much with one expression. I was now a magnet for him. Every step I took he duplicated; he was constantly beside me, carefully placing himself only a few inches away without ever hindering my movements. I had a new shadow.

I never consciously chose to keep him. It was automatic, a foregone conclusion that he was, well, now my dog. On Monday I knew I would need to make some inquiries to see if anyone had reported him missing. But given his lack of collar and abandoned state, this didn't seem likely. Meanwhile, I would need to buy dog food, a collar, and probably some flea and worm medicine. I loaded him up in the Corolla and we headed toward the Farmers' Co-op.

Part farm store, part hardware store, part plant nursery, part men's club, the Co-op was the last bastion of Southern rednecks. It had a distinctive smell of feed, leather, creosote, and fertilizer—a dank and robust aroma that likely hadn't changed in fifty years. The Co-op wasn't a place where you walked around with a shopping cart. You couldn't buy anything without discussing it with someone. Even if you grabbed an item and placed it on the counter along with your money, the salesclerk felt obliged to politely quiz you to make sure you had made the proper choice.

I pulled into the large gravel lot, cracked the windows, and left my new friend to watch the world go by from the safety of the Corolla. The temperature was cool, so I was confident he would be fine. I remembered Nancy Orman had told me to always ask for Junior if I ever needed anything at the Co-op. I made my way inside, walked up to the main counter in the back, and caught the attention of one of the salesclerks.

"Hi, I was looking for Junior."

Simultaneously, four men responded, "How can I help you?"

Not sure what else to do, I spoke to the group. "Where can I find some pet supplies?"

In the Farmers' Co-op, every question was answered with a question. I was immediately bombarded with inquiries of what kind of dog, how big, if was he a drooler, what kind of hunting I was going to use him for, and so forth. There was no shortage of advice—not just from the salesclerks, but also from other customers who happened to be standing within earshot. This prompted infinite stories about hunting dogs, dogs that could climb ladders, dogs that could sing on cue . . . Eventually I was able to make an exit, with dog food, dog medicine, dog treats, and dog toys all in tow. My furry new friend was delighted to see me. Apparently he'd decided to pass the time by cleaning all the interior glass with his tongue, with mixed results.

That afternoon I began to feed him and get him started on the regimen of medications. Despite his thinness, the modest amount of food he ate seemed to propel a quick turnaround in his energy. We spent some time together throwing a ball in the backyard. The innate desire in his breed to retrieve anything and everything was a marvel. I could have thrown the ball till my arm fell off, and he would have endeavored with his last breath to bring it to me.

That evening, when I sat down to watch some football on TV, the golden came and sprawled at my feet, ever my constant companion. I hadn't yet figured out a name for him, having had little experience in such matters. But how hard could it be? I pondered on it for a while, but nothing came to mind.

Engrossed in the game, I hadn't noticed that he had slipped off. It was when I heard a plop at my feet that I realized where he had been. I looked over to see my running shoes sitting askew on the floor at my feet.

"Well, thank you, fellow. But I don't need these right now." I leaned over and patted him on his head, then grabbed the shoes and set them neatly on the end table beside me.

He disappeared and soon enough returned, making his presence known by another plop on the floor. I looked over to find my black dress loafers sitting neatly before me. Just as before, I leaned over, patted his head, and, after wiping off a little bit of slobber, carefully stacked them on the end table along with the others. He repeated this process until my entire inventory of shoes from the upstairs closet had been brought as tributes, including my heavy hiking boots, a feat he was able to manage only by bringing them one at a time. The supply exhausted, he finally lay on the floor with his snout on his paws, his gaze fixated on the pile of shoes on the end table.

I stretched out on the couch. Every so often, I diverted my attention from the game to scrutinize his vigilant focus on the stack of shoes. It cracked me up. That's when the thought occurred to me. I already had a housekeeper; now I had a butler.

It was settled. His name would be Rhett.

CHAPTER 20
The Garage

"Dr. Bradford! Get down here and get down here right now!"

Connie's voice was so loud and shrill, I thought she was standing beside my bed with a bullhorn. It was six a.m. on Monday and I had been dead to the world. Now I exploded out of bed and was tumbling down the steps on my heels, partially sliding and then scurrying toward the entry hall. I arrived to find Connie wielding her umbrella, standing defensively in a corner with a steely grimace on her face. Rhett was several feet away, crouched on all fours in a posture of complete submission.

"Young man, get yourself back upstairs and put some clothes on. This house isn't some Chippendales review. What did I tell you about parading around in your boxers?"

Only now did I realize that I was still in a T-shirt and boxer shorts. "Well, what did you expect? You sounded like the place was on fire."

Connie stared at me placidly, her scowling glare leaving little room for interpretation.

"Okay, just hold on a minute," I said. I stepped into the living room and retrieved a quilt from the couch to wrap around my waist. When I returned to the entry hall, Rhett came over and crouched behind me. The big coward. He'd been perfectly happy to snarl when we first met, but in response to Connie he immediately capitulated.

Connie spoke in a stern, superior voice. "Dr. Bradford, it would have been nice if you had let me know that you had a houseguest."

"Well, it only happened on Saturday. I found him when I was jogging out Summerfield Road."

The disdain on her face was so intense it could have withered a plant. "So I take it you're planning on keeping him?"

I glanced back at Rhett and his imploring brown eyes. I gathered my courage and spoke with as much authority as I could muster. "As a matter of fact, I am. It's my house and now he's my dog. I think a man ought to have the right to a little companionship." I wanted to sound decisive, in control, but something about me standing there in a makeshift skirt didn't confer the command presence I was hoping for.

Connie stood as if carved from stone. She spoke impassively. "You want to try that again, this time making it sound a little more convincing?"

I stood firm, but my words were strangled, barely escaping from my mouth. "No, I'm . . . uh . . . I'm good."

Connie placed her umbrella in the corner and continued to stare at me. Eventually she rolled her head, looking down into Rhett's pitiful face as he peered out from behind me. I was witnessing the slow disintegration of her scornful facade. The tough lines melted from her face and she looked up at me, shaking her head in resignation.

"Oh, come on, Connie. Haven't you ever had the heart to pick up a stray?"

At first she didn't respond, just took off her coat and hung it carefully on the rack in the entry hall. But as she passed by me on the way to the kitchen, she mumbled under her breath, "Mmm-hmm. Last time I gave in to that impulse I ended up being a housekeeper."

It seemed that, by the narrowest of margins, Rhett had found a new home.

October was coming. The winds of autumn began to sweep down the hills that surrounded Watervalley. The flowers that were once a riot of color even in the late summer heat of August were now limp, their backs bowed from the long trial of the hot season. Cool, crisp, starlit nights were becoming the norm. Throughout the valley the trees began to take on the lustrous hues of fall. Entire hillsides became rich collages of orange, gold, and crimson. Fallen leaves filled the yards on Fleming Street, creating a muffled rustling sound. The distant ringing laughter of children at play echoed through the chill air into the twilight hours.

The Fall Festival came, a glorious event put on with much fanfare, a celebration of all things Watervalley. It began early Saturday morning with the annual Hog Jog, a 5K charity run in which all contestants had to wear something emblematic of a pig. Sweatshirts and T-shirts with pig pictures were the most popular, but there were also a smattering of fake pig snouts and pig ears. The Society Hill Bed and Breakfast was booked solid and all the town parks and recreation areas were packed with trailers and travel vans. The entire downtown and courthouse square were a mass of people with tents, concessions, crafts, and children's activities. A few blocks away a livestock judging contest was being held at the county Agricultural Building, along with innumerable contests for best jams, jellies, corn ears, pumpkins, strings of hot peppers, and every other fruit or vegetable known to man. The celebration ended with a large square dance down at the Memorial Building with the main act being none other than Sheriff Warren Thurman and his band, made up primarily of several deputies. Appropriately, they called themselves the Blue Lights.

Watervalley's annual blood drive also took place that morning. Nancy had made arrangements with the Red Cross to ensure that there would be enough volunteers on hand to operate the mobile blood bank. Amazingly, more than two hundred of Watervalley's citizens took their turn in line. I joined in, and jokingly told the volunteer starting the IV to be careful—I was a screamer.

It was an incredible day, a spontaneous outpouring of laughter, excitement, and acres of smiles. Something about Watervalley's agrarian identity imbued this day with a pride that was unmatched by anything I had previously witnessed. I had shied away from participating in any of the events, but moved among the crowds, content to watch and observe and return the constant friendly greetings.

The Fall Festival marked a turning point. I was beginning to see the people of Watervalley in a new light. These were not the champions of brute ignorance that John Harris would have me think. No doubt, events and ideas of the larger world did influence their days. And while they still looked to distant horizons with a genuine curiosity, they chose to hold tight to what they valued most—agriculture, family, and faith—not out of fear or ignorance, but from a deeply felt conviction borne of life's joys and hardships. Their tradition of hard work, their love of the soil, and their tough-mindedness found an exulted voice in the Fall Festival. It provided a collective release from the mundane quality of their lives, an opportunity to revel in the bonds of shared community.

I was coming to realize that Watervalley was far more than some quaint, simple farm town; it was permeated with a complexity wrought by years of tough agrarian existence. I felt a growing respect for those in my small world. But I still counted myself an outsider.

The days of fall came and went.

On the Thursday following the Fall Festival I had seen my last patient by two o'clock. I worked in my office for an hour, finishing up notes for the day and going through the mail. Along with the usual solicitations from various drug companies, there was an envelope from the Red Cross marked CONFIDENTIAL. It was a thank-you note and a summary of the donations made during the recent blood drive. As would be expected, most of the donors were O positive, with a smattering of types A and B. One individual had type AB, a very rare occurrence. I filed all this away.

I sat in my large office chair staring out the large windows at the brilliant fall afternoon. Despite the arrival of cooler nights, some of the mid-October days were still oven hot with only some marginal relief in the humidity. I stacked the day's paperwork on my desk and told Nancy that she could reach me on my cell phone; I had an errand to run.

I had long promised myself that I would get the air conditioner in the Corolla fixed. Summer was over, but the midday October heat had proved to be the final inspiration. I drove the car over to Chick McKissick's garage, a white-painted concrete block building two streets off the city square. It had a fenced-in side lot that served as a graveyard for about thirty old cars and trucks. Most were used for parts, but a few were candidates for restoration at some future, and likely nonexistent, date.

A weathered sign hanging out front read AUTO REPAIR. As I pulled into the parking lot, I also saw a small sign in the front window noting CHICK'S LOCK AND KEY.

I headed for the glass office door. Adjacent was a large, open garage bay that revealed a late-model sedan head high on the hydraulic lift. The surrounding walls had floor-to-ceiling shelves stacked with boxed auto parts, smudged manuals, grease-covered parts and tools, and the requisite wall calendar of a bikini-clad woman leaning suggestively over a shiny roadster.

No one was in the work bay. In the office I found a wrinkled little man with tanned, leathery skin and a cigarette tucked between his fingers. He wore a dirty, faded ball cap, grease-smudged khakis, and a work shirt with the name CHARLIE embroidered on the pocket. I remembered his name. Someone had mentioned it regarding some of the break-ins. Apparently this fellow was suspect, but little about him seemed sinister. He was standing behind the worn counter and staring with squinted eyes at a computer monitor. He greeted me with a well-gapped toothy smile. "Can I hep ya?"

"Yeah, is Chick around?"

"Out back," the man replied, smiling amiably and nodding over his shoulder. I noticed behind the counter an entire wall of brightly colored and oddly shaped keys. The little man refocused on the computer screen and pecked away at the keyboard, his cigarette smoldering above his knuckles.

I nodded and passed through the side door to the garage area. Voices were emanating from the back, so I walked through the large rear bay door. There, to my surprise, I found not only Chick but also Will Fox, engaged in a lively, laughing conversation. Will was seated on a small makeshift bench with his knees tucked up under his chin. Chick was working on an engine block that was lifted on a chain hoist. Their animated conversation came to an abrupt halt when I rounded the corner.

"Hey, Doc! What brings you 'round here today?"

"Hi, Chick. My Corolla brings me around here, but not very

comfortably. The AC hasn't been working all summer. I've been meaning to come by but it just seems that now is my first chance."

"Doc, you gotta be kidding me. Frying pan hot all summer and you just now getting it fixed? What you been thinking?"

"I guess I'm thinking better late than never. How quick can you get to it?"

"I can look at it right now. Hey, you know my sidekick Will here, don'tcha? You two are neighbors."

Will had been sitting silently taking in the exchange and was much less animated than a few moments before. He looked at me slyly, with considerable contemplation.

"Oh, yeah. Mr. Fox and I are well acquainted. How ya doing, Will?"

"Not so bad, Dr. Bradford. Glad to see you're going to get that piece-of-crap car fixed. Why don't you get a new air conditioner with a new car wrapped around it?"

"What, so you're a car salesman now?"

Chick's perpetual smile broke into robust laughter. "I'm gonna let you two have at it while I go look at your car, Doc."

"Keys are in the ignition," I responded. We watched Chick amble toward the front, whistling some random tune. I turned to Will. "So this is where you hang out in the afternoon. I didn't know you had such a keen interest in cars."

Will shrugged his shoulders. "Sure. Cars are fun. Besides, Chick's real nice. I learn a lot from him. He lets me help out."

"Nothing wrong with that. You don't strike me as much of a grease monkey, though. Not an oil stain or smudge or dirty fingernail on you."

"He does all the mechanic stuff. I mostly clean up and help out with other things."

I nodded and smiled, waiting to see if the boy would volunteer anything else. He didn't. "How's your mom?" I asked. "I've seen her out in the backyard a couple of times in passing, but I haven't had a chance to introduce myself."

"She's okay. Stays inside a lot. She . . . uh, she gets headaches and has to lie down pretty often."

"I haven't seen her at the clinic either. I'd be glad to talk to her about her headaches. Maybe I should come over and get acquainted." This last comment seemed to set off an alarm in Will. His eyes darted to the side and he was physically drawing inward, pulling his knees even tighter to his chest and wrapping his arms firmly around them. I could see that he was searching for a response, a carefully worded one.

"She's kind of funny about visitors, but I'll tell her what you said. I'm sure if she needs anything, she'll let you know."

I studied him for a few moments. Will was undaunted, even though it was clear that he was under my full measure of scrutiny. Without doubt, this little fellow was clever, and confident about it.

An awkward silence passed. I realized there was nothing more to gather from him. As with conversations before, the boy seemed evasive, calculating, secretive. Whether he was up a tree or in the back of an auto repair shop, I seemed to always find him out of place. Not in any particular mischief, but somehow in the wrong orbit, not quite fitting into the larger picture. I pursed my lips and nodded.

"Think I'll find out how much cool cash it's going to take to get some cool air. See you around, Will."

He lifted his hand. "See ya."

I made my way to the front, where I found Chick under the hood with an apparatus of hoses and small nozzled canisters. "Chick, what do you think?"

He completed what he was doing and then shut the hood. He

turned to me with a large smile. "I think, Doc, that you are good to go."

I was astonished. "You're kidding."

"Nope. Just needed a little Freon. Can't seem to find a problem anywhere. Pressure's holding fine. It may have some kind of small leak, but should keep you cool till next spring. If it runs hot then, just bring it back. We'll gas it up again and you should be good for the summer."

"Okay, hold it. A mechanic in Nashville told me it would cost seven hundred dollars to replace the AC. So that was bunk?"

"Oh, you know it was. I'm sure there are honest folks in the city, but there's always somebody who will cheat you and figure they'll never see you again. Anyway, I don't want to cheat nobody. 'Cause if I did, I'd have to expect them to cheat me when I buy my groceries or get some new shoes or have my hair cut. A place like Watervalley just don't work that way. We got our differences, but we gotta live together."

I nodded. "I'm sure you're right."

"Now, you can give me seven hundred dollars if you want to, Doc, but twenty dollars for the Freon will be fine."

I shook my head and smiled. Pulling forty dollars out of my wallet, I handed it to Chick.

"Doc, your math is a little off, unless you're planning to go ahead and pay me for gassing the AC up next spring."

"Keep it, Chick. Your time's got to be worth something. Besides, I'm glad to see you keeping my neighbor busy, although he doesn't look much like a mechanic."

"Oh, he's no mechanic at all. But he is crackerjack with making keys and a whiz on the computer. Charlie and me are lost when it comes to technology, but young Will's as slick as a whistle on it. He's good to have around."

I shook Chick's hand and nodded.

"Thanks again." Chick smiled and headed back through the garage bay, once again whistling loudly. I started the Corolla and let the cool air pour over me. It was unbelievable. I spoke aloud to the Corolla. "Well, old girl, I guess I feel about as dumb as a rock." Shaking my head, I put the car into gear and almost felt like taking it for a drive in the country, given my new world of comfort. Then I recalled that Connie wanted me to stop at the grocery to grab a few items for dinner. So I turned left off the square and headed in that direction.

Years before, when I was a little boy, I once heard a Sunday school lesson from Ecclesiastes about how time and chance happen to all men. I was about to learn that they even happen in the canned goods aisle of the local Bi-Rite.

CHAPTER 21
The Grocery

I had pulled into the grocery store's parking lot when I noticed my shirt. Apparently when Chick and I had shaken hands, mine had gotten smudged with engine dust and I'd brushed it against my white button-down. There was a distinct smear the size of a postcard.

Great. Connie was going to love that. Looking around the Corolla, I found some napkins in a side compartment left over from months before when fast food was available in my world. With a little spit, I was able to get my hands clean.

Realizing the stain was altogether too obvious, I pulled my shirttail out to give the appearance of being casual or grungy, as if I had been doing yard work rather than having come straight from the clinic. The idea didn't completely work, but it made me feel a little less noticeable.

Oddly, I actually enjoyed grocery shopping. For most other purchases, my hunter-gatherer instincts kicked in: find the target, pull the trigger, bag it, and then move on to more enjoyable activities. But grocery shopping was different. I liked to meander, take my time. In the early years my aunt would take me along in Atlanta whenever she went to one of the many elaborate shops and bakeries nearby. Although she never cared much for housework, she was a wonderful cook. She loved finding fresh and often rare vegetables, buying unique breads, and crafting delectable sauces. By the time I learned to drive, she would send me to round up the unusual items on her grocery list. Her passion had rubbed off on me.

Shopping at the local grocer in Watervalley wasn't quite so exotic. There were more choices of chewing tobacco than there were of bread, and requests for items like plantains, bok choy, or radicchio were met with baffled faces. Nevertheless, I still enjoyed food shopping.

I grabbed a grocery cart on the way in and proceeded to amble through the produce section, smiling at several familiar faces. As I moved farther along, however, I overheard the intense voice of a young woman coming from across the next aisle. Even though I hadn't heard her in many weeks, I was certain it was Christine Chambers. Despite her disinterest in me, she still haunted my thoughts. As I listened to her speak, I realized she was trying to explain something to someone. The process was fraught with painful but compassionate difficulty.

I looked down at my shirt, dismayed, but just as quickly caught myself. There was really no reason to care about my appearance. Even still, the many lonely days had played more heavily on me than I'd realized, and the prospect of seeing Christine sparked something deep within me. But I decided to remain friendly but aloof and go on with my business. Who was I kidding? Things between us could hardly get any worse.

As I rounded the corner, I saw Christine about twenty feet down the aisle talking with an older woman. They were focused on an item on a lower shelf. I approached unnoticed, leaned over the handle of my cart, and spoke casually.

"Hello."

When Christine recognized me, her first reaction was not the disdain I expected. She looked embarrassed, off balance, vulnerable. Clearly she was caught off guard and not able to fully regain herself. She spoke awkwardly.

"Hello, Dr. Bradford. Hi. Um, Dr. Bradford, this is my mother, Madeline Chambers. Mom, this is Luke Bradford. He's the new doctor at the clinic."

The middle-aged woman standing before me was shorter than her daughter. Although dressed casually, she had a graceful, lovely presence. And like her daughter she was a handsome brunette. I knew that I had never met or seen her before, but something about her was strangely familiar, as if I was certain I knew her face. She held out her hand to me with a delighted smile.

"Good to meet you, Dr. Bradford."

I took her hand. "'Luke' is fine, and I'm delighted to meet you, Mrs. Chambers." We exchanged polite conversation for a few brief moments. I noticed that although Madeline Chambers's natural skin tone was olive, her complexion was pale. During our conversation she would occasionally reflexively squeeze the fingers of her other hand. She was kind and engaging, yet slightly unfocused. Christine continued to appear uncomfortable. She was slipping her finger in and out of a ring she wore on her right hand. It was done unconsciously, a revealing sign of anxious impatience.

The conversation was drawing to a close when suddenly Madeline turned to Christine. "Dear, I need to excuse myself to the restroom." She smiled toward me. "Nice to meet you, Luke."

I returned the smile. "And you as well."

Madeline turned and walked briskly away, leaving the two of us assessing each other warily.

I chewed on my lower lip for a moment, deliberating. I spoke in a soft voice of contrition. "Look, I'm glad we ran into each other. I said some pretty mean things when we talked a few weeks ago. I've been wanting to apologize, but it didn't seem a very smart idea to come back by and knock on your classroom door again."

Christine smiled lightly and nodded. She said nothing but her face expressed a ready acceptance, an indication that perhaps she too regretted her words of our last conversation. We seemed to reach an unspoken agreement to put the matter behind us.

Silence ensued and I was nervously eager to fill the void, to find common ground, to amuse.

"Your mother is lovely. Not near the old battle-ax I expected her to be."

Christine's manner was friendly but still reserved. She smiled, clearly noting that I was poking fun at myself. "Yes, well, you are kind to say so."

"So, you are still here. How is teaching?"

"Still here, and teaching is fine," responded Christine in a pleasant but crisp manner. She glanced at the large smudge on my button-down. "Nice shirt."

I glanced down at it. "Yes, it is. Thanks for noticing. After a busy day at the clinic I try to relax by changing out a transmission or two." This produced a muted laugh but no further response. I filled in the silence. "So, are you heading back to Atlanta anytime soon?"

She hesitated, evaluating her answer. "I've taken a leave of absence and decided to stay a little longer. I'll probably be here through Christmas. Then we'll see."

"Well, if that's the case, my offer to go out and get matching tattoos still stands." I smiled warmly, confidently.

Christine looked away and smiled. For a brief moment I thought she might actually be considering the offer, but she was hesitant. Perhaps she wanted to avoid any relationship that would chain her to this little place. Then again, maybe she just didn't like me. I decided not to consider that possibility.

By now she was no longer fingering the ring on her right hand and had returned to her confident self. Although my request was probably doomed to complete rejection, something in me couldn't resist continuing. "Of course, it doesn't have to be as serious as tattoos. We could get a watermelon here at the grocery and have a seed-spitting contest or go watch a movie on the big TV at Boshers Laundromat. Or hey—maybe even both."

Christine was amused, almost laughing, but she still wasn't budging. She blew out a deep sigh and spoke with soft resignation. "You know, Dr. Bradford, it's a small town, and people like to talk. So if we go out, then people will take notice and the grapevine will start. Anything we might do or say, people will want to stick their nose right in the middle of it. And before you know it, they'll be telling you that we should go down to the courthouse and get 'hitched' so I can be a good Watervalley wife and start making lots and lots of babies and gravy for you. They're sweet people, but that's just the way they think. And frankly, I don't want anyone knowing my business. Besides, I'll probably be leaving in a month or two, so what's the point?"

"Gee. Since you describe it so painfully, I guess there's not much point. But just in case, you think you could bring some gravy by my house so we can decide if that's a deal breaker?"

She rolled her eyes and shook her head. Yet all the while she was smothering a grin. It gave me faint hope that the Bradford charm might be working. "Like I said, Dr. Bradford, it's a small town. I don't think you get it." Despite the exasperation in her voice, something in it expressed a doubt, as if she was also trying to convince herself.

I couldn't stop smiling at her, adoring her. "I'd say on that point you're right. I don't get it. Matter of fact, I don't get a lot of things about this town. All I know is that even though you seem more likely to go out with Bigfoot than with me, I still find you lovely and interesting." I paused for a moment. "So, if you'll excuse me, I think I'll go to the medicine aisle and pick up some Band-Aids for my bruised ego."

Christine grinned and looked away, pressing her lips together.

I continued, feigning a reflective tone. "You know, it's getting harder and harder to find meaningful one-night relationships."

Her defenses were melting. She was almost laughing. "Yeah, well, I think I'll just hold out for Bigfoot."

I looked from side to side as a pretense to speaking confidentially, then spoke in an authoritative whisper. "I don't know. I wouldn't keep my hopes up on that one. I think he prefers blonds."

Finally she laughed. She laughed in a voice that was musical, delightful; it illuminated her face and brought radiance to her eyes. "Oh, so you know him?"

I nodded with conviction. "Absolutely. He was a frat brother. Although he went by a different name to, you know, maintain his cover."

Madeline's voice came to us as she approached from the far end of the grocery aisle. "Christine, dear, do we need eggs?"

Christine grabbed her cart and, for a moment, she searched my face. She was pondering, deliberating, holding on to the moment. If only for a brief second, there was something affectionate, something tender in the way she regarded me, an uncertainty about her persistent rejection of me.

Then again, maybe she was just trying to figure out whether

they did need eggs. She smiled and spoke with soft resignation. "Good-bye, Dr. Bradford."

I stared at her and scratched my head. Even as she walked away, something primitive inside me couldn't but help notice the magnetism of her long lines and delicate curves. I wanted to memorize her, to imprint on my brain the sound of her voice, to remember the rich brown glow of her eyes. I knew I liked her, and was only all the more frustrated our conversation had once again gone absolutely nowhere. More than I knew at the time, Christine was the one thing about Watervalley that felt right, the one thing that made me feel good and fortunate about being there. I was under her spell.

I grabbed the grocery items I needed, checked out, and walked to the Corolla. Even after I was in the car, I was feverishly trying to remember where I'd seen Madeline Chambers before. Her face was so familiar.

When I arrived home, the house was empty save for the cheerful face of Rhett, who, after greeting me at the door and getting a few pats on the head, was content to resume his place on the rug in the living room. Connie had left a note saying there was a casserole still warm in the oven and for me to leave the dishes. Her neighbor had called and needed a fourth for Thursday night bridge. The encounter with Christine had served as a reminder of my self-imposed solitude in Watervalley. I set the grocery bag on the kitchen table and for the longest while stared out the window at the interplay of light and shade in the backyard. Time stretched before me and I stood there locked in a trance.

I could only wonder what life might be like if things had been different, if I had found the money and followed my dream to pursue a PhD in research. I knew in my bones I wanted my career to be elsewhere. But for the moment, as I thought of Christine, I wasn't so sure where my heart wanted to be. All was quiet in the house, but the lilting sound of her voice echoed through my silent rooms, lending an air of enchantment.

I filled a plate with food and, with Rhett at my feet, sat on the back porch steps and watched the last of the October sunset. More than at any other time of year, the fall recalled from deep within me long-forgotten chapters of my life. The autumn air revived buried thoughts, half images, the whispers of ancient voices. The distant glow of the departing sun, the cool damp grass, and the wispy rustle of leaves held old memories. I closed my eyes.

I had blotted out those early years before my parents died. Now I remembered the wide backyard and the open fields beyond it. I remembered playing with neighborhood friends, tackling each other and tumbling in the grass, and the never-ending spontaneous laughter. Distantly I saw the fall sunsets and heard the far-off sound of my mother calling me to come in for dinner.

As it grew dark, I thought about why I had come to Watervalley. The money had clearly been a factor, but secretly I knew there were other reasons as well. Those long-lost voices of my parents, the hopes and expectations of family, had spoken to me from the distant years.

I sat and listened to the familiar noises of the autumn evening. The night sky was now vast and black, yet the symphony of life went on all around me. The rich pageantry of laughter, friendships, and family was unfolding up and down Fleming Street and in the ever-widening circles of homes and yards and farms extending into the far reaches of the valley. Yet my aunt and my parents, the voices of my past—all long gone—were still with me. They counseled my day, edited my thoughts, whispered into my loneliness. I sat and listened to the brooding murmurings of the dark.

The Watervalley I had created for myself was one of quiet

desolation, of deserted streets and empty pavements. Life was still robustly happening all around me, but I had shut myself out from it and insisted on dreaming of a different life. As one by one the stars emerged from the deep, dark bowl of the evening sky, the distant voices of loved ones continued to whisper, advising me and encouraging me away from my loneliness. I wasn't ready to listen.

CHAPTER 22
Relations

The days were growing shorter and I now began my early morning runs in darkness. Religiously, I would force myself out of bed and head onto the pavement. The eminent arrival of morning light had an uplifting effect on me. There was something powerful about witnessing the slow but brilliant progression of the sun over the sleepy frozen fields of Watervalley. The spectacle washed away the muted confusions of the night.

Rhett had made a remarkable recovery over the last couple of weeks, his appetite knowing no limitations. To my surprise, Connie had warmed quickly to him and they had become fast friends. Just as with me, he regarded her with rapt devotion, focusing on her attentively with an open, sloppy, welcoming countenance. On the rare times when she would fuss at him about something, she did so with a cooing, soothing voice. I was almost jealous.

I had fallen into a routine of jogging out Summerfield Road. One of the most picturesque farms was in fact named Summerfield, as indicated by an antiquated but elaborately engraved sign at the entry. Broad wheat fields spread out on either side of the long driveway and in the distance sat a picture-perfect white clapboard farmhouse with a generous, inviting front porch. In the side yard was a vegetable garden and behind it were several brightly painted red barns with the accompanying weathered gray silo. A brilliant white cross-rail fence enclosed the house, garden, and barns. Holsteins dotted the sloping hills that rose behind the boundary of the farmyard.

The faded stenciled name on the mailbox read CHAMBERS. This enchanting place was Christine's family home. The strings of my heart pulled me in that direction every morning. Something in me still believed in chance meetings and new possibilities.

Each morning when I returned from my run, Connie would be in the kitchen and the wonderful smells of a Southern breakfast would hit me as I came through the front door. But this morning was different.

As I passed through the entry hall and into the kitchen, I found her sitting at the breakfast table, drinking coffee and reading the Watervalley paper. Rhett was lying happily at her feet. The kitchen countertops and the stove were clear.

"Good morning, Connie. What gives? Are you on strike?"

She rolled her eyes up from the paper with a deadpan face. "Hardly, Doctor."

"Well, where is my usual calorie-packed, cholesterol-loaded, we're-going-for-full-arterial-blockage breakfast?"

"I am fixing a special breakfast for you this morning. So get your usual stinky, sweaty self upstairs and I'll have it ready by the time you're back down." And with that she returned to her paper.

"Wow, I don't know about this. I'm an addict now. I'm not sure I can go cold turkey." I waited for a response. All Connie offered was a dispassionate, doleful look that told me the conversation was over.

"Okay, but I need to warn you. This may move you down a few notches on the Christmas list."

Connie turned the paper to the next page.

I turned my attention to Rhett. "Hey, buddy, spill it. What's she up to?"

Still lying with his chin on his paws, he wagged his tail a few times and looked up at me with innocent, inquisitive eyes.

I frowned and whispered to him, "Traitor," then retreated upstairs. Rhett followed. Even he knew that we guys had to stick together.

I showered, dressed, and headed back downstairs. Halfway there I was met with the opulent aroma of freshly baked bread. In the kitchen I found the table set with an elaborate presentation of cream cheese, capers, and smoked salmon.

"What do we have here?"

"Sit down and drink your coffee, Doctor. I bought a bagel machine."

"Who are you and what have you done with Connie Thompson?"

She ignored me.

"This morning we are having fresh-made bagels. They'll be ready in a minute." Connie spoke in her standard poker-faced fashion. On the counter next to the stove was a shiny new stainless steel appliance that looked similar to a waffle maker. It was the source of the thick aroma I had so drunkenly inhaled as I came downstairs.

"Well, I'm just speechless."

"You're more likable that way."

"All right, I'm going to hold my response till after I try the bagels. In the meantime I want you to know that I am personally devastated by that comment. I may need counseling."

I took a sip of coffee and reached over to retrieve the *Village*

Voice that Connie had folded and placed on the far side of the table. I had no sooner turned to the front page than she placed a plate of two steaming hot bagels before me. I loaded a generous amount of cream cheese and salmon on one and bit carefully into it, trying not to burn myself. It was heavenly. Meanwhile, Connie was standing sentry over me, awaiting my response.

"So, Doctor, is it to your liking?"

I chewed heartily and swallowed, then grabbed my napkin and closed my eyes for a brief moment. "This is life-changing. When I'm done, Mrs. Thompson, I'm going to kiss you. Maybe even on the lips."

Connie looked at me sharply. "Sweetie, there is some sugar that even you're not man enough to handle." With that she threw the kitchen towel over her shoulder and sauntered her large hips back toward the bagel maker. She was obviously pleased.

I finished eating and hastily grabbed everything I needed to start my day at the clinic. "Connie, that was delicious. Can we have them for dinner too?"

"Get yourself to work and be a nice doctor today and we'll see if you get any dinner at all." She was standing at the sink washing the dishes, her back to me. Quietly I sneaked up behind her.

"Oh, I am *not* feeling the love." With that I grabbed both of her shoulders from behind, gave her a big kiss on the cheek, and leaped back immediately, fully anticipating her recoil. I wasn't disappointed. This show of lighthearted affection had taken her completely by surprise. At first all she could do was look at me with a face of wide-eyed astonishment.

"Dr. Bradford!" Just as quickly she regained her composure, pursing her lips in a thin line and squeezing her eyes to narrow slits. She grabbed the dish towel from over her shoulder and came after me, swinging. "Now git, git, git."

I laughed and scrambled to the entrance hall.

"You're a sinful man, Luke Bradford," she declared to me in mock judgment.

I moved quickly, almost tripping over Rhett, exiting the front door and leaving it open in my rush to escape.

Connie stopped on the threshold but kept up the verbal onslaught. "It's a good thing I've got the love of Jesus in me or I'd be taking a switch to you."

I hopped into the Corolla and pulled onto the street. As I glanced back at her, Connie was still standing in the doorway, arms folded, with nothing short of an ear-to-ear smile on her face. There was definitely something of love in it.

I arrived at the clinic to find Nancy in her normal cyclone buzz.

"Morning, Doctor. Morning, morning." She blew past me with a small stack of folders in her hands.

"Good morning, Nancy. What does the day look like?"

"Oh, not too bad." She took a breath. "But it's going to start getting busy. Our flu vaccines finally arrived yesterday. The notice will be in today's paper, so folks will start coming in for those. Lots of times they want to see you too if they can."

"Okay. Bring on the masses. Better to see them now than when they get the flu."

Nancy nodded and scurried down the hall. I retreated to my office. Something about my encounter in the grocery store the day before had stirred my curiosity and I wanted to check some of my reference manuals.

The day passed without incident. Connie called late in the day and left a message with Nancy that she had made a pizza. All I needed to do was heat it up for dinner.

"Connie also wanted me to tell you that if need be she can have Ed Caswell come over and light the oven for you."

I rolled my eyes. Nancy giggled.

"I guess that's the way it goes, Nancy. You do one goofy thing in a small town and that's what people know you by forever and a day."

Mary Jo, coming down the hall, couldn't resist chiming in. "Nonsense, Dr. Bradford. That's just not true. There are actually a number of goofy things that the folks in Watervalley know you by." She grinned slyly and kept walking. Such exchanges had become the norm between us.

"I can't believe you just said that, Mary Jo. Are you still in that twelve-step program for personality disorders?"

"Cuuuuute."

"Hey, I'm just trying to be helpful here . . . Maybe make you something close to a likable person."

"Don't you worry, Doctor. I've got a little black book full of gentlemen who like me just fine. You know, I was a magazine cover girl once." As she spoke she pulled down the sides of her white nurse's uniform, tugging at the hips, immodestly stretching the material tightly over her and standing with shoulders back and chest out, trying her best to accentuate the curves of her otherwise pencil-straight figure.

"I don't think the cover of a seed catalog counts, Mary Jo."

"Oh, aren't you just the cleverest?" Her words were acidic, but there was a grin pressing up beneath them.

Nancy interrupted. "Dr. Bradford, we've had a late walk-in. It's Sarah Akins with Sam. She came by to get his six-month shots and checkup."

"Sure." I walked to the front reception area, which was empty except for the young mother and her baby. I smiled grandly.

"Hi, Sarah. How's my boy Sam been doing?" I reached for the grinning baby. "Wow, he seems twice as big." I talked playfully with the child, alternating my teasing with questions for Sarah. She looked healthier, stronger, prettier. I asked Nancy to grab Sam's chart and we headed to the exam room. Sarah talked nonstop. I noticed that she was more smartly dressed. Her hair was now fashionably cut and her general appearance was happier. "You feel awfully solid, little fellow, and leaner," I told Sam. "Now, promise not to barf on me like you did last time, huh?"

Sarah laughed lightly. "Oh my gosh. I was hoping you had forgotten about that."

I grinned and bounced Sam as we walked down the hall. He was perfectly content and sucking his thumb, which I noticed was bent backward distally, as if it was made of rubber.

"I think he's grown half a foot," I remarked. "He must be nearly twenty-six inches."

"I can't keep him in clothes. He's really shot up these last few months." In the exam room Mary Jo was waiting with Sam's chart. I spent half an hour examining him and asking Sarah general questions about her health as well. I was pleased to see that both mother and child were doing fine. Once I had completed my assessment of Sam, Mary Jo left the room to gather the things for his next round of scheduled shots. It gave me an opportunity to speak confidentially.

"Sarah, you're looking really well. You seem better off, more content."

She smiled and nodded. "Yeah, I've had some good fortune come my way."

I nodded and shrugged lightly. "Look, I don't want to pry, but I'm guessing perhaps his father has been helping out more? At least financially?"

At first Sarah was reluctant to respond. But then she offered a weak smile and spoke carefully, protecting her words. "Some things have happened and he's come into a little money. Anyway, he's been able to help me and Sam out a lot more. So, yeah, we're doing better."

It was clear she didn't want to offer more, so I let the topic drop. But there was something else I wanted to ask her.

"I know it's been a few months, but didn't I see you the day of Knox McAnders's funeral? You were sitting in a car outside the funeral home."

A subtle but noticeable alarm spread across her face. She seemed slightly flustered, darting her eyes to the side. "Yeah, well, I was there to see someone, but it didn't work out. It was nothing."

Mary Jo returned with the vaccinations just as Sarah had finished speaking. I focused again on Sam and the matter was dropped. His shots invoked another round of bloodcurdling screams, but this time I let his mother soothe him back to happiness. It was a good way to finish the week.

On the way home at day's end I stopped and picked up some beer to have with my pizza. Once home, I threw on some jeans and carefully lit the oven. As I took out the pizza, I realized I really didn't want to eat alone. So I fed Rhett, found a container to keep the pizza hot, grabbed the beer, and hopped in the Corolla. I was headed up into the hills.

I found John Harris sitting in one of the Adirondack chairs reading the paper. The October afternoon was still warm and sunset was yet an hour or so away. I noticed a glass and a half-empty bottle of Scotch on the small table between the chairs. John looked up as I approached.

"Afternoon, Doc. I thought that might be you when I heard a car in the driveway. What you got there?"

"Pizza and beer, but looks like you already have your beverage of choice."

John returned to his paper. "That I do. Thanks for the pizza offer, but I had a sandwich earlier. Here—knock yourself out." John cleared a space on the small table.

"So, what's the latest in the Watervalley news?" I opened a beer and grabbed a slice. John sat silently, studying the paper.

"Here's something newsworthy. 'City Council to Discuss Banning of Beer Sales on Sundays.' If you want a one-sentence example of small-town Southern stupidity, you won't find a better one than that. What's to keep them from buying more beer on Saturday? While they're at it, why don't they ban gluttony at Sunday lunch?"

I chewed on my pizza and offered no response. Then I asked, "How are the apples doing? I don't guess I've seen the orchard since you almost shot me a few months ago."

John folded the paper and looked over at me. He smiled, grabbed his glass of Scotch, and took a long sip.

"All in. Put the last bushel away in the storage cellar last week."

"What are you going to do with all of them?"

"Beats me. I never wanted the damn things anyway. The whole apple orchard was Molly's idea. But I can't very well just let it go to seed."

"All Molly's idea? Yeah, sure, I believe that."

"No, seriously. She loved apples—apple pie, apple cider, applesauce. She made a big fuss about it. Anyway, I'll probably just give them away."

"That sounds rather virtuous of you."

"Doesn't it, though."

"Careful, John. You don't want to lose your standing as a total crank."

"I know, I know, the thought scares me too. But family rituals are stained in, not painted on."

"What do you mean?"

"Ah, it's the South, sport. At least the one I grew up in—an older and, in many ways, a richer South. Old habits die hard. You don't let something good go to waste. My folks knew some tough years, but my dad was always helping people out. He was a postman. Seemed to know who was going through a hard time. We always had a big garden and he usually ended giving half the produce away."

"Why don't you let people just come pick their own?"

John looked over at me. "That means they would have to be on my property."

"Oh, sorry. I forgot that visitors aren't allowed into the Harris Fortress—or 'Summerplace,' as it were. By the way, where did that name come from?"

"Molly's idea. When we lived in Watervalley years ago, we would come to this spot in the summer and bring picnics. It's always cooler up here in the hills. There's always a breeze. It's a geothermal thing. I think the springs and brooks that flow down to the lake form conduits for air to flow back up."

John stared out over the valley. The evening wind began rolling in, carrying with it a faint and wispy chill. A large white moon appeared in the twilight sky above the rim of the far hills. He brought his Scotch glass to his mouth and emptied it, wincing a little as the swallow went down. His voice was beginning to slur a little. His manner and delivery took on a philosophic air.

"Yeah, sport." He paused. "Now I have a whole orchard of apples and I damn near shot you just for walking through it. I'll tell you something, Luke. Marriage isn't just a word; it's a sentence."

"Meaning?"

"Meaning, well, it's a curious thing, that's all. The things you do because the people who loved you wanted it that way."

I mumbled under my breath. "Yeah, I know. Why else would I be here?"

"How's that?"

"Oh, nothing. It's just that my father loved being a doctor in a small town. He had choices. But that's the one he made, and he loved every day of it."

"Is that what he wanted you to do?"

"He never made it a demand, although he mentioned it. I think he was happy and wanted the same for me. It was more my aunt who insisted on it. She loved her life in Buckhead, but she loved my dad and somehow she understood why he wanted to be a small-town doctor."

"So you're in this little hick town because it's what your aunt wanted. That's all noble, but seems like a lot of misery just to keep some dead relatives happy."

"It's more complicated than that."

"Complicated how?"

"Because these people, these 'dead relatives' as you call them, they loved me. Including my aunt no less than my parents. She believed this was something I should do. So I'm doing it."

"Seems to me if she loved you so much, she would have left some money to pay your debts."

"She did."

"She did?"

"Yeah, a pretty sizable estate. But it doesn't come into play until I'm thirty-five. That's still a few years away."

"So this was her way of forcing you to follow in your father's footsteps."

"She didn't force me. I could have done something different, waited it out. But the voices of those in our past—they may not be with us, but we still hear them. At least I do. So it's like you said.

It's just the things you do because the people you loved wanted it that way."

John sat silently, brooding over what I had said. Twilight was passing. Small twinkling lights began to appear in the expanse of dark blue sky. John grabbed the Scotch bottle and poured his glass full.

"Hell, Doc, now you're depressing me. Think I'll drink myself happy." He let out a chortle.

"By all means. But don't use me as an excuse to pickle your liver. I'm not sure I could stand the guilt."

John took a heavy swallow and grimaced. "Ah, too late. The damage is already done. Afraid you're going to have to put that in your basket of burdens also."

"Not to burst your bubble, John, but I'll be sleeping fine tonight."

We laughed and talked into the darkness. I drank another beer and John continued to drink heavily of Scotch. After another hour, his slurred speech and nodding head made it clear he was fading.

"John, come on. Let's get you back to the house. Time for me to go get some shut-eye."

John stood up stiffly. He began to take a step but tilted immediately. I grabbed him.

"Sailor, your ship's rocking a little to starboard. Let's get you back to dry land."

Despite John's mild protest, I helped him up the back steps and into the living room. We walked to the couch, where he collapsed in an outstretched heap. I grabbed a blanket off a nearby chair and arranged it over him. Just that quickly, he was in a deep sleep. I turned off the lights and walked to the kitchen. As I reached for the last switch, I once again saw the picture of John and Molly on the kitchen counter.

I froze, unable to stop staring at the old photo. And it hit me that Molly Harris was the picture-perfect image of Madeline Chambers. My mind was racing. I turned off the last light, locked the door behind me, and walked to the Corolla. Somewhere in the fog of old conversations I remembered that Connie had told me that Molly Harris had had a twin.

It struck me like a shot of adrenaline. "Oh, good grief!" How had I not figured this out sooner? And John had never mentioned it, even though I had asked him about Christine.

I recalled the obscure answer he had given me at the mention of her name some weeks back. I had attributed it to his intoxication. But now I realized that this was yet another hidden chapter in John's backstory, a topic of discussion he had chosen to avoid. The next time we talked, I was determined I would press him on the matter.

Little did I know that the tide of events would delay that conversation for some time to come.

CHAPTER 23

Fields, Farms, and Families

The brilliant October days ended. The last richly colored autumn leaves fell from the trees and carpeted the ground, and as the days passed the leaves were gathered away from the yards of Fleming Street. November came. Cooler days of overcast skies, gray landscapes, and expanding darkness passed one by one. Early presentiments of winter could be felt in the bite of morning frost. In the distant fields the rich, loamy earth stood raw and bare, save for the random stubs of cornstalks. Orderly lines of large, rounded hay bales had been stacked neatly along the farmyard fencerows. The farmhouses of Watervalley were quietly gathering in, preparing for the long nights of winter.

Conversely, the downtown was taking on a new vibrancy. Shopkeepers began to set out Thanksgiving merchandise, quickly followed by Christmas decorations. Ed Caswell manned the fire department bucket truck as the municipal workers hung Christmas banners at downtown intersections and strung lights around the courthouse.

Rhett and I had fallen into a comfortable daily routine. He ate his breakfast and slept all day while I went to work. When I got home, he ate his dinner and then slept some more—that is, when he wasn't constantly following me around the house or methodically dropping a tennis ball at my feet, imploring me to take him out to the backyard. He never failed to meet me at the door with tail wagging and a look of admiration on his face. He had become the perfect companion: accommodating, uncomplicated, and always in agreement with all of my opinions.

At her insistence, I ate Thanksgiving dinner at Nancy Orman's house along with her family, all three million of them. She and her husband, Carl, had a small farm a few miles out from town, and for them Thanksgiving was a massive affair, unlike the Thanksgivings I had known growing up.

In her own innovative way, my aunt Grace had always made a big deal out of Thanksgiving. By the time I was sixteen it had dwindled down to just the two of us, with my parents gone and the last of my grandparents having passed away. Turkey was always in the mix, but otherwise dinner was anything but traditional. Each year preparation of the turkey coincided with the cuisine of whatever country currently held her fascination. One year it was turkey Italian style—shredded mozzarella and ground turkey made into meatballs. The next year, after Grace had taken a trip to China, we had kung pao turkey with a rather strange white rice dressing, as if white rice were not a dish of its own. Subsequent years included an Irish stew with turkey instead of mutton, accompanied by dressing made with soda bread. Perhaps the most memorable was the year she delved into Moroccan cooking, with turkey kebabs and harira soup.

The kitchen was the place where my statuesque aunt threw off her usual reserve and transformed into something of a giddy schoolgirl, full of creative whimsy. She had the incredible knack for making odd combinations of dishes come together in dinners of perfect harmony. She was delighted to bring a note of the international to an American holiday. I often wondered if these dinners were her antidote, a compensation for our small number during a holiday typically marked by large family gatherings.

More than the incredible meals, my fondest Thanksgiving memories were of Aunt Grace's buoyancy and laughter and drama during the daylong preparations. The house would be flooded with random shouts of angst followed by the occasional rendering of the Hallelujah Chorus in Grace's not so pitch-perfect voice. She would playfully nag at me to come help, and then, after I had clumsily executed some of her instructions, she would laugh and throw food at me and banish me from the kitchen, only to seek me out again twenty minutes later. She made the day a party, spirited hours in which we delighted in each other's company, allowing us to ignore the reality that those we loved were no longer with us.

In the years since her passing, I had invariably received invitations to join friends at Thanksgiving dinner. No doubt, I seemed something of a sad case, but inwardly I never felt that way. The years had conditioned me. I wasn't opposed to the idea of engaging a surrogate family for the holiday and certainly wasn't hardened emotionally against it. I had simply grown content with defining myself as a loner for such occasions if not for life in general. Still, I accepted Nancy's offer graciously and was determined to be open-minded and enjoy the gathering.

Nancy and Carl both came from large families and the Thanksgiving meal served as something of a reunion. All told, more than seventy people came together. I had to park in a nearby pasture and could have wandered in uninvited without anyone being the wiser.

They had ingeniously cleared out the concrete hallway of the large barn behind the house and aligned a long row of card tables covered with a collection of pristine white sheets to serve as tablecloths. Carl had provided every necessity, including portable heaters, ample electrical plugs to keep the food warm, and small signs above the side tables identifying the location for vegetables, meats, and desserts. And despite the large number of people, everyone pitched in to help out with the tasks at hand. It was an efficient choreography of serving, preparing children's plates, and then assembling at the long table amid a hubbub of riotous laughter and celebration.

The Ormans were a loud and garrulous group. The men were generally heavyset, with broad faces and broad smiles; they loved to chide and tease and slap you on the back during the thick of the conversation. They all seemed bred to an instinctive generosity and hospitality, and among them I was treated as nothing short of a celebrity. But despite their kindness, I was at a loss to contribute when the conversation turned to farm implements or extending the number of days for bow hunting of deer, topics that brought out impassioned viewpoints from men and women alike.

After the meal, most of the men retreated to Carl's large bonus room, where a football game was playing on his big-screen TV. I obediently followed the pack and sat in a folding chair toward the back of the room. Within thirty minutes I realized I was one of only a few men in the room still conscious. The majority had dozed off into a low symphony of wheezing and snorting catnaps.

Restless, I eased out of the chair, wondering if it was too soon to make my departure, and ran into a game of pickup basketball being played on a small backyard court by the teenage grandkids and some of the young married family members. I was immediately pressed onto a team. Having played college basketball and standing three inches taller than the next closest competitor, I realized it was not the time for showboating. I opted to stand post and constantly passed off, allowing others to make all the points. At least, until the very end of a game of twenty-one, when I couldn't resist the temptation to slam the ball in with a two-handed dunk. This was met with an explosion of whoops and accolades along with universal pleas for me to do it again. I smiled and refused, but I have to say it was a pretty fun moment.

I made my way back to the barn, where Nancy and many of the women were cleaning up. With my aunt Grace, helping out with after-meal cleanup was part of the standard drill. I offered to help but was met with a wave of appreciative but adamant rejection. For these women, this was their time to confide small marital complaints into sympathetic ears, to laugh at the occasional foolishness of their spouses, and to delight in the salty language of really good gossip.

I had also walked into a lively conversation in which I was the central topic. It was Nancy's equally plump sister Adele, a woman in her late fifties, who spoke first. "Dr. Bradford, we were just talking about you. It's just not right for a man as good-looking as you to be single. We need to find you a wife."

I shook my head in amusement and offered a good-natured response. "Well, by all means, line them up."

This prompted a chorus of giggles and laughter from the group, with Adele responding immediately, "We were just discussing that point. That's kind of the problem—most of the girls in the valley are either too young, too old, or too married."

Mary Lynn, one of Nancy's sisters, said, "What about Cynthia Matthews? I hear she and BT are getting divorced. She's real sweet and he's about as worthless as a furball. If you don't mind waiting, Doc, she'd be really good company. Kind of a looker."

Nancy responded indignantly. "Mary Lynn, I cannot believe you are endorsing a divorce just so Dr. Bradford can have a date. What are you thinking?"

Mary Lynn recoiled and replied sheepishly, "Well, they're getting divorced either way. So I'm just saying . . ."

Adele injected enthusiastically, "Hey, what about Shannon Carter? She's in her late twenties and still single."

A collective moan rose from the group. Mary Lynn said, "Good heavens, Adele. Have you been living in a cave? Shannon might as well change her name to Target, because half the men in the valley have had a shot at her."

Riotous laughter broke out among the group until Nancy restored order by saying, "I think choosing a mate is a personal matter for Dr. Bradford and we should leave it at that."

This was met by a long, silent moment of consideration.

"Nah," Adele blurted out. "I don't think so, sister. We need to get this man some help."

Another explosion of laughter followed as I stood with a patient smile. I was striving for nonchalance, but secretly I was hoping someone would bring up Christine Chambers, just to gain some insight from the group reaction. I wouldn't dare mention her name unless I wanted to start a tidal wave of gossip, something that obviously would not improve my chances with Christine. But no one did mention her.

I drifted through pockets of conversation among small groups that had formed between the farmhouse and the barn. Although I was politely included, I spent most of my time nodding politely and finding little of value to add to the conversation. Eventually I thanked Nancy and Carl for being such gracious hosts. Amid a bombardment of handshakes and good-byes, I finally made my way back to my car as the sunset was just beginning to cast an orange layer across the rim of the far western hills. Though the air was cool, it had been an unusually warm day for November in Tennessee.

I stood at the car for a moment, listening to the echoes of laughter, the bouncing basketball, and the collective voices and shouts of all the men and women and children. This was Thanksgiving on a grander order than what I had shared with my aunt. I didn't so much envy the Ormans as I wondered about them. I marveled at their unquestioned bonds of affection and acceptance, their connectedness, their unsparing tradition of kindness to outsiders such as myself. I wondered what it felt like to follow out their lives within the contours of these constant hills and familiar skies, to live so contentedly in one place for all their days. Our common interests had been few, but their generosity was endless.

As the days stepped quietly from Thanksgiving into the Christmas season, the clinic began to wear the rich smell of baked goods as people brought plates of homemade cookies, cakes, and pies. I was invited to a few gatherings that all too often were only poorly veiled attempts at matchmaking. It was the middle-aged wives that hounded me so relentlessly. There seemed to be something in every married woman of Watervalley that felt the call to find a mate for me, irrespective of my thoughts on the matter. I endeavored to avoid them and their persistent mission.

Nevertheless, I dutifully attended the various dinner parties with a mix of enthusiasm and reluctance. Typically, I found myself out of place, despite often being the center of attention. On more than a few occasions, I would excuse myself and leave at the earliest socially appropriate hour. I appreciated the kindnesses offered to me, but within me little had changed. Although I had a general desire to connect, to find common ground, it seemed I still kept myself away.

I enjoyed an occasional phone conversation with old friends from Nashville, but because I was constantly on call at the clinic, I had no chance to visit them. My friends' lives were moving on, while it seemed that mine had stagnated, as I remained sequestered within the long winter shadows of Watervalley.

I maintained my early routine of jogging out Summerfield Road, even though now the mornings were often cold and rainy. Occasionally on the weekends I would see Christine coming out of the public library or maybe walking between the downtown shops, but it was always from a distance. If she saw me, she would politely wave and smile and then, with noticeable effort, look away. I seemed helpless to do anything but stand and stare, following her till she passed from view.

Sometimes in the small hours of the evening I found myself lost in curious wonder about her, trying to understand her. No doubt, her years in Atlanta had given her a sense of style and manner that was all too familiar to me. But beneath her urban veneer was also something rich of Watervalley. It was more than just the rural strength and the provincial hardiness that flowed through the people here. It was something rooted in the wooded hills and open countryside. It seemed that she and the incredible beauty of the valley were natural companions. In the deep, warm brown of her eyes, in the fresh and wholesome light of her face, there was something of the rolling fields, the wind and sky, the billowing grasses of the high meadows—earthy, sensuous, bursting with health. She was intoxicating. While I was supposedly deep in the pages of some novel late at night, my mind would drift to her. She delightfully haunted the margins of my solitary hours.

Connie now came only a few days a week, spacing out our opportunities to catch up on each other's lives. Rhett, however, remained my ever-steady companion. He never failed to look at me with anything short of curious wonder and complete adoration. He was now robustly filled out, his appetite having served him well. Along the way he had developed something of a drooling problem. I told him that if it continued I would have to refer him to an ear, nose, and throat specialist.

The cold, overcast days of winter had set in, the ebb and flow of work continued, and despite the charm and kindness of the people in my small corner of the world, life in Watervalley had become painfully predictable.

Sure as hell, that was all about to change.

CHAPTER 24
Outbreak

On the Thursday two weeks after Thanksgiving, an odd thing happened. During the late morning a man in his mid-twenties named Lewis Clanton walked through the clinic doors. His appearance was so flushed and ghastly that Nancy put him in an exam room immediately. He was racked with aching pain, sweating profusely, and had a constant thick, gurgling cough. He was drowning in congestion and gasping for air. His struggle to breathe had sent him into a panic.

I quickly placed him on oxygen and gave him an antihistamine injection to calm him down, enabling me to do the exam. His temperature was soaring, almost 104. I treated him with an antipyretic, a fever reducer, and Cindy ran a lab test that confirmed influenza.

His condition would have seemed routine to me except for one thing. The onset had been fiercely rapid, almost violent. Lewis had worked his normal night shift at the cabinet factory. As he drove home around seven that morning, he began to ache and cough. He tried to sleep but the symptoms progressed so quickly that by ten a.m. he had felt compelled to drive himself to the clinic. I also knew that the flu typically found a home with either the very young or the very old but not in robust adults such as Lewis, a strongly built man with no history of respiratory problems.

What most confounded me was the fact that Lewis had received a flu shot a month prior. The H1N1 strain had been included in the vaccine, thus ruling it out. It was highly unlikely that what I was seeing was the H5N1—avian or bird flu—given its confinement to the far corners of the earth. Lewis hadn't even been out of the county, much less the country.

I prescribed an antiviral and strenuously advised rest, fluids, and isolation. His case raised the eyebrows of the staff. Outwardly, I remained reserved about his condition but inwardly I was baffled and deeply concerned.

Around half past two, another case of the flu appeared with the same profile. The patient was an otherwise healthy young farmer in his late twenties named Graham Peden. The symptoms and onset were equally severe. He had also received the flu vaccine.

Graham, too, had difficulty breathing and a dangerously high temperature. He was scared. The staff rushed to get him settled in an exam room. After he'd spent several minutes on a rescue inhaler followed by oxygen, his respiration returned to normal. I spent well over half an hour examining him, trying to understand what he might have in common with Lewis Clanton. The two men knew of each other, but had no memory of having had any contact in months. Graham pressed me to explain the cause, but I had no answers.

I could see the frustration in his eyes. He was miserably sick and wanted to know how and why. Graham's wife sat silently in the corner of the exam room. She responded with quiet nods to my instructions. I prescribed the same medications and the same regimen of rest and isolation. Little else was said, but the unmistakable marks of fear and anxiety were clearly evident in their body language, and it was all too clear that their disappointment was focused on me. I told them to call me anytime if the symptoms didn't improve. But they were not consoled, and I couldn't blame them.

For the balance of the afternoon, conversation among the staff was muted. Unoccupied exam rooms and protected corners became enclaves for huddled whispers. The staff had seen the flu before, but not accompanied by the fiercely severe symptoms we were witnessing. Eventually, nightfall arrived and the clinic closed.

Friday came and went with only a few routine gynecological and geriatric visits. Though the rest of the day was quiet, we all still carried the fear that we had not seen the last of this severe strain of the flu.

It rained all weekend. It was a cold rain with a hard, biting north wind behind it. I spent Saturday watching football and reading books. My general mood along with the weather made me a hermit. I took no morning runs and made it out only to buy popcorn and beer. Once during the day I noticed Will Fox and his mother leaving home and returning from errands. I had yet to meet Louise Fox. From the glimpses I had had of her, she was a small, frail woman with rounded shoulders. She had a pinched face that even from a distance looked cheerless and anxious. As I saw them arrive home, I considered going next door to introduce myself, but I felt awkward. I understood as much as anyone the desire to be left alone.

Nightfall came and I thought about where people in Watervalley gathered for casual company on the weekend. There was always the Line Dance and Bingo Club that met down at the Memorial Building every Saturday night. Several of my patients had extended an open invitation, so a month or so earlier I had taken a notion to drop in on one of the gatherings.

I had arrived early—at least fifteen years too early. The crowd was largely geriatric, with only a few as young as their forties. I hung around long enough to be pressed into doing a few line dances, which I did poorly but with a good humor. The experience might have been worth a repeat try, just for vacant fun, were it not for a few fortysomething cougars making less than subtle comments about going to their place to play a game of doctor. It was clear they all had larger plans than the casual exchange of a little spit. I was lonely, but not that lonely.

I knew there were also poker games in the tack room down at the Farmers' Co-op and thought of strolling in. These were penny-ante games played just for fun. No doubt I would recognize a few faces and generally be welcomed. But the few times I had been in the Co-op just to grab an odd item or two, it seemed that the conversation was instantly muted, as if a school principal had just walked in on a group of truants. I knew that at heart this was nothing more than the uncanny level of respect the townspeople had for my profession. It was part of their obliging politeness and was not intended to be unkind. Ultimately, I felt that my presence there would be an intrusion.

There was also a roadhouse on the outskirts of town that was often part of the local gossip. Known as the Alibi, it was located in a wooded area on a chert-topped lane called Indigo Road. The Alibi was known for being a rough bar where locals on the surly fringe would go to blow off steam. It was not exactly my kind of scene. Then again, it offered a place to have a beer and watch a ball game away from the permeating loneliness of my own four walls. It would at least be a place where people would be laughing and having a good time. The idea of a visit had merit.

But soon the drowsiness of the day won over. I fell asleep on the couch and sometime later dragged myself upstairs to bed and to a night of uneasy sleep.

On Sunday morning, the church bells were ringing from the downtown steeples just a few blocks over. I thought about putting on my suit and slipping into one of the services, but ultimately it simply didn't happen. When darkness came early on Sunday afternoon, I once again fell asleep on the couch, bored with my world and wishing Monday would come. Then, at least, I could occupy my thoughts with work. The opiate of responsibility seemed the only cure.

Soon enough, Monday arrived. And with it came hell's fury riding on its coattail.

I arrived early at the clinic and was surprised to see more than twenty cars already parked in the front lot. Entering through the back entrance, I found Mary Jo working up patients in the exam rooms and Nancy scurrying around in a controlled panic.

"Oh, thank goodness—thank goodness you're here. I was just about to call you."

"What's going on?" I asked, alarmed.

"It's the flu, Dr. Bradford. We had eleven walk-ins waiting at the door this morning and from the best we can tell at least seven to eight of them have severe flu symptoms."

"Are they mostly geriatric?"

"No, they're all adults—I'd say all under forty."

I stood in the back hallway, dumbfounded. "Did any of these people get flu shots?"

"Actually, yes. Three I know of for sure. I haven't had time to check on all of them."

This sent off an array of alarms inside my head, but I tried hard not to show it. I spoke impassively. "Okay. Exam rooms one, two, and three ready to go?"

"Yes, yes. Mary Jo has the charts and is getting vitals. What do you think this means, Doctor?"

"Not sure, but I want to find out what these people have in common. Are they family? Do they work together? Go to church together? Are they somehow connected to the two fellows we saw last Thursday?"

"I'm not sure how to get that information," responded Nancy.

"No need. I'll try to figure it out in the interviews." I kept my thoughts to myself, but I was puzzled. How in the world had people who had received the vaccine ended up with the flu?

I grabbed my white lab coat and headed into the first exam room. My patient was a man I vaguely remembered seeing some months before, a tall, gangly fellow in his mid-thirties named Lexie Ingram. He worked in the machine shop at the cabinet factory. When I entered, Lexie was holding his hand over his mouth. He had a deep, gurgling cough that seemed to start from his ankles. The man looked miserable. His breathing was irregular. I listened to his chest and reviewed his vitals. His temperature, over 103, concerned me most.

"When did you first notice the symptoms?" I asked.

"Yesterday afternoon, Doc. I started getting some chills and aching all over. I thought it was just a cold, but by this morning I was burning up."

"Do you remember being around anyone else who was sick?"

Lexie spoke slowly. Conversation seemed to exhaust him. "Hard to say, Doc. This time of year seems like half the people you're around are sniffling and sneezing."

"Anyone else in your family showing similar symptoms?"

"My wife, Candice, drove me here. She said she has a terrible headache this morning. She never gets headaches."

I pursed my lips and thought for a moment.

"We may need to check her also. Lexie, it looks like you've got the flu. It's a viral infection in your respiratory system. Antibiotics don't work on it. I'm going to write you a prescription for some meds. Even still, you're probably going to feel pretty lousy for a few days. The best thing to do is rest, drink lots of fluids, keep the fever down, and isolate yourself as much as possible. This thing looks like it's pretty contagious."

"This is just some kinda forty-eight-hour thing, isn't it, Doc? It will pass in a few days, won't it?"

I knew this probably wasn't true, but I didn't want to panic him further. "It may take a little longer to shake off. If you don't give yourself a chance to get rid of it, it could turn into pneumonia, and that's very bad news. Did you by chance get a flu shot?"

"No, I meant to but never got around to it. Candice did, though. I guess she should be okay."

I knew this provided no assurance. "I hope so. But we'll see."

I wrote the prescriptions, told Lexie to take care, and departed. As I walked through the exam room door, my mind was racing.

This same pattern of interview, symptoms, and assessment repeated itself throughout the morning. More and more patients showed up. For some time it seemed they were literally swarming into the clinic. With every opening and closing of the front door came a clamor, a building storm of concern and subdued fear. Some were terribly sick and had to be placed into an exam room right away. This caused frustration and anger in patients who had already been waiting. Bad news always seems to have a faster stride than the other kind, and by the afternoon the town was in an uproar of gossip.

I worked feverishly, doing my best to convey a sense of calm and assurance to each patient. I desperately tried to find a pattern of contact, a source of connection to the spread of the disease. Only a handful worked at the cabinet factory, so it was not the only point of origin. Beyond that, nothing came up. There were some similar demographics. Most of the patients were male, blue-collar, and in their twenties or thirties, but there were exceptions.

The only commonality seemed to be the speed of onset. The patients were upset and anxious and pressed me to explain what was happening to them. I found myself spending as much time reassuring them as I did assessing them. But it troubled me. My patients wanted answers, and I was clueless.

Considering the normal movements of daily life for most people, the matrix of infection would grow exponentially and any chance of determining its source would be lost in a matter of hours. A random handshake or sneeze in a grocery store, bank, or public place would cross any and all lines. I knew beyond doubt that this matter was deeply serious, and I feared that it was already spinning out of control.

CHAPTER 25
Encounter

By midafternoon, I had seen more than thirty cases. The appearance of extended family members of some of the staff added to the mounting anxiety, and bluntly brought the illness home to the clinic. This was not just an unfortunate condition affecting vaguely familiar names and isolated acquaintances. This was a terrifying reality announcing its presence in the panicked faces of loved ones. My sense of time had been wiped out. Although I was painfully discouraged, all I could do was screw in my determination and make the best of the situation. At half past three there was a slight lull. No new patients had come in for an hour, although a half dozen were still in the waiting area. I finally looked at my watch and realized I'd not eaten any lunch. I found Nancy and told her to get as many patients as possible into exam rooms while I took a quick half-hour break to go home, get lunch, and clear my head. She nodded and patted me on the shoulder.

"We'll take care of everything until you get back, Dr. Bradford."

I nodded and exited out the back door.

The day was gray, cold, overcast. I started the Corolla and

headed toward Fleming Street. As I passed through downtown, I saw people in small clusters of conversation. Their faces were strained. I knew the salty voice of rumor was likely now rampant and would be quickly permeating the talk on streets and in stores. I felt as if a whole parliament of eyes was upon me looking for answers that I didn't possess. As I passed by, a few people recognized me and waved halfheartedly, but all the expressions were somber.

Pulling into my driveway, I stared vacantly at the house. My mind was still churning, absorbing all that I had heard that morning, looking for some connection among all those who'd been infected. My inability to understand the source and violent onset of the disease greatly distressed me. I could think of little else.

As I got out of the Corolla, I noticed an unfamiliar car parked in the Foxes' driveway. A woman was standing on their front porch knocking on the door. It was Christine. We shared a brief moment of eye contact. I offered a nod and a perfunctory wave and then turned toward my porch steps. With the insanity of this day, I was in no mood for yet another encounter with her. But after taking only two steps, I heard her say, "Luke?"

This caught me by surprise and I stopped short. She had never called me by my first name. As I turned around she was approaching.

Looking down at the ground for a moment, I pursed my lips and nodded as I looked up at her. "Hi, Christine," I said, content to let her carry the conversation.

She was wearing a heavy overcoat that seemed to do little to mask her tall, graceful lines. To my surprise, her eyes were full of a soft tenderness. There was almost a beseeching quality to her voice.

"I'm looking for Will and his mother. Have you seen them the last few days?"

"Yeah, I saw them over the weekend a couple of times. Why? What's wrong?"

"He's been very withdrawn lately. He doesn't do his homework and is failing all of his tests. I've sent several notes home, but have gotten no response. He wasn't at school today, so I thought I'd stop by to check on him."

I looked over at the Foxes' house. "I don't think they're home. The car is gone. As far as Will is concerned, I haven't seen or talked to him much lately. So I can't say I've noticed anything."

Christine nodded. "I'm just a little worried. Rumor at school is that there's quite a bit of sickness going around. I was wondering if something had happened."

"Wow. Word travels fast," I said, though I was not surprised. For every patient I saw in the clinic, there were probably two more who were experiencing the symptoms and yet chose to self-medicate and avoid the doctor.

"Actually, I was a little surprised to see you home this early," said Christine.

"As a matter of fact, this is lunch. It has been pretty crazy at the clinic today, so I came to grab a quick bite. I imagine I've got some long hours in front of me."

Christine nodded and looked down, seeming unsure of what to say. "I won't keep you. If you do see Will or his mom, would you let them know I stopped by and ask her to give me a call?"

"Sure."

We both stood there, waiting. Waiting for the other to speak, to open up, to bring life to the buried thoughts and emotions that seemed to whisper in the air between us. Pensively, she looked at me with an expression of strained uncertainty. For the first time in our few conversations it seemed that she was struggling to find some way to prolong the encounter. Ultimately, she simply nodded and turned toward her car.

I watched her walk away, smiling to myself. Her enchantment

over me was unmistakable. There was a sensuous poetry to her movements even from the departing view.

I knew what I wanted to say, but hesitated. Finally I spoke, almost blurting out the words. "Did she have her stomach stapled?"

Christine stopped and looked at me. "Excuse me?"

I walked slowly toward her. The day had exhausted me and my voice and manner were wooden. "Your mother. Did she have her stomach stapled? She did, didn't she?" We were now standing within a foot of each other.

She was puzzled. "Yes, as a matter of fact. About a year ago. But how did you know?" The ardent and protective Christine I had known was beginning to surface.

"Look, technically it's not my business. She's not my patient. But I thought you would like to know that she does not have Alzheimer's or dementia. What she has is a vitamin B12 deficiency. If she had had it all her life, it would have shown up a long time ago. So something had to have happened to her gastric intrinsic factor, the enzyme that absorbs B12. Heavy drinking can do this, but she doesn't fit the profile. So my guess was stomach surgery. Tell her doctor to give her some B12 injections. She should be fine."

"And you know this from meeting her in the grocery store for five minutes?"

The question annoyed me. I responded flatly. "Yeah, I do. The makeup she was wearing didn't hide the anemia and she was rubbing her hands constantly, an obvious sign of numbness. Both are indications of B12 deficiency. I saw the vitamins in your grocery cart, so I know she's getting B12. But the dose is too low for her to absorb it effectively."

"You don't know anything about my mother and I don't appreciate you—"

I held up my hand, cutting her off. Then I spoke calmly,

carefully. "Just stop. Look, get mad all you want. It doesn't matter. All you've done is treat me with suspicion. But I'm right. So do it for your mother's sake. Tell her doctor. Your mother seems like a lovely woman. She deserves it."

Christine was now furious with me, and likely for good reason. I knew I was right, but my patience was gone and she had caught the brunt of my aggravation. She stared at me with the look of a cornered cat, a mixture of fear and ferocity. "All right," she whispered. "I'll mention it."

I turned back toward the house. Now I had one more thing to add to my list of frustrations for the day.

When I returned to the clinic a while later, a new wave of cases had shown up. I wouldn't see my last patient until after seven that evening. Making matters worse, Lewis, the first flu case from Thursday of the week before, had returned. His temperature was still spiking and he was as white as a sheet. I had the EMTs drive him to the hospital in Gunther County to be admitted. There they could pump fluids into him and get him stabilized. I feared the normal regimen of antivirals was not working against this strain of influenza and that more of my patients would need to be hospitalized. I also knew that many in Watervalley would try to self-diagnose or just tough it out, never coming to the clinic or coming too late. It was a potent recipe for needless, meaningless death. I was determined that this would not happen. Not in my practice and not on my watch. But deep inside I knew there were too many factors I couldn't control and the tools at hand simply weren't sufficient.

I could see the deep-seated apprehension growing in the faces of the staff. They were exhausted. I told them all to go home, get some sleep, and cross their fingers for tomorrow. Privately, I knew it would likely be worse.

When I arrived home, Connie was waiting for me in the kitchen, her mood unusually subdued. There was a protective tone in the few words she did say. I was not in a talkative frame of mind either. We had grown to know each other well. Almost like a married couple, we read the moment and moved through the motions accordingly.

I sat at the table, picking at my food in a deep and troubled frame of mind. But even Connie didn't realize what was at the heart of my despair. The flu outbreak, the frustration and fear of my patients, and my lack of answers were all bad enough. But the encounter with Christine had taken me down an even deeper shaft of misery. For weeks I had secretly thought of her. I'd hoped we could somehow find common ground, a way to move upon my tremendous attraction to her. Today she'd been actually kind, engaging. But I had snapped at her. I was confident about my diagnosis of her mother, Madeline Chambers, so I had tried to justify my rude insistence. Yet I knew that I'd blown yet another opportunity with Christine, and an additional one would likely not come along.

"Your food all right, Doctor?"

"What? Oh, sure. I'm sure it's tasty as always, Connie. I've just got a lot on my mind tonight."

"Any ideas what this influenza outbreak is all about?"

"Not a clue. If this keeps up, and I'm afraid it will, I'll need to call the Centers for Disease Control and get them involved."

Connie nodded. "I hear that even patients who got the vaccine are coming down with it. Makes it awfully hard to understand where this strain came from and who brought it here."

"Yes, it does." The heavy breath of frustration was in my voice.

"You can't expect to have it figured out in one day, Dr. Bradford."

"Oh, hell—it's not that, Connie. It's not this flu thing. Although heaven knows it has me baffled. It's just—well, it's something else."

"Heavens, boy. What can you be talking about?"

I didn't appreciate her tone. The yearnings of my heart were my business. "Nothing," I replied.

Connie was taken aback. She realized that somehow she had stepped over into a world that even she knew nothing about. For the first time in our relationship, she sounded humbled. "What is it, Luke?"

This got my attention. I looked at her, and then, with a shrug of resignation, I revealed a small part of my heart. "What do you know about Christine Chambers?"

Connie sat for a few moments staring at me. The question I asked told a story. She could see that there was a whole chapter in my life that I'd kept hidden between the pages of the larger narrative she saw every day.

"Have you met her?" she asked.

"Yeah, I have. Actually, we've talked on several occasions. Not particularly friendly conversations, though. We— Well, we seem to have gotten off on the wrong foot and it's kind of gone downhill from there. But that doesn't matter. What can you tell me about her?"

"Let's see. You mean beside the obvious, that she's quite the looker and independent minded. No steady relationship that I know of. Choosy, I think."

"Yeah, I've picked up on as much."

Connie's gaze went up to the ceiling. She rubbed her chin with her hand. "Christine would be about twenty-eight now. Her father passed away five years ago. He was a farmer, killed in a tractor accident. Anyway, she was Miss You Name It around here."

"You mean like beauty queen stuff?"

"Oh, no. She wanted no part of that. I'm talking about valedictorian, National Merit Scholarship winner, math club—that sort of thing. On top of that, she can sing like a bird."

"Really?" I responded with mild surprise. My mood lightened.

"Oh, yeah. That girl is smart and, Lord, she has the most velvet voice. But that's not what everybody around here remembers her for. Everybody knows her from basketball."

"Basketball?"

"Christine was the best point guard in Watervalley's history. When she was a high school senior, she carried the girls to the state championship, Watervalley girls' one and only. I remember the paper had a weekly column called the 'Christine Watch' to see where she was going to sign for college. She was the pride of the county. Had a full-ride offer to Tennessee, but turned it down. Went to Agnes Scott instead. It upset a lot of folks around here. They wanted her to go to UT and play for a national championship. People in Watervalley can be a little plainspoken, and I think their disappointment was expressed pretty bluntly to Christine and her mother. Ever after that, the Chamberses seemed to keep their business pretty private."

"Really? Agnes Scott? The Presbyterian college near Atlanta?"

"Mmm-hmm. Played basketball there. Studied to be a teacher like her mom. Came back a couple of months ago because Madeline's been sick, or so I hear."

"So you don't know either Christine or Madeline well. No bridge club, mah-jongg, or yoga classes you have in common?"

Connie gave me a perturbed look. "Madeline has always been one to keep to herself. She is as good and gracious a soul as you will find, although I think a little intolerant of foolishness. She's a lot more private, much more so than her sister was."

"And when you say sister, you mean Molly Harris, John's deceased wife?"

"Yes. Why?"

"Help me understand something here. In all the times I've talked with John, he's never mentioned having family here. I even mentioned Christine's name to him once and he played it off, giving me the impression that he didn't even know her. Do you have any idea what that's all about?"

"Oh, I can assure you he loves Christine dearly. But there was a pretty serious falling-out between John and Madeline when Molly died. I don't know the details, but I don't think the two of them have talked since."

"Really?"

"Yeah, the Harrises and Chamberses are headstrong people like that. Very reserved. They tend to nurse their sores in private. Anyway, I imagine Christine is caught in the middle. All John ever did was dote over her. Since they had no children of their own, John and Molly were almost like second parents to her. But as long as Madeline and John are at odds, Christine's going to keep her distance."

For the longest time, the two of us sat in silence. My world was in discord. And now in the late, weary hours came the helpless realization that, among those I had come to know, there were wounds that my med school training could do little to mend.

CHAPTER 26

The Brink

Tuesday I decided to forgo my morning run and arrived at the clinic at six thirty a.m. Within a few minutes, the staff began to appear. The mood was subdued. We moved obediently about our duties, but our faces wore the pallid look of worry. We were soldiers dug into our defenses, awaiting the imminent assault. I called them together, determined to be upbeat. After giving a pep talk, I thanked them for all they'd done the previous day. I encouraged them but also warned them to take precautions, given the easy spread of the disease. We joked a little, smiled a lot, and I did my best to hide my own fear. For the most part, I succeeded.

Some scheduled appointments were scattered throughout the morning, but fortunately the day allowed for ample time to take on the expected storm. To everyone's relief, it didn't happen. Only three new cases came in that morning, and by midday everyone began to exhale a communal sigh of relief. A little past noon I decided to walk over to the Depot for lunch, feeling almost lighthearted.

I took the far seat at the counter, my usual perch. I knew the restaurant was a barometer where one could sense the mood of the town. The tenor of the chatter, the subtle glances, the eye contact, the smiling nods all revealed the telltale temperament of the collective mind. Today, it was mixed. There were a few friendly faces and kind acknowledgements, but also a degree of tension. As people saw me, their conversation changed. Body language became huddled and there was a sudden confidential tone and intensity to the discussions. It didn't help matters that a few of the customers had hacking coughs that erupted occasionally above the low din of the lunch hour. No one came over to speak to me. No one called me by name.

I ordered a meat loaf sandwich and ate methodically, staring at the *Village Voice* before me. There was no mention of the rise in flu cases—appropriately so, since no one from the paper had contacted me for any information. Then again, I knew that the paper generally ran several days behind any real news.

I couldn't know the thoughts of the people in the room, but I believed expressions of doubt were being cast in my direction. I tried not to let it bother me. I was an outsider, and in many ways I understood and even desired that standing. What I most dreaded was a dismissal, the shame of a ruined reputation, a collective verdict of failure. I finished eating, paid my bill, and returned to the clinic.

Two in the afternoon came and went with nothing but a few scheduled patients. By three, only two more flu cases had come through the door, and the staff was easing through the afternoon with the normal deceleration that occurred when the December sun started to fall behind the trees. The methodical pace of the clinic had returned. The crisis was over.

But an hour later, thirteen men and women sick with the flu had arrived. The day shift at the cabinet factory had ended at half past three; most of the patients had come from there along with a few from the Farmers' Co-op. By five o'clock, fourteen more had joined them. Their symptoms were unmistakable. Once again, what most concerned me was the rapid onset and severity of the symptoms. My patients had been fine when they'd arrived at work that morning. By late afternoon they had developed horrific headaches, dangerously high temperatures, and congestive coughs. The disease was continuing to spread.

The staff worked diligently. I moved rapidly from room to room, making uncomfortably quick assessments and working hard not to miss anything important in my evaluations. Tension rose in the waiting room. The misery and pain, the profuse sweating from fever, the exhaustion and fear made hostile creatures of otherwise calm individuals. Family members sat nearby in a state of worry and alarm. People were shuffled in and out as calmly as possible, but we operated in a state of borderline chaos. It had all the trappings of an impending epidemic.

Nancy fielded a steady barrage of impatient complaints. At one point, I had to walk into the waiting room and address the heated crowd. I assured them that I would stay as long as necessary to treat everyone there and insisted that none of them leave.

The hours dragged on. Three of the patients had to be sent to the regional hospital in the next county. In my estimation, several others should have gone as well, but they refused. Pizza was ordered in for the staff, but little was eaten. Word had spread throughout the town. Mayor Hickman came by to talk with me. I had little to say short of the obvious. Watervalley was experiencing a serious outbreak of influenza. Those who had gotten their annual flu shots seemed to be just as vulnerable as those who hadn't. The clinic's in-house lab test proved positive in every case. The staff was doing the best they could. Walt nodded his understanding. There was little he could do. I moved on to the next exam room.

At almost ten that night I saw the last patient. The staff was emotionally and physically spent. I told everyone to go home and get some rest. I would close up. After turning off the front floodlights, I walked to my office. A few minutes later I returned to the front and turned them on again. I was spending the night there. Although I was no less tired than the others, I knew the disease would not discern night from day. I kept my phone on, knowing full well that more cases would likely surface during the night. I was right.

I washed my face and tried to eat some cold pizza. More and more the cabinet factory was turning out to be the hub of the outbreak. The disease could have spread with just one person working in close proximity to another. I was online researching the odd demographic manifestations of this flu when I heard a rapid knock on the front door. I opened it to find a man and woman with a toddler asleep on her shoulder. The man was holding the hand of a young boy of about twelve. It was the boy who was sick.

I brought them in, performed the exam, and gave him some medications for his pain and high fever while the parents stood there anxiously. The young fellow clearly had the flu, but fortunately he did not present the same severity as the adult patients I'd seen throughout the day. It was a demographic change, the first nonadult patient I'd seen. This added another layer of concern and raised more questions in my already fatigued mind. During the course of the exam I received two phone calls from more patients. I told them to come on in; I'd be here.

In between exams I caught a couple of short naps, lying uncomfortably on the sofa in my office. By daybreak, I'd seen eight more patients. Two of them were children between the ages of seven and fourteen. Tracking the source of the disease was becoming impossible. The flu was crossing age and social boundaries.

On two separate occasions during the night I stepped out onto the shadowed back porch of the clinic, hoping to revive myself. The cold air, charged with only the glittering light of the distant stars, shocked me awake. The midnight and shadowed world of Watervalley before me was frozen, bare, rimed with frost: a silent, lifeless town of closed shops and lonely streetlamps. The town was still, voiceless. I stood there numbly in the silent cold. My world had lost its order. This disease was coming at me unexpectedly, randomly, chaotically.

Hunger, worry, confusion, lack of sleep, frustration: all buzzed through my head. Despite the cold air, my eyes closed. Unknowingly, I swayed, listing. Nothing clicked, nothing made sense. I was drunk with fatigue, drifting from reality. The crunching of tires and sweeping headlights of a car pulling into the front parking lot aroused me enough to inhale deeply, filling my lungs with the frozen air, and then move back inside to find my stethoscope and resume work.

Around seven the next morning, the staff began to reappear. They quickly realized that I'd never gone home. Mary Jo confronted me in the kitchen. "Dr. Bradford, have you been here all night?"

I swallowed the last of my coffee and stared at her somberly. "This outbreak doesn't respect office hours. Anyway, I got in a few short naps."

I could sense a sharp-tongued scolding rising within her, but she held it in check. She read my face, my determination, my smoldering frustration. Patients also began to arrive. All of Watervalley seemed to be appearing on the clinic's doorstep. Old, young, rich, poor, black, white, devout and otherwise were touched by the hand of the influenza. The epidemic respected no social bearing, no claims of affluence, no measure of piety.

Around noon I began placing calls to the Nashville office of the Centers for Disease Control to alert them and seek assistance. After being bounced around several times, I was ultimately put on speakerphone to a couple of people who expressed genuine concern but eventually realized that Watervalley was not in their jurisdiction and that the person I needed to talk to was on vacation that week. Furthermore, the idea of a new strain of flu seemed doubtful to them, so their focus settled on tracing the batch of flu vaccinations that Watervalley had received, in case it had been defective. They asked that I send an email detailing the number of cases along with a description of the disease presentation. They assured me that someone would get back to me within a day or so. The situation was insanely infuriating. I hung up the phone and sat for the longest time. I simply was not being taken seriously.

Then another idea struck me. I called the infectious diseases department of Vanderbilt's medical school. The department secretary explained that most of the professors were either on vacation or at a regional conference in Gulf Shores, Alabama, and wouldn't be back until the weekend. At my insistence, she offered to have someone call me. Several minutes later I received a return phone call from a second-year resident who reacted to all I had to say with sympathetic but disengaged curiosity. He agreed to pass the information along but offered little insight and no immediate assistance.

It seemed that I had an ocean of academic resources at my fingertips, but their availability was proving to be only inches deep. Remote Watervalley was simply not high on anyone's list of priorities. To them, my patients were a batch of symptoms and numbers, but I was looking into the faces of panicked neighbors. A small voice of fear was whispering painfully in the back of my head. There would be no quick fix. I was on my own.

Before Wednesday came to a close—some ten hours later—I saw another forty-seven cases along with an array of other patients. I found the strength to deal with them from inner resources unknown to me. Occasionally I slept for five minutes in the chair in my office. I would set the alarm on my cell phone and wake in a confused state, rub my eyes, and proceed to the next exam room. The patients repeatedly asked me if I understood the cause of the outbreak or where it was coming from. I had no answers.

The cabinet factory, the Farmers' Co-op, and a dozen other businesses announced their decision to close; they would reopen as soon as the epidemic subsided. The school system closed as well. The town came to a standstill. All eyes were on me. A reporter from *The Village Voice* made several attempts to talk with me about the crisis, but I had nothing to add to what they already knew. Shortly after eleven Wednesday night I arrived home. I'd not been there since six a.m. the day before.

Connie met me at the door. My defeated and anxious face told its simple story. The town was worried and scared and I had little to offer. I went directly upstairs and took a hot shower. Then I ate a few bites of dinner, drank a glass of iced tea in nearly one gulp, and walked back up to my bedroom, where I collapsed on the bed. Connie and I never spoke a word to each other. She turned off the lights, locked the door, and went home. My body drank deeply of a total and exhaustive sleep.

Thursday brought sixty-nine more flu patients for me to see. No one from Vanderbilt or the CDC had called back. This added to my sense of desperation. I was floundering in a squalling sea of patients who were full of confusion and worry with no end in sight. The exponential growth in cases had caused the disease to blow right past the capacity for a larger public health response. The flu outbreak was a roaring storm that had hit full force without ever showing up on radar. I knew that help would come eventually, but for now it was only the worn-out clinic staff and me. With each new patient I saw came the looming fear of who might be the first fatality. There were simply too many of them who were sick, too many with other health complications, too many who presented severe symptoms. And to make it worse, symptoms were all we were treating. Antihistamines for congestion, antipyretics for fever, a limited list of antiviral medications—these were only holding the disease at bay, not defeating it.

For the staff, tolerance was wearing thin. Tempers flared. Sharp exchanges occurred throughout the day, but they came to a peak when sunset arrived and the waiting room was still full. From inside one of the exam rooms I heard the bitter rise of angry words out in the hallway. It was Nancy, of all people, railing at Mary Jo.

"Jimmy Evans has been in exam room three for thirty minutes and you haven't even gotten his vitals yet. What's the problem?"

Mary Jo responded in a jagged tone. "What's the problem? What do you think is the problem? Just because it takes you five seconds to point a finger to an exam room, you think everything else should happen in a snap. Here—take my stethoscope. Knock yourself out."

Mary Jo's voice could easily be heard by half the people in the building. I left my examination and walked into the hallway, grabbing each of them by the arm and pulling them into my office. I shut the door behind us.

"What's the problem between you two?"

Immediately they both exploded in a tirade of accusations. I held up both hands and spoke in a short, firm voice: "Enough!"

Still stern faced, they were instantly silent, looking at me with lowly, contrite expressions. I wanted to give them a lecture, tell them to get past it. But I completely understood. I bit my lip and stood for a moment, surveying my office as if some buried wisdom could be found within the ancient woodwork. I exhaled deeply.

"Look. Both of you listen. Nancy, tell Cindy to drop off the lab work and go with Mary Jo to each exam and do all the documenting while she collects the vital signs. It's not much, but it will buy five minutes with each patient. Get Cindy to report back to you with the paperwork so you can tell me who is next. You good with that, Nancy?"

She nodded and headed off. Mary Jo watched her leave and then turned to me.

"So. What do you want me to do?"

I stared at her silently for a moment, assessing her question. I spoke as I walked past her. "Just keep doing your job and try not to bite Cindy's head off."

It was a side to them I'd never seen. The aggravation and exhaustion of past days were beginning to strip them of civility. Still they pressed on. The day ended shortly before nine p.m.

I came back to the clinic four times over the course of Thursday night to treat more patients. They looked at me with beseeching eyes, sometimes frightened, sometimes angry, all wanting answers. I grew deeply discouraged. I slept little.

The front page of Friday morning's *Village Voice* read "Flu Outbreak Baffles Local Doctor." It was the final straw. I seethed with irritation. It seemed that the verdict of my incompetence was unassailable. Before the day ended, the staff and I had treated another seventy-two patients. Some of them were repeats whose symptoms had not improved. More people had to be sent to the nearby hospital for observation, particularly several of the elderly patients whose immune systems were more vulnerable, especially those who already had a bevy of chronic illnesses.

After the last patient left, I tried to gather my wits enough to analyze the demographics. Overall, the vast majority of patients from the last few days were adults in their twenties and thirties. But the number had also included nine children and almost a dozen seniors. Still, it was strange that the very old and the very young had less severe symptoms. Based on their comments, the onset was also markedly slower.

Thankfully, no children under the age of five had surfaced. Again, this didn't fit the norm. The only infant I saw was Sam Akins and only because his mother had come to the clinic acutely ill. She apologized for bringing him and explained she had no one to keep him. She'd been sick since Wednesday and had tried to tough it out. There had been more than enough time for Sam to contract the disease, but he was perfectly healthy, as if somehow he was immune. I was thankful, yet still I could not make sense of it.

By the time I arrived home, shortly past eight on Friday evening, my annoyance and aggravation were past expression. What made matters worse was that the paper was right. I knew nothing more about what was causing this influenza outbreak than when the first cases had showed up over a week earlier. The clinic was officially closed and any new patients were being told by the recording on the main number to seek medical assistance at the hospital in the next county. It was a lousy solution, but I couldn't do more. The staff needed a break.

I showered, put on jeans, and drank a beer. Connie had been off that day, so I was on my own for dinner. Now, beyond all else, I was desperately lonely. The four walls of my living room closed in on me. Rhett read my mood and followed close beside me with a hangdog manner. I wanted to be far away from Watervalley, away from the ignorance, the mistrust, the suspicion. But there was nowhere to go, no one to talk to. It was far too late to go visit

John, and experience had taught me that he was not the best person upon whom to unburden my troubles. Besides, while I didn't want to be alone, I did want anonymity. Finally, I grabbed my coat and keys and headed out the door. Pulling the Corolla out of the driveway, I headed toward the north end of the county. I had a pretty good idea where to find Indigo Road and the roadhouse everyone called the Alibi.

CHAPTER 27
The Alibi

The last light of evening had long passed and a full moon hung in the broad sky, casting a soft luminescence over the landscape. I turned the radio on loud, quickly leaving the solemn, sterile streetlights behind, and within minutes I was away from town, into the vast shadowed countryside. Only an occasional light from a farmyard could be seen in the frozen distance. Under the brilliant moonlight, the rolling fields looked cold, raw, barren. I traveled north amid their petrified silence for nearly ten miles.

Soon the narrow road changed from long, straight runs to constant curves and turns, and the open countryside gave way to thick wooded hills. At each crossroad I slowed to find a road sign. I sped past several unpaved lanes with no markings and was beginning to boil with frustration when the headlights caught a quick flash of an old hand-painted sign with an arrow on it. It read THE ALIBI.

I took the next left, following the direction the arrow pointed. After a mile I came upon a barnlike building with at least fifty cars parked in the gravel lot next to it. A neon sign told me I'd found the right place. From inside I could hear the muffled sounds of a live band playing country music. A half dozen people were clustered in the shadows of the parking lot. The night echoed with drunken laughter and reeked of cigarette smoke as couples leaned against the cars, embracing, passionate, oblivious.

I slid through the front door and moved inside, hands in my coat pockets, and was hit with an explosion of energy and sound. The room was a blur of neon beer signs. It teemed with blisteringly loud music, cacophonous chatter, and the musty scent of tobacco. The noise was deafening and the room seethed with the sly, furtive gestures of subtle seduction. The Alibi was the clearinghouse for all passions, the release point of anger, loneliness, desire, and the myriad inventory of human need. As men and women were emboldened by alcohol, all the components of self were potentially up for barter, anything to drown the emotion that had brought them there.

I walked toward the bar, my head down, my gaze sliding from side to side. I received random nods from a couple of men who looked vaguely familiar. I shouldered my way into an opening at the bar. This was a coarser side of Watervalley: large, leather-necked farm and factory workers with powerful arms, ball caps, and scraggly beards. The room had a gamy body smell: unwashed, surly, thick with testosterone. The women tended to be large hipped in tight jeans and low-cut tops, their faces faintly lit from the glow of cigarettes. I ordered a beer. The band blared out a booming song, thick with metal guitars and the unmistakable twang and yodeling vocals of rockabilly country. I settled on a bar stool and drank my beer. The crowd was rough and the band wasn't exactly good, but at least I wasn't alone.

By the end of my fourth beer, I was floating. It was a delicious feeling. I turned sideways to the bar, leaned on one elbow, and surveyed the room, which was a roaring chaos of conversation, music, movement. On more than one occasion, women walked by and smiled. Some were in their twenties, some in their thirties, all of them almost pretty, with well-painted lips and ample curves. One or two even called me by name, giving me the mixed satisfaction of realizing that even here I was known. I smiled and nodded, but showed no interest in pursuing an encounter. I just wanted to unwind and not be alone. For tonight, romance was a distant third.

The throbbing waves of music drowned out any conversation short of yelling. Everyone was full of easy laughter. Two of the more attractive women in their mid-thirties came and posted up next to me at the bar. Hellos were exchanged, but I left it at that. The woman standing beside me was drunk, talking nonstop to her equally drunk friend. She was loud, animated, thick tongued, and bumping into me constantly.

Several pairs of the rural hopefuls approached the two and engaged them to dance. The women were experienced flirts. There was a predatory look about them, a knowing confidence that foretold their mastery of the slow seduction. Skilled in the easy taunt, they yielded only measure by measure to the advances of the rustics in the room, exploiting them for drinks, dances, laughter. From what I could see, their male counterparts were willing dupes.

I drank another beer. The sounds of the room began to blur. The words around me began to lose discernible meaning. Syllables were running together. Some of the men interested in the two women began to crowd my small stretch of the bar. I silently but firmly shouldered against them. This invited some less than friendly responses, but eventually the offenders backed off, returning their attention to the women.

My mind spun in a world of its own. The scene was amusing, a distraction, but ultimately it was just static. I became detached from the noise, the fever and intensity. The earlier euphoria induced by my plunge into numerous beers had now passed and I stood dispassionately at the bar, confronted with the smallness of my life. Within, I was smoldering. A voice inside told me I was getting far too intoxicated, but I was beyond caring. The music blared, the room began to spin, the chaos continued. I ordered yet another beer.

I looked sullenly at my glass and drank it down in one tilt. As I finished draining it to the bottom, a viselike hand grabbed me firmly on the shoulder. I released the mug, almost causing it to go tumbling across the bar. My large frame tensed and I began to turn to confront the aggressor. The hand held me firm, steadying me. It was a calm voice that spoke.

"Careful, Doc. This old wood floor can be slippery. Don't want you falling." It was Toy McAnders. I turned unsteadily and faced him. Toy stood at arm's length, but was now holding my right biceps in a rigid grasp. He looked at me with an easy smile. There was nothing confrontational or threatening in his tone or body language. Rather, he engaged me as if we had long been on friendly terms. It worked. I relaxed.

Toy's smile was infectious. I gave him an affable grin and held out my hand. He took it and we shook. Even in my semi-blistered state, I couldn't help but notice that Toy had an abundance of sheer presence, a confident intensity about him. Even through the fog of beer and noise, I felt a release, an enjoyment at being so openly and kindly engaged.

"So, this place your hangout?" I spoke in a half yell.

Toy grinned and shook his head. "Not really. At least, not that often anymore."

I smiled. I felt light-headed, had lost any measure of focus because of Toy's abrupt entry. I leaned back against the bar.

"Well, drink a beer with me," I said.

Toy's easy smile remained in place. Again he shook his head. "Nah. Not tonight, Doc. I'm more of a Scotch man myself. Might say it's in the blood."

I stood still for a moment. *Might say it's in the blood.* The words were calling up a memory, some conversation from the past. But the alcohol tripped me, redirected me. I couldn't focus. He was speaking to me again. I regained orbit.

"What say we get you home, Doc?"

I gave him a calculated look. Part of me was still floating; the beer had seen to that. The other part of me was rational, discerning, albeit unable to control the world swirling around my senses. I stared vacantly at Toy for a moment. Finally, the rational voice won out. He was right. It was time to go.

I nodded. "Yeah, sure."

"Let me have your keys, Doc. Buddy of mine's going to drive your car. You can ride with me in the truck."

I understood and began walking toward the door, completely forgetting about closing out my tab. Ever since Toy had grabbed my shoulder, the bartender had been standing across the bar from the two of us quietly taking in the exchange. Toy watched me walk away. When I paused, he turned and looked at the bartender. Both shook their heads. Toy placed two twenties on the counter.

"Thanks for the phone call, Eddie. I'll take him from here." The bartender returned a deadpan nod, scooped up the money, and headed toward the cash register.

Outside, the frozen air jolted me to consciousness. For a short moment I thought I could drive myself. But in an instant Toy was beside me, asking for the keys. I handed them over. He took the car key from the ring and walked over to a small fellow wearing a blue jean jacket and ball cap. There was a short exchange that I couldn't discern; then the other fellow nodded and departed into the shadows of the parking lot in the direction of my car. Toy returned.

"This way, Doc."

I climbed into what was clearly a brand-new extended-cab truck. Toy fired up the engine and pulled onto the gravel road. The noise and flashing neon of the roadhouse faded in the dark behind us.

Only a few words broke the silence of the trip back to Fleming Street. Although my bearings were a little disrupted, I felt certain that we were in the general vicinity of Ice Cave Road.

"If I'm not mistaken, your place isn't too far from here, is it?" I asked.

Toy looked over at me, his face illuminated by the glow of the dashboard lights. "If you turn right on this next road up ahead, it's about a mile down on the left." His manner was not clipped or unfriendly, but rather dutiful, as if he was patiently fulfilling some service he felt compelled to satisfy. We rode for a few more miles. The cold of the December night had wrested the beer's dizzying effects from me and I was beginning to feel the drain of pure exhaustion. Even in this clouded state, a curiosity held me.

"You work at the cabinet factory, don't you?"

"Yeah, sure do."

"I hear they shut things down because of all the people out sick."

"Half the people on my shift are out with it. More on the day shift."

"But you haven't had any problems with it? I mean, it's not like you haven't been exposed."

"Well, knock on wood, I guess, Doc. I've felt fine." We rode on in the darkness. Soon enough the frozen streetlights of Watervalley could be seen in the distance. Toy guided the truck effortlessly through the few turns to Fleming Street, pulled up in front of the house, and stopped the engine.

"You okay from here?"

I nodded. "Oh, sure, sure."

I held my hand out to him. "Thanks a lot, Toy." I paused. "Appreciate it." I pursed my lips, knowing full well that I had been done a considerable favor. Headlights pulled up behind us as Toy's friend arrived with my car. He turned into the driveway and cut the lights and engine. Toy took my hand in a firm shake.

"Not a problem. You've taken good care of my people, Doc. Everybody deserves the right to blow off a little steam every now and then. Given the week I imagine you've had, you deserve it no less than anybody else. Grab some sleep."

I nodded, not sure what Toy meant by "my people" but not really caring in the moment. The dreadful beginnings of a monster headache began to creep between my temples. I opened the truck door to exit, and as I did I noticed something roll to the ground that had been stuck between the seat and the door. I reached down to pick it up, steadying myself on the truck frame. It was a small stuffed animal, a brown dog, well worn and fuzzy threaded, with two shiny black button eyes. I held it for a moment, then handed it over to Toy.

"I'm guessing this is yours?"

Toy stared at the object in my hand, his face revealing a brief second of fluster. He collected himself, smiled, and reached for it.

"Thanks," he said, offering no further explanation. By now the other fellow was standing at the truck door, waiting to get in from the cold. He handed me the Corolla key. I thanked him and stepped aside. The truck rolled away.

Once inside my house, I went straight to the kitchen. Rhett

followed me at a soft, lowly pace. Grabbing some Tylenol and a large glass of water, I stepped out to the back porch. My mind was racing. My head was pounding and my throat tugged with a mix of nausea and exhaustion. The evening was now a blur and I was a little mystified as to exactly what had just happened with Toy McAnders.

High above me, the moon had drifted behind the tall trees, giving the stage to thousands of stars. I exhaled deeply and steadied myself on the porch railing, realizing that perhaps I was still drunker than I'd thought. Sleep was now my beloved friend, my escape from misery, loneliness, and the incomprehensible frustration of my life in this town. It was well past midnight. I returned inside to climb the back stairs and fall into bed.

It had been a grand experiment for me, trying to be a small-town doctor. But through the maze of fatigue and lingering alcohol, I knew that it simply wasn't going to work. I didn't fit in and I didn't want to be here. It was time to face that reality. My days in Watervalley were all but over.

CHAPTER 28

High-Water Mark

I was floating in the outer regions, that blissful suspension between sleep and wakefulness, stepping quietly, curiously into an April day of my youth. Light and shadows played across a soft, familiar lawn. Adult voices spoke distantly, calmly. Childish laughter, young, sweet, and innocent, drifted intermittently through the air. The rich smells of freshly mown grass, fruit tree blossoms, and warm sidewalks danced deep within my senses. Balmy breezes poured past. It was a world of tender images: soft, pristine, affectionate.

Then she shook me, hard.

I awoke abruptly. Connie was standing over me with a face of scornful judgment. Her lips were pressed firmly together yet still moving, as if chewing on words that were in danger of erupting. I rubbed my face and eyes, bringing her into focus.

"What time is it?" I asked.

She continued her incessant glare, standing straight-backed with hands on her hips. Then she grunted a deep "humph" and walked in a soldierly step to the windows, where she threw back the curtains, letting in what bleak midday sun could be brought to bear on a December day.

Her words were tart, unsympathetic. "It's time you were out of bed. That's what time it is. And why does this room smell like a brewery? Did you bathe in it last night?"

I looked over at my clock. It was a quarter past noon. Reality of time and place sank in. I had slept fully clothed. I sat up in bed and looked at Connie as if her words had fallen to the floor and never reached me.

"It is Saturday, you know."

"People have been trying to get ahold of you for the last four hours. You don't answer the phone or the doorbell, so I get called to come over and make sure you're okay."

"You may report that I am just fine." I put my feet on the floor and sat for a moment, the fog of sleep lingering. "Anyway, who needs me? I'm not on call this weekend. Any emergencies are supposed to be referred to Regional Medical."

"That's all fine and good, Doctor, but a lot of folks don't see it that way. You're their doctor. They want to see *you*. And what sort of foolishness did you get into last night, ending all tanked up?"

I was now fully awake. Deep within me, the frustration that had been smoldering for the last weeks finally found a voice. "Let it go, Connie."

"Let what go?"

"Your sermon. Let it go. I don't want to hear it. I'm done."

"Whatcha mean, you're done?" Connie was forgoing her usual perfect diction.

"I mean I'm done. I'm quitting. Monday morning, I'm turning in my resignation so they can start looking for someone else. Everything about my life in this town has been a failure. I don't understand the people, I don't fit in, and now everybody wants to blame me for this epidemic. And the worst of it is, by damn, they're right. The paper said it. I don't have a clue what this flu is or where it came from. So, short of the joy of walking around with everyone looking at me like I'm an idiot, I really can't think of a good reason why I should stay. I've tried, but my heart's not in this place. I'm not doing these people any good. So, yeah, I'm done."

Connie spoke her words rapid-fire, on full automatic. "Luke Bradford, that is the most idiotic thing I've ever heard you say. I know every now and then we all climb fool's hill, but right now I'm thinking you want to be king of it. You're all down on yourself and wishing away for the sweet by-and-by when what's really got you is the nasty now-and-now. Lying up here in your man cave is not going to fix anything. Besides, you're all wrong about the people of this town. They like you just fine. It's not them; it's you. You're just like John Harris and his rock wall. You've built one around yourself. Not a wall people can see, like he's got, but a wall just the same. These people care—they care about you—but they're also respectful. If they think you want your distance, they'll let you have it. But it doesn't mean what you think."

Perhaps I should have felt defensive, incensed at her words. But deep down I knew that much of what she had said was true. I had built a wall and I was to blame. But blame wasn't the issue. I certainly wasn't blaming Watervalley. I just wanted to leave. Mentally, I was already in another time zone.

"Look, Connie. I know you're smart, maybe even scary smart. But you're wrong about this. You don't know everything about my life, my thoughts, my loneliness. Watervalley's a great place; it's just not a great place for me. I don't fit in here, and, frankly, these people deserve better. So in the end, I don't want to be here. I'm not a small-town doctor. It's that simple." I spoke the last sentence slowly, announcing each word firmly, deliberately.

Connie stood for a moment. She stared at me, looking deep into my face. Eventually, she nodded in resignation.

"You're right. I don't know your life. I don't know how hard it has been. I just know that right now people are scared and they need you. But I guess we all have to decide our limits." With that she walked from the bedroom and back down the stairs. I could hear the echo of her footsteps traversing the front hall and the careful shutting of the front door. I walked to the windows, pulled the drapes together, and lay back down on my bed, wishing for sleep.

I lay in a half daze for another hour. Rhett had come and propped his chin next to my pillow. We were both hungry. The December day I saw through the kitchen windows was bleak, gray, cold. I fed Rhett, then heated some leftovers, piecing together enough of a meal. I thought about suiting up in my running clothes and going out for a long run, but I didn't want to be seen or engaged by anyone. I wanted my own space. I thought about Connie's words about John Harris and laughed it off, even though there was an aspect of John's life that I envied. John had bought himself the benefits of space, solitude, security. Yet without Molly, he had lost his rudder. Then again, I well knew, everyone adapted and grieved in his own way.

I drifted around the house. Lying on the couch, I caught up on some old magazines and watched some TV. Rhett was my steady shadow, dropping his ball at my feet several times, innocently beseeching me to come play. I rubbed his head and apologized. I just wasn't in the mood.

By half past five it was already dark and I was hungry again. I warmed up some soup and made a sandwich and fed Rhett his dinner. Afterward, I grabbed a quilt and fell asleep on the couch, the exhaustion of the week and the previous night's escapade still drawing against my energy. When I awoke, it was ten thirty at night. I was restless and knew that downtown would be quiet now, all the shops long since closed. I changed into my jeans, grabbed my coat and ball cap, and headed out the door into the dark and dispirited evening.

For several hours I walked the downtown streets of Watervalley. My path held no pattern or direction. I moved randomly from street to street, passing the Co-op, the Society Hill Bed and Breakfast, the old high school, the Depot, Chick's garage, all the churches, the radio station, Maylen's Barbershop, the Merchants Bank, and seemingly dozens of other buildings, names, and signs that had been burned so deeply within me over the last half year. Each yielded up faces, names, conversations, and illnesses that I had carefully logged away. People whose lives in some small way I had mended. People whose stories I knew. But ultimately the streets were filled with nothing but my uncertainty about the future.

All the voices and faces of Watervalley rolled through my head. What Connie had said still plagued me. Everyone built walls and I was no different. Life had proven to me that those you love can be taken away. So you move on, but you also protect yourself.

I stood alone under the pale streetlights of the courthouse square, the center of Watervalley. I breathed in deeply of the December air, and I wondered what it would feel like to live for so long around such familiar people and places. To feel bound to them. My life had not been a broad, stable land of familiar hills and fields but rather a gathering of small islands of love and security, broken apart by the death of loved ones. I didn't have a wellspring of strength to draw upon, the assurance of long years in cherished surroundings. It seemed that I had spent most of my life looking for safe harbor. I had kept myself a stranger. I had built walls. Connie was right.

I thought of the people of Watervalley and could only laugh at myself. Their lives had permeated my hardened shell despite my efforts at detachment. The enormous tide of life, all that I had been and done over the last months, washed over me in graphic reality, and I knew in my bones that I cared for them. I was gripped by the profound awareness of my responsibilities and also by my admission of failure.

I thought of Aunt Grace's words, her voice, the promise she had asked of me all those years ago. My mind drifted back. I had been sitting patiently in her private hospital room. She was gaunt and pale. The cancer had taken her down to less than one hundred pounds. Yet still, she had warm eyes, a handsome face, and a subtle, elegant manner. She spoke barely above a whisper.

I love you, Luke. I want you to know that. I want you to be happy and have a good life, a meaningful one. I want you to make a difference, but that usually never involves the easiest path.

She squeezed my hand.

I hope you'll grow to understand my choices.

She talked on. I remembered hearing her words but not taking them in. The future meant nothing in that moment. I had lost my parents and now I was losing her. All I could think about was the dreadful present and her sad eyes. She had loved life and had dearly loved me. I knew my time with her was passing. Four days later, she was gone.

Even now, years and miles removed, her words haunted me. Something in me didn't just love her, but also trusted her love for me. My head and heart clashed; they were in separate worlds. The night was overcast and I walked alone in the shadows, all the stars shrouded. I found no answers.

Sometime after midnight, I walked two steps into a dark, brick-lined alley between some downtown buildings and sat on a small bench next to a historic marker. The steam from my breath drifted out of the black and lifted into the pale light cut from the storefront. Time and sound were frozen. Then, faintly against the frigid silence, I heard footfalls approaching from down the alley.

Immediately I was alert, tense. Adrenaline shot through me. I instinctively pulled back against the bench and wall, positioning myself in the dark behind the short column of the historic marker beside me. I held my breath. Unaware of my presence, someone came to the end of the alley, then paused and looked both ways before stepping into the light of the street. He turned to the left and stepped hurriedly away. The silhouette was of a boy. The outline of the small shape and the reflection on the heels of the sneakers were unmistakable. It was Will Fox. I could not fathom what he was doing downtown at so late an hour. Was he the same person I had encountered in the dark some months back?

I sat for a couple of lost minutes. Suddenly a strong gust, a cold biting wind poured between the buildings. Then I heard and felt large, icy raindrops begin to fall. They were haphazard at first, landing with dull splats on the brick pavement and crisp, tinny pops against the metal signs. Two breaths later, they came hard and thick in an immediate, inescapable downpour. I pulled my hat down over my head and drew my coat tight around me. I was tempted to run for home but decided it didn't matter. Fleming Street was eight long blocks away and I was already soaked.

The freezing rain dripped into my ears and down my face. I was miserable. Although I walked briskly, moving from streetlamp to streetlamp in an effort to escape the flood, my efforts were in vain. The heavens had opened, washing away the last vestige of my determination. I was beaten. The piercing deluge raged, pelting me, soaking my clothes, drowning me. I walked the last few blocks down the darkened sidewalks in the blinding rain, feeling at my lowest point: despairing and alone, embarrassed and ashamed, wild with conflict, and now saturated and defeated.

And in this bleakest moment I heard distant cries for help.

CHAPTER 29

A Long Night

I began to run toward the panicked voice just as the sound of pounding and someone calling my name also reached my ears. As I arrived at my house the scene before me was blurred by the driving rain. Standing on my front porch was Will Fox. He was soaked through and in tears, beating desperately on my front door and screaming for me at the top of his lungs. Rhett was inside, barking loudly in response.

"Dr. Bradford, Dr. Bradford, please come to the door!" The words were broken by deep sobs and fits of crying. By now I was on the front steps behind him and called out his name. He turned with a face of pure terror. His words poured out. "Help her, help her—please, Dr. Bradford." The boy was pointing. "She's lying in the backyard and I can't get her to move."

The words sank in. I grabbed his hand. "Come show me."

We ran to the Foxes' backyard. In a flash of lightning, some fifty feet out from the house, I saw the outline of Louise Fox in a heap on the ground. She was in her night robe, lying drenched and seemingly lifeless in the mud.

"She won't move. I can't make her move," Will was pleading, his face wet with rain and tears. Another brilliant flash of lightning struck nearby, followed by a booming roll of thunder. I bent down beside the wilted body. She had a faint pulse and was breathing. I smelled the unmistakable odor of alcohol. In a single motion, I scooped her up in my arms.

"Let's get her inside."

Will ran ahead to the back entrance of his house. By the time I arrived with Louise, he had the porch light on and was holding the door open. As I brought her into the dimly lit kitchen, Will was still crying uncontrollably. The shabby room was rife with the stale odor of filth, a chaos of unwashed dishes and dirty utensils, of pots and pans still holding the remains of long-dried food, and stacks of newspapers and unopened mail. A paper grocery bag filled with empty liquor bottles occupied a corner of the counter, along with emptied cans of potted meat and soup.

Cradling Louise's limp, wet body in my arms, I pushed past the kitchen and into the living room. It was in equal disarray. "Will, turn a lamp on and then I need you to clear those cushions off the couch."

Still sobbing lightly, he complied, but all the while he never took his eyes off his mother's limp body. I carefully placed her on the couch, tucking her muddy feet under her sopping nightgown. Again I felt her pulse and listened to her breathing, then sighed a breath of relief. Everything was normal; she was simply passed out drunk. I grabbed a nearby quilt, spread it over her, and turned to Will.

"What was she doing out there?"

Will looked at me with a face of horror. His tears had stopped but his panic had only slightly subsided. He responded quickly, looking to the side. "I—I don't know. I just found her out there."

I bit my lip and nodded. I sat on the coffee table so I could talk to Will at eye level. "Let's try this again. I know you were downtown earlier tonight. I saw you. Your mom's going to be okay, but she's had a little too much to drink tonight. I'm guessing that she somehow came upstairs to your bedroom looking for you. And when she couldn't find you, she wandered outside and passed out."

Will erupted in hysterical tears. "You can't tell anyone. No one can find out. You can't tell anyone. Please, Dr. Bradford—please." Will had grabbed my wrist. I wrapped my arms around the boy and held him in a firm hug.

Will sobbed uncontrollably. He spoke through broken gasps of breath. "I thought she was dead. She wouldn't move. I didn't know what to do."

I closed my eyes. It seemed that the depth of the small boy's fears permeated into me, releasing a wellspring of old emotions. From long-forgotten years as an orphaned boy, I understood Will's desperation. After a few moments I bent down on one knee and held him by the shoulders.

"You're going to have to trust me," I said. "I think I understand what's been going on. We'll deal with that later. But right now your mom needs to get out of that wet nightgown, and I'm going to need help with that. So I'm going to call a friend of mine. Meantime, I want you to go upstairs and change into some dry clothes, then bring me some clean towels. Can you do that?"

The boy nodded. He looked over at his mother, his face still steeped in anguish.

I spoke again. "I'm going to stay right here with her and make sure she's okay. So go on now—head on up."

As Will climbed the stairs, I felt through my coat pockets for my cell phone. Connie was livid at having been awakened in the middle of the night, but as soon as I explained the situation, she said, "I'll be right there."

Incredibly, she arrived in fifteen minutes. She was completely dressed, with full makeup, a rain hat, a raincoat, and rubber boots. Under her arm she carried a change of shoes and some blankets.

I moved Louise to her bedroom on the ground floor. It was cleaner and neater than the rest of the house, but had the thick air of stale alcohol. She whimpered slightly as I placed her on the bed. Connie immediately looked through the chest of drawers for clean sleepwear. I thanked her. She nodded and told me she could handle it from here.

"I'm going to go next door to put on some dry clothes," I said. "Then I'll come back and look after Will."

"That's fine, Dr. Bradford, but you needn't worry. I've got someone coming to take care of him."

"What do you mean?"

Connie waved me away. "Never mind. Just do what you gotta do and come on back. I'll explain then."

I dashed through the rain to my house. Despite the cold, I stripped off my drenched coat and shirt on the front porch. I was down to bare skin when I saw headlights pull up to the Foxes' house. Leaving the wet clothes on the porch, I kicked off my shoes and stepped inside, still in my soaked pants. I finished undressing and threw the remainder of my things in the tub upstairs. Quickly toweling down, I put on dry clothes, grabbed an umbrella, and headed back.

I entered the front door without knocking and proceeded into the living room. There I found Will sobbing quietly, his face buried in the shoulder of Christine Chambers. She was sitting on the edge of a large overstuffed chair. He was half standing, half collapsed into her. Christine and I exchanged silent nods. From across the room, Connie stepped from the bedroom and gently shut the door behind her. She approached me, speaking softly.

"Do you need to give her anything, Doctor?"

I shook my head. "No, she just needs to sleep it off."

Connie nodded. "I got her cleaned up and warm. She's sleeping. But I think I'm going to stay here. She'll be in a terrible fit when she wakes up."

I spoke with resignation. "That's probably a good idea. I should stay too." I looked at Christine. "You okay to stay with him for a while?"

Christine nodded and voiced a silent yes. Then she closed her eyes and ran a gentle hand over Will's damp hair. Connie and I stood in the dimly lit room, surveying the clutter and disarray. Each of us knew what the other was thinking. I spoke first. "Let's start in the kitchen."

We spent the next hour bringing order and cleanliness to the chaos of pots, pans, and dishes. I hauled out several bags of garbage while Connie scoured everything in sight with soap and steaming hot water.

Meanwhile, Christine placed dry blankets on the sofa and got Will to lie down. He was overwhelmed and frightened, begging her not to leave. She assured him that she'd stay until he fell asleep. Once he began dozing, she attempted to bring some order to the living room.

At first, Connie and I moved about silently, speaking little, each aware of an underlying tension between us. Neither wanted a confrontation. I found a clean dish towel and began to dry the pots and dishes that Connie was washing. I stacked them neatly on the freshly cleaned kitchen table. We worked together efficiently. I caught up with Connie's initial stack and stood patiently waiting on a large pot she was scrubbing. I spoke solemnly, almost under my breath.

"Poor woman. I guess I should have picked up on all this sooner."

Connie spoke in a low, kind voice as she focused intently on her cleaning. "I wouldn't blame myself. People have a right to their privacy. Sometimes it's just hard to tell someone your problems." She handed me the pot.

"Yeah, I guess so. Still, it was pretty rough, seeing her lying in the mud like that. By the way, thanks for coming over and helping out, you know, getting her all cleaned up. I didn't mind doing it, but with Will all upset— Well, you understand."

She looked at me and smiled softly. "Of course, Doctor," she said, then turned and grabbed the next pot. Without looking up, she spoke to me in a tone that I had never heard from her. It was humble, affectionate, brimming with a full measure of tenderness and apology.

"Washing someone's muddy feet is scriptural for me, you know. We wash feet because it's symbolic of where we come in contact with this broken world. Jesus cleansed Peter's feet not just as a sign of humility, but to let him know that he could wash him clean of his failings. At times we are all foolish, Doctor. We fail to see or understand, and we inflict wounds on each other. I suppose I've been that way with you. What you did here tonight, what you've been doing for this town the last several months, it's been a gift. But I guess it's one that has come with a price. There's a lot of good in you, Luke Bradford, and a lot of smarts. I know, in time, you'll figure everything out."

In her powerful, rich, deep-throated voice, Connie began to hum a vaguely familiar hymn. The last pot was done. I folded the dish towel and laid it on the counter.

In the living room I found Christine half dozing in the chair. Will was sound asleep on the couch. I touched her shoulder lightly.

"Come with me," I said. "I want you to help me with something."

She followed me upstairs into Will's room. Unlike the rest of the house, it was all in order. The bed was made, clothes were folded in stacks, shoes were paired and lined up. A small desk was scattered with a few books, papers, and a computer.

I shuffled through the papers and found some manila folders stuffed with bills from local merchants along with power and water company invoices. At the back of the folder was a handwritten sheet with the words "Log Ins" at the top. Below was a list of a dozen or more names of local merchants. Christine had been watching as I riffled through the documents on the desktop.

"What is it, Luke?"

"It's a list of computer access passwords to a bunch of the local stores."

Christine surveyed the desk. "Bless his heart. Looks like he is the one responsible for paying the bills each month. That's got to be tough on a twelve-year-old."

I studied the paper for a moment longer. "I think he's doing a little more than paying the bills."

"I don't understand."

I held the paper where Christine could see it. "Look at these. These are not account log-ins; they're system log-ins. I don't think these stores have online accounts for bill paying. If I'm not mistaken, most of these merchants still allow customers to run monthly tabs and send them a paper bill every thirty days. This list isn't about paying bills. It's about hacking into their systems."

Christine was dumbfounded. "But why? What would that accomplish?"

I stared at her. "It's brilliant."

"How?"

"What he does is this. He goes into their accounts receivables program and logs his mother's account as paid. The merchant's cash doesn't actually add up, but the computer printout shows the account settled. So there is no way to catch or rectify the error. Yeah, it's brilliant." The two of us stared at each other in astonishment. We looked back at the paper.

"Why do these four have the word 'key' written beside them?" Christine asked.

I thought for a moment. She could sense me connecting the dots. And yet I said nothing.

"Luke?"

I smiled broadly. "I'll be darned."

"What?"

"That's why he works with Chick McKissick. So he could make keys to get into these four. I'm betting he hasn't been able to remote into them for some reason. So he has to physically get into the store and log directly on to their computers."

"Are you sure about this?"

"Pretty darn sure. Think about it. These four stores are the same ones that have been broken into over the last several months. Their security alarms would go off but nothing was ever stolen. The merchants could tell someone had been in the store. All Will needed was a couple of minutes to cook the books. I took a walk downtown tonight, late. After midnight, I saw Will coming out of the alley beside the drugstore. It's not the first time I've seen him down there. That's why his mother couldn't find him and ended up wandering outside."

Christine shook her head, still amazed. "Poor Will. I guess with his father gone they were having trouble making ends meet. Louise probably thought the merchants were just being kind. Obviously, she hasn't been able to cope."

I placed the paper back in the folder. I thought for a moment and then tucked it into my shirt pocket.

"What are you going to do?"

"Not sure yet." I looked down at the desk at the remaining folders.

"Wow, this is unbelievable. How did you figure all this out?"

I smiled at her and shook my head. "I think the real question is why didn't I suspect something sooner. Things have been odd with Will and his mom for quite some time. I should have known."

I stared at the files a moment longer. "Listen, thanks for coming up here with me. I just wanted a witness to what I thought I was going to find. Keep this under your hat if you would. I'm going to have to let Sheriff Thurman know, but I've got some things to think through before that happens."

Christine nodded. With the rapid events of the night, I had thought of nothing else but the actions before me. Only now did I begin to absorb the full delight of her presence. Wearing no makeup to speak of and dressed in blue jeans and a sweatshirt, she was still hypnotically gorgeous. The moment was filled with a clumsy tenderness between the two of us. Deep, deep inside me, I wanted to embrace her, give in to the incredible attraction I felt for her. To my delight, I saw something vulnerable in her eyes that spoke of the same desire. But I let the moment pass.

I inhaled a deep breath and pursed my lips. "We better get back downstairs."

We found Connie dusting the furniture in the living room, keeping a watchful eye on Will. The three of us discussed the situation and agreed that Connie would stay. She would call me if need be when Louise woke up. Otherwise, after daybreak, she would call some members of her church to come help out.

Together, she said, with simple, unemotional resolve, her church group would work with Louise to help her get her life back in order.

Christine and I walked onto the front porch together. The

rain had moved out and stars glittered faintly in the early morning sky. It was slightly past four and both of us needed sleep.

The moment was awkward. I spoke perfunctorily. "Thank you again for coming over and helping out. It made things a lot easier."

"Sure. I ran into Connie at school on Friday and told her about Will. I asked her to let me know if she heard anything."

The comment caught me off guard. "You ran into her at school?"

"Yeah. Why?"

"Did she say why she was there?"

"I think she's still active with the PTA. It's nothing unusual to see her doing volunteer work."

"Oh, okay. Of course." Knowing Connie as I did, I found the timing suspect and I wondered if she had dropped by the school with another agenda. But Christine's answer seemed innocent enough. I smiled. "Okay, then. Thanks again. Good night."

"Good night."

I stepped down the sidewalk and turned toward my house, but noticed that Christine had not moved.

"Luke." Her voice was crisp against the cold air. There was a subtle, pleading quality to it. I stopped, exhaled deeply, and turned to face her.

"Yeah."

"I need to tell you something."

I walked back toward her. "Okay."

"I need to thank you. You were right."

I looked at her quizzically. "About what?"

"My mom. Turns out the problem was B12 absorption. She got a shot, a large dosage. The difference is amazing. So I wanted to thank you."

As she spoke, she drew near to me. The cold induced us to

move even closer, pooling our warmth. There was a gentle, beseeching quality to her voice. We were separated by mere inches.

I nodded. "I'm glad she's doing better. Thanks for letting me know." In the shadowed glow of the streetlights, the tender outline of her face appeared fairylike, perfect. I wanted to draw closer still, but my head said no. I was leaving town soon, so what would be the point? I smiled, nodded, and turned away.

As I walked up my porch steps, I couldn't help but laugh at the irony. Only a few hours earlier, my heart had been drawing me away from Watervalley and my head had been imploring me to stay. Now it seemed the two had flip-flopped. Things could change so quickly.

CHAPTER 30

House Call

I awoke shortly before eleven the next morning and immediately checked my cell phone on the bedside table. There had been no calls. Apparently, Connie had handled everything. I looked out my side bedroom window at the Foxes' house. Several cars were parked on the street and in the driveway. The people of Watervalley in all their plain and simple decorum had gathered around the family in crisis next door to me. Some were carrying in groceries, others bringing dishes of food. Some were even raking up the leaves long left from the fall season, while others hauled off bags of trash. It was a marvel. A spontaneous outpouring of dutiful rescue carried out with little fanfare or fuss. Watervalley had wrapped its arms around my troubled neighbors.

The downtown church bells started their usual musical prelude shortly before eleven, signaling the call to worship. It seemed that on Sunday the ceremony of life in Watervalley reached its fullness. These were not people who suffered from the pitfalls of negotiating a world of changing and uncertain values. The Sabbath established a time of order and focus. Yet clearly spiritual observance was not confined within sanctuary walls, as demonstrated by all that was happening at the Fox house. What for months had been a dark, quiet place of gloom, secrets, and fear was now a whirlwind of hope, life, and renewal. In their straightforward and unsophisticated way the people of Watervalley possessed an unbounded spirit of charity and, when called upon, the magic of a collective heart.

As I pulled back the bedroom drapes, the sun was bright, pristine. The night's rain had washed all the dreariness from the world. The day was brilliant with a feeling of optimism and expectancy. I stared toward where the downtown buildings and steepled churches stood in stately radiance, like a framed still life painting. The musical chimes from the nearby church continued their song.

The prospect of leaving my job, of leaving Watervalley, brought a new focus to my thoughts. For months I had tempted myself with daydreams of life beyond the town. This glorious morning should have held a fabulous sense of contentment, but it fell short. I still wanted an explanation for the influenza outbreak.

Being the town doctor was the one role I had fully claimed in Watervalley. I didn't want this failure with the flu epidemic to define me, to overshadow my time as their doctor. As I began to think over all that had happened, it seemed I was standing before a great puzzle.

The Sunday morning sun cascading through my bedroom windows faintly illuminated everything, creating an ethereal light. It rendered an elegant, delicate softness to the room. Old conversations, random moments, subtle observations began to stream through my head. I ambled downstairs to the kitchen, poured a glass of juice, and fed Rhett. Then I realized I'd left my cell phone in the bedroom. The musical prelude to the church bells wound down. I moved toward the stairs, thinking, connecting. Then the church bells began their long solemn bongs marking the eleventh hour. As the first of them pealed, I took the first step up the stairs. My mind drifted back to my first day with patients.

Dr. Bradford . . . First patient is a physical, plaid shirt . . . Scotland, 1860, older brother named Carter—no, Cullen . . . war, train.

The second bell sounded. I ascended another step. *I convalesced at Primm Springs . . . Presbyterian roots . . . Scotch . . . Distillery gone from the barn.*

The third bell rang. I took another step. *I hear rumblings at night . . . Grandson lives with me now . . . I walk down to the watermark . . . Use your head and don't give up.*

My mind drifted to other worlds, different days, buried memories. As the bells rang out, I stepped upward methodically, rhythmically.

Hundred-year-old Scotch, a pretty prized possession . . . water of life . . . toxicum . . . family.

The bells continued to ring and I climbed the remaining steps to the top of the stairs. The sunlight beaming through the windows created a visible shaft of light. In the still air I could see a thousand particles floating randomly, effortlessly, yet somehow with a sense of order. I was mesmerized. A thousand dots without connection, yet still they created a pattern. My mind drifted further back.

The large chair in the living room, the men in suits, the light through the transom window. Aunt Grace, crouching beside me . . . You and I are a family now, Luke . . . we're family.

Somewhere within the endless miles of synapses, dendrites, and neurotransmitters of my brain the dots were trying to connect. All I had seen, had heard, had lived over the last months was pushing to the surface. Instinctively, I knew that somewhere in the tapestry of my days in Watervalley there was an answer, a hidden explanation of the epidemic. Yet pieces were missing. Strangely, an odd word bubbled into my thoughts, a word that had no connection to my medical training, my hours spent poring over textbooks, charts, lecture notes. It was a word surfacing in my consciousness as having a place, a key: *reawakening*.

A blaring noise shattered the moment. My cell phone blurted a long, shrill ring, startling me. I glanced at it. I knew the number.

"Hello."

The raspy voice on the other end was gravelly, weak. "Doc, you think you could make a house call?"

"What's wrong, John?"

"I could give you a long list of symptoms, but to cut it short, I think you can bet your ass I've got this flu. How soon can you get here?"

"Let me stop by the clinic to get a few things and I'll head right out."

"That'd be good, Luke. And bring a gun, 'cause if you can't make me better, by damn I want you to shoot me."

"Yeah, I'll bring some medicine too and we'll figure out whether or not to use the gun."

"Thanks, Luke. Get here as quick as you can."

I grabbed my coat and keys and raced out to the car. I made a quick stop at the empty clinic and then headed up into the hills. The whole time I wondered how in the world a recluse like John Harris could have come in contact with the flu.

Knocking on John's front door elicited no reply. I turned the knob and stepped inside.

"John?" Still no one answered. Small alarms were beginning to go off in my head. My senses sharpened. With a hurried pace I stepped through the front hall toward the back living room.

"John?" I heard a low moan coming from the kitchen. Moving

toward the sound, I found him in pajamas and a bathrobe sitting on the floor with his back to the refrigerator. He was holding a plastic bag filled with ice to his head. He spoke without opening his eyes.

"Hey, Doc. You bring that gun?"

"Yeah. But it's just a Winchester replica air gun. It's only good for making people get their butts up off the floor."

John opened his eyes to look up at me and then closed them again. A forced smile crossed his face. "You may need to give it a try. I don't think I can move."

I smiled and extended my hand. "Come on, bubbles. Let's get you to a chair and take a few vitals."

Together we managed to get John into one of the large chairs in the den.

"John, I guess I'm a little shocked. I didn't think you could get sick."

"Why is that?"

"You're so crotchety I assumed even germs didn't like you."

He grinned weakly. "Yeah, yeah, sawbones. Kick a man when he's down. I guess I had it coming."

I listened to his chest and methodically checked him over. The assessment was obvious. Like so many others in Watervalley, John had the flu. His temperature was not as outrageously high as some I had seen, but it was high enough for me to be concerned. I gave him an antipyretic to bring his temperature down and an antiviral that was having mixed results against this particular strain. It was the best I had to offer.

"So when did all this start?" I asked.

"Sometime yesterday afternoon, I guess. Got a headache first."

"Did you go to the bank, the grocery—anywhere in the last few days where you might have come in contact with anyone?"

"Nope. Haven't been in town since Tuesday. Went to the Co-op."

I thought for a moment. It made no sense. The disease had a pattern of presenting itself quickly after exposure, usually within twelve hours. John's situation simply didn't fit.

"And you didn't notice anything before yesterday? No aches, chills, nothing?"

"Nah. At first I thought it was just a little bit of a hangover. Got a little sloshed Friday night but I felt fine in the morning. It was noon when the headache started."

John's story reminded me of my own Friday night escapade. "Yeah, I sort of ended up off the wagon on Friday myself. Thought I'd drown some of the misery of the week, so I dropped by the Alibi—you know, the roadhouse on the north side of the county. Get this—Toy McAnders is the one who ended up giving me a ride home."

Despite his malaise, John perked up slightly. "Did he now? Interesting. He offer you some of his Scotch?"

I was puzzled. "I don't understand."

John's face told the story. He had mistakenly divulged a little-known confidence, but it was too late to retreat. He leaned toward me, his voice barely above a whisper.

"Look, Doc, here's the deal. After Knox died, Toy's curiosity got the better of him, so he got some bolt cutters and a flashlight and started exploring back into the old ice cave. Found an old mortared stone wall that had fallen in."

John's words revived a vague memory. "You know, the day I examined Knox he mentioned to me that he had heard some rumblings coming from the old ice cave. Didn't think much of it then, but now it makes me wonder."

John continued, "At any rate, seems that Toy stumbled across his great-grandfather's old disassembled distillery. The copper was all bent, so it was no longer usable. What he also found were some two hundred plus bottles of Scotch, made around 1910 by the old distillery master himself."

"I'll be darned. So the old legend is true."

"Very true. I got word of it through the grapevine, so I called him to see if I could buy some from him. He hemmed and hawed about it at first, said he really wasn't interested in selling them. But finally we cut a deal. I bought two bottles from him a week ago, two hundred bucks a pop. I opened up the first one Friday night, and I gotta tell you, worth every penny."

John coughed sharply and reached for the glass of water on the table beside him. "I tell you what, Doc. Those two bottles are in the cabinet beside the fridge. There's an unopened one in a brown paper bag. Take it. We'll call it payment for the house call."

I started to refuse, Scotch not being to my taste, but ultimately I agreed for no other reason than to avoid an argument. John slumped back in his chair and closed his eyes.

"Look, I think you could use some rest. I'll get out of here so you can go to bed."

John nodded. Slowly he stood up and began walking with unsteady steps toward the hallway and his bedroom. He cleared his throat, speaking again in a coarse voice. "Thanks again for the pills. I'll let you show yourself out. Oh, and don't forget your Scotch. Cabinet next to the fridge."

He disappeared down the hallway, where I heard the bedroom door shut.

I was confident he would be fine, but I made a note to call tomorrow just to check in. In the kitchen I found the upper cabinet containing John's liquor. The McAnders bottle was unmistakable, having a yellowed paper label with a partially faded MCANDERS carefully stamped in the center. Below the name were the numbers "1910," handwritten with a charcoal pencil. The bottle was still covered in dust and had a sticky film. Beside it was the second bottle John had mentioned, still in the paper bag. I grabbed it, shut the cabinet, and headed back to the front door.

As I passed back through the den to get my coat, something on the coffee table caught my eye. It was a high school annual, the *Watervalley Signal*, dated 1968, opened to a picture of the cheerleading squad. I recalled from past conversations that 1968 was John's senior year, so I couldn't resist scrutinizing it for a brief moment. I picked up the inch-thick book and thumbed through the black-and-white pictures.

The cheerleader picture listed Molly Cavanaugh as the captain. She was an absolutely beautiful girl, shapely yet small in stature with an incredible smile. No doubt it had been easy for John to fall insanely in love with her. Her twin sister, Madeline, was not a cheerleader, but I found her in the pictures of the science and math clubs along with a gangly John Harris standing in the back row. There were also pictures of him on various ball teams.

I was about to return the annual to the table when a full-page picture of John caught my attention. It was an acknowledgement of him as the salutatorian. Curious, I turned to the previous page. Wearing pointed glasses, neatly combed hair, and a white sash across her chest was the valedictorian of the class of 1968. Her face was much thinner then, but even as a youth her pleasant expression had a critical, discerning quality. The caption read "Constance Grace Pillow," the woman I knew as Connie Thompson.

"Well, I'll be darned," I whispered. Putting the annual down, I shook my head, picked up my things, and shut the front door behind me.

During the drive back to Fleming Street, my mind was caught

up in a cyclone of whirling thoughts. Connie Thompson being valedictorian of her class made all the sense in the world—I had no doubt she was that smart. What didn't make sense was why she had never gone off to college. I remembered from months back John telling me there was someone in Watervalley much smarter than him. I shook my head and grinned.

"Unbelievable," I said.

I drove mindlessly down the winding curves, lost in thought about John. Clearly he had the flu, yet he hadn't been anywhere for several days, which meant it had had a slow onset. That didn't make sense. Maybe he had picked up a different strain. I kept trying to wrap my head around all the facts, connect the dots, but the result was more questions, more uncertainty. I came out of my fog only to realize I was sitting in my driveway, the motor running. I might be leaving Watervalley, but this damnable epidemic was not leaving me. I wanted an answer.

CHAPTER 31
The Difference

As I came through the front door, an incredible exhaustion poured over me. Rhett was dozing on the living room rug and offered only a slight flopping of his tail as I entered. The house was quiet, the bright midday light providing little warmth to the silent rooms. The sirens of sleep were pulling at me, moving me upstairs to the sanctuary of my room, the warmth of my bed. Arriving upstairs, I realized I was still holding the brown paper bag of Scotch. I set it on my bedside table, kicked off my shoes, and crawled into bed, pulling the covers heavily over me. Turning on my side, the paper bag was the last thing in view as I drifted off.

I entered the deepest of dreams.

A young boy is running through the tall grass on the high hills overlooking a farm. From the distance he smiles at me, grinning, motioning me to come closer. I know it is Knox McAnders from many years ago, a carefree child playing in the open green fields. He is a make-believe soldier charging the enemy in the trenches, using a tobacco stick as a gun, cheering his triumph. Twilight is approaching. Crisp, cool breezes pass over the cathedral of tall trees on Akin Ridge and waft over him. Heaving for breath, he collapses into the tall field grass, joyous over his victory on the battlefield. He lies there, gazes far into the distant stars, steam pouring off of him. His father calls him from the far reaches of the hill. He runs to meet him but as he comes closer I see instead a man in uniform. His brother. Cullen. He has come home.

Knox runs to him and leaps into his older brother's arms. He laughs riotously and climbs onto Cullen's back. Together they head off down the hill toward home. Knox looks back at me one last time. He smiles, waves, and yells out a single word.

I awoke abruptly.

Daylight spilled richly into the bedroom, but the bedside clock revealed that it was past three. I had slept for two hours.

I threw the covers off and sat on the side of the bed, still hazy in the half fog of sleep. But the dream had not yet dissolved and was still vivid in my head. Knox McAnders. Why in the world would he have been rolling through my subconscious? I stared at the brown bag on the bedside table. Had that been the reason?

Then a thought came to me—an incredible, unimaginable thought. It was the word Knox had yelled to me, the same word that had been rolling through my head earlier that day. With all my training, all my empirical reasoning, the answer was not to be found in what I was seeing before me. The answers were buried in the past, sleeping quietly, patiently waiting for the right moment to surface. It now all made sense, illuminated by the one simple word Knox had said: *reawakening.*

I grabbed the brown bag and headed downstairs, nearly flying over the steps. Finding my keys, I was speeding down Fleming Street within seconds. I was going to Ice Cave Road.

I made my way to the state highway that ran to the northwest of the county. It was a long stretch of straight two-lane blacktop. I pressed the accelerator to the floor. No cars were in sight and on either side of me were nothing but treeless, far-reaching pastures filled with ankle-deep frozen grasses. The cold air rushing by was brisk, exhilarating. The winter sun was still high, bright, commanding, and now almost blinding against the vast sky of cloudless, delicate blue. It was intoxicating. I could barely contain my excitement. A single word, one simple word. How had I not thought of it before? I laughed at myself, not believing the clarity with which I now saw what I'd previously been so blind to.

Somehow—incredibly—the damned virus had managed to lie dormant with the bottles in the cold, wet darkness of the old ice cave for over ninety years. Knox had said that his father had also gotten the flu. He was the one who had placed them there, there in the icy cold, where they had patiently, silently awaited the opportunity for rebirth. For reawakening.

Toy had likely given away or sold a number of those bottles to friends. One after another they had caught the virus. Quickly, the disease had spread. By an odd chance, Toy hadn't gotten the flu. Somehow, he was immune, whether by some random fluke of exposure or, perhaps, something in his genetic makeup. But that realization stirred in me another revelation, one I knew I would need to discuss with Toy.

When I approached the old McAnders farmhouse, I saw Toy's truck parked outside. I pulled up and cut the engine. Leaning forward, I sat for a moment and stared at the house, my arms draped around the steering wheel. Despite the enthusiasm that had carried me out here, I was unsure what my next move should be, how I should approach Toy. Although I had witnessed firsthand a considerate side to the man, I also knew he had a propensity for volatile, unmeasured behavior. I had heard stories.

I didn't have long to decide. Within moments, he was

standing on the side porch peering at the Corolla. Taking a deep breath, I grabbed the paper bag and got out of the car. As I approached, he offered a cautious smile.

"That you, Doc? What in the world brings you out here?"

As we shook hands, I said, "Hi, Toy. Sorry to barge in on you like this. I just need to figure something out, and I was hoping you could help me."

Toy was absorbing everything carefully, his eyes going to the paper bag in my hands. His answer was clipped. "Okay."

I spoke in a guarded tone. "This flu epidemic that's been going around— It's had me baffled. It's not a strain that anyone has seen. The vaccine doesn't work against it and the drugs we normally use have done a poor job helping people recover. Candidly, I'm surprised someone hasn't died from it yet."

Toy was poker-faced. "I understand, Doc. But how can I help you with that?"

"Well, a thought occurred to me. How in the world could a new strain of the flu surface in Watervalley? And that's when I realized it's not a new strain of flu. It's an old strain. The same one that killed your grandfather's brother, and the one that Knox survived. The flu of 1918."

"I'm still not following you, Doc. What are you saying?"

I carefully pulled the bottle of Scotch from the paper bag. "I got this from John Harris. He's got the flu. He told me about the ice cave and what you found there."

At first Toy's gaze sharpened with suspicion. Then a wry grin spread across his face. He rolled his eyes. "That's quite a theory, but I don't see how some old Scotch could be giving anyone the flu."

"It's not what's in the bottles. It's what's on the outside of the bottles." My voice grew firm. "Look, Toy, I'm not a narc or with the DEA or anything. I couldn't care less about you giving away or selling off a few old bottles of Scotch made by your great-grandfather. But here's the point. Both Knox and his father were exposed to the influenza epidemic of 1918. You know the stories. It killed your grandfather's brother Cullen. But Knox was only eight at the time and he survived it, because this strain of flu hits hardest on those with the strongest immune systems. Men and women in their twenties and thirties are the most vulnerable. Their immune systems react so violently that it chokes their airways. It's called a cytokine storm. Knox's dad was fifty-eight and he also survived."

Toy stared at me blankly.

I continued, "So I'm thinking that when your great-grandfather put those bottles away in the cave, somehow the virus got on the outside of them. Maybe he coughed and it was on his hands as he placed each one on the shelf. I don't know. What I do know is that the cold, dark cave provided the perfect place for this virus to sit dormant. For almost a hundred years it has waited for the opportunity to find new victims. I know you haven't gotten it. For some reason, your genetic makeup isn't vulnerable. That's why this is hard for you to believe."

Toy pulled a cigarette from his shirt pocket, lit it, and inhaled a deep breath. He turned and gazed out across the backyard toward the distant bluff and the entrance to the ice cave. He exhaled the smoke slowly, carefully, and rubbed his chin with his thumb.

"Nah, Doc. I'm not buying it."

"What do you mean, you're not buying it?"

"Pretty simple words. You heard me."

"Toy, that's just not going to cut it."

He shot me a hard look. It was clear he had caught the rising anger in my voice. He flicked his cigarette away, a subtle signal that the amiable part of this conversation was over. His eyes grew sharp, sizing me up, assessing me coolly. The Scottish blood in him smelled a fight. His shoulders were firming back. Instinctively he was squaring up to me. I knew from his reputation that Toy was not one for words. Yet now all the weight of misery, disappointment, and defeat that I had known over the long, exhausting hours treating this damn flu hardened me. I wasn't backing down—not now, not after all the hell of the last week, not after getting this close to the answer. Slow seconds passed. The air between us grew tense, explosive.

Then, just as quickly, an easy grin emerged across his face. He exhaled a small, gushing laugh and looked back into the distance. I knew Toy wasn't afraid of a fight, but apparently he had decided that going to blows with me, right here, right now, would accomplish nothing for him. "Doc, unless you've got something else to add to this conversation, I think we're done here."

I stared at him impassively, desperately considering my next move. I nodded and looked out at the high grassy hills rolling in the distance. I spoke as I stared into the vast expanse of Akin Ridge.

"Look, Toy, I know you're smart. You've probably already figured out where you're going to hide the rest of the Scotch now that the cat's out of the bag. I don't care. I just need to confirm the source of the virus. Think about it. Don't do this, Toy. Just because you haven't gotten sick and neither has your son—"

"My son?"

"Yeah, Toy. Your son, Sam. Sarah got the flu, but you know that of course. She came by the clinic and had Sam all in her face. But he didn't get it—still hasn't. I'm a doctor, Toy. I see bloodline connections in more ways than one with you and Sam. So, yeah, I'm sure of it. He's your son."

I turned and looked squarely at him, speaking low and firm.

"You may be a lot of things, Toy, but I don't think you're a liar. You know he's your son and you also know he hasn't gotten the flu. What I'm saying is true. It's the Scotch bottles. Help me here."

For the longest time his lips pressed firmly together. Finally he nodded, clicking his tongue on his teeth. "Well, okay, then, Doc. So what happens now?"

I smiled. It was all the answer I needed.

When I returned home later that afternoon, I went online and found a medical article I had remembered reading. It was a report on the 1918 flu epidemic done by researchers at Vanderbilt. Working with other research facilities, scientists had resurrected an active strain of the virus by taking it from the remains of flu victims who had been buried in the frozen soil of Alaska. The Vanderbilt researchers had taken blood samples from living survivors of the 1918 flu and isolated the immune cells that created the antibodies to it. Thus, they were able to develop an antidote, a cure that would destroy that particular flu strain. As I read the details, I could hardly contain myself.

After spending several hours on the phone and twisting the arm of some old classmates, I was able to connect with one of the Vanderbilt researchers involved in the study. At first he didn't appreciate being disturbed at home on a Sunday evening. But as the facts poured out, I caught his interest. He agreed that the virus could very well be from the 1918 outbreak. He told me to sit tight and he would call me back.

Two painful hours passed. Finally, around nine thirty, the phone rang. It was a conference call with the professor and the local head of the CDC. I had finally gotten their attention.

Other phone calls followed late into the night and ultimately a plan of action came together. By Monday afternoon, staff from the CDC, the state Department of Health, and Vanderbilt's Office of Vaccine Sciences converged on Watervalley. Lab results confirmed that the strain of flu was, in fact, a resurrection of the 1918 virus.

By Tuesday a mobile clinic had been brought into town to help assist with administering inoculations to those with the flu and to give vaccines to those who had not yet fallen sick. The staff at the clinic once again worked nonstop, but this time there was an exuberance in our efforts. Our patients began to improve within twenty-four hours and no new cases took hold. It was an incredible, ecstatic victory. Just that quickly Watervalley was on the mend.

CHAPTER 32
Conspiracy

The week passed and by Friday life at the clinic had returned to a steady and wonderfully predictable pace. I had decided to wait until after Christmas to disclose to the mayor that I would be leaving town. Christmas Day was less than a week away, the following Tuesday. At noon on that Friday I pulled Nancy aside and told her I had some things to take care of and would be gone for several hours. The mobile clinic was still set up and assisting where needed, but in reality the crisis was over.

"In fact," I told her, "I might not be back at all for the rest of the day. The nurse practitioner in the mobile clinic should be able to handle anything that comes up. If not, give me a call."

Nancy nodded, but appeared puzzled. I was no actor, and even though I hadn't mentioned anything, my polite detachment had probably given the others some cause to suspect I might be leaving. Despite the great relief of having ended the flu outbreak, I'd lately been reserved, distant. Now, taking off in the middle of the day was yet one more thing out of the ordinary, and I couldn't help but think the others would take notice.

I drove the Corolla the few blocks from the clinic to the downtown stores and city hall. The day was cold but bright and sunny. For the first time, I paused to admire the Christmas decorations. The streets were filled with banners, large tinseled balls, and holiday garlands, and many of the churches had constructed magnificent nativity scenes. On the lawn of the city hall was a beautifully lit Christmas tree. Storefronts glowed with displays of red and gold ribbon, bright holiday colors, and twinkling lights.

The normally languid pace of downtown had quickened to a lively step and a feeling of mirthful anticipation filled the air. The stores were vibrant, bursting with activity. Shoppers were everywhere. People greeted each other with exuberance, easy laughter, and the embracing warmth of shared lives. The cold, the sounds of Christmas carols, the brilliant displays, the imminent joy of parties and gatherings had permeated the hearts of Watervalley's inhabitants. The whole town was held in a collective enchantment of the delight and mystery of Christmas.

And the flu outbreak had had the unexpected benefit of serving to blur the hard lines of social distinction. Its indiscriminate hand had respected no degrees of intelligence, wealth, or virtue. It had been a great leveler of aloofness, pride, and privilege. Having been washed in a common fear, the people of Watervalley had exhaled a communal sigh of relief.

I found a parking space in the downtown municipal lot. Normally this small area was half vacant, but the heavy shopping day availed only one or two open slots. I pulled up the collar of my wool coat and warmed my hands in the large side pockets. Rounding the corner toward city hall, I encountered a bell-ringing Santa Claus standing beside a small, colorfully decorated metal bucket. He was calling out a lively "Ho, ho, ho" as he gathered donations for the local food pantry.

Peering out from under his fake beard was none other than Chick McKissick. With his toothy grin, thin frame, and black skin contrasting the red and white of the Santa suit, he was not an image one could easily overlook. Chick was loud, and laughing, and loving it, and seemed as entertained as anybody about the unconventional Santa he made—he was anything but a plump elf.

He recognized me and spoke robustly, extending his hand. "Merry Christmas, Doc!"

I grinned, returning the handshake. "Merry Christmas, Chick. Aren't you a sight?" I began to reach for my wallet, wanting to make a donation.

He became even more animated. "Ho, ho, ho, Doc! Ain't this something? How you like me in this getup? Crazy, huh? Anyway, I'm just doing my part. All the guys in the volunteer fire department are taking turns to raise money for the food bank." He bent toward me and spoke in a confiding tone. "Truth is, Doc, it's hard to ignore a skinny black Santa. I get twice the donations anybody else does." He reared back his head and released a hearty laugh. His joy was contagious.

I laughed and tossed a couple of bills into the bucket.

"Thank you, Doc. Thank you muchly."

I held up my hand in a gesture of departure. Once again, Chick leaned in toward me. "Hey, Doc, let me ask you a question." He looked to either side of himself, ensuring that his next words would be in confidence. "What's going to happen to my little man Will?"

"So I guess he told you everything? About what he's been doing?"

"Yeah, I told him that he and I and his mom needed to go talk to the sheriff. I felt pretty bad, like I was an accessory or something. I had no idea. But he promised me that you were handling the situation. He said he gave you the account details about all the stores and the money. Is that so, Doc?"

"That's right. I am handling it. Matter of fact, that's why I'm here. I want to present an idea to Sheriff Thurman and see what can be done to get this worked out."

"Okay, Doc. That's good. Let me know if I can do anything to help. He's actually a good boy, you know."

I nodded. The cold was starting to penetrate, so I waved goodbye. "I'll keep you posted."

He smiled. "Merry Christmas!"

To my surprise, it seemed that many of the passersby I encountered either smiled or spoke outright to me. One elderly lady I had never met before stopped me, took my hand, and patted it. She simply smiled, thanked me, and wished me a Merry Christmas.

I actually had two matters to discuss with Sheriff Thurman. As I neared the steps to city hall, I stopped and reached into my pocket and felt the leather cover of my checkbook. That would address the first matter. Satisfied, I pursed my lips and walked briskly up the steps to the large wooden front door.

Before the afternoon was over, I'd tied up the loose ends of the second matter with a visit out to Ice Cave Road. My final stop before home was the Foxes' house.

I arrived home a little past five and noticed Connie's car out front. Whether intentionally or not, we had seen each other only in passing for the past week and had spent no time in real conversation. I came through the front door and found her sitting in the living room watching one of the financial news channels. Rhett was lying cozily at her feet. As I entered, she remained fixated on the TV and spoke without looking up.

"Mmm-mmm-mmm. The Dow is dropping like a rock. I need to get online and move some assets around."

I looked at her for a moment, and then at the TV. With a military stride I walked over and hit the off button and turned to address Connie face-to-face. "Constance Grace Pillow, we need to talk."

Connie lowered her head, amused, and looked at me above the tops of her gold-inlay glasses. "I see. And what might we need to talk about?"

I walked to the far side of the room and grabbed a small wooden chair that I placed in front of Connie. I took a seat and rubbed my chin for a moment. "I need to understand something."

A cunning smile tweaked the corners of Connie's mouth. "Well, well, Doctor. Ask away. I see you've learned my full Christian name. No big secret there. I would have told you if you had asked."

"*Watervalley Signal*, valedictorian, class of 1968."

Connie looked away, her mouth pressed tightly, suppressing a wide grin. "So I guess you saw the picture. My heavens, that was back in my Afro Sheen days. Just where did you find one of those old relics?"

"Coffee table, John Harris's. When he came down with the flu he asked me to make a house call. He must have gotten the annual out for some reason. Anyway, I saw it sitting there and thumbed through it for a few minutes. So, you want to fill in some gaps for me?"

"Such as?"

"Connie, look. Actually, it's no big surprise to me that you were valedictorian of your high school class. Watervalley's average IQ is probably not equal to the square root of yours. But what I don't understand is why you never did anything with all that mental horsepower you have."

Connie laughed out loud. "You've got it all wrong, Doctor. At least partly wrong. True, I never did go off to college. But I've put what gifts the good Lord gave me to great use. I have four brilliant children, all of whom I homeschooled for part of their education. You already know one's a nurse. Two of the others have PhDs in chemistry and philosophy respectively. And my oldest, Rayford, works for Goldman Sachs in New York. He manages one of their bond funds. I'm proud of him just like the rest, though I wish I could see him more often."

I shook my head. "Well, that's all fine and good, Connie. But I don't get it. Don't you understand the limitations you've put on your life? You get by on your husband's pension and work as a housekeeper. It seems you could have done so much more."

Connie flashed a mischievous smile and straightened the cuffs on her blouse. She spoke in an unaffected tone, never making eye contact with me. "Not everything is as it appears. Who do you think taught Rayford how to manage a bond fund? My portfolio has more zeros than you have letters in your last name."

"Hold it. You're telling me you're rich?"

Connie looked up at the ceiling, pondering her answer. "Conservatively wealthy would be more exact. It runs into several million."

I was astounded. "Then why, *why* do you work as a housekeeper?"

"Because it is what I choose to do, Dr. Bradford. I enjoy the things money can buy, but I have all that I need. I love this town. It has its eccentrics, its simpletons, and its fair share of just plain mean people, but it also has a lot of good folks too—kind, reliable, and good-hearted. I have history with them, a shared life. We needed a doctor and you needed a housekeeper. It's that simple."

I was awash in amazement. "I don't know what to say."

"You can start by saying where you've been all afternoon. I

called over to the clinic to ask Nancy what time you'd be home and she said you had left for the day. That was hours ago. So?" She tilted her head down, looking at me above her glasses again.

"I went to talk to the sheriff about a couple of things."

"And?"

I grinned. I knew Connie was going to pry the whole story out of me eventually.

"I got it worked out with the sheriff that none of the merchants Will Fox stole from are going to press any charges. Will has to show them how he did it and help them improve their security systems. Besides, Warren says all of them feel a little like a heel pressing charges, given the circumstances."

"What about the money that's owed?"

I hesitated. "Let's just say that's been taken care of."

"Taken care of?"

"Yes, taken care of."

Connie readily gathered that it was not a matter for further discussion. "All right, fine. What was the other thing?"

"What other thing?"

"Stop holding back. The other thing you needed to talk with Sheriff Thurman about?"

"Oh, that. Well, I just wanted to make sure that charges were not going to get pressed in another matter."

"Would this have something to do with you going out to Ice Cave Road today?"

"What, do you have a tracking device on my car or something?"

"No, I was just coming back into town from putting flowers on Mr. Thompson's grave and saw you driving on the north road out in that direction. The rest was a guess. Anyway, I presume you wanted to make sure no charges were being pressed regarding those deadly Scotch bottles. I heard the sheriff confiscated all twenty-five of them."

"Actually, not exactly. Toy and I had a long talk when I confronted him on Sunday. He was pretty shaken up when he realized the Scotch bottles were the carriers of the flu. He took me back into the cave. Showed me everything. That was after I confronted him about Sarah Akins."

"Sarah Akins?"

"Yeah, Toy is the father of Sam, her little boy."

"He admitted to it?"

"Yep."

"How in the world did you figure that out?"

"It first occurred to me at Knox's funeral. I saw Sarah sitting waiting in her car about a block away from the funeral home. She was dressed to attend, but for some reason she was nervous. She seemed undecided about whether to go in. Sarah wasn't related to Knox, but the thought hit me: what if Sam was? After that, there were some small clues. I also noticed at Knox's funeral that Toy had a hitchhiker's thumb. So does Sam. It's pretty rare and Watervalley is a small place, so the odds seemed pretty good."

"And you figured it out from that?" Connie's tone was disbelieving.

I hesitated. "Not exactly. There was more."

"Mmm-hmm. Keep going, Doctor."

I leaned back in the chair, crossing my arms. "It was the flu. Sarah got it; Sam didn't. Toy handled all the bottles. He was in the middle of all the cabinet factory workers with the flu, but he didn't get sick. That level of exposure and no flu couldn't be a coincidence. Maybe something in their genome makes them immune. There's no way to know. But it bugged me and I started digging a little deeper. That's when I discovered the other link. Toy gave blood in the fall blood drive and I had Sam's medical records. They're both AB negative, which happens in less than one percent of the population. Again, it was a huge coincidence for such a little town. I wasn't completely sure, so I bluffed him a little and he opened right up."

"Well, Sherlock, you may have missed your calling. Anyway, what's this got to do with the sheriff?"

"You remember Sarah was underage when she got pregnant, and Toy was twenty-four. Technically, under Tennessee law, that's statutory rape. She's eighteen now and the two of them want to get married, quit hiding everything. But they've been afraid Sheriff Thurman might still want to press charges."

"So I take it he agreed not to."

"He did. Saw no need to stir up trouble for the two newlyweds."

"Praise the Lord for all that. I'm glad to see Toy McAnders is coming around to being a solid citizen. That boy's been a little too crafty and secretive for too long."

I laughed out loud.

"What's so funny now?"

"I think Toy wants to be a responsible husband and father. And I can personally attest that he has a generous side to him. But I wouldn't go so far as to say he's up for sainthood just yet."

"Why's that?"

"You said that the sheriff confiscated all twenty-five bottles from the cave."

"That's what I hear."

"When Toy took me back into the catacombs there were over two hundred bottles in the old distillery room. Sounds like a few of them vanished before the sheriff got there."

"Oh, you don't mean to tell me?"

"I wouldn't worry. Toy's smart enough to make sure the

bottles get disinfected. Besides, for him I guess they're like a family heirloom."

Connie was not pleased with this conclusion. "Humph. I just hope you're right."

I smiled. "Only time will tell. Anyway, it was a good afternoon. Good to get those things settled."

"Sounds like you're tying up loose ends, Dr. Bradford. What now?"

"What now as in . . . ?" I left the statement hanging, inviting Connie to finish it.

"As you recall, Luke, in a previous episode you said you were leaving Watervalley. I haven't told anyone what you said. So I guess I'm wondering if you are still considering this foolishness."

I answered slowly. "I'm not sure. I guess I'm thinking through my options."

"While you're doing all that thinking, I've got something I want you to do for me."

In all the time we'd known each other, I couldn't recall a single time she had asked me for help. "Okay, sure. What do you want?"

"I want you to do what you promised me."

I was puzzled. "And what would that be?"

"When I interviewed with you that first day, I asked if you ever went to church. You said you did. Now I may be mistaken, but I don't think that has happened since you've been living in Watervalley."

I exhaled a deep breath of resignation. "Guilty as charged."

"Okay, then. Fine. This coming Monday night is Christmas Eve. Every year Watervalley has an interdenominational service at one of the big churches downtown. It's a big deal with a huge choir, string quartet, the whole works. This year it's at the Episcopal church at seven."

"Fair enough. I'll be there."

"Good. But there's more."

"More?"

"Yes, each year at the service they recognize one of our citizens who has made a contribution to the community. It took a lot of debate, but this year the interchurch council agreed to honor John Harris."

"Really?"

"Yes. They think it's about time to extend an olive branch to John. Time for forgiveness on both sides."

"I hate to break this to you, Connie, but forgiveness doesn't mean much to a man who doesn't think he's done anything wrong. Anyway, how does this involve me?"

"I need you to get him to come."

"Oh, sure—no problem. Are you *kidding*?"

"No, I'm not kidding. And furthermore, the award is supposed to be a surprise, so you can't tell him."

"Connie, do you have any idea what you're asking? John Harris would rather eat a green bug than be around those people. He hates them. I'd have to anesthetize him and carry him in over my shoulder."

"Whatever works, Doctor."

"Tell me you're not really serious."

Connie stood up and headed toward the kitchen, walking behind me. She stopped and turned back, putting her hand on my shoulder. "Dr. Bradford, you promised me, and just how many times have I asked you to do me a favor?"

I looked over at her hand, then up at her. She was staring down at me with that same look of detached disdain that had defined her from the first moment we had met. I exhaled deeply.

"Well, okay."

"Good!" Connie responded with a large smile. She patted my shoulder and leaned over to me, speaking almost in a whisper. "My, my, Doctor. It seems that we are now bonded in the web of a dark conspiracy." She released a low giggle and continued into the kitchen to prepare dinner.

I sat there wondering what in the world I had just agreed to do.

CHAPTER 33
Valley of the Shadow

I spent Saturday organizing, taking inventory. I checked the attic for boxes, did an assessment of each room, and sized up the effort needed to pack up my life and leave. It was a decision that was still mine to make, one that seemed to teeter precariously in one direction and then another, hour by hour. For over a week, I had told myself I was leaving. At first I had felt relieved, at peace with my decision. Yet each day I found myself faced with divergent voices, alternate thoughts and perspectives. Now leaving was no longer a foregone conclusion, but more of a possibility I was pondering. I was still greatly conflicted and I knew it.

It was three days before Christmas and I still had some shopping to do. In midafternoon I went downtown to pick out a few gifts for the clinic staff. Just as on the day before, there was a spontaneous richness of spirit that permeated the streets and sidewalks of downtown Watervalley. The holiday streets were alive with shoppers, the December air biting cold as people in coats and scarves hurried along loaded down with packages. Many of them smiled and nodded as they passed me. On more than one occasion, people pointed discreetly and whispered with animated faces to their companions. Although the glances and stares were typically friendly, the attention I was receiving seemed out of the ordinary, and I wasn't sure what to make of it. Still, I enjoyed myself.

Late in the afternoon I returned home. In addition to gifts, I had bought a few holiday decorations, including strings of small white lights. I had to laugh at myself, recognizing the illogic of decorating a place that I planned to move out of in a matter of weeks. But the season had caught my sense of wonder.

I had also bought a live evergreen wreath from Hoot Wilson, who had set up shop on the town square, using the open bed of his pickup as a storefront. I hung the wreath on my front door and carefully strung the lights along the porch railing. With Rhett by my side, I walked out to the street to take a look. The cottage glowed with a nostalgic warmth. I was pleased.

Then I noticed the decorations of my neighbors up and down Fleming Street. Although one or two had clearly gone overboard, their yards cluttered with Santas and sleds, reindeer and wreaths in all shapes and sizes, most homes were tastefully but grandly adorned with lights and garlands and a few well-chosen displays. They made my modest decorations seem miserly at best. But I didn't care; mine suited me fine. I made my way back inside to warm up some canned soup for dinner. By nine, I was in bed and sound asleep.

I awoke with a start on Sunday morning to the clanging of church bells. I sat straight up in bed and looked at my bedside clock. It was nine in the morning. What besides the cold weather could account for my newfound capacity for sleep? I had been dead to the world. The church bells had guaranteed an instantaneous resurrection. But why were they ringing so early?

Then I remembered what Nancy had told me. As had been the

custom in Watervalley for decades, on the Sunday before Christmas all the downtown churches rang their bells at the same time for five whole minutes. It was an explosion of sound.

Shafts of morning sunlight bore through my bedroom window. I sat staring at the myriad of dust particles suspended in the air, caught in the path of the illuminating rays. Now fully awake, I pondered all that had happened in the last week, how things had changed so greatly. I recalled this same moment a week earlier, standing in my room and seeing the random particles in the light. Yet now they appeared to have an order, a pattern to their movements. I laughed under my breath. How ironic! The design, the infinite balance had been there all along. The only thing that had changed was my ability to see it.

Ambling over to the window, I gazed out over the town, this little place where I had lived for the past half year. I felt lighthearted. I thought of my aunt and my mother and father and their shared conviction that I would find a home in a small town. I thought of how my aunt had always seen me as a lost little boy in the big city, how her choices regarding my inheritance had deliberately nudged me to a place like Watervalley. In the bright light of that Sunday morning, I felt a new contentment, a sense of belonging that I had not previously experienced, one I found difficult to capture in words.

It seemed strange to me that this glimpse of understanding had grown out of my own experiences in Watervalley rather than from the wise words of loved ones from many years ago. It was something of an epiphany. My parents and my aunt had encouraged me to find purpose as a small-town doctor, to engage in the modest lives of poor and otherwise. Their words had been with me all along, but I had resisted. It seemed that their wisdom had found only lukewarm value without the experience of the journey. Something in me had been asleep for many years. Knox's singular word from my dream had captured it for me. It was a reawakening.

I took care of Rhett, who continued to amaze me with his ecstatic delight over a couple of scoops of dog food. I showered, made breakfast, and spent some time on my computer, hitting a few social sites and catching up with friends. But their names and voices seemed distant. Restless, I decided to grab my coat and walk over to the clinic. Slipping around the Episcopal church, I came in through the clinic's back door. Despite the frost in the air, the hall was warm. All was quiet. I moved to my office, turned on a small desk lamp, and began to sift through the stack of unopened mail and medical journals. Eventually I turned toward the light of the windows behind me.

I stared at the nativity scene on the church lawn next door. My mind was elsewhere. This last task, this ridiculous request that Connie had laid before me, had surfaced through my subconscious and was now consuming me. I knew that sometime today I would have to drive up into the hills and convince John Harris to attend the Christmas Eve service, a task I had no idea how to accomplish. I sat for almost an hour, pondering, brooding. It was nearing noon. I gathered a few papers, turned out the lamp, and locked the back door behind me. While I was walking home, once again the church bells rang loudly in the distance, marking the end of morning worship.

At a quarter past three I pulled into John's driveway. Having heard the car, John was standing at the open front door as I approached the porch. He tried not to show it, but I could discern his subtle delight at having some company.

"Hello, sawbones. You bring me a Christmas gift?"

"Actually, I did. I brought your bottle of Scotch back. But don't worry. This one has been disinfected, so it should be flu safe."

"I don't know, Doc. I'm a little conflicted. Not sure it's good etiquette to take back a gift of a gift."

"Ah. I thought maybe a little later we might both try a glass. Sounds fair enough, doesn't it?"

The surprise on John's face was obvious. I'd turned down all his previous offers of Scotch.

"Okay by me. So come on in."

We sat in the large chairs in the back room, with sunlight pouring in through the wall of windows. A robust fire was burning in the large stone fireplace, giving the room the feel of a rustic but comfortable lodge. Conversation flowed easily between us. John was fully recovered from his illness and the days of isolation had left him pleased to have company. For over an hour we talked about recent events, the weather, and various projects John had in the works. All the while, I was looking for some point of easy entrée to the topic of the Christmas Eve service. None was readily apparent.

At one point, there was a lull in the conversation. John sat staring out the large windows. "Today would have been Molly's birthday, Doc. She would have been fifty-eight and this place would be filled with wreaths and decorations and scented candles from floor to ceiling. She loved doing all that stuff, but it really wasn't necessary. She had the most radiant smile. She lit up the room by just walking into it. It's hard to describe how much life she brought to the place." His voice was matter-of-fact, absent pathos.

"I hate that I never got a chance to meet her."

"Me too, Doc. I think she would have liked you—you know, the way people take a liking to stray dogs."

"Thanks, John. You've just made my whole day. I had no idea you had a capacity for such kind analogy. You and Connie must have the same joke book."

He glanced sideways in my direction with a contented smirk. "Anytime."

"So I guess that means today is your sister-in-law Madeline's birthday."

This brought a slight snarl to his tone and yet another sideways glance. "Yeah. I guess you finally figured that one out. No doubt you also figured out that the in-laws and I are not exactly on the best of terms."

"And why is that?"

"Ah, long story. Probably has something to do with me being a horse's ass. I could go through it all, but to cut to the chase—it's pretty much my fault. And I'm rather content to leave it at that."

"That all sounds very noble."

John laughed. "Careful, Doc. If I didn't know better, I'd say there was a little sarcasm there."

"No, you would be wrong. There's actually a lot of sarcasm in it."

"Yeah, well. It is what it is." John swallowed a low chuckle. He then looked at his watch. "Grab your coat. Let's pop open that bottle and get some fresh air."

John grabbed two glasses and we moved outside. He poured a tall amount of Scotch into his glass, but I halted him after he'd dashed about an inch into mine. "Easy there, bartender. I'll have to drive back in a little while."

He shrugged. "Suit yourself." John carried the bottle with him as we walked out to the far end of the deck and leaned against the railing. We gazed out over the town tucked distantly away in the valley below. Sunset and darkness were rapidly approaching. In one tilt, John emptied the contents of his glass and exhaled deeply.

"Oh, that's good stuff. Doc, you've got me at a disadvantage.

Can't say I've got a gift for you." He proceeded to fill his glass again.

It wasn't much of an opening, but I took it as my best opportunity to broach the subject. "Actually, I do have a favor to ask."

He glanced sideways over at me. "Okay, shoot."

"Well, I'm thinking about going to the Christmas Eve service tomorrow night—you know, the one the town puts together every year."

"Christmas Eve service, huh. Well, now. That doesn't sound like you, Doc. You trying to get a little grace on the cheap?" John took another huge swallow of the Scotch and reached yet again for the bottle to refill his glass.

I laughed nervously. "No, not exactly. Just seems like a good thing to do. And this Christmas gift in return you mentioned—I want you to go with me."

John turned and looked at me deadpan, trying to determine if I was serious. After a moment, he turned his gaze back to the sunset and took yet another large swallow of the liquor.

"No damn thanks. I'm just fine with hiding my light under a basket."

I continued to stare straight ahead, out across the valley, struggling to speak casually. "Oh, what could be the harm? Might even be enjoyable."

"Nah, not for me. I'd rather be a bad example than a hypocrite." John wavered a little. The Scotch was taking effect.

I was frustrated. It was now clear that John was not going to agree to go as a simple favor. We both stood in silence.

John took another swallow. "What's got into you anyway? I didn't think you went for all the Bible-thumper stuff."

"I don't. At least not the way you describe it. But don't mistake reticence for lack of conviction. I'm at peace with what I believe.

If you'll notice, I don't think I'm the one in this duo who feels the need to bring the topic of God up so often."

That last comment bought a wry grin from John. He knew I was right, but he was reluctant to concede the point. "Well, well, well. Touché, Doc. Sounds like you've been putting some thought into the matter."

"I have. With all that's happened here, with everything that, well, that I've been through, I just think I see things more clearly now. That's all."

John scoffed, laughing under his breath. "It just goes to show you're never too old to learn something stupid."

I spoke coolly. "Oh, that's right. I forgot. You're the one who's got all the answers. Did it ever occur to you that you might be wrong? Maybe there is some higher thinking than yours."

"That's just by damn grand, Doc. You've got it all figured out now, huh? So you've decided that the universe isn't random and meaningless, and you're going to tie all the loose ends up in some wonderful what-it-all-means theory. Hell, did it ever *occur* to you that maybe life is just one damn thing after another and all you can do is bow your back and muddle through it?" He was drunk and I knew it.

By now I had turned to face him fully and spoke bluntly, forcefully. "No, John. You've got it all wrong. There's more. There's more than just the day-to-day. Tell me you don't see it. You spend all these hours looking down into the valley looking for something. You don't get it, do you?"

"Oh, screw you. You think you've got all the answers? There's nothing down there for me. But if you're so damn smart, why don't you tell me? Show me what I'm looking for."

Something in me snapped. I wasn't dealing with a man of intelligence and a broken heart. For all his wealth, his intellect, his commanding presence, John Harris was nothing more than a sarcastic jackass. I was furious. I grabbed him by the back of his coat and stood him up from where he was leaning over the porch rail.

"Okay, fine. I do want to show you something." In my muted rage I held his coat firmly with one hand and pointed down toward Watervalley with the other. "You see that? You see that town down there? It's not just a bunch of buildings and cars and people moving aimlessly about. It's life. That's what it is. *Life.* You sit up here and look at Watervalley from a great height, close enough to hear the church bells, see the lights, feel its rhythms, watch its movement. But you don't want to be drawn into the middle of it. Then you might be vulnerable to their thoughts, subject to their opinions. You'd rather box up your pain and cover it in a thick wrapping of cynicism. So, yeah, you were married to a wonderful, beautiful woman. You had something great. I get that. But as much as you say you hate these people, all I see you do is draw as near to them as you can without getting burned, because you're trying to hold her memory warm and keep it as close to you as you can. You think you've got your eyes wide open, but you don't. You're blind and don't see it. You're part of this place."

"So what's your point?" John shouted. He grabbed my arm and yanked himself free of my grip on his coat. Fire was in his eyes.

"The point is, you could make a difference. Bring some light and life into a small corner of the world. I'm sure that all sounds just hokey to you, John, but that's all any of us can do. But no—not you. You're too damn busy being angry at the past. Look, I've been doing the same thing. Just in a different way. All my life I heard what a brilliant doctor my dad was. He could have been a department head at Emory or Vanderbilt or anywhere. But instead he chose to set up practice in a small town in rural Georgia, to take care of people who half the time did nothing to take care of themselves. And all he ever got for his trouble was to be killed by a drunk driver. I never understood. But now I do. He made a difference, and that meant something to him. He made a difference in the lives of people who had no other choices."

John leered at me. "Well, good for you, sport, on your recent enlightenment. If a little hunker-down time in a church pew gives you a warm fuzzy, then knock yourself out. But leave me out of it."

I looked at him sharply, speaking coolly, firmly. "You say you have no use for God and faith and all the church stuff down in the valley. Okay. Fine. But answer me this, since you're the smart one. How is it that you can be so mad at a God you don't even believe exists? Why are you more than willing to take a pill for a virus that's invisible but you give no chance to a God you can't see and no forgiveness to people you can?"

John took a step back and squared himself up to me. For a moment we stood a fist's throw away from each other, seething with anger, taking in and exhaling deep, powerful breaths. His eyes, cold and piercing, were fixed hard upon me. The dulling effects of the alcohol now seemed cast aside and he glared at me with a venomous fire I had not seen before. He stood straight, his powerful shoulders pulled back. The lion of strength within him was finding full fury. In that moment, from the burning glare in his eyes, it seemed that I embodied all the betrayal, all the pain, all the loss that had been tearing him apart and he wanted nothing more than to lash at me, to find in me a tangible object for his anger.

Then his gaze drifted down toward the town. His broad chest heaved with deep, forceful breaths. With only the slightest of motions, he gradually began to nod his head up and down. For a brief second, he looked up at the stars. Without ever looking at me, and without saying a word, he turned and picked his steps slowly up the short rise to the back door of the house.

Without moving, I watched him. I heard the heavy click of the back door latch as John disappeared inside. I stood for a moment longer, looked down, and sighed. I stood silent in the dark. Nothing remained for me to do but go home. I had failed.

I walked to the Corolla. There I paused and looked at the great majestic home one last time. All the lights were out. It stood in the silence, joyless. With all its beauty and splendor, this house was nothing more than a lifeless shell, a walled castle John had made for himself, filled with ghosts of anger and loss that he could not see and refused to acknowledge. Regardless of all his genius, all his rational insight, John had not found the means to change.

High above, the cold stars twinkled brightly, bringing their glimmer of light into even this dark place. I stared up at them and marveled at their unspeakable beauty, the grand, raw perfection of them. Oddly, they offered an unexplainable feeling of consolation that warmed the frigid night air. Despite the swallowing loss, the angry confusion of the last few minutes, I felt that all around me was enveloped in a larger order. It seemed the universe still inspired hope.

Once more I looked back toward the house. I thought of John and felt a pang of grief. I wasn't prepared for this end between us. I realized more than ever that below the acidic veneer, in his own way, John had been an unfailing friend. I would miss him and his constant wit and insight. I would miss the hours of conversation in the small pulpit of his Adirondack chairs, pronouncing on the ebb and flow of life in Watervalley. It seemed my roots in town had reached deeper than I knew.

But we had reached an impasse. The ever-changing tides of life had washed John under and he seemed no longer interested in searching for answers beyond his hardened certainty and a bottle of Scotch.

Inhaling deeply of the frozen air, I thought of John's love of quoting Shakespeare. In a low, whispered voice, I spoke a melancholy salute to my lost friend. "'There are more things in heaven and earth, Horatio, than are dreamt of in your philosophy.'"

I started up the Corolla and began my descent into the shadowed valley before me.

CHAPTER 34
Revelations

It was the morning of Christmas Eve and I awoke once again to the rich, permeating smells of breakfast. A cold front had moved in during the night and my room was chilly. I pulled the covers tightly around myself and closed my eyes for a few moments longer. I yawned. The aromas grew stronger. Buried deep in the warmth of my blanket, I smiled.

Connie, I thought to myself. *You gotta love her.* I could hear the sounds of cabinets closing, pans clanging, and Connie humming a Christmas tune loudly. She was in full acceleration mode and not being very quiet about it. I finally threw back the covers, hastily put on a sweatshirt and jeans, and ambled barefoot down to the kitchen.

Connie was in an unusually cheerful mood. "Good morning, Dr. Bradford."

I stopped at the bottom step and stretched, my hands reaching the stairwell ceiling above me. "Good morning to you too, sunshine. You seem all giddy this morning."

"It's Christmas Eve, Dr. Bradford. Or did you not get the memo?"

I smiled warmly. "Yes, and so it is. Merry Christmas Eve to you, Connie."

"And to you too, Luke."

Rhett came over to the steps and enthusiastically greeted me, his tail wagging and his tongue flapping rhythmically in cadence with his panting. He had been attentively focused on Connie, who no doubt had been slipping him a nibble of egg or bacon. With both hands I grabbed his big hairy head and rubbed behind his ears.

"Hello, big fellow. Food and loving, food and loving—that's all you want, isn't it?"

Connie glanced over her shoulder at me. "He's male. Go figure."

I continued speaking to Rhett. "Pay no attention to the woman in the apron, buddy. She has issues." I stole a glance at Connie, who never looked up from the stove but was clearly smirking and subtly shaking her head. Rhett finally pulled away, no doubt now on a mission to find his throwing ball and bring it to me.

"Is that coffee I smell?"

Connie nodded toward the counter. "Help yourself."

I poured a cup. "So, I was going to offer you some kind of Christmas bonus, but now I'm thinking anything I come up with won't even rank as petty cash on your balance sheet."

Connie's back was to me, but my comment made her laugh. Privately, she loved that I enjoyed picking on her.

"Yes, yes," she said. "Have a good laugh there. Since that cat is now out of the bag, I was thinking about giving you some stock pointers for your Christmas gift. But just keep it up and you can kiss that one good-bye."

"Wow, that's just harsh." I paused, then spoke in a lighthearted ceremonious voice. "But no matter. It is better to give than to receive." I pulled out the small wrapped box I had carefully hidden in the cabinet the night before.

Connie beamed. "Luke Bradford, now just what have you done here?"

"Just a little something for the woman who already has everything—and I do mean everything."

"My, my, my, Doctor. Aren't you the thoughtful one?" She beamed with a rare glow, a suppressed smile that bespoke a moment of pure joy.

"Go ahead and open it."

She carefully pulled away the ribbon and wrappings to reveal a modest white box. Inside was a sealed envelope. Connie unfolded the two papers within it. She stared at them, puzzled. "Well, what in the world is this?"

"Gift certificates. One is for a first-class round-trip ticket to New York. The other is for a three-night stay at a Lower Manhattan hotel. You mentioned a few days ago you never get to see Rayford, your oldest son. I figured you could go see him sometime soon, on me, meals not included."

"Good heavens, Luke. This is too much. Where in the world did you find the cash to afford this?"

"No cash needed. I've had a gazillion miles saved up over the past years. All through school my loans never came through in time to pay for classes. So I paid tuition with a credit card and immediately paid the balance off with my student loans. I racked up a ton of miles. Anyway, I figured you would never fly there on your own, so here you go. Merry Christmas, Connie."

As my words sank in, Connie's face became like a child's, full of wonder. She thanked me profusely, hugged me, and looked repeatedly at the papers in her hand. I was greatly pleased and satisfied that my gift had hit the mark.

Abruptly we both noticed the smell of burning bacon. Connie rushed to the stove, now in a total fuss. She managed to salvage breakfast, and when it was all ready, she sat at the table with me.

"So, Doctor, expecting a busy day at the clinic?"

"Not really. No appointments are set up. The staff is coming in to exchange gifts and enjoy a little Christmas Eve brunch. Should be out by noon. What are you all about today?"

"I'll be down at All Saints Episcopal Church, right next to the clinic, finishing the decorations for tonight's service."

This comment resurrected my memory of the conversation with John Harris. "Oh, yeah, speaking of that. I talked to John yesterday about coming tonight. It didn't go well. I didn't mention that he was to be honored, because candidly the conversation never got that far. But, well, sorry. I tried. I really did."

Connie pursed her lips and nodded. "God made him just like he made you and me. If he doesn't see it that way, that's his affair."

"Yeah, it's a sad business. And, unfortunately, it got a little heated. I spoke to him pretty harshly. Don't think he took it well. I may have botched up any chance of a reconciliation with one of my few friends in this town, all in one short conversation." I actually laughed.

"And this is funny because . . . ?"

"Look, Connie. You may be one of the most amazing people I have ever met. Knowing you has been a real treat, but, beyond that, for me Watervalley has been pretty much a mixed blessing. This falling-out with John is the coup de grâce, the final straw. There's a better fit for me elsewhere, I'm sure. Meanwhile, Watervalley will get along just fine without me."

I didn't let on, but even as I said the words I found them hard to believe myself. I was still deeply torn about leaving.

I expected a lecture. Instead, Connie smiled at me with adoring eyes. "I know your head wants to leave Watervalley, Luke, but

I'm not so sure your heart does. Distant pastures always have a glow, but you're needed here and you know it. Give it some time."

I smiled. "I don't blame you for trying, Connie. I'm even a little flattered. But we'll see."

She rose from the table and began to clear the dishes. "Doctor, the service starts at seven tonight. I assume I'll be seeing you there."

I hesitated and exhaled deeply. "Sure, a promise is a promise."

I showered, dressed, and drove over to the clinic. The staff had brought plate after plate of snacks and cakes and baked goods. Mayor Hickman and Fire Chief Caswell stopped by, bringing fruitcakes and holiday greetings. Only a couple of patients showed up. Both had simple colds, for which I prescribed some medications and gave the usual advice of getting rest and drinking plenty of fluids.

The morning was festive and lighthearted. Gifts were exchanged and the staff spent a little time roasting me about favorite moments from the past half year. I took it all well and felt somewhat guilty, knowing that I was already planning my departure. They were good people. I had shared both joyful and desperate hours with them. I would miss them.

By one that afternoon all the staff had left. I locked the doors of the clinic and drove home. The afternoon was gray and cold. The morning's fog lingered. Even still, the mood of Christmas was in the air. I came through the front door, took off my coat, and stood in the entrance hall. Having come from all the laughter and life of the clinic gathering, home now seemed lonely and empty except for Rhett's cheerful face and wagging tail.

In the previous week I had made several phone calls to some old contacts in Nashville, who assured me there was plenty of emergency room work I could pick up if I decided to move there. Meanwhile, I had received a couple of invitations for Christmas Eve and Christmas Day gatherings from various Watervalley acquaintances, but I had refused them all. Having made the decision in the previous week to leave after the first of the year, it seemed really bad form to do anything but retreat from my connections to the people I had come to know. But now that the day was upon me, I was having regrets. Once again, I had imprudently been the author of my own loneliness. I needed to put this mix of emotions behind me. I needed to get busy with the task of wrapping up my life in Watervalley.

I moved from room to room, unsure of what to do with myself. I decided to gather a few boxes and began to pack some of the books on the shelves in the upstairs office. I examined piles of old magazines, throwing most of them away. I filled a few boxes and then came across a small leather-bound book of poems by the Romantic poets that my aunt had given me, a present celebrating my acceptance to med school. I remembered thinking at the time what an odd gift it was; poetry and the science career I was about to embark on seemed a universe apart. They still did.

Aunt Grace had written an inscription to me in her refined, elegant hand. I opened the front cover and read the words slowly out loud. I could almost hear her strong, tender voice.

Dear Luke,
Wherever you go you will find broken people in your path. Medical school will teach you how to mend their bodies. But never forget simple acts of kindness and the beauty and power of words. Words can give them hope and joy and courage. With words you can mend their hearts. A simple kindness, a simple word, is like a single drop of water. Gathered over a lifetime, they form an ocean of healing.

Love always, Aunt Grace

For some moments I thought of her and the incredible dichotomy she represented, with her sometimes detached and indifferent manner yet her ability to love unconditionally. The inscription was seven simple sentences, yet they embodied who she was and what she wanted me to be: a man capable of using my head without forgetting to bring along my heart. Though they'd never met, she and Connie seemed to be in collaboration. I closed the book and placed it in the packing box. The house was quiet save for the whisperings of voices from long ago.

Nightfall came. I fed Rhett dinner, then made a sandwich and stepped out onto the back porch and was met with an overcast sky. A light misty rain had fallen earlier, but now the temperature was dropping, and any new moisture would surely turn to snow. I thought about the Christmas Eve service and was torn. I knew I should go. I even wanted to go. I did not want the stares, the furtive glances, the myriad reminders that I had kept myself a stranger, an outsider. But even now, the powerful story of Christmas kept me devout, and I had made a promise. I thought of my aunt's words. I knew I would go despite the awkwardness. My heart would simply have to follow.

Around half past six I noticed large flakes falling on the front lawn, illuminated by the porch light. I stepped out the front door and for a short moment watched in wonder at the transformation of Fleming Street into a world of hushed splendor. As seven o'clock approached, my stomach churned. I deeply wanted to avoid this last reminder of my solitude. I decided to go late. The service would last at least an hour, and it was only a ten-minute walk. So at the stroke of the hour I made my way up the stairs to find my hiking boots.

I was lacing them up when I heard a pounding on the front door. It startled me. It had to be some emergency. A dozen panicked thoughts raced through my head. Tumbling down the stairs and into the front hall, I yelled loudly, "Hold on—I'm coming, I'm coming."

I swung open the door, and standing before me with a broad and mischievous grin was none other than John Harris.

"Evening, Doc. Nice place."

"John?"

"In the flesh. What? You look surprised?"

"That would be because I am. I didn't expect to see you here."

"I understand. I didn't expect to see myself here either. But here I am. So, we doing this nod to God or not?"

I shrugged. "Well, sure."

"Come on, then. Hop in the truck. We're already late."

Dumbstruck, I grabbed my coat, closed the door behind me, and nearly skipped to John's idling truck. I was flush with excitement, speechless. By the time the truck had made the first turn onto Church Street, John had taken notice of my silence.

"So how's it going, sawbones? You're not your normal chatty self."

I laughed and shook my head. "I guess I'm in shock. I mean, I'm glad, but I just never would have predicted this."

The truck pulled into the church's packed parking lot and we hopped out.

As we approached the front steps through the thickly falling snow, John looked at me with a sly smile. "Well, it's all a little hard to explain, Doc, but I figure if God is watching everything, the least we can do is act entertaining."

I laughed again. I was still astonished, elated beyond words. I could hardly catch my breath.

We opened the large front door of the church and stepped into the empty narthex. The doors to the sanctuary were closed and since there was no sound coming from inside, I immediately assumed a prayer was in progress. As we approached the sanctuary doors, I grabbed John's arm.

"John, look—I'm really glad you came, but you need to know something before you go in. Every year, you know, they recognize someone who's been important to the town. Well, I was told it was to be a surprise, so I didn't tell you yesterday. But this year, it's you."

John had abandoned his jovial mood. He stood expressionless. Then slowly the wily grin returned. He put his left arm around my shoulder and with his massive right hand he pulled open the sanctuary door. "No, sport," he said. "It's not me. It's you."

"What?" By now he had ushered me into the cavernous, candlelit sanctuary. Every pew was full and a large choir sat behind the distant pulpit. The room was silent. Everyone was seated except for one person. Standing in the center aisle just inside the sanctuary doors was Connie. She nodded to John and approached me with her typical disdainful gaze. She turned and stood beside me, taking my elbow. "You're late. Come with me, Dr. Bradford."

We began to walk down the center aisle toward the front of the church. At first I resisted, but in my shock and with Connie's firm grasp, I began stepping along with her. As we passed the back pew, I saw Toy McAnders sitting with Sarah Akins and Sam. Toy immediately stood up and began to clap loudly and methodically. Then each successive row gradually rose and began to clap. By the time we were halfway down the aisle, the applause had grown to a thunderous roar. I recognized a sea of familiar faces: Sheriff Thurman, Leo Sikes, the librarian Herbert Denson, Maylen Cook, Lida Wilkins, Chick McKissick, even Polly Fletcher, and dozens of others. They were all smiling at me. Connie was looking straight ahead and now wore a beaming grin.

I could not grasp what was happening. "I don't understand," I whispered to Connie. "I—I don't understand."

Connie tightened her grip on my elbow. "Just keep walking, Doctor. It will all be fine."

The roaring applause continued. All the people of Watervalley turned to me as we passed. They formed an ocean of smiles. My heart rose with an unspeakable joy.

I became filled with the spontaneity of the moment and leaned over to Connie. "Are we getting married?"

She stifled a snorting laugh and immediately regained her stoic face, whispering to me, "You're in the Lord's house. Act like you're housebroken."

Connie and I arrived at the front pew, where two spots had been saved for us. Already seated were Will Fox and his mother, Louise. Her face was filled with healthy color and she gave me a soft, grateful smile. Following Connie's lead, I sat.

The crowd continued to stand and the applause echoed even louder. Finally, one of the ministers standing at the front approached the pulpit. I recognized Frank Whitfield, pastor of the Episcopal church. He smiled warmly at me and held up his hands to the crowd. The applause slowly receded and everyone sat down again.

Pastor Whitfield spoke. "Dr. Bradford, just as on your first day in Watervalley, you make quite an entrance."

This brought a ripple of laughter from the crowd. I looked down with a smile of embarrassment.

"As many of you know," he continued, "each year we give thanks for one of our own who has touched our lives. I can think of no time when the community has been so united on choosing that individual." He turned to me. "Dr. Bradford, thank you for coming to Watervalley and being one of us. You've listened to us, cared for us, and used the gifts God has given you to cure us. We count ourselves blessed to have you among us."

As he finished these words, the entire choir rose in applause. Once again, everyone in the sanctuary stood and clapped. Connie's face was full of generous pride. It was all overwhelming. Those directly behind me patted me on the shoulder and I sat completely humbled. Tears of irrepressible joy welled up in my eyes.

Finally I stood and sheepishly held up a hand in thanks to the crowd. Then I sat down again.

Pastor Whitfield motioned for the congregation to sit as well. He then nodded to the organist, who began the opening strains of "O Come, All Ye Faithful."

I was relieved that the service had finally started and the focus was no longer on me. As the choir and congregation sang the verses of the song, I sat in complete wonder. A startling thought suddenly hit me, hard. I leaned over to Connie. "Hold it. You lied to me. You did. You lied to me. You told me John Harris was being honored."

Connie glanced sideways at me, unmoved by the accusation. She whispered in return, "I knew it'd be good for you to ask John to come. Let's just say I was killing two sinners with one stone."

I absorbed Connie's response for a moment. Again I whispered, "Humph. Doesn't change anything. You still lied."

Connie frowned, facing straight ahead. "Whine all you want, Doctor. Jesus is on my side on this one."

I had to swallow a grunted laugh. I smiled and whispered playfully, "What makes you so sure?"

Again Connie glanced sideways over to me but this time she did so with a confident smile. "Jesus loves us all, Doctor. But I'm his favorite."

It was all I could do not to laugh out loud. I shook my head and smiled, then reached over and squeezed Connie's hand. She sat looking straight ahead, but reached over with her other hand and placed it on mine, giving it a good squeeze. Then, releasing my hand, she brushed the corners of her eyes. My astonishment was complete—Connie Thompson moved to tears.

The service continued with hymns and prayer and a short message. I was humbled and thankful to be once again in a place of worship. It had been too long. I was also shocked to note that John Harris had taken a place in the back row of the choir, among the basses. Apparently he had slipped in there after handing me off to Connie.

During one of the hymns, I whispered to Connie, "Look at John up there in the choir. What got into him anyway?"

"Apparently you did," she whispered. "He called me early this morning and wanted to know the details. He practiced with us this afternoon. He probably never told you, but he used to sing in the choir every Sunday."

I shook my head. It was all so unbelievable.

As the service was drawing to a close, I noticed on my program that the final song featured a short solo by none other than Christine Chambers. All along I'd been watching her in the choir, where she looked radiant and beautiful. She eventually met my gaze. I couldn't bring myself to break away from staring. She looked down, but was noticeably smiling. The time for her solo was coming up.

In the soft candlelight, Christine's clear voice sang "Advent Come." The velvety, almost distant sound of the quartet of strings, the deep, low pitch of the organ, and the muted but perfectly blended harmony of the choir warmly joined in. As the soft, melodious notes filled the church with calls for a new heaven and a new earth, I closed my eyes and could feel around me the swell of life that was Watervalley. The people here knew sickness and setback and disappointment. I had seen that firsthand. But along with the faith they expressed within these walls was a fundamental belief in the goodness, the value, the beauty of life. These people of Watervalley had forgiving spirits, a sense of optimism, and a joyousness that lifted them over the muck and routine of their daily lives. At that moment I fully realized the importance of my life here. There was a larger agenda that transcended my small plans and gave my life a significance it would not otherwise have. Many miles away were bright lights, glamorous places, art, entertainment, and endless possibilities of new relationships. But I was here, with these people, and I found myself thankful to be counted among them.

After the service, I walked out onto the steps and sidewalk in front of the church, shaking hands with well-wishers, exchanging holiday greetings, and receiving an endless stream of thanks. I felt someone come up from my side and gently grab my arm with both hands. It was Christine.

She pulled the length of my arm tightly in next to her, wrapping it in a delightful hug, and whispered softly, "Do you remember what I said to you the first time you asked me out?"

My mind was still in a spin. I exhaled a soft laugh. "Wow. Um, no. You got me. Help me out here."

Christine gently placed her finger on my chin, pushing my gaze toward the steps of the church where her uncle, John Harris, was in a robust and laughing conversation with the mayor and his wife. She whispered deliciously into my ear, "I told you the devil would be singing Christmas carols before you and I hit the town. Since it looks like you've pulled that off, give me a call sometime." She squeezed my arm again, yielding herself into me. Then she smiled and lightly ran her finger down the length of my nose, and with a teasing grin she walked away. She joined her mother, who stood waiting nearby, and they departed toward their car.

After a few steps Christine glanced back at me with a most luxurious smile. About that time I heard a voice behind me. It was Connie, leering at me with her standard judgmental face. No doubt she had witnessed the brief conversation between Christine and me. She shook her head from side to side and forced a low hum between her closed lips.

"Mmm-mmm-mmm."

"Okay, what?" I responded in a puzzled tone. With all that had passed, I no longer lived in dread of Connie's scornful glares, although secretly I still had a healthy respect for them. "C'mon. Why the frowny face?"

Connie broke into a robust laugh. "Well, well, well, Doctor," she said as she reached over to straighten the collar on my overcoat. "You're just in a dream right now, aren't you? You held off an epidemic and the whole town adores you. You quietly solved a series of ongoing crimes. You got the meanest man on earth to sing some praises. And suddenly the prettiest girl around is taking a serious interest in you. Now what you got to say for yourself?"

I paused for a moment to look up into the night sky, at the beauty of the snow falling thickly and gently upon the world around me. Then I flashed an irrepressible smile at her and said, "Well, Connie, if it is a dream, then wake me up in Watervalley."

POSTLUDE

Luke walked home from church. Alone, but not lonely. Passersby yelled, "Merry Christmas, Doc!" The streets echoed with the sounds of laughter and carolers and distant ecstatic conversations as people made their way home through the muffled beauty of snow and streetlights. The moment was filled with an unexplainable serenity. As he neared home along Fleming Street, he couldn't help but notice the incandescence of all the houses. Each of them had a warmth and a glow and he could feel the excitement, the anticipation, the spontaneous mirth of the people inside. Luke felt that he could go up to any one of these homes, knock on the door, and be ushered in with shouts of welcome and delight. Just knowing that was enough. He smiled deeply. Then slowly he climbed the porch steps and unlocked the front door. Rhett greeted him warmly with an excited face and a wagging tail. He turned on a few lamps and put on some old familiar Christmas music. His thoughts were merry and reflective, and he pondered happy memories of Christmases from years gone by.

In time he walked out onto the back porch for one last look at the muted tranquillity of the falling snow. Now only a few scattered flakes were coming down. He tried to catch one of them on his tongue as he had done as a child, but had no luck. So he held out his hand and managed to catch a single large, beautiful flake in his palm. He stood there marveling at its symmetry and design. It spoke of an order in the universe, of patterns he had been unable to see before. His eyes were drawn upward, where the first faint flickers of distant stars were visible in the clearing night sky. Eventually he turned to go back inside. That was when he noticed that the snowflake that had been in the upturned palm of his hand was now a single drop of water.

ACKNOWLEDGMENTS

The journey from idea to bookstore shelf is never one an author travels alone. Many have directed and supported me along the way, some without ever knowing it.

Many thanks to my dear friend Buck Young, who always encouraged me and whose gift of storytelling I have always envied. A hearty thanks to Karyn and Paul and all the rest of the cardiac surgery team at Sacred Heart Medical Center in Springfield, Oregon, who provided a wonderful place to work during the months in which much of this book was written. Many thanks to David Hagberg, who saw a spark of possibility in the early manuscript, and to Susan Gleason, who agreed to take me on despite what I suspect was probably her better judgment.

And finally, tremendous thanks to Ellen Edwards, my delightful and demanding editor, and the talented team at Penguin, who have shown such great enthusiasm for this project. For a son of the South, my red Solo cup runneth over.

Photo by Amanda Hagler

After growing up on a farm in rural Tennessee, **Jeff High** attained degrees in literature and nursing. He is the three-time winner, in fiction and poetry, of an annual writing contest held by Vanderbilt Medical Center. He lived in Nashville for many years, and throughout the country as a travel nurse, before returning to his original hometown, near where he now works as an operating room RN in open-heart surgery.

CONNECT ONLINE

www.jeffhigh.com
www.watervalleybooks.com
facebook.com/JeffHighWriter

READERS GUIDE

MORE THINGS in HEAVEN and EARTH

A NOVEL OF WATERVALLEY

JEFF HIGH

READERS GUIDE

A CONVERSATION WITH JEFF HIGH

Spoiler Alert: The Conversation with Jeff High and Questions for Discussion that follow tell more about what happens in the book than you might want to know until after you read it.

Q. This is your first novel. Have you always wanted to write, and what took you so long?

A. I studied English literature as an undergraduate and have always had a love of writing. For decades I worked on various projects, including some poetry and a couple of novels, strictly for my own entertainment. Then, a few years ago, on a whim while working at Vanderbilt Hospital, I entered the medical center's annual writing contest. To my surprise, I won—three years in a row! That affirmation convinced me to pursue writing with greater determination, and I eventually completed *More Things in Heaven and Earth*. Even still, despite my long gestation as a writer, I think the timing was right. What I would have written about and how I would have written it would have been very different ten and certainly twenty years ago. The passing years have tended to sharpen my perspective.

Q. What were your sources of inspiration for the novel?

A. There were several, but perhaps foremost is that I wanted to write about what I believe is fun and good and wonderful about life in a small Tennessee town. I also wanted to write a story about seeking home, about finding our place in this world. We all have moments when we struggle to understand the direction our lives are taking and the forces that are shaping them. Just as the title implies, *More Things in Heaven and Earth* endeavors to bring light to these questions in the unlikely, unsophisticated setting of Watervalley, Tennessee.

Q. Where did you get the idea for the title?

A. The title is taken from Act 1, Scene 5 of Shakespeare's *Hamlet*, when the ghost of Hamlet's father has just visited him. As the ghost is departing, Hamlet's pragmatic friend Horatio barges in on them. Hamlet insists that Horatio not tell anyone what he has seen. Horatio sees the world only through a lens of rationality and is uncomfortable with the whole business, calling it "wondrous strange." To this Hamlet replies, "There are more things in heaven and earth, Horatio, than are dreamt of in your philosophy." In essence, Hamlet is telling him that there is more to this life than what we see before us.

This idea rings true for Luke Bradford as he comes to understand his role as the new doctor in Watervalley. The events of his first six months in town help Luke to eventually realize that there may be a higher order at work in the ebb and flow of his life. The antithesis to this perspective is that of the emotionally hardened and rational John Harris, Luke's best friend. One of the pivotal points of the story occurs when Luke confronts John with the possibility of a higher order and later remarks that there are "more things in heaven and earth" than John's cold, caustic nature will admit.

In addition, although he does not appear as an actual apparition, the long-lost voice of Luke's dead father is quietly at work in his thoughts, counseling him by day, inspiring his dreams by night, affecting the choices he makes. These parallels make Hamlet's quote a fitting title.

Q. You mention some negatives but mostly praise the virtues of small-town life. What do you particularly like about living in a small town?

A. Having grown up in the South, I have known plenty of people, both black and white, whose economic station in life was far beneath their exceptional wit and wisdom and intelligence. I always admired these people and wondered about their lives. In the small town in which I grew up, there was a permeating goodness, a genuine sense of community that was part of my everyday world. Don't misunderstand me—bad things happened. There was crime and prejudice and social exclusion. But there was an overriding common bond among all of us, a connectedness to one another that found expression in the simple acts and gestures of daily life. Perhaps it was an outgrowth of our agrarian roots, but the people I grew up with had a tough-minded independence coupled with a devotion to community. We had to work together to overcome life's difficulties. Tennessee's moniker as "The Volunteer State" is not just a slogan to attract tourists. It is a description of the mind-set, the attitude of the people I knew and have known all my life.

Q. Your medical background is an obvious asset in writing about a doctor, but where did you get the idea for the revival of the flu virus of 1918? Is such a thing really possible?

A. In the August 22, 2008, edition of the *Reporter*, a Vanderbilt University Medical Center publication, there was an article about researchers who resurrected an active strain of the 1918 flu virus from victims of the disease whose bodies had been preserved in the frozen soil of Alaska. Conversely, by taking samples of blood from living individuals who had survived the 1918 flu epidemic—all were between ninety-one and one hundred and one years old—they were able to isolate antibodies to the virus that could be used as a cure.

I was fascinated by this work and greatly struck by the idea that the virus had remained dormant for nearly a hundred years, waiting for the right conditions to reemerge. It was powerful, real-life science and made for a captivating aspect of my story.

Q. Who are your favorite characters in the book? Did any take on lives of their own and surprise or confound you with the direction they made the story take?

A. Without doubt Connie is the most fun. There is a very real intensity about her as a force to reckon with, and yet she can be a humble, selfless person. Her remarkable intellect not only gives her personality tremendous depth but also allows her to have a very sharp, dry wit. Connie is a fusion of several women I have known who were intelligent, clever, and insightful but worked in modest circumstances. Their lack of education and opportunities had limited their career potential, but not their wisdom, their moral grounding, or their sense of purpose in everyday life. And, man, were they funny.

Q. You were raised in Tennessee and have returned to it in recent years. Would you share with us what makes the state special to you?

A. Tennessee and Tennesseans typically invoke some iconic images, but the state is actually incredibly diverse. Most people don't realize it, but it is farther from Mountain City to Memphis than it is from Nashville to Chicago or even from Nashville to New Orleans. The geography is different, the people are different, and, notably, the music is different. In Tennessee we have bluegrass from the Appalachians, blues from Memphis, rock all the way from Elvis the King to the Kings of Leon, and of course Nashville is well known for country. And common to every region of the state is an incredible depth of gospel music. Music is the Facebook wall of daily life for Tennesseans. It is where we find expression.

I am from Middle Tennessee, which has beautiful rolling hills and endless woods and open fields. As in much of the state, agriculture has historically been the economic mainstay. And while this is changing, the values of that agrarian culture are still firmly rooted. That is why, even though I have lived on the East Coast and the West Coast, Tennessee will always be home.

Q. Do you have any funny or astounding stories about life in a small town that you didn't include in the book but are willing to share here?

A. Wow. I could fill up several books with absolutely wonderful and hilarious stories of life in small-town Tennessee. In the community where I grew up, there was (and still is) a daily radio show called the *Swap Shop*. People call in with something they want to sell or buy—everything from tractor parts to bridesmaid dresses. Often bizarre, the items can absolutely crack you up. And even though I talk just like them, sometimes you can't help but laugh at the thickness of the callers' Southern accents.

Q. Are you as high on reading as you are on writing? If so, what kinds of books do you gravitate toward? What writers have inspired you?

A. I am very much a classics guy and probably don't read as many contemporary authors as I should. My greatest love is the Romantic poets up through the work of Tennyson. I also love a wide array of British and Irish novelists, including Henry Fielding, Sir Walter Scott, Robert Louis Stevenson, and James Joyce. I find myself going back and rereading these guys over and over again. And, of course, who doesn't love Jane Austen?

Southern gothic writers have also had a huge influence on me, particularly Flannery O'Connor, William Faulkner, and Thomas

Wolfe. Conversely, however, even though I see the same depravity that they did, I tend not to write about it in the same light. I'm inclined to see the more redemptive aspects of Southern life and, invariably, that is reflected in my writing.

Q. Can you tell us something about your process as a writer, and how it's still evolving?

A. Situations and words from everyday life and everyday people seem to find their way into my books. Perhaps it is from my affinity with the Romantic poets, but the lives of ordinary people—their trials, their delights, their foolishness, their wisdom—fascinate me. As well from the Romantics, my writing will likely always reflect a love of nature and a devotion to the soil.

Also, somewhere along the line it occurred to me that whatever I wrote couldn't be anything my mother would be embarrassed to review with her book club. Even though she is eighty-three, I would never hear the end of it. For this reason, my writing will probably always get a PG rating.

Q. What do you most look forward to about being a published writer? What has surprised you about the publishing process so far?

A. Without any doubt, the possibility of connecting with people who perhaps in some small way have been entertained or enlightened by my words is a very exciting prospect. My hope is that the book will find a broad audience and that it will resonate with those who do find it. What a wonderful gift that would be.

Candidly, the publishing process has been delightful, albeit sometimes a slow one. As a writer, having a team of professionals on hand for editing, cover art, and advice is an absolute ride, a wonderful thing. The biggest surprise came when I was told I would need to create a social media presence for the book. Ultimately, this led to the creation of WatervalleyBooks.com, which is a great place for readers to learn more about Watervalley. It will allow me to do what I love best: share more about small-town Tennessee life.

Q. You obviously plan to write more Watervalley novels. Can you give us some hints of what to expect next?

A. The next book will likely pursue the evolving romance between Luke Bradford and Christine Chambers, but it will be even more about events in Watervalley's past that bubble to the surface in the present. The story will evolve around an unsolved murder mystery (the only one in Watervalley's history) from a half century ago and how dire events surrounding that murder have secretly rippled through lives in Watervalley over many decades. Redemption of life's injustices will be a central theme.

Q. Where can we go to learn more about Watervalley?

A. Readers can go to WatervalleyBooks.com to catch up on everything happening in Watervalley. The Web site has monthly short stories and articles where readers can learn more about the characters in Watervalley and the history of the town. They can also learn about upcoming Watervalley events and news, get some of Lida Wilkins's favorite recipes from the Depot, and obtain invaluable automotive and fishing advice from Chick McKissick. There will be plenty to put a laugh in your day.

QUESTIONS FOR DISCUSSION

1. What do you think you will best remember about this book six months from now?

2. Luke Bradford feels like a misfit in Watervalley. Are there concrete reasons for that, or does his attitude color his perceptions? How do his thoughts and feelings about the town change over the course of the novel?

3. Discuss how Luke's past has shaped him. In honoring the wishes of his family, is he hopelessly old-fashioned and out of touch with the times? Or do you think he is a model and more people should follow his example?

4. Who is your favorite character, and why?

5. Connie Thompson is starchy and dignified on the outside but has a heart of gold on the inside. Have you ever known someone like her?

6. John Harris has allowed his anger at the townspeople to drive him into seclusion. Do you find his turnaround at the end convincing? Why or why not?

7. Discuss Will Fox—the challenges he faces at home, his computer hacking, and how Luke and others in town resolve these issues. Do you know kids who are troubled, or in trouble? How have their problems been resolved, and what does that suggest about the communities they live in?

8. Discuss the miracle that saves Hoot Wilson's life. Have you ever experienced a real-life medical miracle?

9. Have you ever lived in a small town? How does that experience compare to life in Watervalley?

10. What makes Watervalley Southern? How might a small town in New England, the Midwest, or the West differ?

11. How does Jeff High's Watervalley series compare to other series you might have read, such as Patrick Taylor's Irish Country series or James Herriot's veterinarian series?

12. The flu of 1918 plays an important role in the story. Unlike the original epidemic, which killed millions around the world, everyone who becomes sick in Watervalley recovers. Discuss why that is. Can we depend on medical advances to prevent such loss of life in the future?

If you enjoyed

MORE THINGS in HEAVEN and EARTH,

then we hope you'll want to return to Watervalley by reading Jeff High's next Watervalley-set novel

EACH SHINING HOUR

coming in October 2014
in paperback and e-book.

Turn the page for a sneak peek at an event that occurred long ago but still affects the current-day residents of Watervalley, and catch up with Luke Bradford just as he's about to meet a lively new resident in town . . . in a most peculiar way.

PRELUDE

Watervalley, Tennessee
April 28, 1944

The grass was taller here, moist and cool in the dark April night, only a few sloping steps away from the road. He would rest for a while, keeping his hand pressed firmly over the small bullet hole above his right hip. But the handkerchief . . . the handkerchief was getting soaked.

"It must have been a low-caliber pistol," he whispered. "Perhaps a twenty-two." It was only a small wound.

He had been running. His suit was drenched with sweat. As he lay in the fresh, delicate grass, steam rose from him and drifted elusively into the soft air. He breathed in great heaving gasps, staring up into the vast, silent sky, an eternal canopy pulsing with a million radiant stars.

It was the telegram. He had come back for the telegram. He'd thought it was with everything else. But when he'd buried the box, he hadn't found it.

In his agony, he whispered softly: "Oh, Elise; dear, precious Elise."

He would tell her everything. Explain everything. His mind drifted. His eyes wanted to close. Then, down the far reaches of the road toward town, he heard the long, slow wail of a police siren. He stiffened. His thoughts raced. They were coming. Someone at one of the farmhouses must have heard the gunshot. He flattened himself deeper into the tall grass.

The car blew past, flying headlong toward the lake and stopping in the distance, the headlights pouring across the bandstand. No one had seen him. He would have to wait before moving again.

Once more he stared briefly into the infinite heavens. But now the stars were fading. "Elise; darling, beloved Elise. I will . . . I will tell you. . . ." His breathing slowed. His eyes were surrendering. They grew tired, heavy, and in his delirium, he spoke tenderly, sliding into the distant language of his childhood. "I will tell you. . . . über die Diamanten.*"*

I will tell you about the diamonds.

CHAPTER 1
Estelle

As I approached, I could see that getting past her was going to be difficult. The woman, bless her heart, was large, blocking part of the grocery aisle. Her askew and drifting cart was barricading the balance of it.

She seemed lost to another world, intensely focused on a midshelf item. And there was something about the red spandex covering her lower half that was difficult to ignore. Even though her vibrant and oversized Christmas-themed sweater hung sloppily past her considerable hips, the spandex was clearly not the most complimentary fashion choice, like memory foam that had lost its memory. For anywhere in the South, and especially for Watervalley, the outfit took unabashed flamboyance to a new level. Moreover, although the scent was pleasant, she had apparently chosen to marinate herself in perfume.

Absorbed in the moment, she was oblivious to my presence. I was about to utter a simple "Excuse me" when suddenly the woman bolted upright. She jerked violently with a convulsion that seemed to start at her ankles and rippled viciously up through her entire body, ending with a fierce shuddering of her head and hands.

"Sweet Jesus," she exhorted, "that was a big one!" She took a deep breath, regaining herself.

After a stunned moment, my doctor instincts kicked in. "Ma'am, are you okay?"

I had startled her, if that were possible, given what I had just witnessed, and she gasped lightly. Then, just as quickly, she responded with radiant animation.

"Oh hi, sugar! I did *not* see you standing there."

"Ma'am, do you need to sit down?"

She smiled broadly and flipped her hand airily toward me. "No, no, no, I'm fine, sweetie. I was just having one of my moments." I gauged her to be about fifty, and despite her robust size, she had a lively, pretty face with near perfect chocolate brown skin. She wore no shortage of holiday-colored bracelets and beads and ornate earrings, all of which were adventurous by Watervalley standards but just short of gaudy. And despite her gushy delivery, she spoke with a subtle articulation that wasn't the norm for around here. It had definitely been molded in an urban setting.

She reclaimed her wandering shopping cart and smiled warmly at me again, speaking with another quick gesture of her hand. "You have a nice day!" Then with an emphatic, cheery nod, she proclaimed, "Happy holidays," and was off.

I returned the smile and nodded cautiously. "And you as well."

She continued at a leisurely pace down the aisle. I paused for a few moments to give her some distance. But after five or so steps, she once again halted and stood straight up at rigid attention with her entire body quaking and shuddering so violently that she rattled her grocery cart.

"Sweet heavens!" she announced in a loud voice.

I immediately left my own cart and dashed to her side. "Ma'am, something's definitely not right here. I'm a doctor. Are you having some kind of seizure?"

She regained possession of herself, and regarded me with the same engaged, bright face. "Goodness, sugar, are you Dr. Bradford? I have heard just *so* many wonderful things about you."

"Well, yes, I am Luke Bradford, but right now, ma'am, I'm more concerned about you. You seem to be having some kind of neurologic episode. Are you epileptic by chance?"

She dipped her head, pursing her lips in a beaming smile. "Listen to you. Aren't you just the sweetest? No, honey, I'm not epileptic. It's just my silly pacemaker. Sometimes it gets a mind of its own and shocks me for no reason. It usually quits after two or three times. So I'm fine, just fine."

"Ma'am, if the ICD on your pacemaker is shocking you, it may mean that your heart is in a lethal rhythm. I think we need to get you over to the clinic." Numerous times in my brief medical career, I had had to deal with patients in cardiac arrest. But the heroics needed to care for someone in remote Watervalley made this situation an absolute adrenaline shot. This lady needed critical medical attention, and fast.

"Oh, that's not necessary. I can tell when I'm tachycardic because my hair tingles." She gave a light pat to her head and increased the wattage of her smile.

"Well, you may be right, but I still think it best to get you over to the clinic immediately. We have a pacemaker programmer and I can analyze yours in a matter of minutes."

She studied me for a brief moment with no break in her effervescent smile. Then she shrugged her shoulders. "Dr. Bradford, it's *really* not necessary. But something tells me you're not giving up on this, are you?"

I grinned, shaking my head.

She exhaled in resignation. "Well, okay, if you insist. So, look, I've got four more things on my list. Let me just grab those and I can follow you over there."

I stood dumbfounded. Given the gravity of what was happening to her, this idea left me incredulous. "Ma'am, I was actually considering calling the EMTs and having you taken to the clinic right away."

Once again she flipped her hand at me in dismissal. "Oh, sugar, it is not worth that much trouble. Just let me grab these few items and I'll meet you in the parking lot."

Despite what I considered a potential disaster, it was clear that I was not going to win this part of the argument. I sought compromise. "Okay. I'll help you round up what's left on your list and then you can ride with me over to the clinic."

She folded her arms, giving me a look of complete adoration. Her words began in a high pitch of inquiry and then descended lower. "Really? You're willing to do that? Well, darling, if that's the case, then you may need to pucker up 'cause I might be laying a little bit of heaven on you."

I paused, slightly taken aback. "Well, thanks. But I'm sure that won't be necessary." I wasn't certain what to make of that comment or of this incredibly colorful, unreserved woman. She was patently unconcerned and, admittedly, was showing no symptoms of cardiac distress. "So, tell me what things you need," I said.

I grabbed the last few items on her list and met up with her in the checkout line. Wanting to move quickly, I grabbed her bags and headed for the door. But the woman had other ideas. Her top pace was more of a saunter and her jovial manner was a clear indicator that she saw no urgency in the situation. With pained effort I bridled my steps to keep even with her. Meanwhile, she was talking nonstop about how happy she was to be back in Watervalley, and about the warm day, and about starting a new business, and occasionally injecting some adoring commentary about how kind I was being. But truthfully, I felt more duty-bound than kind. As the only doctor in Watervalley, I knew full well that this woman's ill health was mine to deal with, either now or later.

Impatiently I walked toward my old Corolla. But as we neared she spoke up. "Oh, that's my car next to yours. Do you want to just take it?" Beside my shabby Corolla was a late-model BMW with a license plate that read "BonBon1."

Driving her car threw too many variables in the mix, so I insisted that we take mine. I tossed her few bags of groceries into the backseat and opened the passenger door, only now realizing that my pocket-sized car might be an uncommonly awkward fit for a woman of her heft. To ease the process, I took her hand and arm to help her squeeze in. With some effort she maneuvered into the front seat and swung both feet inside.

I was just about to release her when a lightning bolt jolted me to attention and zipped up my arm. The whole world went black.

When I awoke I was seeing double, lying with my back on the pavement and my face pointed skyward. The large woman was peering over me, but she had two faces. One was leering at me with scornful disdain while the other regarded me with a wide-eyed look of innocent anticipation. Then I realized I wasn't seeing double. Standing above me was none other than Connie Thompson, my devoted, critical, and—ironically—wealthy housekeeper, and beside her, the walking Christmas-ornament lady from the grocery store. Against the clear blue midday December sky, they looked like twins.

I pushed myself to a sitting position and rubbed the back of my head, where a considerable knot was rising.

Christmas-ornament lady bent over and held my cheeks

between her plump, fragrant hands. "Oh, sweetie, I am so sorry. My silly pacemaker went off while you were holding my arm. The car tires insulated me, but the jolt must have grounded through you. You fell back and bumped your head on my Beemer."

Connie, on the other hand, peered at me sternly through her gold-inlay glasses. She spoke in her typical expressionless, no-nonsense manner. "Dr. Bradford, do you need medical attention?"

I sat there for a moment with my arms crossed over my knees and eventually looked up again at the two women, one with the face of an eager puppy, the other with that of a disapproving schoolteacher. I pondered Connie's question and responded impassively, "Yeah, looks like I have a lump on my head. What say you kiss it and make it better?"

Connie rolled her eyes and regarded me with placid disdain. Her voice was absolute deadpan. "Why am I not surprised that you would use even this situation to exhibit some foolishness?"

I rose to my feet, lightly rubbing the tender bump. "How long was I out?"

Christmas-ornament lady responded, "Only a couple of minutes. I called Connie immediately. Fortunately she was only a block away."

I stood for a moment, gazing back and forth at the two women. There was something odd about them. They were complete opposites in both manner and dress, but strangely, they looked similar.

"So, you two know each other?" I inquired.

This brought a shrug and a giggle from the colorful one while Connie tilted her head and regarded me with modest disbelief. "Dr. Bradford, have you two not met?" She exhaled with a tiresome frown. "Then by all means, let me introduce you. Dr. Bradford, this is my younger sister, Estelle. You two have something in common. She got her doctorate from Vanderbilt also."